NEW YORK REVIEW BOOKS
CLASSICS

A FAIRLY GOOD TIME

MAVIS GALLANT (1922–2014) was born in Montreal and worked as a journalist at the *Montreal Standard* before moving to Europe to devote herself to writing fiction. In 1950, after traveling extensively she settled in Paris, where she would remain for the rest of her life. Over the course of her career Gallant published more than one hundred stories and dispatches in *The New Yorker*. In 2002 she received the Rea Award for the Short Story and in 2004, the PEN/Nabokov Award for lifetime achievement. In addition to *A Fairly Good Time*, New York Review Books Classics publishes three collections of Gallant's short stories: *Paris Stories*, *Varieties of Exile*, and *The Cost of Living: Early and Uncollected Stories*.

PETER ORNER is the author of two collections of stories, *Last Car Over the Sagamore Bridge* and *Esther Stories*, and two novels, *Love and Shame and Love* and *The Second Coming of Mavala Shikongo*. He is also the editor of two books of oral history, *Underground America* and *Hope Deferred: Narratives of Zimbabwean Lives*. His book of nonfiction *Am I Alone Here?* will be published in November 2016. Orner has received Guggenheim and Lannan Foundation fellowships, and two Pushcart Prizes. He teaches at San Francisco State University.

OTHER BOOKS BY MAVIS GALLANT
PUBLISHED BY NYRB CLASSICS

The Cost of Living: Early and Uncollected Stories
Introduction by Jhumpa Lahiri

Paris Stories
Selected and with an introduction by Michael Ondaatje

Varieties of Exile
Selected and with an introduction by Russell Banks

A FAIRLY GOOD TIME

with *Green Water, Green Sky*

MAVIS GALLANT

Introduction by
PETER ORNER

NEW YORK REVIEW BOOKS

nyrb

New York

THIS IS A NEW YORK REVIEW BOOK
PUBLISHED BY THE NEW YORK REVIEW OF BOOKS
435 Hudson Street, New York, NY 10014
www.nyrb.com

A Fairly Good Time copyright © 1970 by Mavis Gallant
Green Water, Green Sky copyright © 1959 by Mavis Gallant
Introduction copyright © 2016 by Peter Orner
All rights reserved.

Library of Congress Cataloging-in-Publication Data
Names: Gallant, Mavis, author. | Gallant, Mavis. Green water, green sky.
Title: A fairly good time / by Mavis Gallant ; introduction by Peter Orner.
Other titles: Green water, green sky.
Description: New York : New York Review Books, [2015] | Series: New York
 Review Books Classics
Identifiers: LCCN 2015040639 (print) | LCCN 2015048276 (ebook) | ISBN
 9781590179871 (paperback) | ISBN 9781590179888 (epub)
Subjects: | BISAC: FICTION / Psychological. | FICTION / Humorous. |
 FICTION / Literary.
Classification: LCC PR9199.3.G26 A6 2015 (print) | LCC PR9199.3.G26
 (ebook) | DDC 813/.54—dc23
LC record available at http://lccn.loc.gov/2015040639

ISBN 978-1-59017-987-1
Available as an electronic book; ISBN 978-1-59017-988-8

Printed in the United States of America on acid-free paper.
10 9 8 7 6 5 4 3 2 1

CONTENTS

Introduction · vii

A FAIRLY GOOD TIME · 1
GREEN WATER, GREEN SKY · 275

INTRODUCTION

THE BOOK jacket copy of the Random House first edition of *A Fairly Good Time*, Mavis Gallant's second and last published novel, and among the most neglected masterworks of the last century, begins with this sentence: "The setting of this deliciously funny and heartbreaking novel is the Paris of the 1960's and its endearing protagonist is a vague, warm-hearted, untidy girl named Shirley Perrigny." The jacket goes on to call Shirley myopic and gauche before praising the novel's delightful barrage of wit and finally concluding that, in spite of Shirley's faults, you'll end up siding up with her against a shabby world.

Of course, jacket copy is by nature ridiculous. How to distill into a few lines what needed many years and a whole book to express? Marketing will always be a product of its time, in this case 1970. Forty-five years from now, jacket copy written today will probably sound just as goofy, though there might not be any jackets. Even so, I have a notion that this particular copywriter read (or didn't read) a vastly different novel than I did.

Deliciously funny? It's true *A Fairly Good Time*—the title comes from an Edith Wharton line ("If you make up your mind not to be happy there's no reason why you shouldn't have a fairly good time")—is funny, very funny. But the tone, the message being sent, is way off and suggests: This is light stuff, you'll really like it, and then you'll probably forget about it. But won't it make a wonderful gift for a witty friend? Had I been the copywriter, I might have tried something catchy to the tune of: *Think of this book as a new wave* Sun Also Rises *written by a woman with a better sense of humor*.

vii

And vague? Shirley? She's brave, exuberant, bewildered, wounded, fickle, mistake-prone, meandery—all this and a lot more. Including, yes, untidy. But isn't there something inherently logical about Shirley's theory about making one's bed? Why make something when you're only going to unmake it in a few hours? There is nothing hazy, nothing fading away, about this character. Shirley bursts forth as she entered the world in the first place. As her own mother puts it in the hilariously bizarre letter that opens the book: "To think that when you were on the way I believed you were a tumour! But you were you—oh, very much so."

I have a tendency to fall deeply in love with fictional characters. Call it a flaw in my critical judgment skills. When I was kid, I liberated the neighbor's rabbits after reading *Watership Down*. Perhaps you might not want to take books so literally, my mother said. Gallant once wrote, recognizing the odd relationship that fiction has to our lives: "I still do not know what impels anyone sound of mind to leave dry land and spend a lifetime describing people who do not exist."

I think writers create people who don't exist in order to fend off a permanent, nagging loneliness, and by some strange alchemy these people—and rabbits—keep us readers company, too. I'll be lugging along Shirley now for the duration.

It is 1963 and newly remarried Shirley, a bookish, twenty-seven-year-old Canadian living in Paris, returns to her apartment one Sunday morning, after being out all night, to discover that her husband, Philippe, has apparently moved out.

She'd told him she was going to a party, but she'd spent the night watching over a friend who'd attempted suicide. Renata hadn't tried that hard (the pills were crushed aspirin and she may have been only wanting to play at being Marilyn Monroe, who *did* kill her herself a year earlier), but the circumstances are real enough. Shirley can't tell Philippe the truth because then she would have to tell him about the illegal abortion Renata had on Friday. Any knowledge would have potentially implicated Philippe under France's strict antiabortion laws. Abortion didn't become legal in France until 1975. It's complicated, even convoluted, but doesn't this characterize so many of our entanglements—our friendships, our marriages? It's important to note that these characters are all still in their twenties, when drama for drama's sake is at a premium.

Not that Shirley is some saint running around Paris helping desperate friends. Well, in some ways she is, but let's say she's no wifely saint. A few days after Philippe leaves (he's only decamped to his mother's but for a Frenchman this is distance enough), Shirley sleeps with her upstairs neighbor, a Greek architect named James whose greatest fear is that Shirley will attempt to have a conversation with him, and whose idea of a book is the thesaurus he uses to prop open the window. But I can't help preferring shallow James to over-serious Philippe, a journalist who, in one of the novel's more brilliant send-ups, is said to have written numerous articles on different subjects, all under the same title: "A Silent Cry." Infantile drunkenness in Normandy: "A Silent Cry." The Berlin Wall: "A Silent Cry." The Canadian question and the liberation of Quebec: "A Silent Cry." It is Philippe, the author of "A Silent Cry," who believes that Shirley's most damning fault is her openheartedness. "Your life is like a house without doors," he says.

Still, for the duration of the novel Shirley aches for Philippe.

In an essay written during roughly the same period as *A Fairly Good Time*, Gallant says, "The question of what people see in each other defies analysis." She was introducing a book of the prison letters of a French schoolteacher, a woman who was held in preventive detention after being caught in an affair with a sixteen-year old male student. The teacher committed suicide shortly after her release from jail. The case of Gabrielle Russier and Christian Rossi mesmerized France in the late sixties, and while Gallant skewers a French legal system that punished a female teacher but would have excused the same crime if committed by a man, men being men (deliciously funny?), it is the conundrum of love that drives her probe. She goes on to write: "The mystery of what a couple *is*, exactly, is almost the only true mystery left to us, and when we come to the end of it there will be no more need for literature—or for love, for that matter."

This is Gallant's inexhaustible subject. In story after story, book after book. Her work is a living bulwark against the notion that there could ever be a final word said about the behavior of people in love, out of love, seeking love, rejecting love, enduring love, conjuring love...

In *A Fairly Good Time*, Philippe's worst crime is absenting himself from the novel itself. For instance, Philippe misses out, among so many other experiences, on munching éclairs with Cat Castle, an old family friend, in town on "grand tour" from Canada.

> "You've messed up two marriages now," said Mrs. Castle. "Why are you always in such a hurry to get married, I wonder? You seem to get married in a rush, then you rush the other way."
> "Pete died, Mrs. Castle."

A lesser writer would have milked the moment. Gallant knows better. The ghost of this first husband, Pete, hovers over the book without suffocating it. Shirley mourns like real people mourn, that is, erratically and with much forgetfulness.

A reader is swept along as Shirley drifts one way and then another. Every day without Philippe is a day open to encounters with other people. In a café, she meets Claudie Maurel, a young mother who emerges to play an increasingly important, if at times baffling (even to Shirley), role in the novel. But first, Shirley has to pay her tab, as Claudie has no money to pay the waiter. Those who admire Gallant's shorter work might be perplexed. Unlike the stories, *A*

INTRODUCTION · xi

Fairly Good Time refuses restraint, and Gallant almost gleefully luxuriates in digressive opportunities. Shirley's brain wanders as much as her feet. But this is what makes this novel such a revelation. Here, in a book overlooked for nearly half a century, a reader experiences Gallant at her most experimental and spontaneous. At the center of this spontaneity is a character who will not, in the face of grief, repudiate life.

All her screwups, all her losses. Shirley gets up in the morning and goes at it again. And when you might least expect it, in the boldest of narrative maneuvers, the scaffolding of the very book gives way, and Shirley begins (in a letter she never sends) to speak directly for herself about all the things Philippe could never understand, including her first marriage. The result is so affecting that I felt myself drop into a free fall. If I could have, I would have reached into the novel and tried to hold her. It is, as I've said, this sort of novel.

For Gallant, I believe, the business of having to begin again, to quote the title of one of her most magnificent longer stories, is "the cost of living." And when I think of her work, I think of the immense number of opening lines she set in motion. Gallant published a hundred and sixteen stories in *The New Yorker* alone. In a brief story called "In Transit," published in the magazine in 1965, a character named Philippe Perrigny and his new wife, Claire, are stuck in a waiting room in the Helsinki airport. A squabbling older couple ("What I wonder is what I have been to you all these years") prompts Claire to ask about Philippe's ex-wife.

> "Why did you leave her?"
> He had been expecting this, and said, "Because she couldn't concentrate on one person. She was nice to everybody, but couldn't concentrate enough for a marriage."
> "She was unfaithful."
> "That too. It came from the same lack of concentration. She had been married before."
> "Oh? She was old?"

The earlier story acts as a kind of pre-coda to the novel and in the course of it, Philippe does, in a sense, read the letter Shirley never sends. For a moment, he thinks of how Shirley must have looked before he had known her, when she was even younger and in love.

Green Water, Green Sky, published in 1959, is as desolate as *A Fairly Good Time* is crowded. There's humor—nothing in Gallant is ever free of humor. Yet here the comedy lacks buoyancy. And the edge is far deadlier. Both novels are set largely among expatriates in Paris, except now we have actual Americans as opposed to wrongly accused Canadians. Both books culminate in August in Paris, that month when the city empties out and in theory only lost souls remain. Unlike the longer novel, which is about marriage, friendship, and everything else under the sun, including the etymology of flowers and the Algerian War, this earlier work is focused nearly exclusively on family. If *A Fairly Good Time* is a messy, anarchic daydream of a novel that will ravage your heart, *Green Water, Green Sky* is a spare and undiluted nightmare.

At one point in *A Fairly Good Time*, Shirley says, "I prefer dark to daylight or any kind of light." Don't believe her for a second. Florence Harris, on the other hand, the character around whom *Green Water, Green Sky* revolves (to call her a protagonist would be to suggest action), truly hungers for all-consuming darkness. It doesn't make her any less riveting. At a party among strangers, the sort of party Shirley would enjoy and Florence would loathe, Florence would get all the attention.

Divided into four distinct parts, *Green Water, Green Sky* is radically compressed, a precursor to Gallant's later stories where she moves, seemingly without effort, and often with hardly a transition, back and forth across decades and space, capturing, as so few ever have, the weight of memory on a page. We first meet Florence, or Flor, as she is called by her family, in Venice as a fourteen-year-old, worshipped and feared by her younger cousin George. They are the kind of cousins who only see each other once every few years, and yet the image of Flor breaking apart a necklace burns into George's memory.

> She unstrung the beads still in her hands and flung them after the others, making a wild upward movement with her palms. "Oh, stop it," her mother cried, for people were looking, and Flor did appear rather mad, with her hair flying and her dress blowing so that anybody could see the starched petticoat underneath, and the sunburned thighs. And poor little George, suddenly anxious about what strangers might think—this new, frantic little George ran here and there, picking up large, lozenge-shaped beads from under people's feet.

George has held on to a few of these beads as good luck charms. Eleven years after this scene along the Grand Canal (in the novel, only a few pages later), he brings the last remaining bead to a party in New York to celebrate Flor's marriage to a man named Bob Harris. (Bob Harris is never just Bob; he's always Bob Harris as if his name is a single word.) But when George tries to present his sacred treasure to his cousin, a talisman rescued from oblivion, Flor is puzzled. A necklace? "I'm not a person who breaks things," she says.

An eternal disconnect. The one person we thought would have remembered a life-defining moment has no idea what we're talking about. George is left gripping the bead in his sweaty palm. But Flor's connection to her family, to her very life, is a lot more tenuous than your average cousin. And her descent into debilitating mental illness—back then the diagnosis might have been more quaintly called a nervous breakdown—is as startling as it is quick. While walking along the Boulevard des Capucines, Flor feels the motionless sidewalk erupt under her feet.

As Flor's frantic sense of desolation increases, all the energy she can muster is used to push other people away. At a café, Flor begins a letter to her psychiatrist. "What help can you give me?" she writes.

"I have often been disgusted by the smell of your dresses and your rotten teeth."

In *Green Water, Green Sky*, as in *A Fairly Good Time*, minor figures achieve indelibility, often in as few as one or two sentences. In part three, when the book retreats in time to the courtship of Flor and Bob Harris in Cannes, a fraud named Wishart—who is a friend of Flor's mother, Bonnie—nearly steals the show. Yet, above all, it is the book's relentless examination of the impact of Flor's mental collapse on herself, and on her mother and husband, that is the source of the novel's bleak power.

Both novels employ letter writing to remarkable effect, but there's a moment in *Green Water, Green Sky* when Gallant takes this nearly vanished, intimate art to an entirely new level. Bonnie writes to George's parents, breezily thanking them for the new hat. She reports some of the latest news and casually mentions that George might want to postpone his trip to Paris in August, as she and Bob Harris will be out of town, and Flor, you know, never likes to go out these days. Georgie simply wouldn't have any fun. Inside this "official" letter, Bonnie slides a small note card where she makes an attempt tell the truth: "Polly, Flor is getting so queer, I don't know her any more." Can you imagine? An e-mail within an e-mail, or a post within a post, where you tell it like it really is? Bonnie is abominable in so many ways. She's a controlling, vain, incurable anti-Semitic snob, but she's also somebody's mother.

And Bob Harris—a man who is referred to by the family as "the Seal" because he can't prevent himself from charming people—he, too, injects the story with raw sorrow. Pathetic Bob Harris, the Jew who Bonnie always thought was unworthy of her daughter, Bob Harris who will never touch his wife again—it is this Bob Harris who, while sitting beside Flor in their dark bedroom, remembers her and mourns her at the same time: "Still, remembering, he said, 'I do love you,' but he was thinking of the hot, faded summer in Cannes, and the white walls of his shuttered room on a blazing afternoon, and coming in with Flor from the beach."

Again, love, who's to account for it?

—PETER ORNER

A FAIRLY GOOD TIME

"There are lots of ways of being miserable, but there's only one way of being comfortable, and that is to stop running round after happiness. If you make up your mind not to be happy there's no reason why you shouldn't have a fairly good time."

—EDITH WHARTON, *The Last Asset*

To Doyle

I

Montreal, May 26th, 1963

DEAREST GIRL:

The sadly macerated and decomposed specimen you sent me for identification is without doubt *Endymion nutans* or *Endymion non-scriptus*, or *Scilla nutans* or *non-scriptus*. Also called wood hyacinth, wood bell, wild hyacinth.

It is, in short, the common European bluebell.

In French it is called *Scille Penchée, Jacinthe-des-Bois, Petite Jacinthe, Jacinthe sauvage*. I am wondering why you couldn't have pried this much information out of Philippe, though I know the French know nothing whatever about Nature and do their best to turn gardens into parlors. It was your father's opinion that they do not distinguish between trees and statues, and are completely taken aback every Spring to see all these statues putting out leaves. I know that they have only one word for currants and gooseberries, and as for birds!

In German, it is *Hasenblaustern*, also *Englische Hyacinthe*. In Flemish, though this won't be useful to you unless you get married for a third time, and this time to a Belgian heaven forbid, it is *Bosch Hyacinth*!!!

Your father always thought *Bosch Hyacinth* very funny, it completely fitted in with his sense of humor which it was not given to everyone to grasp. He picked up the phrase when he was an M.O. in the last war (and please do not write back asking "Which war?" because you know perfectly well the war I mean). Your father thought less than nothing of the Flemish. The other lot of Belgians were "given over to being entirely French-minded" but on the whole a cut above. It is surprising to remember he was in uniform, considering the age he was at that time.

Of course you had never seen *Endymion non-scriptus* in Canada! I am assuming this is what your nine-page letter was about. I could not decipher what seemed to me to be an early Teutonic alphabet. Neither of your marriages ever improved your writing. You may retort that legibility is not the purpose of marriage. I am not sure it has any purpose at all. Your father and I often discussed this. We felt that marriage would have been more tolerable had we been more alike—for example, had both of us been men. But no Church or Govt that I know would approve. The idea has been interestingly taken up in "... And Again the Cosmos" by B. P. Danzer. A disgusting photograph ornaments the dust jacket. "Courts fail to prove obscenity" was, you may remember, the upshot of a long case involving the jacket (not the book). I am one of the few persons to have read the book all the way through. I recommend it. You can remove the jacket, or turn it back to front.

Endymion non-scriptus does not occur wild over here. Nor does any similar plant. A competent authority will bear me out but when I say competent I mean that, and not just some Pole. It has a southern cousin, *Endymion hispanica* or *Scilla campanulata*, which is larger and stronger but has NO SCENT. It grows wild in Spain, Portugal, possibly southwest France. Don't know about Morocco. You could look it up, or ask Philippe. They hybridize when planted in gardens. The true wild bluebell always has a delicious SCENT. It also occurs white, and sometimes pink. It loves woods. It almost never grows in the open.

The *Campanulata*—synonym for the Spanish form—is merely descriptive and means "like a Campanula." But it is in fact NO RELATION. It is of the Lily family, of which, of course, the lily-of-the-valley (*Convallaria*) is too! I finally had a letter from Cat Castle. She has an unfavorable impression of Europe. Some young man has made "a bad translation" of a movie in Rome. Some person she met mentioned this to her. Some conductor she heard about in London was "disgracefully bad." She hears that none of our embassy people "can spell." She herself saw two films about Eskimo fisheries whilst in Titograd that were "a shame on the country." Our image is hopelessly blackened in Montenegro, "perhaps forever."

Hope all this is not so, as her trip is costing her children a lot of money.

Your bluebell is found wild only in the British Isles and Northern France and in Northern Belgium. Holland? Look it up. When your father was over there he saw woods full in *South* Belgium.

I can see you from here making a long face at all these old memories and at any reminder of the War. Well, nothing can alter the memory I have of the gloriously sunny day when Canada rallied to the Mother Country. I held you on my lap, near the radio, so you could hear the news, and even though you were not three years of age, I was sure your inner mind would retain the impact. I was, am, and always shall be a pacifist, but that War was different. It came along when a lot of people were down and out, especially out West, and it saved countless others from futility and boredom. Your father said that if he had been younger it would have changed his outlook. I exclude it from colonial wars, crusades, wars for gain, and wars fought out of nervousness. The men in particular enjoyed it, and many of them felt it ended all too soon.

In England, on our wedding trip, your father and I picked bluebells one morning and tied them to our bicycles. But they died within the hour.

You did not say where you had found your specimen, but as it seldom grows in the open—I should say never that I know of, though there will always be some Pole ready to quibble—I take it you must have found it in beech woods. Next time you send a specimen press it between two sheets of clean paper and please don't forget the leaf.

I hope my letter tells all you need to know. I counted a dozen question marks and took them to indicate anxious queries re *Endymion non-scriptus*. As far as I can remember, you never asked me a question about anything until now, not even the innocent questions children usually put about their origins—whether they are truly the children of their parents or have been adopted; whether they are not really of noble or aristocratic descent and have been brought into this dreadful family by mistake, as part of the process of reincarnation; and so on. You never once asked why time exists, and when time began, and if it is necessary. Or, if the Creator is only an Idea, then in Whose mind did the Idea originate? I could have answered any of these questions easily.

Your letter was stained and blotted. The envelope was unlined, and the paper a dirty tone of gray, where it had not turned slime-green because of the rotting stem. The pages did not fit neatly in the envelope. The writing was a model of cacography and I think that unless you learn patience and penmanship you had best forget your manners and use the machine, as I am doing now. I want to know if you have or have not seen Cat Castle in Paris. Please answer this. She ought to be there this week some time. Make an effort. She has known you since before you were born. Do not encourage her to have streptomycin shots. Daughter Phyllis says they "enervate Mum."

The North American bluebell is botanically *Mertensia*. No relation to *Endymion*. Don't cry whilst writing letters. The person receiving the letter is apt to take it as a reproach. Undefined misery is no use to anyone. Be clear, or, better still, be silent. If you must tell the world about your personal affairs, give examples. Don't just sob in the pillow hoping someone will overhear.

> Nuns fret not at their convent's narrow room,
> And hermits are contented with their cells...

I made you learn this by heart, but you never had much of a memory.

I was able to make out the odd phrase here and there. Of course I don't "understand" you. Have I ever invited anyone to "understand" me? You can't "understand" anyone without interfering with that person's privacy. I hope you are not forever after poor Philippe and torturing and prying to get at his inmost thoughts. The more a man has to conceal the more he is likely to proclaim himself "a very private person" and you had best settle for whatever knowledge of him this affords you. You always had a key to your room, the first diary I ever gave you had a key, and I never bothered you. To think that when you were on the way I believed you were a tumour! But you were you—oh, very much so.

Your affectionate
Mother

P.S. Re flowers, wedding trip, bicycles mentioned above—that was the year of the death of George the Fifth, who was notoriously stingy, mean, a stranger to culture, and hard on his children, but who otherwise resembled my own father in every way.

2

THE BUILDING across the courtyard must have been removed by someone playing with bricks, for the light of morning, which had been suppressed until now, blazed through a gap in the bedroom curtains, shot along a wall, set on fire a mirror framed in snapshots, notes, post-cards, out-of-date reminders to and from Philippe, and revealed a small scarlet translucent spider hanging on a rope of the stoutest silk. A milder luminosity—of imagination this time—surrounded two middle-aged persons cycling steadily up an English hill. In homage to morning and to the splendor of new beginnings they carried an offering of blue, but the blue was perishable. It turned to indigo. The petals rotted. The flower fragrance altered and resembled the scent of the aging lovers, of soap and of death. The cyclists were dressed like each other in Fair Isle sweaters and breeches. The woman's hair, reddish in sunlight, fine and silky to the touch (although scarcely anyone knew that), was short as the man's. That had been in the year of the funeral of George the Fifth. Who was he? He was crown, beard and profile on twenty-five Canadian cents—at one time, Shirley's allowance. Once she found George the Fifth on a beach and brushed the sand away, saying, "What can I buy with this? Can I keep it?"

"You can't buy what you could have bought ten years ago," was her father's answer, as though Shirley knew what "ten years ago" meant.

Her parents, a lost pair, cycled off into the dark. They became smaller than a small living spider. What she required this morning was not a reminder of the past but a harmless substitute for it. When

Philippe came in he would address her with a breezy cordiality that was, at its worst, his way of showing indifference: "Well—where have you been? Where did you spend the night? Did you sleep at Renata's?" Or he would cross the room and pull the curtains open as if Shirley did not exist, which would mean that in his heart he wished she had never existed. Anticipation of a vague calamity drove her to invent, "Look, I know this is quite the worst thing I have ever done…" No. Wait. Facts were essential: they were the ground, the basis for flight. This was the morning of Whitsunday, the second of June. She sat in the bedroom with a letter in her hand, still dressed for a Saturday party in black chiffon that some ill-intentioned woman friend had urged her to buy. Over the dress was a Burberry with a button gone and a long thread dangling. A handbag, green velvet, a present from her husband's sister, lay on the counterpane spilling cigarettes. Wrenching it open just now to hunt for her glasses she had broken the clasp. The house was perfectly quiet, as though the other tenants, Philippe included, were all away attending the same funeral. A summing up, or a preliminary? It seemed to her at once military and lame, precise and hobbling: for where was Philippe? No use accusing *me*, she said, with the kind of nonchalance she could assume in his absence. Where did *you* spend the night? A light left burning, a scorched brown stain on the lampshade, meant that he had either dressed and departed before dawn (an assignment? a summons from his mother?) or had never been to bed at all.

The room was neat, the bathroom looked as if no one had ever used it, but none of that signified: rushing, say, to his dying mother's side Philippe would have stopped to cover his tracks. The immediate past was eliminated; it had something to do with picking up one object, one feeling, one idea, at a time and finding another place for it. If a place does not exist then you must invent one. Before her marriage Shirley had never bothered to make a bed: Why make what you were bound to unmake in a few hours? She had worn the same clothes until her women friends decreed them unwearable, and then she simply gave them away. Clean sheets, towels and pillow cases were piled on a chair in the living room and the used linen thrown in a convenient recess between the end of the bathtub and the wall. When one hillock became greater than the other she would pack all the dirty clothes in a large suitcase and have herself driven by taxi to a laundry on the far side of Paris. Her experience of Parisian taxi drivers had taught her to dread rudeness or a sharp refusal, both of which were eliminated by the promise of a long and costly journey. She could not understand why this system, which worked successfully and required only an occasional effort, seemed irrational to Philippe. At any rate he had put a stop to it. Now a boy trundling a sort of trunk on wheels came to fetch the washing every Saturday morning and brought it back torn, worn, stiff as the kitchen table and reeking of chloride bleach. Every face cloth and potholder had to be counted, examined and checked against a list. She was never prepared, never on time, never had the right inventory or the change needed for tipping; and the clean linen, corseted in hard brown paper, held with murderous pins, had to be undone, sorted, placed on shelves she could barely reach only to be taken down again; a repetition of gestures that seemed to her lunatic but that Philippe assured her were almost the evidence of life.

Be sensible, she said to herself. One step at a time, like unwrapping the laundry. Ring his office—no, for God's sake, don't. He'd never forgive it. No switchboard on Sundays, I'd hit one of his friends, and later it would be said... he probably did explain where he would be, and I must have forgotten. He has left a note. Look for it. No, that isn't it—the blue envelope is from our neighbor James Chichalides, whom Philippe hates. It probably contains an invitation to a party, which is the last thing either one of us needs just now. Look on the pad beside the telephone, in the frame of the hall mirror (Renata's wedding present), on the blackboard in the kitchen. Look on his desk in the box-room—look *in* the desk. If he catches you just say, I was only... After you find the note telling you whose funeral he's at run a bath and change. Get out of your Saturday clothes. Put them away so he won't see them and be reminded. Don't leave your dress on the floor—he will walk on it on purpose. The kitchen: There's a question needing an answer. He must have eaten his breakfast standing up—you can't sit on either of the chairs. Since when have I left dirty plates on chairs? Since yesterday. Bundles of newspapers the Salvation Army was supposed to call for. Bread, a cup half empty, a carton of powdered milk. He hates that but I forget to get the other. A salad bowl and two yellowed slivers of chicory pasted to a wooden fork—an ugly bit of evidence about my housekeeping; but I was comfortable in chaos, and he knew it, whereas that unwashed cup left by Philippe seems like a moral slip.

A windowless recess off the living room, probably once intended to be a child's sleeping quarters, had become Philippe's office. They had named it the box-room because the term, a hangover from English novels about little boys growing up and going to Cambridge, sounded comic to Shirley; and Philippe, who was grave mostly, unconscious of the origins of all that she could hate and yet think laughable, accepted it as one more of the Anglo-Saxon mysteries. Accepted only, which was not what she had intended; for it was like saying "We are sharing an apple because I have cut it in half." When visitors looked in the box-room Philippe said, "This is my desk and my wife works at that one," without explaining even to Shirley what her work was or ever could be. Between the two desks shelves climbed to the ceiling. A pair of neon strips hummed, flickered and spread their bilious light on stacks of *Le Miroir*, the fortnightly review that employed him, on coffee mugs filled with pens and pencils, over twin typewriters tucked up in plastic blankets made by Philippe's mother, upon a temperance poster Shirley had stolen out of the Métro. The poster was a dead weight in the room; it sagged like a laboriously translated anecdote impeding a dinner party. For what was so humorous about a fragile child and his plea of FATHER DO NOT DRINK! THINK OF ME! when you considered that France had the highest number of alcoholics in western Europe and the greatest number of deaths resulting from drink? Philippe had written a series of three articles on infantile drunkenness in

Normandy called "The Children of Calvados: A Silent Cry," the first of which began, "It was a silent cry torn from the heart, rending the heavens, searing the universe, and ignored by the middle-classes," before going on to say what took place when a baby's formula was half applejack, half watered milk.

"Would you tell me what is humorous about cirrhosis, diabetes, congenital heart disease and feeble-mindedness?" he had asked, unrolling the poster.

"Funny? Nothing. I don't know."

"Then why are you laughing?"

"I'm not laughing. Am I? I'm sorry, I'll throw it out."

"No, leave it. I don't mind. How did you remove it from the Métro?"

"With Renata's nail file. We were together."

"You were drunk?"

"Philippe! No. It was in the middle of the afternoon."

"Did none of the passengers try and stop you?"

"They pretended not to see. We were very serious and Renata gave me serious instructions in French. It was terribly f... I was going to say funny."

"Two women of voting age," said Philippe.

"We can't vote in France."

It was his practice to let Shirley have the last word, usually when she had just shifted ground. This meant that the last word was really the start of a new subject. She was about to tell him how she had never voted in her life, what the circumstances were that had caused this omission; how women had chained themselves to lampposts and been forcibly fed in prison hospitals, women in shirtwaists, wearing pince-nez that must have been dashed to the stone floor and smashed during the struggle with the attendants, against the hideous tubes and the monstrous feeding; all this for Shirley who had never once voted, never at all. Philippe's mother voted for General de Gaulle; Philippe voted against him; his sister voted, but would not say how. She made up her mind on the way to the polling place whose vote she wanted to cancel, her brother's or her mother's. She gave it thought, and thought up until the last second, when her hand went without wavering to this stack of bulletins or that. "I have accomplished my electoral duty," said Shirley's sister-in-law, but no one ever knew whose vote she had canceled. She had immense power, and Shirley had none, for she could not vote in France.

Of course, no message had been left for Shirley on Philippe's desk. It was a working place, not a repository for explanations. Urgent letters, bills and projects for *Le Miroir* were piled like bricks in stacked plastic trays, each tray another color—industrial blue, industrial yellow, the red that, used on machines, is said to keep workers in factories from sleeping, and the green meant to keep them calm and from hurting themselves. One desk drawer (Who invited Shirley to pull this open? Not Philippe) contained the typescript of a novel written by a close friend of his named Geneviève Deschranes; another—once you have opened one drawer you try the second—revealed a volume of Mother Goose and sheets of yellow paper covered with English nursery rhymes.

He had typed on a sheet one of many remarkable versions of Goosey Gander:

> GOOSIE GOOSIE GANDER
>   WITHA WALTHA WANDA
> UP THE STARES DOWN THE STARES
>   WITHA WALTHA WARES
>
> SHAME TO YOU GOODSIDE'S GANDER
>   WE'VE CAUGHT YOU UNAWARES
> HOW CRUEL TO KICK A POOR OLD MAN
> AND THROW HIM DOWN THE STARE'S

Underneath in Philippe's small sloping handwriting was "Poor old Man—Churchill? Goodley Gander—the Greek inheritance?"

Philippe's spelling of "Goosey," his belief that the rhyme held a prophetic meaning, and above all the second verse, whose authenticity Shirley would not accept, had long been a source of argument between them. Philippe shared a common French presumption that English nouns were automatically possessive, or that it did not matter much if they were or were not, and that the orthography of English names was subject to whim. His source was not a dictionary, not his wife, not his education, and not even the book of Mother Goose Shirley had given him and begged him to consult, but his friend, the authoress Geneviève Deschranes. Many years ago Geneviève's intellect had been nourished by an English governess named Miss Thule. It was Miss Thule who had maintained that Goosey Gander held a universal key. Life, love, politics, art, death, explanations of the past and insight into the dreadful future were there for the reading, and she had made Geneviève repeat, until the child remembered it, "Goosey Goosey Gander, Whither shalt thou wander…" in July 1947, next to the Medici Fountain in the Luxembourg Gardens. That the little girl's lisp, or her wavering attention, had produced "With a Waltha" was almost inevitable. But this Philippe would not accept. Shirley's comment, "Geneviève heard it wrong," was dismissed as incompetent, as was her insistence that even if the second verse were genuine it would read "Shame on you" and not "to you." Philippe merely replied, "Did you learn your English from Miss Thule? From any English governess?"

"I never had to learn English," Shirley said.

He had begun his research on the enigma of nursery rhymes as part of an investigation his magazine was conducting into the Parisian sub-society of soothsayers, prophets and demonologists spawned during the Algerian War. That war had ended but the city had not settled down: bombs, tracts, threats, blackmail and vengeful trials were a diminishing cause of excitement, for which one substituted tales of royal babies switched in their cradles, medieval monks who turned up reincarnated as atomic scientists, Christ sent back to earth and working hard at the hydroelectric station of Krasnoïarsky Kraï in central Siberia, continents that sank like stones, swarms of bees commuting regularly between the planets Neptune and Venus, children raised by wild beasts and revealed to be without neuroses, cancer cures suppressed by powerful interests in Berne and

Washington, Shamanism among the clergy and Freemasons in charge of banks. As for politics, this had been removed to the domain of magic. Once Philippe had taken Shirley to a meeting at which the language probably spoken by the aristocracy on lost Atlantis had been discussed, and during which someone tried to prove a link between the name Mao and the noise made by a cat. Shirley had stolen a look at the two guests of honor, both Chinese, and discovered it was untrue that Asians were able to conceal their true feelings whatever the circumstances. Later, from a stray remark of Philippe's, she learned that Geneviève had been at that meeting too, which meant that she and Shirley had been in the same room and had not been introduced.

The quest for mystery in ideas seemed to Philippe to eliminate certain problems of behavior, while the mystery of behavior seemed to Shirley the only riddle worth a mention. The riddle of his attachment to Geneviève, for instance: Was Philippe in love with her? No. He said that he admired her because her whole life was a sacrifice, and he pitied her because of her useless courage, much as he admired and pitied his own mother. But Philippe's mother was widowed, fifty-four and half-crippled with arthritis, while Geneviève was not yet thirty, was married to an ethnologist in excellent health, and her personal finances were such that she had never had to share a bathroom or wait for a bus. Still, Philippe said that Geneviève's strength was built on fragility and that, though timid, she had the dauntless heart of an Early Christian martyr—all of which made Shirley crave the compassion he did not think she required and the approval he had evidently never found any reason to voice. She was driven to obsessive conjecturing about Geneviève. She imagined her pallor, her bruised-looking eyes, her Botticelli hair, her Mexican silver earrings, her unusually small vagina—an attribute Geneviève mentioned in her letters from time to time and which Shirley took to be a sign of refinement, like having no appetite—and her tightly tuned speaking voice. She knew from an assiduous reading of Geneviève's letters to Philippe that she suffered in both spirit and body because of her ethnologist husband's persistent conjugal demands, which were made "quite without provocation, on the contrary," in trains, in the cinema at Orly Airport, in the Peugeot 403 "alongside the Western Autoroute, where it is forbidden to park," in the dining room while waiting for guests to arrive, in the Egyptian section of the Louvre on a winter afternoon just before closing time and, finally, in the presence of their four-year-old son whom the ethnologist was trying to goad to a parricidal fury in order to prove, or disprove, some incursion the Freudians had made in ethnology's private field. Shirley also knew that part of Philippe's life—his collection of records, four thousand of them, or forty thousand, or perhaps four hundred thousand were stored in Geneviève's country house. Did he go there to listen to them? The frequency of her letters suggested that she and Philippe did not meet very often. Perhaps Geneviève's husband was jealous and would not let her talk on the telephone.

Of course Shirley's mother had been right to say nothing except *Endymion non-scriptus*: what was all this snooping and reading except a heartless pursuit of Philippe? On the other hand, what was privacy? What did it mean? Where was the line between intimacy and privacy? How could Philippe claim one and insist on the other? Even this morning, with Shirley's sensible program still in the air (change clothes, run bath), she could not stop turning papers over on the pretext of looking for a message though she knew this was the last place she would be likely to find one. The truth was that the written evidence of Philippe's daily, routine life—his correspondence with Geneviève, who also sent him, chapter by chapter, a termless novel in which he figured; the notes he made before composing even personal letters; the scribbled drafts for the jazz column he wrote once a month under the pseudonym of Bobby Crown; the book in which he noted his appointments and the smaller diary to which he transferred the same reminders; the copies of typewritten complaints sent to garages and television repairmen; the folders full of research for pieces on the state of unrest among artichoke farmers in Brittany or the decline of the Foreign Legion—was a source of unflagging interest to his wife. Just as other women were driven to the refrigerator or to orgies of overspending or to daytime sleep, so

Shirley scratched through wastebaskets and coat pockets to find jotted trivia about plane departures and the names of foreign hotels. She was not trying to discover where he had been or where he was going: she usually knew. She was searching for enlightenment he could not willingly provide. His tranquil belief that because he was French he was logical meant that she was in the desert. She craved a broken horizon now—stones, trees, danger, relief. The evidence of his letters was that Philippe could be mean, petty, vain, gullible and subject to pique. This afforded her an inexplicable feeling of cheerfulness, and had he not so steadily objected to her perusal of his private papers she could have discussed her findings and told him how his faults were superior to her own, for she was willing to learn from anyone, and especially from him.

Now a church clock like a gong struck the half-hour—half-past nine or ten or eleven: Her watch was somewhere or other, perhaps in a pocket of her raincoat. She tried the game of placing herself, as she had done earlier (facts!). The church must be St. Clothilde; at half-past something, the time of day was confirmed in the Ministry of War, the Ministry of National Education, the Soviet Embassy, the Italian Embassy and the National Geographical Institute. Charwomen and secret service agents, left behind like Shirley on the holiday weekend, were in tune with the minute. She would have taken pride in this precise and panoramic image of a young woman and the web of streets around her except that Pons Tearoom, which was all of two arrondissements away, came nagging in its place; instead of seeing herself she saw a large iced pudding shaped like a sand castle and composed of garnet sherbet, vanilla ice cream and pale green marzipan. Oh God, she said, with all the trust and fervor only an unbeliever can express, clear up my mind. Why did I come into this room? What am I looking for? Word from Philippe to say where he is. No, not really—I am looking for a message from Geneviève. None today—only the most recent installment of *A Life Within a Life* (pp. 895–1002).

This lay on top of a mile of typescript in the drawer Philippe reserved for his friend's novel. One day he would not be able to shut the drawer and that would remind him to bundle up the whole thing and take it to a publisher. Through the pages wandered Flavia, a lonely girl; Bertrand, her husband, a third-rate anthropologist; and Charles, a brilliant journalist. Charles had once been married to a North American slut by the name of Daisy, but Daisy had died of a combination of drink and disaster long before Chapter One. Skipping through the new passages, reading only phrases that seemed essential, Shirley learned that Flavia, though ground down by daily contact with the inferior Bertrand, managed to keep a grip on her spiritual values thanks to an exchange of letters with Charles:

> I looked at myself in the mirror   I saw the delicate face and soft unruly   Upstairs I saw my face in the Venetian dressing table with its charming   the face of Saint Veronica after she
>
> I remember wandering over the grass trying to find my adorable underclothes   "See how pretty   with the trimming of creamy lace   but he was already unfolding the road map   to him so trivial   As he lit his cigarette without offering me one, I saw my small face in the black windscreen   I looked like Lazarus risen from the dead   bruised arms   acute discomfort   no hot water   The dignified tragedy it could have been   wanting a bath   rest   understanding   conversation on a level unknown to him   A mere performance   an operetta now   His absurd assertion that the Oedipus complex has never existed outside Vienna   In the restaurant I saw my small blanched face in the bowl of a spoon
>
> even upside down   the face of a small, hunted   I felt so weary, so exhausted   I wondered if I would survive until the end of the
>
> and that it affected no one save middle-class Jews   on and on   parricidal hatred impossible except   if he would start up again on the way home   He ate grossly   coarsely   swallowing leek soup   mutton stew   apricot meringue   with cream   with sugar   more brandy

> coffee   corrupted by the American way of life   drank gin
> fizz after gin fizz   until   no regard for my small   tired or
> even for his own liver   blood pressure   With Bertrand I
> dined in the most expensive restaurants   I was invited to
> mingle with celebrated people   actors   contributors to   I
> drove to   in fast luxurious   pure white sand
>   every gala performance at the   and yet all substitutes
> for his professional non-being   as I stood in front of
> the mirror   my hand resting lightly on the carved   I saw
> eyes   framed by   whose courage   did not yield under his
> stare   Only a letter from Charles could rouse me from my
> habitual boredom and apathy

Whatever Philippe's feeling for Geneviève amounted to, there was no doubt that Geneviève's language was a situation in itself, and it was one that no foreigner could hope to penetrate—not even Daisy's ghost.

Language is Situation, Shirley said to herself. The Silent Cry.

When Philippe talked about Geneviève he used the vocabulary of her novel. It was a form of expression the two roused in each other, as if some third, gassy, invisible presence—a substitute for passion—occupied each of them in turn. If Philippe was the possessed, he could say, without smiling, "She was a corn fairy."

"She was a what?"

"A goddess is what I mean. A feminine deity. A goddess of corn."

"Oh, Philippe, what do you mean? Say it in French."

"I mean fertility. Abundance. Warmth."

"I do wish you would stick to French. It sort of sounds all right then."

"She was a Demeter. An adorable Demeter. She was Persephone. Charming nature. We never quarreled. Always saw eye to eye. Marvelous cook."

"Why didn't you marry her?"

"It wasn't like that. She was the incarnation of the dreams a small boy..."

"A small *boy*?"
"Who had lost his father..."
"Oh, Philippe."
"Alone..."
"This is terrible. You sound like her. What about bed? Her, I mean."
"It wasn't like that. It didn't matter. She was the incarnation of—"
"No, please, you've said that. Back to bed."
"Well, you see, she'd hardly known anything before me. Only two other men. One she loved, but he—"
"He was married."
"No, he became a priest. The other one was only... anyway, she hated it with both."
"Don't forget her husband."
"She hates it with her husband."
"If she hated it she'd move out."
"Her religion prevents her."

Her religion! Hear it, St. Joseph! Send a shower of pins on Geneviève! Make her grow a beard! Geneviève loses her hair and wears a polka-dot turban with a glued-on fringe. Geneviève gets frostbite on the Trans-Siberian. Curse Geneviève. Screw Geneviève. No, I take that back. It wouldn't help.

This conversation, which Shirley had started to scribble all around the margins, petered out. Shirley, or Daisy, was only the phantom of a slut and had no rights whatever. Here was the lowest point of a marriage—the ocean floor: On Sunday morning, June the second, neither of them knew where the other was. Geneviève was a ghost too: she was merely what Philippe wanted her to be, a perpetual past. Shirley picked up the scattered pages of her mother's letter and shut *A Life Within a Life* back in its drawer. Nothing had been gained by this fiddling, not even time. It was not at Geneviève's that Shirley had spent the night; it was unlikely that Philippe was with her now. If Shirley were to perish at this instant, struck by lightning (if guilt were lightning), the report on her death would say, "She ate her last breakfast standing in the kitchen. The chairs were stacked with rubbish she had kept meaning to throw out." No one looking back to lost Atlantis would ever believe that the person concerned with the unwashed cup had been Philippe. She wondered if he had been trying to frighten her and if the lamp left burning, the two sleeping pills, the slum kitchen, were fragments of a final opinion.

With the spider for company she shed her Saturday clothes, then ran water in the ocher-stained bath. Drops fell on her head from a pipe coiled on the ceiling. Her mother's letter had said, The death of a king, don't sob in your pillow, hope all this is not so. All what is not so? Cat Castle's bad opinion about Europe. She is in Paris; make an effort to see her. But I know she is in Paris—she rang me. We talked and her ugly prairie accent brought tears of pleasure to my eyes. We talked, we said we would meet. Meet when? "Oh my God," said Shirley. I am supposed to be with Mrs. Castle now, this minute. Breakfast with Mrs. Castle.

The courtyard filled up with a soft Sunday murmur of voices and radios. Everyone is listening to news about the weather because this is the long weekend. Deaths on the roads: those left behind enjoy hearing the figures. Now a guitar: against a recording of "Nuages," which the entire neighborhood knew by heart, Sutton McGrath played a counterpoint of his own devising. It must be Sutton McGrath, for she had seen the name on a petition drawn up and circulated by Madame Roux of the antique shop downstairs. A complaint against musical instruments and the presence of foreigners (McGrath was an Australian), the petition wound up with an eloquent plea concerning the rights of others. Shirley had not signed it precisely because of those rights. Neither had Philippe, but on grounds of a native prudence: Don't sign your name, at least not legibly; if noise disturbs you, shut your window. Later Shirley had been assured that the slighting remarks in the petition about strangers had not been meant for her. What difference did that make? It turned out that Madame Roux could barely hear the guitar down there on the ground floor. Her reason for protesting, like so much of normal living, had been exclusively concerned with principle. Let me tell what I have to say about principle, Shirley declared, until she remembered she was without money and that there was none in the house. She could run upstairs and borrow from the neighbor Philippe disliked, but she imagined meeting Philippe either coming or going, he wearing what she called when he frightened her "his Mean Catholic Face." "Where are you off to *now*?" he might ask her. It would be a poor time to mention money. No matter: Mrs. Castle, old friend, would give her whatever she needed. There would be no problem of language and none at all of ambiguity. Shirley thought, She will understand every word I say. She turned over a page of her mother's letter and wrote in large capitals, HAVE GONE TO PONS TEAROOM FOR BREAKFAST WITH FRIEND OF MY MOTHER'S MRS CASTLE SORRY I MISSED YOU THIS MORNING DIDN'T HAVE TIME TO CLEAN UP THE KITCHEN, WILL DO LATER PLEASE SAY WHERE YOU ARE BACK AS SOON AS POSS LOTS OF LOVE S (SORRY ABOUT YESTERDAY) But it was not part of Mrs. Norrington's letter at all—it was a page of Geneviève's novel, which meant that Mrs. Norrington's good counsel had become part of *A Life Within a Life*. Shirley sat down on the edge of the bed, wrapped in a damp towel, and read, without skipping this time, the description of how Bertrand, the incompetent anthropologist, had eaten his post-coital supper of mutton stew. The sound in the streets was of cars rushing to leave the city.

3

SECALG was what Shirley could read on the wrong side of the awning at Pons. Beyond SECALG were plane trees and a Sisley sky.

"I've just this second remembered something," said Shirley. "Oh Jesus. Sorry, Mrs. Castle. But it's come back to me. I'm supposed to be having lunch at Philippe's mother's today."

"Call 'em up and say you'll be late," said Mrs. Castle. Ignoring all that her travels must have taught her by now, she said, "Tell that waitress to bring you a phone."

"I remember now. That's where Philippe is. He went to collect his sister at the airport early this morning. She's been in New York. They must have gone straight from the airport to his mother's. I was supposed to join them there. They'll say I forgot on purpose. He's at his *mother's*..."

"Bad place for a man," said Mrs. Castle, drumming her ring on the table for a waitress. "What'll it be, Shirl?"

He had not been trying to frighten her. If she had looked carefully instead of mooning over Geneviève, she would have found a note. She imagined his writing on the pad beside the telephone: "Colette is back, with a lady wrestler from Hamburg she met in the Museum of Modern Art. Maman hopes the wrestler has a brother and that this strange adventure will lead to marriage. We are expecting you for lunch."

Yes, they were expecting her for the Sunday roast veal and to hear Colette's contemptuous account of the meals, clothes and manners of another city. They would wait for Shirley and then, having made up face-saving excuses in aid of Philippe, begin Colette's favorite hors d'oeuvres of egg in aspic. "This is the worst thing I could be giving my liver," Colette would remark, mopping up the yolk with a bit of bread. They would eat sparingly of the veal, for meat created cancer in Madame Perrigny's anxious universe. Much of the conversation, once New York had been disposed of, would center on the danger of food, of eating in restaurants, of eating anywhere but here, and finally of what even this luncheon would cost in terms of languor, migraine, cramps, insomnia and digestive remorse. Philippe's mother cooked well but only because she could not cook badly: she did not know how it was done. Yet the fact of eating alarmed her. Peristalsis was an enemy she had never mastered. Her intestines were of almost historical importance: soothed with bismuth, restored with charcoal, they were still as nothing to her stomach in which four-course meals remained for days, undigested, turning over and over like clothes forgotten in a tumble dryer.

Colette sympathized with her mother's afflictions, often shared them, and added to them one of her own—a restless liver. If Colette's quiescent liver were suddenly roused by an egg, an ounce of chocolate, a glass of wine, or even one dry biscuit too many, it stretched, doubled in size, and attempted to force its way out through her skin. By locking her hands against her right side, just under the ribs, Colette would manage to snap it back in place. Shrinking the liver was something else again: this meant lying down and drinking nothing but unsalted water in which carrots and parsley had been boiled for two hours, until the enraged liver subsided. Every second weekend as a matter of course, Colette went to bed for forty-eight hours, drank her broth and got up with a liver considerably weakened though never permanently vanquished.

Soon after she met Philippe, Shirley invited his sister and mother to dinner. She had not known the degree of involvement this invitation suggested or even that only uneducated persons entertained on a Saturday night. Curiosity goaded the Perrignys across Paris on a common evening. They arrived twenty-five minutes too soon. Colette bore a ritual bunch of carnations strangled in wire and wreathed with asparagus fern that shed fine green needles all the way up the stairs. Goya people, Shirley had thought when she saw them grouped together on her landing—the frail, arthritic woman with her dark gypsy's eyes, and Colette, carved and fringed and dipped in gold, like an antique armchair, and there, behind them, a new, watchful Philippe. Fifteen minutes before their arrival, if only they had been punctual, Shirley would have made her bed, emptied the ashtrays and cleared the living room of its habitual scruff of scarves, newspapers, coat hangers, rainboots and dying flowers. She was barefoot, dressed in a towel bathrobe she held shut with her left hand. She knew that this meeting was irreparable. She remembered how the parents of her first husband had looked at her and how she had seen herself in their eyes.

"Philippe, give them a drink, will you?" she said in English. "This damn robe hasn't got a belt and I can't let go."

"They don't drink. Don't worry but please, please put some clothes on."

She heard them murmuring as she dressed. The tone was only of small talk. She said to the no one in particular she named St. Joseph, "Do something. Help me out."

She made them sit around her living-room table and she solemnly lighted candles, which led them to feel, she learned later, that her notions of elegance had been obtained in Latin Quarter restaurants. They then looked at the large dish in the center of the table and said this of it:

The Mother: "What is there on that dish that could harm us?"

The Daughter: "Everything."

They picked their way through the four kinds of herring and the potato salad dressed with dill. Glasses of aquavit remained untouched before their plates. Philippe was courteous but bewildered: Whatever had possessed Shirley? What had made her think they would enjoy an outlandish Scandinavian meal? He had told her about his sister and mother: Shirley had listened, but had she understood? She caught these questions across the table, or thought she did, and signaled, "I am sorry," which it seemed she had always been saying and would say forever. The Perrigny women in the meantime tried to eat some of the pork and prunes. They looked at the pastries and looked away. They nibbled black bread and pretended to sip the Danish beer. They were not shocked or offended; they were simply appalled, distressed and terrified of being poisoned.

The disastrous first meeting had not prevented the marriage but merely made the Perrigny women prudent. When they came to visit now, they accepted nothing but china tea. They bowed their heads and exchanged looks Philippe never saw and murmured opinions he never intercepted. For Philippe the sole result of the Scandinavian dinner was his fear that after he and Shirley were married they would never be able to invite normal people to share a meal: their guests would go away anxious and hungry or else stricken with colitis and botulism. He began her education. He taught her not to serve spaghetti because it was messy to eat and made it seem as if they could not afford to pay a butcher. He discouraged any dish in the nature of a blanquette or a bourguignon partly because he did not trust her to prepare it and because it might seem to others that the Perrignys were disguising second-rate cuts of meat. As he took his place at the head of the table and watched the passing round of the approved anemic veal and the harmless sugary peas he would say, "My wife is a North American, but I taught her about food."

Discreetly, so that Mrs. Castle would not misunderstand and be offended, Shirley stole a look at her watch. Fifteen used plates were now rinsed and stacked in her mother-in-law's kitchen. Boiling water dripped through coffee grounds into a china pot. If Shirley hurried she might arrive in time to be forgiven. She imagined herself here, in Pons, summoning a portable telephone. There was no such thing; nevertheless, clean, light, a new sort of foreigner, it circled the table and alighted between Mrs. Cat Castle's two guidebooks and her tapestry-covered handbag. She saw herself dialing her mother-in-law's number, listened to five or six shrill signals, and gave it up. She was afraid of the Perrignys; that was the truth of it. The Perrignys, when they fixed their sceptical brown eyes on Shirley, were like the people in Italy who long ago had stared because Shirley was wearing shorts. She saw today's sun shooting straight over Paris. It missed Madame Perrigny's dining room, which remained dark as the sea, and bathed instead the houses across the square in a wash of yellow-gray. The Perrigny windows were shut against drafts and the noise of traffic, and their white net curtains were drawn tight lest someone flying low in a helicopter try to peer in and see what the Perrignys were having for lunch. The phantom telephone on the table at Pons dissolved. Shirley said to herself, I tried to call them but they wouldn't answer. That was the way to disburden oneself—to move away from guilt and disaster! Her mother-in-law's dining room at once became sweetly sunny, as friendly as Pons. Shirley put together the bunch of flowers she would dispatch by way of apology. Freesias, daisies, primroses and white violets were borne to their destination by a boy on a bicycle; they were lifted out of crackling paper by Madame Perrigny herself, who then, while thriftily trying to save the three pins that kept the paper fast, ran one into her thumb. She was rushed to the police station, from there to a hospital, and given anti-tetanus serum. Shirley's excuses were disposed of: she was free to obey her mother's letter and pay attention to Mrs. Castle, who had known her forever—had known her before she was born.

Poor odd old Mrs. Castle had undergone a European tour with all its discomfort and loneliness in order to show her children back in Canada she did not need them. She had acquired a Salzburger cape and hat. Beneath the hat, butterfly spectacles flashed. She dropped the menu, which she had been studying as if it were in code, adjusted the hat so that it sat jauntily, tucked back her sleeves, and said on a long Western note and in a single breath, "Well, Shirl, I am surprised a smart young lady like yourself had never heard about Pons Tearoom, the best pastry in Paris."

"I've heard of it, I've even been here. I just didn't know it was so famous."

"Let's hope it meets your standards."

Sarcasm made the old woman familiar; her voice might have risen out of this morning's letter.

"We are from Canada," said Mrs. Castle, preparing to turn the waitress to stone should she attempt to deny it. "Tell her what you want," she said to Shirley. She opened a notebook, spread it on the table and wrote "Pons." When she had completed the word she drew a line through it, saying, "That's done."

"Coffee!" she shouted suddenly.

She continued writing: "Went there seventh Sunday after Easter (Pentecost) with Shirl." Looking up, she said to the waitress. "Have you got any of those Scotch pancakes? It so happens I've been in Scotland." She spoke sharply to Shirley, "Translate that, will you? Don't be shy. Never be shy about who you are or what you might want." She wrote: "Green walls. Wicker. Red plush seats. Red carpet, pattern Prince of Wales feathers (or ferns?). Morning sun does not come from park. Comes from entirely opposite direction. Fielding wrong. Satin shades on wall brackets. Like my bedroom. Geraniums—kind of peaky. Artistic tables. Mirrors look like old silvering."

"Don't read upside down," she said, flashing the maniac glasses. "If you're interested in what I'm writing, speak up and say so. It happens to be for a long story I'm going to tell into a tape recorder once I get home. I'll put the whole thing on tape and I'll get my family together and they can spend a Sunday listening and then they'll have had it. Nobody looks at pictures and even with pictures I'd have to talk. I've thought it out. What'd she say about the Scotch pancakes? Never mind. I eat any old thing. This is my third breakfast today."

Eclairs replaced Scotch pancakes in the visitor's memory. She recalled having been told to try the éclairs at Pons. She chose the two that had the thickest and glossiest icing and began to eat them at once, remarking to Shirley that she had always sacrificed herself for others. She had put her own wishes low on the list. Her children understood that now and they were remorseful. The boys were married to selfish little snobs, and Phyllis hadn't done all that well either.

Shirley, drinking black coffee as if it were black poison, saw the panic of old age and the need to eat everything soon.

"There's only one mother in anybody's life," said Mrs. Castle. Her triumph sounded slightly mournful: Would Mrs. Castle's children love her better because she was unique? "Your mother has been dragging around the whole winter, Shirl," she said. "Only stomach flu—so she said. Nine times out of ten, stomach is cancer. What do you hear from her?"

"I've just had this long letter."

"Speak up, child. I can't hear when I'm chewing."

"I've had this *long letter*. It came yesterday but I didn't get a chance to read it until today. It's about bluebells, all the history of bluebells. I don't know why. She says she can't make out my handwriting."

"She's great on botany," Mrs. Castle said.

"I told her I thought I was messing up my marriage, doing all the wrong things. I can read *her* writing but I don't always know what she's driving at. One time she asked me to mark the Grandes Rousses on a map and send her the map airmail. Who was to know they were mountains? They could have been nude dancers. Philippe knew but he was away on an assignment, and by the time he came back and said they were mountains she said it was too late. Too late for what? Another time she wanted a picture of the castle and dungeon at Nogent-le-Rotrou. Philippe knew about that too, or he found out, and he did get a picture for me. But it was a couple of weeks later and she didn't even thank us. She may have been looking for Jericho again. The original Jericho, the one that was destroyed, well, she says it was really in Europe. She didn't say, so I never knew."

"You shouldn't have mentioned that part about marriage," Mrs. Castle said. "Margaret wouldn't like that. She's a spiritual kind of person. She wouldn't appreciate it at all. Your father was a very affectionate man. He'd try and hold her hand and that at the beginning, and she'd stare him down and say 'Teddy, don't be dirty.' She's more for the spiritual side of things. Teddy got used to her. I think he even got so he liked her."

"I never heard her being like that," said Shirley. "She was sensible about everything, except England, and she'd talk about anything I wanted so long as it wasn't personal."

"Why didn't you bring him along?" said Mrs. Castle. "I invited the two of you, as I remember."

Shirley tipped her cup back and forth. She said, "I forgot to tell him." Before she could be asked to repeat she shouted, "FORGOT! He couldn't have come anyway because of meeting his sister. Anyway I didn't know where he was. When I got home this morning he wasn't there. He'd left a light on, as if he'd gone out before daybreak, and there were two sleeping pills for me. When we have a fight he never fights. He just listens and corrects my French sometimes and then he gives me a couple of phenobarb. When I saw them there in a saucer I knew he meant there was no fight, or else the fight was over."

"What do you mean, when you got home this morning? What do you do all night—ride round in buses? Put your cup down. If you want more coffee say so, but don't play with cold food."

"It was so simple, Mrs. Castle. It was simple for me but I've made a mess of it. I've got this friend by the name of Renata. She's not Italian. That's just her name. She had to have this abortion so I got her the address and I went with her. Don't tell Mother, by the way. That was Friday. Next day, which was yesterday, she called up and said she needed me and to tell Philippe anything, to say I was going to a party, anything at all. You see, the person involved, the person responsible, I mean..."

"I can safely say that I don't want to hear about him. From the word go, Shirl, what did it have to do with you?"

"To *do* with me? Nothing, except she said she needed me. She tried to kill herself and all that. Not very hard, but still... it might have surprised her and worked. I couldn't tell Philippe anything because abortion is serious here. You can be in trouble just for knowing about it. I wouldn't ever want him to guess I was the one who got her the address. I'm never quite sure just how Catholic he is. I know one thing—he thinks Renata is a pest and that I waste my life and my time over people who aren't worth a thought. But how can you tell what somebody's worth? What's the measure?"

"All this is your mother's doing," said Mrs. Castle. "Her whole family was like you. Honest to God, any old bum your grandfather could pick up off the street he'd bring home. There was always some deadbeat eating fried eggs in your grandmother's kitchen. And your grandmother used to read the Word of God at them till there wasn't a Christian left among the unemployed. Well, you'd better tell your poor dumb husband something."

"I think I'd better tell him the truth before it gets any more complicated."

"No point," said Mrs. Castle, calmly. "If you start on a long-winded story like you keep doing with me, he'll just drop off to sleep. If you want to make him pay attention then write him a letter. That's always a shock to a man. It seems like the last word. He can take it to the place, and have a good read, and think it over. In my experience, that's effective provided you don't try it too often. Keep your letter short. Only crazy women write long letters. Tell him the truth if it sounds realistic. Otherwise invent something better. You don't have to go through life saying any daft-sounding thing just because it happens to be true. Keep it plausible but mostly keep it short."

"A party is plausible. He thinks we're always drinking and racketing around."

"Who's we?"

"Oh ... Americans."

"I'm not American. To the best of my knowledge you weren't born one. If you're going to be that way, forgetting your heritage, I don't want to hear any more. I guess he'd be against suicide because he's a Catholic."

"It isn't that so much. Philippe's sick of my friends and their troubles. He thinks you should keep things to yourself, unless you can make them sound like sums. Philippe isn't anything like Mother's family. More the opposite, in fact. I'd sooner tell him I'd been to a party than looking after a friend. I do go out without him, sometimes. We suddenly started living that way, with my going to parties on my own, because he'd be working evenings or else be out of town on an assignment. Even when he's here he won't go anywhere if it's a Saturday. But I think Saturday night is lonely just staying home. To tell you the truth, Philippe scares me. I'm scared to go to my mother-in-law's now. When he's with his sister and his mother I'm nervous all the time. I feel I'm being judged for things I don't understand. If I understood what they were maybe I wouldn't care."

"Has he ever laid a hand on you?" said Mrs. Castle. "Ever hit you?"

"*No.* Oh, no. He's nothing like that. But if you could see him with his sister you'd realize what I mean. Right from kindergarten they were told they were better than other people. We weren't ever told anything one way or another, so I've got nothing to fall back on."

"You've messed up two marriages now," said Mrs. Castle. "Why are you always in such a hurry to get married, I wonder? You seem to get married in a rush, then you rush the other way."

"Pete died, Mrs. Castle."

"So he did. Now *his* mother was American."

"He didn't die of that," said Shirley, seeing herself in miniature in the other woman's glasses. "You get over things," she muttered suddenly.

"Married in a rush" seemed to Shirley wide of the mark. It had taken weeks to collect the documents needed for the marriage of a French citizen to a foreigner. She remembered, among a dozen stone-faced officials, a woman who seemed to have the power of life and death over Shirley, and how this woman had licked a stamp, placed it just so at the foot of a letter, initialed the stamp, sat down, typed three words, taking her time, before looking over the brown counter that separated her from pleas and petitions. "Why can't you marry someone in your own country, miss?" she asked. "Aren't there any men where you come from?" Fat toad in a greasy nylon smock ... her nails were gray. When Philippe approached his own godfather to ask if he could use influence toward having the wedding speeded up, giving as a reason that Shirley was pregnant, his godfather answered, "She is certainly lying," and did nothing. Then had come the warning letter from Shirley's mother: "Remember that they are sacred in their own minds. God looks out for them. God interfered on their behalf through Joan of Arc. I have heard that she was really a man, or a lunatic, or a royal by-blow, but I've never read one word that put the divinity of her mission in any doubt. That nation is directly beholden to the Almighty, and direct lines are always dangerous. Anyway, dear girl, do THINK!"

Shirley and Philippe read the letter together, laughed over it and one day were married in the mairie of the sixth arrondissement, not in a church. The next day they set off for Berlin in Philippe's Deux-Chevaux. Philippe had an assignment there: "The Wall One Year Later: The Soundless Cry." They had trouble crossing the East Zone because Philippe had to make frequent stops where no one was supposed to so that Shirley could get out and throw up. He noted all this, intending to weave it in as something both poignant and comic, but in the end found it was no use to him. He could not really describe a honeymoon where the wife was some twelve weeks pregnant, while referring to Shirley as someone easily carsick made her sound tiresome. In the end he eliminated Shirley altogether. In the long first-person account of the trip that appeared in *Le Miroir* it was clear that Philippe had traveled alone.

"I was in a rush to get married because I thought he was sent from heaven," Shirley said abruptly. "I thought he was too good for me, that I didn't deserve him. I was twenty-five and all the men I knew were married or childish or neurotic or homosexual."

"Safe," was Mrs. Castle's comment, perhaps of the latter.

"Oh, Mrs. Castle, it isn't. What's safe about it? Everything between two people is equivocal."

"Equivocal as you like, Shirl, but no morning sickness."

"Look at Prince Albert," Shirley said. "Queen Victoria had nine children and she was sick with every one."

Expecting to be challenged or, at the very least, asked to deliver evidence, she began to prepare a case—the well-known but hushed up affair of Baron Schwartz-Midland would do to begin with—but Mrs. Castle merely answered in her normal Western whine, "Your grandmother Woodstock had Prince Albert on a very old authentic milk jug. Stood in her kitchen at the end of a shelf. Always looked like it was going over the edge. You'd see celery in it. Parsley. That jug, which should be in your possession, is now in a museum in Buffalo. So much for our national treasures. For this reason I've brought you something. It belongs to me, but knowing how your family is, I feel if I don't give you this you'll never have anything."

One of her two guidebooks was what she meant. She pushed it across the table, opening it, as she did so, to the flyleaf. With sepia ink, in a lilliputian hand, someone had written:

> For the Fifth Birthday of
> Charlotte S. Mackie
> from
> Shirley Ann Horsburgh
> November 5th, 1873

Beneath this, in a somewhat fresher color was:

> To Little Cathie Murray Pryor
> From Her Godmother
> Charlotte S. Woodstock
> Regina, July 2nd, 1892

Then, with a biro pen, came Mrs. Castle's long scrawl:

> For Shirley Norrington, souvenir of a meeting in Paris, this book comes back to by rights.
> Catherine M. Castle, Whitsunday 1963

"Lots of women, eh?" said Mrs. Castle. "If I waited another ten years I'd be giving you a real antique—one hundred years old. But I can't wait that long. I found this last winter when I was doing out the house before coming over here. I put a lot of stuff in storage. Anything my children couldn't agree about—who was to have what, I mean—I just stored. They can fight after I'm dead. I told them that before I move into a small apartment and spend my old age babysitting..." She lost the thread of whatever she meant to say. "The book...I've got a sentimental attachment to it. But I figure you ought to have something from your own people, and knowing the

Woodstocks like I do I think it's all the heritage you're likely to see. Don't look so blank. Don't any of these names mean anything to you? Why, Shirl, with the exception of my name, and your mother's being skipped because she was overlooked, this is your female line. It sure shows it's a man's world. I'll bet you know every surname on your father's side!"

"I know Woodstock—not that it means anything to me. Pryor, now... Look, there's a Shirley! I was always told I was called after a maid we had."

"Pryor's me," said Mrs. Castle. "I was Cat Pryor. Mackie's your grandmother—her maiden name. I put you down as Norrington because I can't keep track of you. You've been what? Higgins? Perrigny?" She pronounced the latter name with great sureness, with the accent on the second syllable. "Norrington was at least how you started off. Your grandmother wasn't really my godmother. She was self-appointed. I was created, christened and confirmed an Anglican, and to your female family that was practically the pope's pocket. A lot of them have got more respectable since, though. Your mother doesn't believe in anything except reincarnation any more. That's respectable. I mean, no one would attack it, though I'm darned if I want my soul to come back in any form but me. *Me*, Shirl—me all the way. I didn't think that way before, but I advise it. When you get up in the morning say to yourself, 'Me now, and I'll see about the rest later.'"

It was not a guidebook Mrs. Castle had given her but perhaps the very text Shirley's grandmother had read to the unemployed: the price the poor had been obliged to pay for fried eggs in the Woodstocks' kitchen.

The Peep of Day
or
A Series
of the
EARLIEST RELIGIOUS INSTRUCTION
the
Infant Mind is Capable of Receiving

"I don't mean you've got to *read* it," said Mrs. Castle, sounding offended. "You can do that later. There can't be anything there you don't already know." But Shirley was already immersed.

> How easy it would be to hurt your poor little body!
> If it were to fall into the fire, it would be burned up.
> If hot water were to fall upon it, it would be scalded. If it were to fall into deep water, and not be taken out very soon, it would be drowned. If a great knife were run through your body, the blood would come out. If a great box were to fall on your head, your head would be crushed. If you were to fall out of the window, your neck would be broken. If you were not to eat food for a few days...

"... in the train coming up from Rome I fell in with a French-Canadian," said Mrs. Castle. "Nice boy, round your age, maybe younger. A *lot* younger most likely. Went to the diner with me. Drank white wine, said he was allergic to the red. Gives him a rash on the neck. Father a dentist. This boy kept running down his own family till I didn't know where to look. Said they were vulgar. Well, I haven't met them so I wouldn't know. I told him there were vulgar people in Saskatchewan and any place else he cared to mention. He said, 'Well perhaps you always were vulgar. We only became vulgar because of our contact with the English.'"

"What English?" said Shirley, leaving *Peep of Day* with reluctance. "What did he mean?"

Mrs. Castle shrugged. She began gathering together her notebook, her pen, her gloves. "He let me pay for his lunch," she said.

"Half the men I know are like that. Is that vulgar?"

"Careless. It might have been all I had in the world."

"I suppose it was rude. Was it? I'm never sure what rude means." She tried to see the train, the hand around the glass of wine.

"Oh, I don't know," said Mrs. Castle quite cheerfully. "From his point of view I think it was just sociable. He was trying to make the conversation interesting for me. Well, Shirl, you've got plenty to read now, so don't let me keep you."

"Mrs. Castle—I've loved this. Aren't we going to see each other again?"

"There's no real need, is there? I've had a good look at you and I'll know what to tell your mother. We've been here, at Pons, which I was desiring to see. I'm going to Fontainebleau with a group from American Express this afternoon. I liked those éclairs."

"What are you going to say to Mother?"

"Nothing I couldn't put on tape for others to hear. That you're thin as a rail and you seem to know a lot of people. You're about like you always were, to tell you the truth. Reading instead of listening. Life isn't books. Did you know you were born feet first? If we see each other again sometime I'll tell you a lot that might interest you."

On the street Shirley felt as if she were a stranger in Paris and that Mrs. Castle had been here all her life. She saw her heading purposefully for what certainly must be the right bus stop. Had they said good-bye? Mrs. Castle swung back and called, "What'd your Italian friend—Gina?—what'd she do it for?"

"Renata—she's not Italian."

"Never mind. Why'd she try the suicide? To see what comes next?"

"Why, I think I told you, Mrs. Castle. She said she felt lonely, and she had a pain."

"Your mother had *you* without so much as an aspirin—feet first. Your husband is right. That girl is a pest. Keep away from her."

Under a shifting lace-pattern of leaves and sunlight, Mrs. Castle disappeared. Where she had been now stood a man carrying a folding chair. Shirley was myopic and accustomed to watching people vanish. She spoke confidently into the light and shadow: "Oh, Mrs. Castle, I left the house without any money this morning. I've got nothing on me, not even a bus ticket. Could you lend me something? I'll bring it round to your hotel tomorrow."

"Now, that's something I'd just never do," came the prairie voice. "Couldn't and wouldn't. You've had your book, and you've had your breakfast, and that's all I'm good for. Anyway, Shirl, your mother would be the first to remind you that a lady never needs anything. Never needs, never wants. Anyway, never asks."

4

SHIRLEY never failed to expect her mother's letters to contain magical solutions, and never failed to be disappointed. The correspondence between mother and daughter, Montreal and Paris, was an uninterrupted dialogue of the deaf. Shirley would beg for advice, only to be assured that her questions were unreadable; having solicited answers, she was afraid of what they might turn out to be, even though she envied the clairvoyance that must surely have inspired them. Sometimes she let the envelopes lie unopened for days, as though she feared that some form of unsatisfied justice might leap out of them and claw her to death. For that was the way she envisioned justice—a leopard in the dark. As for Mrs. Norrington, if she had chosen to ignore Shirley's last letter on the pretext that it was scrawled in rune, that did not mean she had failed to grasp what it might be about or that she lacked an opinion. Shirley's mother was one of a family of militant, university-trained prairie women. Long before Shirley was born she had published a thesis entitled "What Ruskin Missed," which dealt not so much with Ruskin as with an insignificant aspect of the Italian Renaissance: all Ruskin had missed in life was one or two painters. (Years later Shirley came across her mother's thesis filed In a university library under "Scottish Chieftains" with "Gray Family" as a cross-reference, which did not displease Shirley, for it meant that only the most persevering and gifted students would trace their way back to the proper century.)

Mrs. Norrington had emerged from her years of research far more affected by the lamentable story of Ruskin's marriage than by the history of art, for which, in spite of herself, she felt much of the prim contempt of her part of the world. For some time now she had been accumulating material for a second work she intended to call "What Effie Didn't Say." This would be a pamphlet—Shirley saw it in stiff, olive green covers—and would deal with Effie Gray's capacity for suffering and for forgiveness, with her sexual innocence, her long married virginity and the possible reasons for the final stroke of gumption. Time and passion moved in circles. Mrs. Norrington understood Effie, though an inborn prudence kept her from understanding Shirley. Now Effie and Shirley had somehow overlapped. Some seven months ago, in November, Mrs. Norrington's birthday present to her daughter—a pillow stuffed with pine needles—had arrived with a message skewered to its iron heart: "Well, dear girl, you are now twenty-six, the age Effie Gray was when she finally got rid of that Ruskin." It was not her mother's innocent obscurity that Shirley found dismaying, but the bland dialectic that led her to judge two men as one. In vain Shirley composed blotted, coffee-stained assurances that Philippe and Ruskin had nothing in common except the basic error-as-to-person that haunts every marriage. Mrs. Norrington continued to hint that although an unfulfilled union must be the most restful of all relationships, it had no spiritual merit if the husband were merely impotent or homosexual. No, it had to be more complicated still. An unshared religious vow would have received her approval even though she had often assured Shirley that she herself was and always would be "an extremely calm-minded agnostic."

I ought to stop bothering my mother, Shirley said, leaving Mrs. Castle with her principles and her independence at the right bus stop. She will never want to understand my handwriting. Why insist?

She had nothing to look forward to now except a long walk home. She thought of taking a taxi to Philippe's mother's house and asking the driver to wait while she tore up several flights, rang a bell, was inspected through a peephole, and then breathlessly asked for money. The picture was so terrifying that she was thankful to be here, penniless, crossing the road and entering the light and shade of the Luxembourg Gardens. Today's letter had at least assured her she might use a typewriter: it had been Mrs. Norrington's habit until now to tear up, unread, any message not written by hand. Some sharp drifter, some cunning neighbor, had probably talked her into believing that the progress of mankind depended on those who still wrote with a ballpoint pen. This person had then produced a broken-down Remington and sold it to her at an exorbitant price. On such encounters were based, usually, her mother's changes of heart.

Here is the fountain next to which Geneviève memorized Goosey Gander, Geneviève's green chair trustingly drawn up to Miss Thule's, Geneviève's bare knees against Miss Thule's postwar utility skirt. Shirley selected a chair in the consecrated spot and opened her guidebook, her true Word from home, *The Peep of Day*. "Could your father die?" she read. "Oh yes; many little children have no father. I have heard of a little child whose father fell down from a high ladder, and was killed. Another child's father was kicked by a horse, and died. Another father was digging a deep well, and his breath was stopped. Some children's fathers fall sick, and die." Shirley was pleased to be told something at last that seemed irrefutable. At her feet two children who did not appear to know each other crouched back to back drawing in the dust. She heard a whey-faced park mother asking in a sly whinny, "Are both of them yours?" Only then did she notice that one of the children was dark, perhaps North African. She shut the book, keeping a finger between the pages.

This is where I have been since last evening, she began all over again, trying to make some sort of story stand up for Philippe. I came home this morning from Renata's by Métro (true) and I stopped in the rue du Bac to shop for food for our lunch (plausible). I have been shopping. That is what I have been up to for the last sixteen hours. I've got olives and anchovies and garlic sausage and two sorts of cheese ... But no, because she had no money, not even a centime, and they would not have needed the anchovies because every second Sunday they went to Philippe's mother's for lunch. Today was a gala Sunday, with a gâteau St. Honoré fourteen inches high, studded all over with candied violets, stuffed with the very lightest cream until the cake seemed to float, all because Colette was safely home from her visit to New York. Colette, who was a hairdresser with an almost exclusively foreign clientele, had been taken there on the whim of a client who wanted her to show this woman's coiffeur exactly how Colette had obtained a certain shade of russet brown— so Colette had explained to her mother. Shirley imagined the three Perrignys around the gâteau St. Honoré. Whenever she saw Philippe and his family together, even in her mind, she thought she had been meant to save him and that this was what their marriage was about. "I was afraid of becoming like Maman," he had said once, which was alarming, for in his eyes his mother had no detestable qualities. Not long after their wedding Philippe had read Shirley's future in the lines of her hand, which perhaps meant he had not been able to see it in his mind. She lay on a high hospital bed in Berlin and looked past him to a leathery sky. His back was to the window. He said that her head line was shallow and the fate line broken in two; it took up an uneven course a little after the break. A choppy life, an American life, he told her. She thought that he was attempting to make her pain seem inevitable because he felt responsible for it. He had dragged her across half of Europe in a Deux-Chevaux. He thinks he has caused the miscarriage, she said to herself. But it was an accident, both our faults. This wasn't the reason why he married me. Was it?

"Perhaps you had a religious crisis once, and that explains the break," he said, not mocking her, but trying to find in her hand a subject she avoided. *We have been abandoned* was all she knew about the universe. She shook her head. "Or else it means you will do something foolish." He pressed her fingers back until her arched palm resembled a leaf.

"I may have done it, the foolish thing."

"You will forget it," he said gently, thinking she spoke of today. "I see you with seven children."

"Good. So do I." Why did he say he could see her and not himself? She could speak without weeping about her dead father, she never mentioned her dead young husband, she was not crying now, and so he believed that she cast sorrow off easily and that grief was a temporary arrangement of her feelings. He thought this to be an American fact which made for a comfortable existence, without memory and without remorse.

She was not as careless as he seemed to want her to be: at least she knew what she dreaded. Her accident had shocked him. He felt culpable, but misunderstood what the feeling meant. She had considered Philippe invulnerable and, because he was accurate, superior to herself. None of the wretched friends she had received so willingly into her affections had ever known how unclean she thought them. Now she saw that Philippe was still learning: aged twenty-nine, he discovered that the best of days contain wicked surprises. Her easy sympathy, her quick good faith and ready remorse were going to be of no use to him. Obsessed with the hidden meaning of ideas, he still believed people to be as they seemed—worse, that they were as they had to be. He thought that secrecy of mind was essential and that attitudes of the heart were easily defined. She had expected him to build a house for her, intellectually and sentimentally, and invite her inside. But as it turned out, it was she who invited him. The housing shortage in Paris, which now spanned two docile generations, created rules: one of the partners was supposed to provide an establishment. Two homeless persons simply never married. Philippe left his sister and his mother for an apartment where there was plenty of space but no room for anyone but Shirley. She made a place for his clothes by flinging her own across chairs, and they might have stayed there forever if Philippe had not put them back where they belonged.

The day moved: she dragged her iron park chair a few inches out of shadow. She remembered you had to pay to sit down in parks in Paris, and wondered what she would say when the slut with her paper tickets came by. She read, "There is no night in heaven, for the angels are never tired of singing, and they never wish to sleep. They are never sick, and they will never die." Each time the story she was composing for Philippe touched on the truth, it became improbable. Who would ever believe that her mother's oldest friend, Mrs. Cat

Castle, had refused to lend Shirley so much as bus fare? Perhaps Philippe was right and it was best to imagine other people only as they ought to be. Shirley would then be described by any of the Perrignys to survive her as naive, puritanical and alcoholic, for in their eyes that was the North American makeup. At least it was explicit; she had no firm picture of anyone. Early this morning, dragging her way home after the long night at Renata's, she had caught sight of herself in a charcutier's plate-glass window. She expected to see the face of someone easily exploited (how reliable Geneviève's mirrors turned out to be!) but the reflection said, "This is what you are like," and gave her back ruthlessly. Also, she was absurd. The belt of her macintosh trailed. On a glowing June morning she was prepared for rain and for night. Not caring for this memory, she rearranged it, and had herself proceeding up the rue du Bac adequately clothed and as daunting as her sister-in-law Colette. She backed up and saw the street from a distance. Across the road, pursuing Shirley in a bumbling sort of fashion, came a melancholy follower, a Turgenev hero with undone shoestrings. Properly managed it could take up to twelve minutes of any boring European movie. For an American film either of the two would have to be screaming. She laughed, and one of the children crouched at her feet thought she was mocking him. He tried to cover whatever he had been tracing in the dirt, but his hands were too small. He had drawn a lion or a sphinx with large feet; his creature was wearing boots. He said to Shirley, "It's a gentleman."

"I knew that," she answered. "I could tell because of the boots."

I was wearing those plastic boots from Canada, she would say to Philippe. I had the raincoat your sister has described as looking like part of a Boche uniform. We had all been promised a weekend of rain a few hours earlier, but as always I was the only person in Paris who had taken the forecast to heart. I was dressed for one or two events that never took place. *You* had said I shouldn't wear the macintosh because it was dirty. But you wouldn't let me give it to anyone, which would have been so easy and sensible! No, you advised me to take it to a cleaner's and have it dipped in embalming fluid.

My mother wrote, "If you marry him two things will always separate you—hygiene, because he is bound to be unwashed, and a way of considering worldly goods, because he is sure to be stingy." Wide of the mark. I think so. What now? Cross the park. Walk home. Find some money. Where? James, of course. My neighbor, James Chichalides. Philippe will be furious. All right, she said to Philippe. I can't keep on apologizing. I know you think my friends are trashy and I suppose they are; but where are yours? Another thing my mother wrote was, "Remember, they have no friends." You've got Geneviève, but I have never seen her. There is Hervé. School together, military service, Algeria together, but now you have wives and your wives pull you apart. I could describe a Geneviève, though I haven't seen one, but how to describe a Hervé? Hervé wouldn't know his own name if it weren't typed on a card and stamped by the police. He doesn't look in a mirror—he looks at an identity photo. If the police have sworn that face is Hervé, then of course it must be. If the police couldn't see him then he would either be invisible or he'd be somebody else. I have done something foolish, she said to Philippe. You said in Berlin I would. You saw it in my hand.

It stood to reason that all of her telephone calls could not be imaginary. In the shuttered living room she dialed his mother's number. The exchange (Galvani) conjured up heartless streets and dentists' wives wearing gloves as they lined up at bus stops. Colette answered and said, "Oh, it is you," with a new rasp to her English. She let Shirley ramble, or chatter, for a minute or two before breaking in with, "Dear Shirley, don't have the bother to come now unless you are hungry. I am tired after my journey and I am going to bed. Maman is resting. We are all tired here. Why are you sorry? Sorry about what? But no, but no. A friend of your mother's is equally important. No, Philippe has not gone to *Le Miroir* at all. He will not be working. That I can tell you without error. Wait, please, he says to me ... no, he says that he says nothing. Furious? Even not. What dramatic language you use. Apologize for what? No need, no reason, so please stop. I must leave you now. That is it. I leave you. Good-bye.

Shirley, please say good-bye, it is simpler than so much apology. Now I leave you. I hang up."

She could smell his cigarettes and something resembling the scent of her mother's house, which was of herbs drying, apples, dark books and camphor. She was smiling, as if the conversation with Colette had been something of a joke. In the bedroom the spider had vanished, but here was a reminder that Shirley had friends. She had to hold James Chichalides' letter close to her eyes because someone had told him once that a tiny hand was the sign of an intellectual. As she had guessed, it was an invitation to a party. "Bring anyone," he wrote, as if Philippe were anyone. His first message to her, almost two years ago, had pleaded, "Your records drown out my radio. Don't you think such noisy neighbors should get together?" He liked writing in English, which he spoke haughtily. "Donhent yo thenk?" was how he would have read his own phrase aloud. She remembered how often she had climbed two winding flights, always in search of something. Pressing the doorbell (chimes) she would remember that today was Sunday, that Paris was empty, and all the Saturday parties were over.

James answered the door, sure of himself and sly, smiling with his head down, and she thought, as when she had first seen him, "Black fox." She held out his letter. "All right, I'm here," she said. "But you ought to stop addressing letters just to me. Philippe doesn't understand things like that. That's partly what I came up to tell you."

He took the letter and stuffed it in his blazer pocket as if he intended to use it again. His front door opened straight onto a living room in which two fair-haired girls sat with their shoes kicked off and a heaped amber ashtray between them. On a card table were a tray of drinks and the remains of a large untidy breakfast.

"We were expecting you last night, Madame Perrigny," said Rose O'Hara, rising to meet her. "James said he gave the invitation to your husband. I told him it wasn't tactful to address it to you."

"Philippe never comes," said James, "so why bother?"

"He hates parties," Shirley said.

"I know," said Rose. "And we bore him. I'm sorry."

She and Shirley, comfortable in each other's presence, smiled, excluding the others. Rose was tall and awkward. Her mouth was large, her skirts too long, and she wore her soft, floppy hair Gin Lane style, held with combs, pins and even what seemed to be bits of string. Once, sitting on the edge of James's bathtub, Shirley had watched Rose hopelessly trying to fasten the limp strands, and she had listened while Rose told her that there were not enough men to go around, that clever men chose stupid women because of their restful qualities, and that anyone left over was subaltern. She meant James and herself; that was what Rose was talking about. But Shirley had taken it as a reference to Philippe, and she understood that she was the uninteresting girl keeping an intelligent person out of the hands of a woman more suited to him. She said she was sorry, to which Rose replied, "Oh, you needn't feel sorry for *me*."

The second blond girl, who had kept her eyes closed until now, as if hoping to be surprised, suddenly opened them. "Oh, a woman," she said, in a light German accent. "Why not a man, finally?"

"You mean you couldn't hear me?" Shirley said.

"It is Sunday, my dear, and Madame Perrigny has dropped by for an aperitif," James said, trying to provoke a new decorum. He stared at the girl as if to say, Don't do anything that can shock Madame Perrigny or frighten her away.

"James, are you and Rose adopting children again?" Shirley said. "You're going to be in the most horrible trouble one of these days."

"What you have just said is not interesting," said James. He had a long nose and slightly troubled skin, as if he had scratched at chickenpox. His hair gleamed like a freshly washed blackboard; his hands had been given middle-class European care, which meant their owner did not wish to be thought of as someone who had ever had to change a tire. He moved in this atmosphere of women like a bird in air. "What nationality would you think I was, if you didn't know?" he asked Shirley.

They must have been debating this when Shirley rang the bell. He wanted to be taken for something he was not, but what was he? "That Greek upstairs," was what Philippe called him. To Shirley, "Greek" took in everything at the other end of the Mediterranean. Greeks, Turks, Egyptians and Lebanese were to be encountered at large cocktail parties with smart, dark wives covered in lamé and Chanel pearls. When a group formed and drifted out to eat supper somewhere, the Greek or the Turk always was along to pay the check. He never seemed to feel slighted; all he wanted was to be seen, with his wife, paying for a crowd of strangers in an expensive place: but seen by whom? Concentrating on James, whom she knew well—perhaps, in a sense, better than Philippe—and on Athens, which she had never visited, she cast up "Byron" but could get no further. James's French had been inculcated by a self-exiled provincial schoolmaster. He sounded like those stateless Egyptians who always replied, when asked what they were, "My culture is French; I have read Racine." James's clothes were English, but so flawless that they could only have come from a Merrie England boutique on the continent. At least James has a name, she thought: the Lebanese banker or the Alexandrian lawyer ordering champagne for twelve strangers never tells his name, or no one asks.

"I'd say you looked sort of French-English," she said.

He lifted a hand as if to bless her. Sunlight poured into the room. "More French, or more English?"

Thinking of Philippe, she said, "More English."

"There," said James to the other two. "*She* knows."

"You hate them because of Cyprus, you said, and because they never did anything for the Christian community," the German girl complained.

"It is true," said James. "They built playing fields and encouraged young boys to wear baggy gray shorts and never to change their underwear and to run round and round to no purpose, but other than that they did nothing for the Christian community. I agree. Everyone hates them. Everyone likes being mistaken for them."

"Oh, James, I don't think so," Shirley said. "Not any more. Perhaps in hot countries. Even there..."

"Not in one cold country I could mention," said mild Rose fiercely. She stood up and shook ash from her skirt. "Give Madame Perrigny a cigarette, James, instead of standing there preening and embarrassing her with questions."

James saw Rose out as far as the landing; Shirley could hear a whispered quarrel.

"She had missed Mass this morning," the German girl explained. "Now she had gone to her own home to pray and to have a bath. She will not use James's bathtub."

"Does he still keep books in the clothes hamper?"

"Only *The Whip Angels* now. We know it by heart. It was written by a very moral lady who had seen strange things in her youth. The English is without fault."

"Was her name Miss Thule?"

"I cannot say."

"Does James read aloud to you or do you read in turn?"

"Why? You think he is not like other people? Oh, it is not so, I assure you. *Er nimmt schon Frauen, aber es muss doch immer einer dabei sein.*" She spoke scornfully, with her head tossed back, as though copying James. When she slipped into German, she evoked the thick white stockings and buckled shoes, the laced bodice and the petticoats of a postcard costume. It was nearly a dialect; for *Frauen* she had said something close to *vrown* and Shirley had not at first understood what she meant. "We have all slept here because it was so late after the party," the girl continued, "and we are believably tired."

"You mustn't tell me things about Rose," Shirley said.

"I am telling you of myself," said the girl. She repeated her own name—it sounded as if it might be Crystal Lily. In her mind Shirley corrected it to "Christel." "You have nice hair," said Crystal Lily, presently.

"Have I? My husband won't think so when he sees it. I cut it with someone's nail scissors around three o'clock this morning."

The girl was slightly offended. "I have often been told *I* have nice hair." She paused, accustomed to some tradition of reciprocal compliments: none came. "So has James," she said presently. "Very nice natural hair. Rose used to admire his decadent Roman head, as it is called, though he is without error a Greek. Now she is tired. Every evening he goes to her after work. After *her* work. We do not know James to work. He carries an English newspaper, which he inspects, and a bottle of wine which he will not let her put on ice, though she is made sick at heart by warm wine. She will not drink it warm, so he drinks it all. He says, 'A gentleman looks after the drink.' This is said to be English. Rose buys a chicken already roasted and frozen peas. James can eat a whole camembert. Rose dislikes the smell, and she has to leave the table. They make love à l'Américaine; at first it was so as to save time, but now she has taken advice from her father, and she will no more. And so she prays, and she has several baths a day.

"James leaves her after supper and comes home. He sleeps alone because he is afraid he might snore and be laughed at. Rose is anxious because of her father and because she is religious. I do not think they are suitable together. Their happiest times are when I am with them. I sleep between them so that Rose has the impression she sleeps with a sister, you see, or with a beloved friend from schooldays. James says he gets no sleep, but I have heard him dreaming and grinding his teeth. Last night at the party he asked Rose if she would consent to wash the windows because his two sisters are here for a visit from Greece. I feel that James is not consistent and he is looking for another girl." She looked at Shirley and said, "How long have you known him?"

"I'm married," Shirley said.

"James would not mind," said the girl. "You are about his age, no?"

"A year or two younger maybe. I'm twenty-six."

"Oh," said the girl, who was perhaps seventeen. She fell silent and sat smoothing her own hair, staring at the wall.

James, returning, walked twice around the room. Silence was too much for him. He said, "There is no happiness. She is in a state of grace three days a week. She writes to her father every day and tells him what and why and how she regrets, and the aged voyeur writes back that he is sorry his little white lamb has been dragged in the mud." He stopped before Crystal Lily and said angrily, "I see you are admiring my apartment. Perhaps you have never seen it in daylight before? It has been furnished by my landlady, who is anonymous. She is the richest woman in Paris but she rides in the Métro second class. Her sole extravagance is Nescafé with which a former husband keeps her supplied. It is widely believed that he mixes poison in it, but so far only her guests have died. The furniture is hers. The accessories are my own." He meant the corrida posters, the ashtrays lifted from cafés and the doll in evzone costume on the television set. The doll was a lamp. James switched it off and on rapidly now to show the lightbulb concealed under the skirt. Electric wires dangled, hung and stole along the walls, leading to lamps, stereo speakers and a record player the length of a rowboat. He also owned an air conditioner and a propped-up and forgotten electric iron. "One more drink," said James, though he had not given Shirley anything until now. The glass became cold in her hand as he poured ouzo over ice.

The progress of this day was toward disaster; she had known it in the park. She heard her mother saying, "You might be twelve, but you do act nine." You might be twenty-six, she told herself now, but you do act fourteen. Not even a clever fourteen; a sharp fourteen, entangled in some other person's bogus suicide, would not have sat drinking all night in the suicide's kitchen: she would have found where the bedsheets were and made herself a bed, and in the morning she would have eaten bacon and toast and marmalade, without dismay, stepping over Renata's dead body to get at the butter. In front of the Rodin museum a refugee had once asked Shirley something. His situation in Paris was complicated, she remembered; what she recalled of his person was a graying crew cut. "You can call from my place," she had said. "I live about five minutes from here." Half an hour later she hit him with the telephone, meaning to kill him. He thought she was mad, and she was afraid because she sensed he thought this. He was the ugly product of city life and of chance encounters. The shocked, foreign man sat trembling. She would have done anything for him at that moment—nursed his wounds, found money if he needed it; she saw the shape of a cloudy feeling she must always have had about people.

"Why did you bring me here?" he said.

"I brought you here for the reason I said on the street—to see if I could help you."

"How old are you?" He held his ear, palm flat. "To look at, you have no age. You could be a child, anything. I thought you were thirty, then twenty, now I don't know. I think you are young and hysterical, or old and mad."

"I'm twenty-four," she had said.

"Then, miss, you are still young, but much too old to be innocently helpful."

The direction of her life had snapped in two; one of the lines in her hand shifted. The refugee was on the new, disjointed line. She was independent, but she had never wanted such a thing.

"Another drink?" said James.

"I haven't eaten anything since yesterday at lunch," Shirley said. "My kitchen is so full of dishes I can't even get in it. James, may I ask you something privately?"

"Go and read in the bathroom," said James at once to Rose's friend.

"You know you've always begged me to ask you a favor..."

"Yes," he said. "Because I owe you something. I should have married you, but perhaps that would not have been a favor."

"Look—I'll tell you quickly. I haven't got a franc and there's nothing in the house. I haven't eaten anything since yesterday at lunch. You know—I've been with Renata. No, I don't want cold toast from your breakfast, thank you. I'd feel better if I just had some money in my purse, until I see Philippe tonight...or until Tuesday, because tomorrow is a bank holiday."

"Only money? I thought you wanted a favor." Like a woman, James kept money all over his flat in odd hiding places: the evzone doll had a fortune in his boots.

"That's too much," said Shirley, squinting and counting. "More than I need."

"Take it," said James. "More than you need does not exist." For what he knew of women was that they were at the beck and call of necessities that bored him—social and economic—wanting to be married because of these last two, and wishing to be loved for some quite other reason. "Poor old Crystal," he said. "So nasty and so obedient. She will sit now on the clothes hamper reading books until she is called, but what she really is doing is thinking of something to say to me. Something that will tick and ring an alarm bell and blow up the house. Then she will say to Rose, 'James is in pieces—let us sell him to a butcher.'"

"Wait, I want to tell you one thing. You know about Renata. When I came in this morning I didn't know where Philippe was and he didn't know where I was. It's all wrong. My mother and father managed that part of it better."

"My father respected my mother and my mother did not desire a secret life," said James, meaning that this was as things should be. He walked around the room again, switched the television on to a white snowfall, touched the side of a coffee pot—it was obviously cold. He would rather have talked about clothes (his own); a safari in Kenya; this day and the next—nothing further; about the permanent partouze in a flat on the avenue d'Iéna and the member of parliament who walked in fully dressed, wearing the Legion of Honor, and who clapped his hands and said, "*Allez, allez, Mesdames*—I have an important rendezvous in twenty minutes with the Turkish foreign minister."

She knew this, but was still impelled to go on "Now he's at his mother's and won't even come to the telephone. He must be more than angry—I'm scared of seeing him now."

"Rose has never met Renata," he said, which was not irrelevant. It meant he wanted Shirley to stop talking about last night. She remembered his fear of being left with any one person. He would give time, money, rapid advice, an introduction, whatever would stop the problem, anything so as not to hear any more.

"She may not have met Renata but she seems to have met Crystal Lily," Shirley said.

"...who is free to meet anyone else. You can take her away, if you want her."

"No thanks. I've already told you about that. She looks seventeen. One day you'll be in trouble." He thinks I am jealous, she realized. He thinks I am brainless. No, he is bored. Five minutes ago he had three women. One went home, one is sulking in the bathroom, and the third has said, "Lend me money. Where is my husband? You have no right to that young girl." And so he hums and sits with the points of his elbows on the breakfast table, and snaps his fingernails on the coffee pot, first one hand then the other.

More decorum: Rose, returning, made a performance of handing James a key, so that no one would think she had casual access to his flat.

The Crystal girl, wandering in when she heard the new voice, nursed an arm as though someone had hurt her. She said to Shirley, "He has said mean things about Rose."

"Don't be stupid," Shirley said. "Rose was never mentioned."

"He does complain about you, Rose," said the girl, with casual spitefulness her friends appeared to accept. This was the bait, the start of a game. "Last night he complained to me about your cooking and many similar aspects."

In a voice like Mrs. Castle's, Shirley said, "I'd better leave you. I'm going to...What am I going to do? Oh, yes, I'm going to a restaurant to eat an enormous meal on James's money. Then I'm going to bed. Though I'd better do something about the kitchen before Philippe gets back. It's a pigsty, and why argue over a kitchen when there are so many..."

Crystal Lily, who had inherited someone's cold, sea-blue eyes, said, "Is marriage happy? Does it take too much time? Would you cook a meal only for yourself?" She had momentarily lost interest in her captors. Briefly she examined a future without either one of them.

Rose, whose father had sometimes worn a wig, who had bequeathed an understanding of loud melancholy laughter, said, "Of course it is happy."

"He says whatever *you* cook tastes of blotting paper," cried the girl. "Gunshot peas. Blotting-paper chicken."

"Be careful, Crystal."

None of them noticed Shirley take her leave. In a few minutes, she thought, they will have Crystal's head in a teapot and she will say drowsily, "Twinkle, twinkle." Only by reducing the scene to children's folklore could Shirley be rid of it. And if Crystal ever wants rescuing, she went on, why, she knows where I live and who I am.

5

A CONNECTION between life and pleasure could only be found from hour to hour; Shirley knew it, just as she knew that appeals to memory were never perfectly answered. Nevertheless, because of her mother's letter, still more because of her conversation at breakfast with Mrs. Castle, she thought of her parents. Eccentric, uncomformable, entirely peculiar by Canadian standards, they had never doubted themselves or questioned their origins or denied the rightness of their own conduct; they could be judged but never displaced. Whereas she, ordering breakfast in a café-restaurant in the middle of the afternoon, paying for it with borrowed money, was a refugee. It had nothing to do with one's being foreign or ignorant: Mrs. Cat Castle, without a word of French or of regret, had got on the right bus—has been on the right buses all over Europe, in fact. Philippe was at his mother's, where he had said he would be, even if it was, as Mrs. Castle had mentioned, a bad place for a man.

She remembered how her elderly father had called her Belle, first because he disliked the name Shirley, then because Belle corresponded to a generation and a measure of female beauty. It had been his habit to replace every second meal with a raw onion in milk, explaining whenever he was asked about it, "It moveth the bowels." Sometimes he brought his milk-and-onion to the table, but on a fine day he liked eating out of doors, crouched on the back steps in sight of five backyards. She could not bear to suppose that the old man who sat there chewing bits of onion and spilling milk could be her father. "I am adopted," she told the neighbors, but no one believed her. Once, seeing that the child minded, he said placidly, "Well Christ, Belle, who's eatin' it?"

"You will never live a life of reason," Philippe had told her. "Not unless you learn logic and order." Well—who's eatin' it? She imagined the two of them, seven years from now, aged thirty-three and worse, sailing past the sugar-lump coast of Yugoslavia on the annual August adventure. "We picked bluebells and tied them to our bicycles; but they died within the hour."

And so she was here, a refugee in a restaurant, on a red leather banquette. She sat between two silent strangers, a man and a girl. The girl had built a barrier against Shirley; it consisted of a worn, stuffed, costly handbag; a copy of the weekly guide to Paris entertainments opened to a page of movies, with a penciled cross next to *This Sporting Life*; a white chiffon scarf; a pack of Craven A, which Philippe also smoked; a bunch of violets that had been sprayed with a vehement synthetic scent; and a dog's leash. The dog, a brushed, docile cocker spaniel, lay in the narrow lane formed by Shirley's table and the girl's. The waiter now stood over them, recording Shirley's order for orange juice, beer, coffee, ham and eggs and buttered toast, to be brought all at once, together; he read this back to her with disbelief. While they struggled for understanding, the girl sat back and listened and seemed delighted. Her hands were as large as a boy's; she placed them on the table, palms down, as though preparing to defend a position. She is French, Shirley decided, because she is so self-contained. On the other hand, what is she doing alone, lunching in a public place at such an unusual hour? There must have been serious family business behind it—an old grandmother who has to be visited every Sunday and who is on a diet of slops and so never gives the girl enough to eat. She is at ease with money, otherwise she'd have gone home, no matter how far away it might be, and catch the cold mashed potatoes left over from lunch. She is not quite French. She is at loose ends. She is Swiss, with a paranoid mother. Her father has brought her to Paris where he is attending a congress on Persian theology. No—her parents are divorced. She lives with a

Hungarian mother in Lausanne in one of those streets full of traffic signals. Her father works for Pan-American. He lunches with his American mistress then takes his daughter to *This Sporting Life*.

The waiter put before her a plate holding two slivers of ham and a pickle. Shirley formed a sentence, but she had been daydreaming in English and by the time she remembered the French word for "toast," which was "toast," he had vanished. From the table on her left, her second neighbor silently passed across a basket of bread and a pot of mustard. "Oh, thank you!" Shirley cried, with the eager exaggerated gratitude that Philippe found so unnecessary.

"It was an ordinary gesture," he would have told her. "You must not give it more significance than it contains."

There are no ordinary gestures in cities, she told him now. Even the most simple courtesy has a meaning. She was pleased with her answer and added it to a conversation they would have on the Yugoslav cruise seven years from now.

Of the man on her left, she had seen only a nicotine-stained hand and an enormous signet ring. She stared quickly at the girl, perceiving her ironed blouse and freshly washed hair and the faintly Slavic lift to her cheek bones. There was never any knowing how St. Joseph would strike. The girl slid a cigarette from the pack and began rummaging through her handbag, which was her first untidy gesture and led Shirley to say to herself, Oh, she's American. It seemed to her that there had been some business going on between her two neighbors before her coming had put a stop to it. She expected the hand with the ring to reach across and snap a gold lighter under the girl's nose, but presently the girl produced a folder of matches bearing the name of a restaurant in Bougival. She had the loaded handbag of someone who camps out and seldom goes home, or who imagines life must be full of emergencies. Shirley's own purse contained nothing but a pencil, a latchkey, James's francs, a comb, a paper handkerchief and her sole heirloom, *The Peep of Day*. Breakfast now proceeded with orange juice and two quivering undercooked eggs on a cold plate. "Toast," she said correctly.

"I know, I know," said the waiter, disburdening his tray of a pat of butter.

She drank the orange juice, rejected the eggs, and began to read *The Peep of Day* in a furnace of neon.

"One day God will burn up this world we live in," she read. "It is dreadful to see a house on fire. Did you ever see one? But how dreadful it will be to see this great world, and all the houses and trees burning! The noise will be terrible; the heat will be very great. The wicked will never be able to escape from God. They will burn for ever and ever. The world will not burn forever; it will be burnt up at last, and God will make another much better than this."

"Plain common sense," Shirley said. She closed her eyes, saw her bed in the curtained room as Philippe had left it. She dreamed she was sleeping and that someone woke her by breathing through a wall. She sat up sharply.

The girl smiled at her and said softly, "You were dreaming."

"I'm afraid so. I hope I didn't talk."

"I wouldn't have let you. I'd have woken you, discreetly." Her voice was lower in pitch than the Paris level, but unmistakably French. "I dream, too. Last night I had such a nightmare that my mother had to come to me." She blew smoke and sent ash all over Shirley's butter. "It was about a rosebush growing in a pot on a radiator. It had the shape of a Christmas tree and was covered all over in pink flowers. I turned it so that it could get light on all sides, and I saw that the roses that had been next to the wall were a mass of dust and mildew."

The man pushed his table away from the banquette, tossed his napkin down, and walked heavily away.

I don't blame you for leaving us, Shirley said silently. I envy you, in fact. She tells her dreams. Only one of her in Paris and Saint Joseph put her next to me.

"I did not ask him to buy me cigarettes or violets," said the girl. "It was his own idea."

"Together?" said the wild-haired waiter loudly. "Are you together?

One bill or two?" To avoid any further telling of dreams, Shirley had gone back to her book. "You, madame," he said. "I'm off duty now—if you wouldn't mind paying. Are you and this young lady together? Is it one bill, or is it two?"

"Why, no, of course we aren't together," Shirley said. She was surprised by the question and even more by the way the girl glanced at her, waiting for an answer. Why doesn't she speak up? Shirley wondered. She was eating up a chocolate pudding when I came in, and she's been sitting, smoking, making pickup conversation as if she were waiting for some other person or just killing time.

She paid her own bill, feeling uneasy, as if she were responsible for something imperfectly explained. She paid for eggs she had not eaten and for beer and coffee the waiter had forgotten to bring. She forgot that she would be expected to return the francs James had given her; they were only stage francs, of no real value. The girl watched her, smiling. Then she said softly, "Watch the comedy."

The act is what she means, Shirley thought. In English we would call it the act.

To the waiter, now adding up a second and quite long list of figures, the girl said "Don't bother going on—I can't pay." She said it two or three times, laughing up at him, until he stopped and made slow-motion of looking up, pencil pressed hard on the pad. He was an actor too.

"No," he said. "No. The second time today." Loudly, to the boy clearing away ashtrays, "Olivier! Fetch Madame. And tell her why."

"Oh, *Madame*," said the girl; it was plain that an edifice fell.

Shirley saw herself getting up, as the man had done, and pushing her table out of the row; she heard herself saying, "Excuse me" and "Good-bye." Instead she remembered the money that was not hers and so had no importance or meaning, and said, "It's all right. Don't trouble Madame. I can pay."

Well, that is what it has become, she said to herself, this business of caring for strangers. If I dared, I would sleep on the stained tablecloth, the way refugees who can't pay their hotel bills try to sleep in cafés; but first I shall settle up so that this Russian-looking girl needn't face Madame. I can't face my mother-in-law or even Philippe, and when I'm with my sister-in-law I spill wine and talk nonsense, and so I shall pay up. Madame frightens her—she smiles, but see how she twists the match folder in her fingers. She has money somewhere; even the spaniel looks as if he had a private income. Today was an accident. She wanted to do something daring and then she took fright. Four thousand francs? I wonder what the spaniel ordered?

Just as the waiter snatched up Shirley's money, Madame arrived. She was short, square, lame and mustached, as the girl had surely expected.

"They came in together," the waiter said, including them in the sweep of his pencil. "Or almost. Mademoiselle was waiting for someone, and madame or mademoiselle here," indicating Shirley "seemed to be looking for someone too."

"We were both waiting," said the girl. Her attitude now was such that her conscience obliged her to be accurate. "Actually, I do not know this lady well."

"If you weren't expecting this lady, why did you go on eating after you knew you had no money?" said Madame. "You might have caused trouble."

"The dog had creole rice, carrots Vichy, a hamburger with a fried egg, and coffee with milk," said the waiter, reading his record of the meal. "Four lumps of sugar. That I saw."

"Why shouldn't Bobby eat?" said the girl, with grief in her eyes. "He is innocent."

"The two of them came in together," the waiter reaffirmed. He looked with some tenderness at the girl. Shirley was the delinquent—she had enticed her here. Shirley was a predator; his glance said so.

"I shall tell you the truth," said the girl. "I was not sure my friend would turn up. Also she was not sure that *I* would come. Our appointment depended on each of us remembering the other." She smiled and folded her large hands and looked down at them. Delicately she begged Madame and the waiter to understand: this was a private and particular situation. She added, "Don't blame the dog."

"Certainly not," Madame said. "If people were as simple as dogs there might be some pleasure in running a restaurant."

"And now," said the girl, turning her eyes to Shirley, "will you accompany me to my home? I live nearby. My father will want to settle this. He does not want us to owe money."

The waiter sneered, Madame had gone red as a radish, and only the bus boy seemed to have some grasp of what had really taken place. He looked at Shirley with a sympathy that lasted until she returned his look; then he turned away. She began to understand what these strangers were thinking: the girl had been too innocent, too pure, or else too clever. Got a meal out of it—good girl. Lesson for the other one. The foreigner doesn't dare face the father, of course.

"Why do I have to see your father?" said Shirley. She began lettering her name and address inside the cover of the Bougival match folder. "He can send me a check if he wants to."

The girl pocketed the address and wound the dog's leash around her wrist. Her smile and her gesture to Madame and the waiter (both were waiting to see the outcome of this) meant she was leaving the violets for them. "I insist," said the girl. "I live nearby." She was taller than Shirley. Shirley followed her because she could not bear to stay here one more second under the eyes of their audience, and because it would be easier to say good-bye on the street. Outside, the girl said, "Are you parked nearby? Oh. Then we shall have to take a taxi. It is hours by bus."

"You told me you lived in the neighborhood," said Shirley, but then, hearing in her own voice a petulance she despised, she decided she must have understood nothing of the kind. "I have been wondering one thing," she said. "Though it would be too perfect to be true. It is because of the way you speak and the cigarettes you smoke. Is your name Geneviève?"

"No, it's Claudie. Claudie Maurel."

Their taxi rushed them westward along the left bank of the Seine until they came to a waste country of filling stations and shut, blind-looking factories: here the Seine was a dirty river on which floated refuse and oil and an oil-stained pigeon. In Shirley's calendar of time this was a Sunday in the past. She fixed a point, a beginning of time, and put a finger on the circle as the minute hand began its sweep round. "You never once asked me if time is necessary," her mother had complained.

The girl gazed out the window in a kind of enchantment. She seemed waxen, as if she had died young and had been preserved. Pete and Shirley had seen an embalmed infant under glass in an Italian church. "She still has her own original hair," their guide had told them.

The girl sighed. "It isn't every day that I ride in taxis."

Because her father has a chauffeur, Shirley had to suppose. Shirley's mother thought that shady people cruised around in taxis to pick up schoolgirls and stun them with hypodermic needles. Perhaps the girl had been taught the same story. She tried to remember how she had met Renata: Renata had been a pickup—like this girl; like Philippe. The taxi seemed to be leaving Paris. Perhaps they were driving to her family's weekend cottage—"the secondary residence" was what it was known as in Paris. Even Philippe used the expression with a straight face. Or the drive might end on a half-moon of gravel edged with those ketchup-colored sage flowers, before the brick packing-case crowned with Victorian towers that Parisians imperturbably called "a château."

They crossed the river between red-and-white barriers and blinking lights; the bridge, like much of the capital, was under repair. A wall of stopped cars halted them. "Sunday drivers," said Claudie, marveling, as if she had heard of such creatures but never had seen any evidence of them until now. Shirley had glimpsed between a sign reading "Autoroute" and wondered once more where they were going. She wanted to speak to the girl, to question her, but she was dulled and silenced and depressed now; and in any case the day was lost. Perhaps they would end up in Versailles or Chartres or Le Mans. She recalled a large ugly square in Le Mans and a restaurant where, her ears bludgeoned by a jukebox, she had sat over her cooling coffee while Philippe paid the luncheon check. Just as now, she had embarked on the wrong ship; she had drifted away from shore and to the wrong destination. There had come over her a wild and urgent need to be attractive to provincial louts with ducktail haircuts lounging along the bar. The long, alcoholic and affectionate lunch with Philippe had not ended in bed, as they had intended, but in talk. Philippe had confided that one of his secret dilemmas resided in his inability to attract women of great distinction or beauty. Oh? Yes, he said, and when an unattainably lovely girl did become accessible, why, then he was afraid of becoming impotent—of failing to please. Impotent *mentally*, he added—whatever that meant.

Really? She said. You never were with me. Of course, I was available from the first day on, and not very pretty. Oh, *mentally*. I wouldn't have known. I mean, I would not have thought of asking, How is it in your mind? She had cured another person of a similar fear, she said. It had been no trouble at all—no effort. She had never been certain what she had said or done to make the difference; but the person had assured her there was a difference, for which he had been grateful. He was still grateful, in fact, and so friendly. Who? Oh, the Greek in the apartment two flights up from us. That Greek with the rancid hair who invites us to parties? Yes, that one. Was this recent? Fairly recent—that's why I remember it. It was before we were married, of course. Before we were married but after you met me? I can't remember. It may have overlapped. Outside was a dull Sunday. They had been driving back from Brittany. Philippe had said, Shall we wait until Paris or take a room? Oh, take a room.

Past the Renault factories, closed and dark, she and Claudie shot along an empty street and paused, alone, before a traffic light. From a half-wrecked house came screams of fear or of hilarity. "Tramps live in there," said Claudie. "Men, and women too. When the house is torn down they will have nowhere to go. My father says they will survive the summer and perhaps the autumn, but luckily for society the winter will finish them off. Alcoholics are susceptible to pneumonia. That is nature's way of protecting the rest of us."

New-looking houses with mean, narrow balconies appeared on

the fringes of Shirley's numbed vision. She saw a lawn, a Swiss gnome fishing in a bucket, a used-car garage with two Volkswagens behind a cobwebby window; prefab army barracks—no, these were dwellings; their rooftops were hanging gardens of aerials. The girl spoke quite happily: "You will meet them now. They despise me and made me beg for everything. Everything I wear or eat. They have stolen my son. After he was born they took him away. He believes I am his sister. At least I *think* that is what he thinks!"

"Well, you have a child," said Shirley. "How nice." She was uneasy with people who talked about stolen children. Swedish films had given her the impression that conversation in an unknown tongue consisted of nothing except "Where is God?" and "Should one have children?" although, in reality, everyone in those foreign countries was probably saying "How much does it cost?" and "Pass the salt." Knowing that Shirley was not French, the girl might have been trying to sound foreign and enigmatic too. It made conversation as easy and aimless as swimming.

"Yes, a little boy. And *you* have a husband," said the girl, looking at Shirley's ring. Her eyes turned away from the ring with a sharp, catty expression— a Renata sort of look.

"He is often away," Shirley muttered. She seemed incapable of bringing out a few needed phrases, such as "Good-bye," or "It doesn't concern you." She went on to say stupidly, "He is traveling," thinking, He might as well be.

"I wish my father would travel," said the girl. "We are all cowed by him. I am afraid that one day he will beat my mother, who is so fragile and small. Sometimes I think he already has beaten her. Those are the dark corners in a woman's life."

The driver had not once turned, or even glanced at the mirror. When he pulled up in a street planted with frail, new trees, Shirley saw that he was Algerian. She and Claudie must have sounded to him as anyone did who could not speak his native language. What Claudie had said was not rubbish—it was merely foreign. The girl strolled away from the cab as if it would have been impolite to see what Shirley had to pay. Then she drew a new breath and went on.

"They despise me because I have no money. My sister made a good marriage when she was nineteen. Well, they will all be pleased and surprised to see me with *you*. Wait till they see what a nice friend I have now! We live up there."

"Is yours the balcony with the flowers?"

"No, that belongs to mad people. Maman says they won't be able to pay for their own funerals, yet they waste money on plants."

"What a funny thing to want money for—for your own funeral." Shirley, beneficiary of a legacy from her first mother-in-law, wondered what one did want it for. She next wondered if she could possibly have come all this way merely to collect a few francs from the girl's father.

In a cement lobby filled with perambulators, the spaniel made a show of character by talking at the elevator and baring his teeth. "He doesn't trust it," Claudie explained. "You take it. I'll have to walk up with Bobby. Sixth floor, on the left."

"No, I'll come with you." They all three climbed together—Shirley, the girl and the dog. Between floors they had to pause because of Bobby, who, developing more and more individuality, was revealed as a dog with a heart murmur. They were in twilight. The windows on each landing, grudgingly small, as if only the meanest point of a bylaw had compelled the builder to provide any light of day at all, were of pockmarked glass and covered with a wire grille. Before a brown door on the sixth landing, the dog came to a halt, sat down, and began panting violently. No names were to be seen anywhere. From behind the door came a sound as of dry leaves flung, and someone screamed, "Bobby!" The door was pulled back. Of the faces that appeared, one above the other, only the smallest looked at the dog rather than Shirley. No one said "Hello" or "Come in." She felt as if she were facing a class of children left without instructions, but now the teacher appeared—a prim, slim woman of about twenty-nine in a light suit, with a green felt beret pinned to her head. This woman pushed the children aside, as if walking in long grass, and slapped Shirley's new acquaintance twice with the palm of her hand and the back of it.

"I am with a friend," was all the girl said. Her head jerked. She did not exclaim or hit back.

"You don't know what a friend is," said the woman. "No one would want you. How dare you take Bobby away? And my handbag! What sort of creature could ever be your friend?"

In eyes gray with hatred, Shirley saw reflected the eyes of the police. She saw cruel young girls at the prefecture bullying foreigners; she heard them cry, "What's the matter, can't you read?" to someone who could read in Spanish, in Arabic, and who did not know what had gone wrong or how to answer. The iron tubing of the stair rail slid cold under her hand. She thought, in her headlong descent, that each turn would send her smashing into a wire-covered window. Once as she stopped to catch her breath, she saw the lift, lighted and sinking, with a dark figure inside. She waited for her heart to quieten. Her way was barred by a blond woman who stood looking up at her as if pleading. Her face twitched. She seemed frightened.

"I came down so that I could catch you," she said. "I am so sorry. My daughter is too spontaneous."

"I can't stand by and see anyone humiliated," Shirley said, coming down slowly now. "I didn't find her spontaneous. She's calculating if anything. Anyway I've brought her home to you. She is safe."

"No, I mean my elder daughter," said the woman. "You are speaking about our little Claudie. You brought Claudie home."

"She brought *me*. Excuse me, I must go. My husband is waiting." If only Philippe had been at home this morning Shirley would not have been here now. She clung to the thought of Philippe's traveling somewhere—say, in Hong Kong. The woman clutched at a brooch she was wearing as if "husband" caused her the greatest possible nervousness. From high up, dropping down the iron and cement spiral of the stairs, fell a command: "Maman! Come back at once! And bring the lady with you." The elevator flashed a light on and off and disappeared skyward.

"This is the first time she has brought home anyone decent," said Claudie's maman. "I regret this. Marie-Thérèse was distressed because of Bobby. She pays a fortune to be told by the veterinarian that

Bobby has a bad heart, and we did not know where Claudie had taken him or how far she made him walk."

Miles across Paris, Shirley thought. Unless Claudie was sharp about getting lifts. Then she remembered the taxi and realized that, of course, Claudie need never walk. Shirley suddenly said in English, in the dark, "It wasn't just because that other one in the green beret was roaring that I ran away, though I do hate yelling. But what am I doing out here in the suburbs, being misunderstood by someone else's family?"

"My husband had gone out," the woman replied in French. "Oh, not to look for Claudie. In his anger he never wanted to see her again. I mention this because Claudie has certainly spoken of it too. *I* don't mind about the dog, but when Claudie makes her father enraged, he refuses to eat. He simply stops eating. He walks the streets. He comes home weak and exhausted and the next day he is angrier than ever."

"They won't give me the money I owe you—the camels," said Claudie, emerging from the lift. "But you can come back when Papa is here and get it from him." She held the dog's leash and struck it idly against the stair railing. "What are you staring at?" she roared to a row of heads up above them.

"Forget what you owe me," Shirley said. "I wouldn't come all the way back here just for money. I don't even know where I am. Never mind about the taxi. Forget everything."

"Taxi?" a voice cried. "Did Claudie ask for a taxi?"

"Papa will give you the money," said Claudie, undisturbed. "But until he has seen you for himself he will never believe my story."

Claudie's mother held on to her gold brooch as if her strength were drawn from it. She said, "It is impolite to oblige madame to collect a debt. The money Claudie owes will be returned by post. How much is it?"

"Oh, hardly anything," said Claudie. "But I would like my friend to come back."

"No, it is wrong," said the mother. Her facial tic became so strong now that it prevented her from speaking for a moment or two. She said, "Claudie has your address?"

"Naturally," said Claudie. "How could I *not* know where my friend lives?"

"Then, Claudie, accompany madame to the bus stop."

"A taxi," said the other voice, nearer now. "When I think that the tart rides in taxis. Bobby might have been sick."

The mother spoke quickly, in confidence: "And I would like it if you are free, and if you would consent to it, if we could—no, if *you* could—come here to lunch with us next Sunday. Then you will meet my husband and all that will be civilized."

Silence filled the stairwell. A man's voice broke it with, "That's courage." A judge wearing heavy shoes was descending slowly.

When Marie-Thérèse's face came into view it was stiff with authority. A few steps above the group of three she halted until they were looking up at her, faces tilted at the respectful angle she evidently needed and desired. "Now, Maman," she began, as though dealing with a moody child. "Gérald cannot give this young lady the sum she says Claudie owes her..."

"I haven't said anything," Shirley objected.

"...Because if Gérald does so he will never get a franc of it back from Papa. Papa will say more fool you, and there it will end. And we have four children. Claudie must confess to Papa and apologize and see what he will be willing to contribute. As for madame, she will not want a meal with a family she doesn't know."

"No one asked you that!" Claudie cried.

"No one," said the mother to herself, as if she were describing herself too. The backwash of this would overwhelm her.

Shirley's alarm at the sight of Marie-Thérèse those eyes!—had driven her around Maman and thus nearer the door to the street. "That part wouldn't have bothered me," she said earnestly. "About not knowing the family, I mean. But my husband is away and I have quite a lot to do at home. I have to put away all our winter clothes and get out the summer ones."

They stared—they were astonished. The invitation had been a means of saving face, a version of having good manners: Claudie has a debt, it is bad of her, but this woman is a careless stranger and if the debt is written off through a sham invitation no one will mind. The mother once had known of another system of behavior, but it had been washed away. It was almost with coldness that Claudie's mother addressed Shirley in the third person: "Madame must do as she likes." The three looked at Shirley as though she had been annoying them, interrupting, asking for advice or a job or a place to live. First she had been a help, then a curiosity, then finally an intruder.

Claudie caught up with Shirley. She still carried Bobby's leash and hit at trees with it. "Don't run, you will stumble," Claudie said. "I can see you aren't used to walking. You drive a car."

"I used to. But I saw an accident once, and it scared me. I might be over it now, but my husband drives and so I never have a chance to find out."

"I hate living far from the center of Paris," said Claudie. She waved the leash at stucco villas, billboards masking vacant lots, odd, lost little houses with late spring gardens. "All this is going," she said, "and then it might be better out here. There is a magnificent supermarket nearby. My mother has looked through the door. She hasn't had enough courage to go inside and begin helping herself. She is afraid she will be accused of stealing."

On the rim of a traffic circle, contradictory signs directed them back to Paris. Claudie maneuvered into the queue waiting at a bus stop. "Any bus here takes you anywhere," she said, quite sure of herself. "Now you know my name and where I live. Claudie Maurel. When you come to lunch next Sunday I shall come and fetch you at your home."

"I didn't say I would come."

"Yes, you must. It will make Marie-Thérèse so angry when she sees you again! I can hardly wait to see her face. Will your husband still be traveling?"

"That's what I don't know," said Shirley.

When a bus drew up, the queue broke and became a crowd. Everyone except Shirley carried babies or shopping bags filled with branches and flowers. "Priorities! Priorities!" the conductor called. Important cards in plastic holders flashed under his nose, signifying that the holder had a great many children or had been wounded in any of several wars. Shirley let herself be carried forward until she felt a tug on her arm.

"Let it go," said Claudie. "I have something else to say to you. The next bus will be empty."

"That's not how it works!" Shirley shook free too late.

"I want to tell you," said Claudie, impassively watching the bus depart, "that my father paid fifteen million francs for that apartment, but he hardly ever lets me buy a new toothbrush."

A few minutes later Claudie, who was stuck to the day like a postage stamp, followed Shirley into a taxi. Seine, Eiffel Tower and deep sunlight flashed out of the late afternoon. Claudie said, "I felt I had borne a child for them. Marie-Thérèse has four boys but she keeps them to herself. My parents took mine, and he must not be brought up as she was or I was. Do you see why? Did you hear Marie-Thérèse? I am the other kind of product of that upbringing, and I am not proud of myself, believe me. I would do anything to get away, but I have no money. They never let me study anything. When I was pregnant my father wouldn't hear of an abortion, but afterward my mother reproached me for not having had one on the quiet. She said she and my father need never have known. Even if they had known, we could have pretended I wanted the abortion money for something else. We could all have played a game. I was seventeen."

Shirley said, "Why do you live with these dreadful people? Why have anything to do with them?"

"Why, they are my family," said Claudie, staring at Shirley, "What funny questions!"

"When you are unhappy anywhere with anyone, family or not, you walk away and never look back." Shirley believed every word she was saying at that moment.

"I never minded for myself," said Claudie. "Now I mind for Alain."

"Take him away. Work."

"Yes, I shall work," said Claudie passionately. "Doing what?"

"I'll think of something," Shirley said, as her own mother had often said before her to any number of Claudies.

In the courtyard of her house she suddenly remembered she had not paid for the taxi. When she came back to the street it had disappeared. She supposed that the driver and Claudie would come to some sort of an arrangement. Claudie, who seemed lazy and helpless, was clearly more competent than Shirley in some domains. She thought that she and the girl were alike; both of them probably denied all experience unless it hinged on chance and chance encounters.

Philippe had not returned. From the kitchen doorway Shirley considered the stacked dishes, the frying pan and the stove, which was buried under casseroles and saucepans. "I don't mind helping with the dishes," Philippe had once said. "We both have more important things to do, so these inferior tasks can be shared. I do not consider women lower in quality than men."

"Neither do I." Mrs. Norrington's daughter was quite astonished at the suggestion that anyone might. She did not dare ask what the "more important things" were. He seemed to imagine that she was gifted but overly modest. He often said that his own work bored him and that he was repeating himself. The magazine that employed him wasted his energies, exploited his intelligence, blunted his reasoning powers.

If that were true, then they were both exhausting themselves in the wrong activities, Shirley said. She did not enjoy keeping track of laundry and making certain there was enough butter for each day's breakfast. Perhaps they ought to make a change.

"Change what? You mean that you want me to shop and cook while you work for us both? You haven't yet shown what you can do, except for your funny little jobs here and there." He teased her, laughing, and because of the teasing she became mean-spirited and decided it was impossible to talk to a man who took everything literally.

She tried again. "I meant change everything. Go away from here. Change flats, for instance."

"That is the paint-the-kitchen theory about marriage," he said. "When we have painted the kitchen everything will be better." When, not long after that, she began to paint the kitchen and he refused to help, which was unlike him, she remembered this conversation.

6

BECAUSE of the system of numbering houses in Paris, where a collective address sometimes took up half the block, Shirley's friends never could find her the first time they called on her. The double doors leading to the courtyard were closed and looked as if they had never been unlocked. There was no concierge to guide anyone: the squalid quarters of the last of these had been fumigated a year ago and turned into the office of a Japanese importer. A blue-and-white plaque reading "44" seemed to belong only to Madame Roux's bric-a-brac antique store. Visitors inevitably would blunder into the wrong building, lose themselves up the wrong urine-smelling staircase, and be driven back to the street by a guardian like a cloud of wasps. Madame Roux was then careful how she chose to answer the pitiful, "Is this number forty-four? I mean, is it the real forty-four? Because there seem to be a couple of others."

If the stranger were French, or for any other reason unlikely to be bullied easily, Madame Roux would send him away with clear instructions about doors, stairs and light switches; but when the visitor had the manner both she and Philippe described as "Anglo-Saxon," and that combined, in their eyes, extreme ignorance and a total absence of charm, she would smile before she replied. The smile, men had told Shirley, informed the stranger he was in the presence of a true woman. A true woman was one who could tend a shop eleven hours on end without showing fatigue and still have time to wander about the museums, climb up to the top of the Arch of Triumph to take in the view, and spend the rest of the day in the many picturesque markets of her beloved city. She would return from her excursions with a kilo of peas, a bunch of marigolds, and a large drum of detergent for washing socks—the stranger's, if he were lucky. Her nature was a unique mosaic of art, thrift and sensuous generosity. She would shell the peas while talking wisely and amusingly, and when she took someone home to bed it was always for his sake and never her own. The Anglo-Saxon world, devoid of such women, was headed for nothing but sterility and defeat—so Shirley's friends said.

Madame Roux had great hips and fragile wrists. She wore a soft cardigan draped on her shoulders and she knotted the empty sleeves while she talked. She favored turquoise, to bring out the color of her eyes, but had thought of switching to something safer after having read that the sight of blue inspired the Japanese to rape. The Japanese importer had the habit of parking his car in front of her shop, and she wondered if he was not hoping for quick voyeur pleasures every time he glanced at the windows. She was tolerant of men but did not wish to give satisfaction to an Oriental. Explaining this, she would slip her hand inside her blouse and absently stroke the skin between her shoulder and breast.

"*You* may go straight through the shop and out the back," she would tell those friends of Shirley's she had elected. "Yes, behind the bead curtain—you will find a door to the courtyard. My shop is not a public highway, but for Mrs. Higgins what wouldn't one permit?" (Even after her marriage to Philippe, Shirley remained to most people "Mrs. Higgins." It was a name that suited her, whereas "Perrigny" seemed merely borrowed.) Madame Roux aspirated the "H"—she had somewhere in her past entertained an English husband or lover. Her short fair hair was reddish at the roots. She smoked a long Pall Mall that moved when she talked. She buttoned the blouse where it had slipped open at the straining point and murmured, "Mrs. Higgins is my friend. Oh, don't bother looking at the silly treasures I keep to sell. They are not for such connoisseurs as you." She hugged herself, pressed her arms under the loose sweater, and watched the connoisseur bump against a tray heaped with crystal bottle tops that rolled everywhere. She did not put out a hand to save the toppling books that were labeled "For Decoration" and that were sold by the meter. She laughed, as if her shop and her livelihood were nothing worth speaking of.

"But I am interested," the victim would protest. "You've got some lovely—euh—stuff here." In terror and embarrassment his hand would settle on a decayed pincushion or a disgusting mouse nest of a purse worked by a Victorian child. "A present for you," the friend would tell Shirley later. "I dropped into that store downstairs to look around. She's got some interesting…"

"Yes, I know. Thanks a lot."

At the beginning Madame Roux had not trusted Philippe. It had seemed evident to her that any Frenchman who chose to marry a foreign widow of modest income, of no great beauty, settled outside her own country for no apparent reason, must himself be a swindler or a fraud. When Shirley had said months before, "He wants to marry me," Madame Roux had answered, "Are you sure he is French?" Then she said, "Does he think you own your apartment?" That seemed important. Did he know it was a mere rental, a warren of short halls broken by doors leading nowhere? The bedroom was on a court and never saw sunlight except for ten minutes on certain June mornings. The bathroom, large as a drawing room, had a fine view over a convent garden but it was virtually unheatable. The kitchen and the lavatory were separated by a partition that did not reach all the way to the ceiling, and the doors to both yawned in the entrance hall except when Philippe was there to keep them shut. A rotten scruff of carpets and curtains enabled the place to be called "furnished," which meant only that the tenant could be expelled at the landlord's liking.

Shirley had paid eight hundred and fifty dollars for the use of these mothy draperies before she was allowed to set foot in the place. She had inherited the flat from a girl at NATO, who had used it as the base for a miserable love affair. It was considered an unlucky place to live; but to Shirley it was simply one more apartment set apart for foreigners who would pay any rent asked, who never demanded or were given a lease, and were often expected to swear to the police (as a favor to the landlord, for the sake of his income tax) that the flat was not rented at all but had merely been lent as a favor. Shirley had never known who the proprietor might be, and had never inquired. Like her predecessor, the NATO girl, she slipped her rent inside an envelope each month—in cash, again out of delicate concern for the unknown landlord's income tax—and gave it to Madame Roux, who was kind enough to pass it on. The sole information Shirley had ever obtained was that the owner was a woman; the only name she had seen was a scrawled signature that might have been either "Curlew" or "Coulan." Shirley imagined her landlady to be old, eccentric, avaricious, obese, half-crippled and chauffeur-driven. Once she had decided this, she accepted it as the sole possibility and thought of it no more.

Madame Roux's obsession with Philippe's motives drove her to nag at Shirley: Shirley must never quit the apartment overnight, for that was known as leaving the domicile and it meant that Philippe could put her out if he so wished.

"But I don't want to know about things like that," Shirley protested. "The less you know, the less can happen."

When Madame Roux next discovered that Shirley did not understand what a marriage contract was about or what was involved in a separation of property agreement, she slid low in her chair and sank her head in her hands. This was not one of her mocking gestures, but a sign of true, feminine desperation.

At first Philippe had been just as suspicious of Madame Roux, and there had been some snobbery in his attitude, which Shirley minded. It made her want to seem fonder than ever of her friend, as if Shirley's affection could increase Madame Roux's stature. She protested that Madame Roux was useful: now that there was no longer a concierge, Madame Roux was obliging about taking in parcels, signing for registered letters, and directing visitors. Philippe replied that she was a busybody and a presumptuous bore and probably in the pay of the police. Shirley then admitted that Madame Roux was an intermediary between herself and Mademoiselle Curlew or Coulan. She meant that to be a clinching argument; instead it sent him downstairs to the shop intending to have a menacing interview with this undeclared agent and informer. He emerged from the interview her admirer for life. He too now spoke of Madame Roux as "a complete woman," as if other women had parts missing. He said that she knew how to be a good friend and a clever businesswoman and still retain her feminine nature and her respect for men.

"You mean she knows her place?"

Yes, that was what Philippe meant. He thought it was a complimentary thing to say about Madame Roux, though he might have found it a vulgar remark applied to a servant.

He began dropping into the shop and Madame Roux brewed her endless supply of Nescafé for him. Like Shirley, and gradually replacing Shirley—though neither of them quite realized it at first— he sat with Madame Roux behind the bead curtain at the back of the shop. From here one could see the door without being seen, and it gave the guest a feeling of being slightly more privileged than an ordinary customer. Sometimes the two Perrignys and Madame Roux were all three together, and then Shirley watched the others as though lip-reading. Philippe was no longer a man she had ever known intimately and Madame Roux had never said, "What he wants is the apartment." They talked about Shirley as if she were their child.

"Everyone confides in Shirley," Philippe said once.

"And Shirley confides in everyone too," said Madame Roux, always good-natured.

"She does not gossip," said Philippe.

"She is not looking for ordinary gossip. What is she looking for, our little one? I often ask myself."

Their little one sat with a cup in both hands, wishing her hair were long enough to cover her face. She felt slightly cross-eyed because she did not know where to look except in the cup.

Something else that Ruskin missed, she thought.

The class difference Philippe had once implied between Madame Roux and himself dissolved; and Philippe, who never breathed a word about his private feelings, Philippe the prudent, the discreet, had a topic in common with the woman in the shop downstairs—

his marriage to Shirley. But it was not gossip either: Shirley knew that he considered it merely as a problem in logic.

It was Madame Roux who on the morning of Whitmonday brought Shirley news about Philippe. This was the news: as Philippe had stood waiting for his sister at Orly airport on Sunday morning his throat became inflamed. The pain worsened during lunch and then became a crisis that spread to his liver. He was nauseated—even his mother's cooking made him sick.

"He has the temperature of a horse," said Madame Roux. "It is infectious hepatitis. So the doctor says." She stood in Shirley's doorway huffing and panting with a hand upon her heart. She seemed to have gained weight these recent weeks; the exertion of climbing only one flight of steps had turned her crimson.

Today was a national holiday. Shops and banks were closed, which meant that Madame Roux had no logical reason for being in the neighborhood since she lived in the suburb of Saint-Maur, which she pretended to love, and praised bitterly for its quiet and the quality of the air one breathed. Gasping, she glanced all round her now with something between amazement and wonder, much as Claudie Maurel had seemed astonished at the sight of Sunday drivers.

It is because she never comes up here, Shirley guessed. We have all confided in her, laughed at our friends and our lovers, but always down in the shop. Within that limit. I never once asked her to a party, and I ask anyone—any dog without a collar, as Philippe says.

Madame Roux had been leaning against the wall; she straightened up and, still uninvited, astonished Shirley by pushing past her and stalking, as best someone short and rounded can do, straight into the living room. *She* was not a concierge, her attitude said for her, even if she did deliver messages—*she* was not to be kept standing in doorways. Her bold, interrogative staring continued; she might have been inspecting the advantages of an abandoned house, seeing beyond the trash and the litter and the bread left to molder what she could make of the place. Madame Roux had an eye for the value of ruins. If something could not fetch money in a devastated form she patched it up, but only to be better rid of it. When anything ceased to interest her it was only because she had ceased to make it pay. She was a devoted buyer of broken toys, blistered mirrors, indelibly stained teacups and slum dwellings: some people are born to own them.

"How did *you* find out about Philippe?" said Shirley. She tied the sash of her bathrobe and yawned, trying to adjust her sleeping mind to the news. "My God, what time is it? Noon? It can't be! Am I supposed to be anywhere? Maybe not." Because she and Madame Roux had been friends once, she found it impossible to be formal. She shook a cigarette out of a pack and tossed the pack over to her former sympathizer, who let it fall to the ground. "It's true, you don't like French cigarettes," Shirley went on, trying to make the rudeness seem normal. "Did you come all the way in to Paris just to tell me about Philippe? You could have called me—that's what phones are for. *He* could have, for that matter. I wonder why Colette...oh, it doesn't matter, I suppose."

Of course it mattered. Her first mother-in-law, Mrs. Higgins, rose up in her memory, and she heard Mrs. Higgins saying quietly, "...just be dignified." Shirley said, "I'll make us some coffee, shall I?" in English, because when she and Madame Roux had been friends they had talked English together. But Madame Roux had no time for harmony. She said, "Philippe will remain at his mother's until he has completely recovered. He is overtired and undernourished and he has many mental problems."

"I suppose he has." Shirley felt humbled. Her voice had an extraordinary sadness. She considered Philippe's mental problems, one of which must have been his wife. But what was all his new intimacy with Madame Roux about? What was it? He used to despise her, Shirley remembered; then he started taking her seriously. They would talk and stop talking only when they noticed me; then they would smile as if that was all they had ever been doing. Until this morning Madame Roux had spoken of him as "your husband." To his face she had called him "monsieur." Now a new Madame Roux, with new ash-blond fluffy hair and new tight underclothes sat crossing her short legs in Shirley's parlor, discussing "Philippe." That was a change, that and her recent hatred. Shirley could not understand being hated: she could not keep it in mind. Surely there must be a line of behavior to follow when someone hated you, a new vocabulary to try to learn, an ear to train for new music. How easy it seemed for Madame Roux, who must have been taught from childhood—in affection you think this, in enmity you mean that. She wanted to tell Madame Roux about yesterday, about Mrs. Castle and *The Peep of Day*, about the children in the Luxembourg Gardens, and the girl in the restaurant, the flight to the suburbs, the dog and the staircase and the frightened woman wearing the golden brooch, but Madame Roux sent one final scorching look around the walls and got up to leave.

"I wouldn't call too much, if I were you," she said. "The telephone disturbs his mother."

The door closed behind Shirley's new enemy. Why an enemy? Only because Madame Roux could not like two people at once. She heard Madame Roux halting, pausing for breath or for a look at something freshly discovered on the stairs. She has found out about Saturday, Shirley decided. Someone has told her. She knows I didn't come home. That law she was always telling me about—it's in Philippe's favor now. Can they put me out of here, even supposing that Philippe would so much as touch on the idea? There was no settlement. He owns everything. But what if I had asked for an agreement—wouldn't that have been a rude, suspicious thing? As if I had always been prepared for a bad ending? With Pete nothing like that ever came up, probably because he had everything and I had nothing. What if Philippe expected not to be trusted and has been despising me because I did trust him?

Something about her own living room began to trouble her now. She felt that eyes might appear in the wall or Doré faces peer out of the leaves of wallpaper. Shirley felt a sharp pain, as though someone had thrown a stone between her shoulder blades. Her head was a weight: her neck did its best to give this leaden burden support. She pushed off her slippers and lay on the sofa. She was going to be twenty-seven. Madame Roux had told her it was a desperate age, one in which women made disastrous choices.

"'A woman of seven-and-twenty can never hope to feel or inspire affection again,'" Shirley had quoted, answering her.

"Say it in French," said Madame Roux. Shirley did her best with it. "True," said Madame Roux, "but, at the same time, nonsense. The truth lies in the picture the woman has of herself. Only the objective truth can prevent her from behaving like a madwoman." Madame Roux was partial to phrases like "the objective truth," which she picked up from the front-page editorials of her morning newspaper, and which Shirley did not understand at all. "Who were you quoting?" said Madame Roux, rather severely, afraid of having been caught out. "Balzac?"

Jane Austen had said it.

Who was Jane Austen? The author of *Wuthering Heights*?

No—Jane Eyre was the author of *Wuthering Heights*.

Had Laurence Olivier played in that?

Yes, Shirley thought he had. It was an old movie—almost as old as the book. In that case Madame Roux knew about it, though she could not remember when Laurence Olivier had made that remark.

A legion of older women had been waiting their turn, trying to catch Shirley's fickle attention. Mrs. Castle, Mrs. Higgins and Mrs. Norrington, her mother, said in chorus, "Do you mean to say you're going to lie there moping just because that bleached-blonde hussy told you not to call your own husband? You mean you're going to stand for that? Do you think any of us would have given in?"

No, none of them would have, but who were their husbands? Shirley's father had admired his wife; Mrs. Higgins had been quiet and secretive—she and her husband had never quarreled. Mr. Higgins had never taken a holiday away from her. Her death, it had been thought, would kill him. Shirley knew nothing about Mr. Castle, but she could not imagine Mrs. Castle, at Shirley's age, receiving news of her own husband by way of a nearby shop. She swung her feet around, sat up, pulled the telephone onto her lap. She dialed

Galvani again. Oh, who was he? Who was Galvani? One of Napoleon's generals? Married to one of Napoleon's sisters? Ringing flooded the Perrigny dining room, where the table had been cleared. Someone—Philippe—was watching television. On and on, waves of ringing filled the room. Madame Perrigny bent over her sewing. Her plum-colored curls, dyed by the expert Colette, slid onto her powdered cheeks. Shirley saw all this, saw large spools of black and white thread and the old-fashioned snap case for Madame Perrigny's glasses open, adrift, on the gleaming table. Assaulted by the ringing, still no one moved. Colette slept, sighing; her face was bloated. Then the ringing stopped and Madame Perrigny smiled over her sewing, smiled with her mouth turned down.

"I'll give him time," Shirley said aloud. Yes, I had better give him time to get over being sick or being mad. I'll give him until next Saturday. That's enough time. She dialed eleven then and asked for the Paris message service, which would deliver words to his door. The message would resemble a telegram; he would be certain to open it. To a clear-voiced person, who repeated her words back to her, she said that she would call on Philippe next Saturday after work. She was about to sign it "Shirley" but remembered the confusion this would create; it would be spelled wrong and thus make her message look foolish. So she gave "Perrigny" instead, spelling it with the official alphabet—Pierre Eugene Raoul Irma Gaston Nicholas Yvonne.

7

THE NAME that no one in Paris could spell, pronounce or appreciate had been chosen by the doctor who attended Shirley's birth. Mrs. Norrington would have called her infant daughter Michael, had her husband not objected. She was of a generation that believed the subservience of women would come to an end if girls were named Anthony, Jonathan, Walter or Ralph. It was difficult for Shirley to imagine her mother's having ever been subservient to anyone: even in childhood pictures Mrs. Norrington seemed nearly six feet tall, with hair parted to form sloping curtains on each side of a severe and elderly face. She was middle-aged when the signs of pregnancy occurred; she took them to be connected with the menopause. After twelve weeks she supposed she had developed a tumor. Rather than worry her husband by mentioning it, she simply made her will. Her dismay when she understood the truth was not based on dislike of the incipient Shirley, but on her own ignorance of children, of whom she knew nothing except that they were loud-mouthed and dirty in their habits. She was prepared to be open-minded, but her husband was elderly now and he could not imagine a third presence in the house.

In one of her regular birthday letters to Shirley she said, "I feared that your advent might bring my mental activities to a close, for most mothers seemed to me provincial and stupid." At one time these "activities" had been innocently political, almost without her knowing it, for the word "politics" suggested to Mrs. Norrington a kind of blundering male obsession, or else someone beefy, Irish and drunk. Though passionately conservative on one topic—England

and the British royal family—she was a natural revolutionary when it came to virtually anything else. Soldiers' firing on workers' houses in Vienna, the siege of Madrid, they-shall-not-pass, the Socialist martyrs of Rome, Saccovanzetti (one name and, to Shirley, one person), still colored a personal monologue in which abhorrence of pain and a fierce defense of virtue prevailed. Later on, "justice" came to mean avoiding meat as food and refusing vaccination because the enemies of man embody life. She was surprised when Shirley told her that the Higginses, Shirley's first parents-in-law, had spoken of her as a socialist. All she had ever done was draw the line between possible and inconceivable behavior, which were her personal substitutes for right and wrong. In a society where eccentricity was not encouraged, she had acted out her beliefs; native of a country that welcomed neither passion nor poetry, she was shown to be naturally endowed for both, but she had somehow made her daughter suspicious of either.

Shirley had not inherited her mother's moral temper: she wanted life to be passionate in itself and could only imagine this in terms of being loved. She had seen how a mind as strong as her mother's collapsed when faced with a sentimental obstacle, and this reinforced her own hostility to ideas. For her mother, the limit of reason seemed to have been 1940, the White Cliffs of Dover, and the introduction into the Norrington household of four small British refugees and their nymphomaniac mother. Shirley felt and resented a new, slavish quality in her mother where the Team-Browning family was concerned. It embarrassed the little girl and made her ashamed. By the time she was seven or eight she was heartily sick of the flaxen heads and adorable accents her mother admired; nor did she share Mrs. Norrington's delight in the four cases of precocious intelligence the Team-Browning children were said to constitute. It occurred to the child that four loud, finical, humorless voices were passing for brains, and she wondered whose fault it was that she had been taught nothing more piercing than a Canadian mumble. At nine, she was old enough to judge the flight back to England and to piece together an attitude out of a few dropped words. Mothers who had not paid a penny in private school fees now discovered the inadequacy of the schools and rushed their children away "to be educated all over again." The word "heritage," which had been lying in the corner like an old tennis ball, now bounced everywhere. The independence children had acquired in Canada was suddenly known as "growing up too soon," and so they were repatriated "to learn to be little boys and little girls all over again." There was no doubt in Shirley's mind that the purgatory of the Team-Brownings had shortened her father's life; for once the children's mother had seduced those neighbors who were still civilians, then a postman, two headmasters, several taxi drivers, and the accountant who prepared Dr. Norrington's declaration of income tax, there was no one left except her own sons and her host; but Shirley's father was old and ailing, and the sight of Mrs. Team-Browning waggling her bottom along the passage from bath to bedroom merely made him feel that no one understood him any more. Long after his death, when the correspondence with the Team-Brownings had trickled down to an exchange of Christmas cards, Mrs. Norrington would still feel called on to justify her act of kindness. She attempted the abstract terms she liked, but as Shirley immediately assumed a deaf face at the mention of "our traditions," her mother had to remind her that refugees from *any* society and castoffs of *any* political turnabout had her sympathy. Being displaced was so contrary to Mrs. Norrington's notion of the way people should live that the fugitives had to be either criminals or victims. Criminals could always benefit from the example of disinterested assistance, she reasoned, while victims required it. And yet she was not instinctively generous. A crust of bread given away made her heart swell with anxiety. Her own father had been one of those Westerners who will deprive his family for the sake of outsiders, so that her early memories were there, nagging and repeating that even old shoes worn by others mean food out of one's mouth. Still, she gave, wincing and flinching. What she preferred, for her own tranquillity, was a pretense at exchange. She would buy anything if the seller were poor enough. She became the protector of a family of Bulgarians who painted flowers in oil paints all over rough linen. Material thus decorated was eminently useless, but that did not prevent Mrs. Norrington's buying yards and yards of it and having it made up into frocks. Her long figure encased in a linen tube, a support for clambering roses, once seen could not have been imagined otherwise. No one laughed. Her appearance was always inevitable. And she was at peace, because she had rewarded the Bortoloffs for having spent their time around the kitchen table employed in producing something preposterous. Shirley thought that her mother's charity lay chiefly in the way she seemed to understand suffering, though she would not always acknowledge its importance. Mrs. Norrington was an attentive listener; only Shirley had ever failed to catch her ear. No family voice could ever find the right pitch, probably. On hearing a recital of woe and abuse, Mrs. Norrington would at once look for its confirmation in poetry. Her comprehension of other lives came out of literature—the only form of art she trusted. As a result, Shirley's suspicion of ideas was as nothing to her dislike of poetry: the very sight of her mother's books, their dark green and maroon bindings, their tarnished gold titles, and the opaque bricks of words they contained, could raise but one desire in her mind—Resist! She had too often seen her mother pushing through the pages until her long hand stopped at the lines she wanted. She read aloud, flatly. Every variation of grief and anguish had its summing-up in Herrick, Bunyan or Pope. Shirley had been told from tricycle age, "But die you must, fair maid, ere long,/as he the maker of this song," and "He that is down needs fear no fall,/He that is low, no pride..." and "A heap of dust alone remains of thee,/Tis all thou art, and all the proud shall be!" and her rage, resentment and jealousy because of the presence of the Team-Brownings had produced frequent readings of Wordsworth's disgusting "Ode to Duty"!

"'Stern Daughter of the Voice of God,'" announced Mrs. Norrington, equably, proceeding on through the repulsive "'Denial and restraint I prize,'" to the final, nauseating "'Give unto me, made lowly wise,/The spirit of self-sacrifice;/The confidence of reason give;/And in the light of truth thy bondman let me live!'"

Never, never, said Shirley to herself. Aloud she responded, "Thank you, Mummy, that was quite helpful."

Now that she was in her middle-twenties and closer to her mother in social stature—for in theory Shirley was now an adult—she understood that she had inherited her mother's uneasy generosity as well as an idiosyncrasy of dress she did not desire. The difference between Shirley and her mother was that while Mrs. Norrington did not see how other people were or guess that her own appearance was in any way unusual, Shirley longed to dissolve in a crowd but did not know how to go about it. The same climbing roses that had been lent distinction by the very person of Mrs. Norrington had turned the child into a freak, and she grew up with the idea that this could never change. In time Shirley discovered that no woman ever liked the way she had been forced to dress as a child, and that each was inclined to trace her fears and anomalies of feeling back to the fact that she once had not looked like other people; but what had become of the girls who *were* those other people? What had become of Ruth Griffith, of Elizabeth Macfarlane and of Margaret Rose Wagner? Perhaps they had died of sameness before reaching maturity. She suspected that in her personal peculiarity she was less distinguished than her mother had been. Still, it was part of her inheritance and perhaps all of it, which meant that Mrs. Castle had not been mistaken in handing over *The Peep of Day* with the remark, "It's all you're ever likely to see."

Shirley's father, recalled as mild, kind and obstinate, had put his foot down on having her named Ralph, Michael and the rest, but his own choice could have been just as disastrous. He favored Isadora because of the dancer—a fine healthy woman, no corsets, and an excellent mother from all accounts. But this, in turn, her mother opposed for fear of nicknames. Shirley was born at home in her mother's bed. Mrs. Norrington had wished to be attended by her own husband or by no one at all, for she had read that birth was as simple as breathing and that the umbilical cord could be bitten in two by any agile woman. She believed that a child produced under such conditions would be lively and intelligent and able to read music from the age of two. Conviction gave way to panic with the first contraction and became hysteria within the hour. Her husband, who had foreseen this, had already arranged for a colleague to come when summoned. Dr. Norrington then went downtown to St. Catherine Street and saw an American travelogue about Berlin in which there was no trace of Hitler, the news, which was too loud, a Donald Duck that kept him awake, and a movie that annoyed him from beginning to end but in which Ann Harding figured and she looked, to him, like his wife. He then took the precaution of eating a mixed grill at Drury's, fearing that home would be chaos for some time and that he would need a solid base of protein. He then returned by streetcar to find that Shirley existed, was very ugly, and had not been named.

For the next twenty-four hours he and Mrs. Norrington remained locked in courteous but immovable discord and so the naming of the infant fell to Dr. Hector Walsh, who was to register the birth. Dr. Walsh cast about him for the nearest saint and discovered the Norrington's maid, who was called Shirley Smart and came from Newfoundland. This squat, tranquil girl was one of a family of sisters who replaced one another in the Norrington household like annual plants. Winnie, Mary, Violet and Dot had arrived in turn in Canada (a foreign country), learned the Norringtons' tiresome ideas about hygiene, survived their balanced diet, realized they were grossly underpaid even for Quebec, and departed to a factory after ensuring that a younger sister would follow, as though the Norringtons were a necessary initiation. Dr. Walsh had been grateful for Shirley Smart's assistance. She had remained stolid and attentive throughout, chewing licorice to keep from vomiting and limiting her comments to the occasional "Jesus!" He asked her name, and understood it to be "Shirlum Smatt." She wrote it down and he thought of the Brontës, and then of his own mother whose name had been Anne; and so he registered the birth of "Shirley Anne," which was the name of one of Mrs. Norrington's ancestors, and which Dr. Norrington wholeheartedly disliked.

The name created trouble for Shirley in France, where it was not on the religious calendar. It had no equivalent that anyone could find, either saint or heroine. Its spelling was a mystery and its pronunciation obscure. Philippe had enchanted her by saying "Shelley"; her first mother-in-law had said something like "Shay-Lee." Canadians wrote it "Shirl" and pronounced it "Shurrul." James Chichalides, meeting her on the staircase on Tuesday morning, said "Ah, Shairlee!" She had wakened a few minutes earlier in a room as cold as March, pursued by the faintest remnant of a dream, remembering a painting her mother had made of birch trees and snow. She could smell the cold varnish of her old bedroom. In the picture a shadow of each tree, depicted as a rod of steely blue, lay as neatly as Mrs. Norrington thought shadows ought to in nature. Her mother had taken up painting not to make a fortune, not to develop a latent talent, not to expand her personality, but to prove how terribly easy everything is. The memory of the picture was mixed up with the death of Dr. Norrington and the extreme frugality that followed; for Mrs. Norrington's unstinting contribution to the war effort, which included not only the entire support of the Team-Brownings for more than six years but also the turning over of all her uninvested savings to a Spitfire fund, had left the family very much on the edge. Her husband's last coherent sentence, "Don't touch your god damned capital, Margaret," took on an added poignancy when it became known how depleted it was. Economy had sent them—mother and daughter—south of Montreal to a house warmed by two Quebec heaters, one upstairs and one down. The icy mornings, the sound of the stove shaken down by her tireless mother, the sight of the daunted landscape framed and hung over her desk, rushed together and evoked one more sensation—the feeling of a bumpy rag rug underfoot and the glacier linoleum beneath it. She opened her eyes and saw a blue sky through a pitiless coating of ice, and it was seconds before she knew that she was grown, in Paris, in June, and alone; that Philippe had jaundice and had told Madame Roux; that he would not so much as bother to come to the telephone; that Saturday was irreparable, Sunday a confirmation of disaster, and Monday... on Monday she had seen Madame Roux, taken Philippe's two sleeping pills, and crept back to bed. This was Tuesday, the end of the catastrophic holiday weekend, and now, with luck, they would return to normal life.

James Chichalides, wearing a spy's raincoat, carrying two croissants in a square of flimsy paper and a folded copy of *The Times*, put on his English face when he saw her. He had two favored English remarks, which he could make apropos of nothing known to his hearers. These were "Brains, my dear fellow, brains," meanwhile tapping his forehead, and "What, may I ask, is the meaning of this?" She tore down to him, equipped as always for floods, dams bursting, torrents in the streets.

"What, may I ask…"

"I'm late, that's what. My husband usually looks after the alarm and he's away traveling and I forgot about it. Usually he hears the seven o'clock news on one station, then the half-past seven news on another, and he makes the coffee and brings me some, but he makes me drink a glass of cold water first so I won't forget the coffee and go back to sleep. Then the cleaning woman comes. Nothing happened this morning. Even she isn't there. I remember now he said she'd stolen something. I'd sooner not know. Even if I knew I'd pretend I didn't know, rather than talk about it. I mean, I'd rather be stolen from. She couldn't go on and on stealing. Finally she'd have just stopped out of embarrassment, and then we could have gone on as before—don't you think? After he fired the poor old thing she came to the door and I just shoved some money in her hand and shut the door and she was still trying to tell me something. I've always had thieves and drunks working for me. Madame Roux finds them. Unmarried mothers from Brittany with idiot children, and shuffling old female winos wrapped in stinking sweaters. And I feel sorry for them, or maybe I'm just lazy—I don't know."

"Fasten your watch," said James. "You are losing it. Why do you say 'my husband' all the time as if I have never met Philippe?"

The painting of birch trees in her dream, the magpie cleaning woman, Madame Roux and Philippe, something to do with discomfort, the wrong principles, and the mismanagement of living had brought her close to weeping.

You are someone who never cries, she had to remind herself.

"God, I'm so late," she said. "I've got my old summer job again, one I had years ago. Not bad. About five hundred francs, or fifty thousand, depending what kind of francs you count in."

"A week, of course."

"No, a month. A *week*! I'm not trained for anything. Why, I couldn't even get a job as a mother's help. All I can cook is coffee. I majored in French lit., though I don't expect you to believe it. I know some German. I got married the week I graduated..." She colored, afraid that her admission of knowing a little German might be taken as boasting. "I don't know anything," she said firmly, once and for all.

"What is this job?" said James, who did not understand why women should work.

"What's yours? I mean, what is it really? I used to wonder. Philippe supposes all sorts of shady things where you're concerned."

"But you and I know all about each other," he said, trying a different voice.

Why does he say that, she wondered? Because we used to sleep together? What she had liked about Philippe at the beginning was that he had not instantly moved from *vous* to *toi* on the conceited assumption that now they were intimate.

James became haughty and English again. "You know I am an architect, though *you* may not believe it. Here I buy apartments and sell them. I wanted to live in Paris while I was still young enough to enjoy it..."

"Enjoy the *au pair* girls, you mean. I'll bet you've never had a French girl, ever. Well, I'm an interpreter in a store. I wanted to stay here while I was still young enough to enjoy it too. Let's stick to our stories. Here we both are, in Paris, in the middle of a staircase, young enough to enjoy it." James, attempting to re-create an atmosphere he had invented or that existed only in crowded recollections of other women, moved closer to Shirley. She felt as she had when Claudie's mother had blocked her path—alarmed and frustrated, yet obliged to seem polite. She showed him the plastic-covered label she wore on which was printed "Mrs. Higgins." "It's the same one I've always had," she said rapidly. "I kind of like the work. You take these people round the store, where they want to go, the washrooms and all that, and to look at the gloves, and they like to smell all the perfumes before they finally buy their Chanel 5. The men are nice. They go to so much trouble for their wives."

James was staring, more and more anxiously. "Is the term for Chanel not 'scent'?"

"If you like. Scent is what immigrants buy in Woolworth's." Having said something extremely petty, she began to feel more cheerful, as if she had discharged part of the burden of constant concern for others.

"...in Woolworth's," James went on repeating to himself, privately. "You shouldn't have to rush out in the morning for five hundred francs," he remarked.

She took this to mean a criticism of Philippe. She could not explain to James how it would have been wrong for her to stay at home and do nothing while Philippe worked. He gave all the money he could spare to his arthritic mother, for one thing. So did Colette, who kept back only as much as she needed for her two-tone jersey costumes, her lumps of gilt jewelry and an occasional holiday in Taormina. Shirley supposed that Madame Perrigny invested the money for her children, or else made green tomato pickle out of it, or else was saving up for three lavish funerals. Her children never asked. They had been trained that way—pay-conditioned. Another reason why Shirley worked was that Mrs. Higgins, her first mother-in-law, had expected her to use up her life. Shirley, the survivor of Pete, inheritor of his mother's affection until Mrs. Higgins's death, had been called on to complete his life for him. That she did so incompetently, and to invisible witnesses, was not James's affair. She snatched off the watch that would not stay on her wrist because the strap was frayed. "For once I'd love not to be late. You're supposed to be on time in that place."

"My sisters long to meet you," said James. He stepped aside so that she could descend. She went by slowly, her hand on the bannister.

"They've heard about *me*? What did you tell them?"

"I'm having a party at five," he said. "You can meet them then."

"I'm still working at five."

He bent over the railing. She looked back and up and remembered something of the old secret shared. "Wear your uniform," he said. "It's so funny, and it is smarter than any of your dresses."

As this was her own opinion, it could not offend her. "All right; I need a party," she said. "I'll be there. I promise." Out of earshot she added, "Depending on Philippe," which was said as one would touch wood; it was a conjuration.

Sun bleached the gray street. Her arctic morning had been dissolved in rain and re-created with sun, leaves and the smell of honey. She saluted the marble bust of an entirely forgotten figure of the Third Republic. She and Philippe had given him a name—Rigobert Arcadius—and acknowledged him their private high priest. This was a game for two, not one, but she bowed to Rigobert Arcadius all the same, for luck, and she did not feel absurd but only happy. She heard sparrows whose chirping was a country sound—had to be, for she had no other reminder. Wearing the blue usherette's uniform she was strictly forbidden to take outside the store, she lined up for a bus and was carried on a cloud across the enchanted Seine. She had something to look forward to—James's party—which meant that her life was not finished. Anything promised was reason enough for living. She beamed at her fellow passengers and did not care when they looked contemptuous and withdrawn. Even the children won't smile, she reminded herself. The reason you pay so much attention to clouds and light and monuments and the shape of rooftops here is simply because no one ever smiles and you have to look at something.

As she had explained to James, who already knew but could not be bothered remembering, she was an interpreter in a large old department store. It was a creaky building with splintered floors, and cockroaches in the employees' dining room. Wearing her Higgins label, she was a lifebuoy for holiday hordes of bewildered, put-upon tourists. Often they came from small towns and knew little about cities, even in their own countries. They were afraid of being a nuisance, they longed to be liked and admired, and became confused when they inspired insolence. Their lack of fluent French did not lead to amusing chatter with policemen but was taken as a personal insult. They had read the advertisements telling them how friendly the chefs of celebrated restaurants would be, and how they would be invited to postmen's weddings. No one had warned them that in 1963 Parisians were not happy-go-lucky but dour, reserved and irritable even with one another. Some of the visitors were hurt, most were startled, and several were rude back. Today's first victim was a man of about forty, wearing a hat quite like Mrs. Castle's. He said suspiciously, loudly and clearly, with a pause between each word, "Do you speak any English at all?"

"Try me."

"Are you sure you understand?"

"I have to—it's my job."

"Well, I want to know where I can get some fresh orange juice. I can't get what I want anywhere."

She would have walked straight out of the store, taken him home, and prepared his breakfast for him, but the thought of Philippe put a stop to any such fancy. Philippe had never recovered from the first party she had given after they were married and his discovery that she had not known who half her guests were. "Your life is like a house without doors," he said. She saw cold dashes of rain coming in and wondered why he had not thought of building her a proper house.

After the man wearing Mrs. Castle's Salzburger hat had wandered off in quite the wrong direction (she had learned that strangers did not often want the information they asked for and seldom heard her explanations), she began planning a new party. Philippe showed his records to Shirley's friends and spoke of musicians whose names sounded so strangely Irish, such as Kullman O'Kings. There were records Shirley would never hear because they were stored in Geneviève's country house: the importance of this today was the size of a poppy seed. Her mind raced round the party all day. In the stuffed bus that carried her home she invented a dress cut out of a sari, then destroyed it when she realized it was something her mother would have worn. A new note from James, a reminder about tonight, made her feel he had taken away a party belonging to Shirley, something she owned.

She was halfway up the stairs to James's when the telephone rang in her flat. Someone is trying to prevent me from enjoying myself, she said. Someone wants to spoil the party. She paused and came back slowly, one step at a time, like a child clinging to a bannister. Before she had taken out her key the ringing stopped. She knew it had been Philippe crying for help and that she had let him drown.

No one knew about this.

Later she heard James saying, "Somebody, I can't tell you who it is, has bought every apartment in the house."

"The Japanese importer?"

"I can't tell you, but some of us are going to have to get out" was his answer. "Shirley, you will soon receive a letter telling you to buy your apartment or move."

"Is it you?" said Shirley. "Are you the person? Have you bought the whole house as a present for Rose?"

No, it was not James. He knew about it because it was his business to know everything. "It can't make a difference to you," he said. "You could find another place just as ugly and inconvenient for the same rent."

"I don't want to move." Nothing he might have said could have frightened her more. If I move, Philippe won't know where to find me, she thought. One of James's brothers-in-law told the last line of a joke and, laughing, trembled violently. She had been wrong about the telephone, she had deliberately slowed her steps, she had said, "They want to spoil my party."

At that moment Colette had been in the Métro reading the dummy of the new women's page *Le Miroir* was planning to introduce and which Philippe had lent her. Colette's lips moved silently: "Covered in washable tartan or plain and harmonious in black, it cracks nuts, shreds carrots, sterilizes, washes, dries..." Madame Perrigny pulled on her gloves and, the prescription for Philippe's medicine in hand, consulted the calendar of pharmacies open on Sunday, remembered this was Tuesday, and pursed her lips because the days were running together. In June the days were too long. White light suggested a wide conspiracy of pleasure. She hooked her black glacé patent leather shopping bag over her wrist—like the rest of her, it was in deep mourning—and shut the door softly behind her. Philippe, who had been simulating sleep, at once padded in bare feet to the other end of the apartment and called his wife. The ringing flowed around the rooms that were in chaos. The laundry was back in the parlor, the bed unmade, and a heap of orange peelings clogged the sink. She, on the staircase, turned slowly and said, "Nobody wants me to enjoy myself."

"My holidays are over," James explained.

"What does that mean?"

"That I am going back to Greece in August. So the sale of the apartment doesn't affect me."

"Don't say it so happily!" Shirley cried, thinking of Rose. The house is empty and Rose is left behind. But Rose glanced at her, smiling, and she understood: Rose believes he will marry her and take her to Greece. She remembered their conversation about subaltern men.

Alone with Rose, they combed each other's hair. Shirley said, "Let's see if we can write in blood, or in lipstick, the way they do in novels." And Rose replied, "You can't—I have tried it. The lipstick squashes down flat and too much blood is needed."

"Let me see." Shirley wrote with lipstick above James's bed, CORO DI NINFE E PASTORI.

Rose squinted and said, "What are they singing about?"

The climate in the room changed, as though a page of calendar had fluttered and turned, showing a picture of wet lilacs. The two moved to the window, which looked onto the street. Every inch of pavement had been rained on. Rose's soft hair came down and covered her face.

"I suppose that in Athens it is always sunny and dry," Shirley said.

"I shall never know," said Rose, which meant that Rose knew what would happen now. She lifted her curtain of hair, knowing everything.

"Oh, what is all this leaving and being left?" Shirley cried.

"That is what your chorus is singing," said Rose, smiling and drawing back from the window. "That is all it can find to sing about. And do look at what you have done to my lipstick, Shirley." Neither of them cared about the wall.

The women at the party drew armchairs close together, sat with their feet tucked up, and talked to each other about their husbands. "Mine seems to have left me, for the moment," Shirley said. Because of the way she told her stories, disaster sounded gay. She described the way Madame Perrigny had been abandoned by Philippe's father and had gone into mourning, and how, when he did die in the last year of the war, she had said, "My choice in clothes was finally justified." Once he stopped existing, she had made a hero of him; and even though Philippe knew his father had died of heat-stroke after an abundant black-market lunch, he thought of himself as someone half-orphaned because of the turnings of history. "Now tell about Colette," said James, who was nobody's husband and could gossip with the women. "Tell the story you told Madame Roux about the American officer and the milk. Madame Roux tells it almost better than you do."

"Shirley may not want to tell," said Rose, standing, seen in smoke somewhere outside the circle of chairs.

"An American officer..." said James, prompting Shirley.

"...rented a room in the Perrigny's flat just after the Liberation," Shirley said rapidly, watched by Rose. "Colette was just six or seven and rather delicate. Being kind-hearted, he persuaded the little girl to drink powdered chocolate milk. As milk is notoriously bad for the health..." Shirley paused, wondering if milk was bad for the health in Greece.

"She would drink this milk in secret in his room," said James. "Shirley, tell it properly. Do the voices."

"She may not want to," said Rose again.

"Colette began having bilious attacks," said Shirley, gathering speed. "One day she told her mother the truth, and her mother sent for a doctor."

"No," said James, "do the dialogue, the different voices. First she just said she had been in the officer's room quite often. It was only after she told she had been drinking milk that her mother..."

"The doctor examined her and said to her mother, 'I regret to say that the little girl *has* been drinking milk in large quantities. Her liver is thoroughly diseased as a result and will never be normal again.'"

"No, what he said was, 'Her liver is the size of an elephant's and it will never be normal again,'" said James.

"You tell it, then," Shirley said. It became an agitated recital. He was like a woman shaking a mat and calling to a neighbor. That was because he was copying Madame Roux. He missed telling what the story was about. Well, the progress of it was true—the doctor took Madame Perrigny's hand and placed it close to the child's ribs, and there, as Madame Perrigny was to say to Shirley years later, "I could feel Colette's liver beating beneath the skin."

The women listened seriously now. One or two men had joined them—a brother-in-law, and a man who had owned a cork factory in Algeria and had been dispossessed. America was to blame, said the brother-in-law. Of course, for the officer had been an American. The hypocritical milk trick was held up, a mirror in which they saw reflected Americans shipping arms to Algerian rebels, Americans interfering with the weather.

This much of the party Shirley remembered the next day. She found a spray of lily-of-the-valley on the doormat, either an offering or a discard. James had been pleased with her; he had drawn his sisters' attention to Shirley so that no questions were asked about Rose. Jo-Jo, the fat boy of the two brothers-in-law, had not found Shirley's store uniform amusing, but her lack of artificial elegance was in her favor—it meant she would make someone a reliable wife. The sisters, Pucci parrots, screamed and defended the young woman who was in no way their rival. That she was already someone's unreliable wife escaped them; perhaps no one had said so. And so Shirley became excited, nervous, frightened. Faces went around and around her—she was the sun. She described her mother-in-law, her husband, her hopelessness as a sensible wife, and understood too late that she had taken these strangers on a tour of an invalid's bedroom; they were laughing against drawn curtains at the sight of a spoon in a glass. She saw Rose, her soft buttercup hair slipping out of tortoiseshell combs as she handed caviar on squares of bread. Rose was silent and no one said, "Who is she? What is her role?" for they were looking at Shirley, they were turned to Shirley, they were being shown an invalid's bedroom and were waiting to be made sick with laughter. Jo-Jo (was it?) said they must all of them put ads in the Paris *Herald-Tribune* personal column reading "Philippe come home" and the like. She saw herself in the dreadful future. She and Philippe sat facing each other on two kitchen chairs. She said again and again, "I am sorry. Of course I am sorry. It was stupid. Worse than stupid. No, I can't explain myself. Yes, I was drinking, but that isn't all. I knew it was sad, and yet it also seemed funny at the time."

There was no sign of Philippe. Perhaps Madame Roux had been mistaken and had garbled some quite simple message. Afraid to call his mother again, Shirley rang *Le Miroir* but after she identified herself she was passed from one impertinent voice to another. Someone told her he was in Egypt and another person said Philippe Perrigny was away on a holiday "with his wife."

"I am his wife," said Shirley.

"Then you ought to know where he is," said Philippe's friend.

Before the end of the week, advertisements began to appear in the *Herald-Tribune* signed with her name. She wondered who had bothered—who had taken it seriously. She suspected everyone except Rose and James, even though they were the only two with enough command of English; but Rose was prudent and James was careful. No mail arrived for Philippe. No one asked for him on the telephone. That meant everyone knew he was somewhere else, either in Egypt or at his mother's. Opening the medicine chest in the bathroom one night, she saw that everything belonging to him had disappeared. The discovery sent her to his desk. Both typewriters were in place, but it seemed to her that some of the work projects in colored folders were missing. *A Life Within a Life* still occupied a whole drawer. She leafed through it and read, with her usual delight:

> You know that I am a reasonable little person   resign myself to the universal betrayal   calm   despair   nausea   to go forward, expecting nothing.

But a day later the manuscript was gone too.

She had not been unjust. It seemed to her there could never be enough injustice now. In rooms flooded with June light someone came and went. He was forcing her to guess at his plans and divine his intentions. Perhaps it was Madame Roux who smuggled his belongings away, in Philippe's order of importance: everything in the medicine chest, and then Geneviève. She saw Madame Roux on the sofa making surreptitious telephone calls, sliding drawers open, unfolding letters and putting them back without a crease, looking, peeping, waiting to find a mistake. She imagined Madame Roux transformed, shrunken, with six spider legs and a spider's eyes. One day toward the end of that week Madame Roux came out of her shop as Shirley was going by. Shirley turned, stopped, smiled, ever willing to be a spider's friend. But all Madame Roux had to say was "A young lady left this for you," and she handed Shirley a folded scrap of ruled paper. It was from Claudie Maurel, reminding Shirley that she had been invited by Claudie's mother to lunch.

"On Sunday you will be fetched by car, by my brother-in-law, Gérald Ziff," Shirley read. "My father yearns to make your acquaintance and as for my mother, she talks of no one but you."

"I'll bet," said Shirley. She dropped the note on the pavement, not far from the shop, so that if Madame Roux decided to collect it and keep it she would not have far to walk. Shirley was prepared to forget Claudie and the Maurels, and she hoped they would forget her too.

8

ON SATURDAY after work, as her message had promised, Shirley called on Philippe. She had a present for him—a bottle of champagne, which they had often agreed to be a cure for everything. In the bus she found a seat next to a small old man whose hands were clamped on the silver head of a walking stick. All at once, in a fit of elderly private annoyance, he pounded the stick on the floor three times. It was the beat that signaled a curtain rising; it heralded the entrance of mourners at a Mass for the dead. When Peter Higgins had been buried in an Italian graveyard, women unknown to Shirley had touched her sunburned wrist and said they were sorry. They were the remains of an English colony, summoned by an Anglican clergyman. One of them laid a hand twisted as a vine root on the girl's sleeve and frightened her by whispering "I am the Resurrection and Life." Resurrection? No, she was the shadow of Madame Perrigny thrown before, a mistake in time.

A row of cypress trees swayed in Shirley's mind. Their shadows rocked over untended Protestant graves. She heard a woman's cracked undertone muttering "I am the Life." She was the Life and Shirley was only a penitent in a strange house now, tapping her heels along a strange marble floor, standing finally with her offering (champagne) before a brown-painted door. This was a door equipped with three locks, one above the other. Drilled at dead center, at eye level, a hole fitted with a magnifying glass and known as a Judas enabled Madame Perrigny to be sure her husband's ghost was not there in the hall, whimpering and cringing and offering apologies. After Madame Perrigny had decided the visitor was indeed Shirley and not just someone pretending to be, she opened the door a few inches, though she still kept a chain on the latch from within. Her system of precautions had seemed necessary when Philippe and Colette were still small and their mother had been afraid Monsieur Perrigny and his infamous mistress might kidnap them, pervert them, teach them to steal in the streets, and abandon them in the Bois de Boulogne when their usefulness had come to an end. She had imagined a black Citroën trembling at the curb with a sly Corsican at the wheel. The children, warned and ready, would clutch each other's hands whenever they saw such a car and run home. The whole family would sit quietly then, not even turning on the radio to hear the war news, listening for the sound of a motor or a step in the hall. Shirley could now glimpse a dark eye, a few thimbles of glossy hair, and a hand as white as talcum. The smell of curried mutton came out of the dark flat.

"But of course you would not have made him a curry, he has hepatitis," was the first thing Shirley said. It was for such remarks that her husband's relations considered her well below par, almost feeble-minded. She dropped her gaze to the hand and the inch of black cuff that indicated Madame Perrigny's perpetual mourning for the living. She, exasperated by Shirley's dismal simplicity, began easing the door shut. It seemed to be moving irresistibly, of its own accord. "You needn't do that," Shirley said. "I'd never force my way in." The Judas glass, no larger than an infant's fingernail, terrified her. She felt as if another presence were behind it, silently watching and judging her.

What Shirley had at first taken to be curry was disinfectant, the background scent of the twice-monthly Sunday luncheons here. It wafted out of the looped, carpet-thick draperies and the tapestry rug that hung from a rod between the parlor and the dining room as a barrier against drafts. These rugs, decorated with scenes of an extraordinary Araby, were reminders of a colonial past. Philippe said he detested everything in this apartment; he had told Shirley how nothing ever changed and that even the rusty can opener in the kitchen had been there as long as he could remember. But he had grown up with the rugs and the stiff net curtains and the cold chandeliers and had never thought of leaving them or changing them until he was nearly twenty-nine. One day he and Colette would probably fight like wildcats for everything in the place, even the useless can opener, each of them wanting to own their common past. Shirley supposed Philippe to be behind the Arab curtains now. Darkness was above and behind the Arab on his white horse and the wild-armed women he trampled to death. Behind the barrier, steadily inhaling disinfectant, Philippe, safe from fresh air, listened to his mother dismissing his wife.

"It is only champagne," he must have heard Shirley pleading. "It's something he likes."

"It would finish him off," said his mother. "Even a child would know better."

"Doesn't he want to see me?" No answer. "Doesn't he need anything from home?"

"He is home," said his mother and shut the door.

On a Saturday night less than a year ago Marilyn Monroe had committed suicide. Tonight, in a bright square where restaurants displayed trays of oysters, where a soft rain that was almost fog wet her hands and hair, Shirley tried to give away a bottle of champagne. No one wanted it, not even the drunk sprawled on a flight of steps going down to the Métro. A concierge ran after Shirley crying, "Miss, it is forbidden to abandon bottles in our courtyard!" She was afraid of throwing it in the Seine lest a policeman see her and suspect her of getting rid of a gun, a Molotov cocktail, or a home-made plastic bomb.

I shall give it to James, she decided; but when she came along her street a little later she saw that his windows were dark. Madame Roux's shop was softly lighted so as to show off her wares, but Madame was out in Saint-Maur with her feet on a coffee table, watching television and drinking an infusion of orange flower mixed with rum.

Well, this is Saturday, she said to her empty apartment. I'll drink it myself. The wine by now was tepid, but she could cool it with ice cubes, for Philippe was not there to call her a barbarian, or James to exclaim "What is the meaning of this?" Letting water run over the tray of ice, she remembered other Saturday voices—Maureen Clune's yapping in a rhythm that sounded like Ya ya. Yahayahuh. Yayuh. She turned off the tap and thought of Maureen yelling, "Hey Shirl, where ya wanna eat?" Maureen's voice slid down as Shirley appeared with new ice and fresh drinks: "Philippe's working. I guess he's just too busy to eat, huh?" Shirley's guests treated him with respect because he was French. The men they knew were flabby and neurotic. Her friends envied Shirley; sometimes they displayed the acid jealousy also aroused in them by far prettier and more fortunate women, such as Mrs. Kennedy or Brigitte Bardot or even Marilyn, until she gratified everyone by being unhappy and dying. They wondered why Philippe had married Shirley when it might so easily have been one of themselves.

"You've got everything taped," said Gertrude Schram, who had worked herself into a situation of anxious drama with a married Negro lover. "I wish I could settle it all *your* way."

Philippe's dislike of sharing the proletarian Saturday night was so deeply ingrained that Shirley had either to force him to live in a way alien to his feelings, or abandon him to his records and his writing. A winter's compromise had brought to their living room a succession of babbling feminine strangers who, on sitting down, immediately removed their shoes (a ritual gesture he noted under "Anglo-Saxon—significant movement"), who drank more whiskey in an evening than he could imagine anyone's consuming in a year, and who displayed their lives without much wondering if their lives were interesting. He listened to Maureen Clune describe an infatuation with the image of her great-uncle Desmond, who had been put down a well by the Black and Tan long before she was born, but whose picture had hung in her room and dominated her fantasies. When Philippe laughed, Maureen looked shocked; she was serious. He begged her to imagine Great-Uncle Desmond as he might have been if life had spared him—senile and dull. That brought her close to hysterics, and so Philippe gave up. There had also been Renata, golden-haired and full of calculated malice. Everything that happened to Renata was as dramatic as possible; for either she was beaten blue by her neo-fascist lover, who was smaller and younger than she was, or she caught an obscure amebic ailment after having eaten pineapple and had to fly to Zurich for treatment every Monday, or she was pregnant and suicidal. "Have nothing to do with her," was all Philippe would say. "Keep away from Renata." If Renata fleetingly caught Philippe's attention it was only because their political ideas overlapped; but he seldom listened for long. She might as well have been a budgerigar, a creature that talked without requiring answers.

He was kind to poor Gertrude Schram, however, perhaps because she laid her tear-stained love story before him in a manner so blatant that benevolence was the only response. She would begin from the beginning and then rapidly turn in circles. First of all, no one must know: she implored his discretion. She would rather have been thought an old maid or a lesbian than have the truth get about. "The minute anyone sees you with a Negro all they think about is sex," said Gertrude primly. Secondly, the man was married to an Armenian from Cairo—all *she* had wanted was the American passport, Gertrude said, and could she really be Armenian? Her name was Lorna—I ask you, now—

"He is married," said Philippe, even when it seemed best to say no more.

"Yea, to this Lorna. She threw spaghetti all over me in a restaurant. She told Alroy she was brought up in an orphanage, that way she got his sympathy. I happen to know her father had chain stores before Nasser threw them out."

But there was more than any of this: Alroy had lived in Paris more than seven years, he could not speak a word of French, he had quarreled with everyone. This meant that if Gertrude married Alroy there would be no social equivalent for the life she was likely to lose.

"You would not lose us," said Philippe, giving an imagined Alroy a friendly glance. There were a thousand reasons why he would have preferred Alroy's company, with or without French.

"Well, he's never mentioned marriage," said Gertrude, coming around to something Philippe had been suggesting all along. "She's one of those doormats. Puts up with anything."

"Don't cry," said Shirley as Philippe rang for a taxi. He would see Gertrude safely downstairs and give the driver her address, for she was sobbing too convulsively to speak. He was afraid the chauffeur would think he had enticed Gertrude into drunkenness so as to seduce her and that she was weeping now because he had not been much of a lover.

The long decadence of Saturdays had touched bottom a week ago, when Renata called and Shirley said softly, with her hand cupping the telephone, "I can't come over now. Philippe's here; we're just having lunch. I'll see later. I'll try. No, what I mean is, it's a promise. I said, a *promise*."

"You know what I'm going to do, don't you?" said Renata.

"No, don't. At least don't say it. Though if you say it, it means you won't do it."

"You're all bastards, every one of you," Renata said.

Shirley hung up cursing the sun and good weather. This should have been the day of a general strike, pouring with rain, filled with foul-mouthed drivers and scratched cars. Once James had called on the morning of a general strike to say, "The electricity is off and I can't see to shave up here. Could I shave in your bathroom? You have light from the window."

"No," she had said proudly. "You can't just wander in like that now. I'm married." Though Philippe had certainly heard her end of this, he had never asked, "Who was it?" just as, weeks later, he had not commented on her conversation with Renata. He seldom asked questions because he hoped none would be asked of him. Their marriage was conducted in a truce of privacy (at least on his part) and a white silence.

After lunch that Saturday she had expected Philippe to depart on some business of his own; he took her instead to the Select in Montparnasse, where he was to meet someone who had promised to fetch him a camera from Germany. They sat on the terrace of the café and

Philippe, who had perhaps begun thinking back from Renata to an earlier nuisance, who was James, suddenly said, "What would your father have said about that Greek if he had known him?"

"My father?"

"Yes. You should think about it. It is important. I always wonder what my father would have said or done when I am not sure of myself."

"'Bloody time-server' I think he'd have said. James is kind and Canadians don't like men to be too kind. They can just barely stand kindness in women, though it's all right to be nice about animals. They don't mind it if you say you appreciate trees and all that."

As usual she had lost his attention. Why my father? she wondered. Philippe didn't know my father. He doesn't know my father called me Belle. Doesn't he know *his* father was a swindler, a crook, a con man? But Philippe is honest. Colette is too, for that matter. Colette will say sincerely to someone, "But I think of you every day!" before turning her back and never speaking to that person again.

Philippe was smiling now and saying that it was a holiday weekend and would Shirley please look at the weather? He was free today, he would go anywhere she liked, do anything she wanted. He offered the names of restaurants and kissed her cheek.

What shall I say? What shall I say to avoid saying "Renata?" Conversation: Acid, vegetarianism, the food at the Coupole, Victorian silver.

She perceived at two or three tables pushed together young Germans who had been chosen to play SS men in another film about the war. "You'll have to stand on your feet for a change," a make-believe officer yelled at them. "We'll show you how to stand, what it means to walk."

At that moment the man Philippe was waiting to see, Helmut, moved out of the group and came toward them. He said something to Shirley—something perfunctory, polite, hands on their table, bending down, the tweed sleeve grazed her shoulder—but his eyes flicked past her to Philippe, whom he admired. Philippe had helped him out once—had written about one more cry or injustice. He drew up a chair and sat between them, slightly turned to Philippe, which was useful; it excluded her and gave her time.

"I told them," said Helmut, "that for fifteen thousand francs a day I would wear a uniform. I look like something they want. It's funny, isn't it? They said you are not an actor, don't try to be one, just repeat what you know. What I know? I was born in 1940 on Hitler's birthday. The sign of the ram." The two men spoke entirely to each other. Helmut was going to Germany for the first time in years. He wanted to see his mother, though they did not get along. A sad story was wound around this meeting. Helmut spoke as if Philippe knew all the details and as though Shirley simply were not there. What he described was violent and political and concerned with abstract justice, and she shut down her mind. Helmut was to bring back a camera for Philippe—that was what today's meeting was about. She sipped her beer and tried to find the trick, the excuse, that would release her and send her across the city to Renata, who was alone, and who needed her, and who Philippe considered sly and unimportant and a waste of time. She watched a dark, doll-like man choosing extras and pretending, yes, pretending that it was the "selection" in a concentration camp; he knew and even Shirley knew, but these young Germans thought it was a game and they laughed at him. Once he said to someone, "God, you've got the face of an animal. You're in—saved!" He meant a scarred man, older than the others, slightly overweight, like an athlete out of training. He laughed immoderately.

The chosen one grinned. "Did you hear? I've got the face someone wants."

"He was in the Foreign Legion seven years," said Helmut without turning. "The *brain* of an animal—an ox. The face is normal. A face..."

"Would you bring me a flag from Germany?" Shirley suddenly said.

When Helmut realized she was speaking to him, he asked politely, "What sort of a flag do you mean?"

"Why, *your* flag, of course. The..."

Philippe said quickly, "About the camera ... do you want dollars? Because I can..."

"It's for this person I know, Karel Brock," said Shirley. "He collects all that sort of thing."

Helmut stood up, said to Philippe, "I don't need dollars," bowed to Shirley briefly and departed. Philippe stared straight before him at the cars rushing to leave the city.

"I'm sorry," she said. "Why should I do Karel a favor, come to think of it? I was only trying to get into the conversation. I didn't think he'd be so touchy about the flag. I was thinking about Renata and that made me think of Karel."

When Philippe spoke to her next it was about something else entirely. They walked along the boulevard toward the rue de Rennes, where he said he had left the new Simca parked on the wrong side of the street. He would never quarrel: he would look for a way around quarreling. He had wanted a way of being that was unlike his mother's and now (Shirley thought) he knew that Shirley's way was based on nothing but daydreams and incompetence. But she was part of his life, he had accepted her, and he would not quarrel. He was endlessly patient; his discretion was limitless; and she was in the desert.

He said, "Where shall we go? I know that you like the crowds on Saturdays." He was teasing but his voice was kind. He was concealing something—his anger at her gaffe with Helmut. If only he would talk about it! He held her hand, which, in her guilt and distress, she had clenched to a fist. She knew, because Madame Roux had told her, that this habit of holding her hand in public was a compliment. None of Madame Roux's French husbands would have considered doing such a thing.

"I have to go to a party," she muttered. "Renata absolutely needs me." She added, "You could come too," knowing he would not.

"What?"

She said it again, or something like it. He made her repeat it a third time. She looked up and saw behind his head the light summer sky. He did not make a point of releasing her, but presently they walked apart. He did not so much draw away as let her fall.

"You hadn't said anything about tonight until a few minutes ago," she said. But she had lost everything, even his interest. He examined the parking ticket pinned under the windshield wiper, then unlocked the door on the driver's side. He slid behind the wheel, reached across and opened the other door.

"When we got married you said we'd be free, not like those other Noah's Ark couples," she cried, but if she was arguing in a motor car on a Saturday afternoon then they *were* like those other couples. "For example, if I weren't your wife you wouldn't leave me there on the sidewalk like a . . . a horse. You'd unlock my door first." Who is speaking through me? she suddenly wondered. My mother? Never. Some yappy wife in a movie? The dead "Daisy" Geneviève so wisely killed off before her novel even opens? "I'm sorry," she said. "Look, let me call Renata. Or, I'll go for a minute and come right back." No, it was no good: he had left her.

Oh, how much easier it was to talk to one's friends or to someone in transit.

Every thought that crossed her mind now was proof of bad faith or hypocrisy or cowardice. Words became toads as they sprang from her lips. "You live by plans, you're always making lists," she said, trying to find the same affectionate, slightly teasing voice he had used earlier; but she was an amateur actress, her voice was not "placed," what she had to say came out in a woman's whine: "I didn't know today was on a list."

"You are right, I did live to schedule," he said, without looking at her. "But Renata was never on any list of mine, which means I can't cross her off. And so you had better go to her if she can't be happy without you."

"It is normal for women to have women friends," she said. She had not meant this to be the last word, but he let it be.

Before dawn, uninvited, she rang James's doorbell. She knew she was indiscreet and might not be welcome. She was dressed as she had been when she had left the store and boarded a bus to go and visit

Philippe. James opened the door after he had combed his hair and placed a blue handkerchief just so in the pocket of his dressing gown. He was alert and ready for any dawn caller, whether it was a young girl hysterical with love, a slightly tight neighbor, or the vice squad. She half-expected him to send her away.

"The thing about champagne is you can't drink as much as you want to," she said. "You start to gag on it. And Geneviève's novel has vanished, all but a few pages. Maybe they won't be missed."

He surprised her by taking it for granted she had come to borrow money again, but she wanted nothing but company. The apartment downstairs was condemned and she was afraid of seeing the first cracks appear in the walls. Nothing could save the house now except a blessing. Lovemaking was exorcism in its simplest form. She undressed casually, saying, "Where is Rose?" CORO DI NINFE was still scrawled with lipstick on the wall. His only failing, for her, was an edge of sentimentality that made her laugh. Her laughter worried him—he had forgotten what she was like. He did not know if he ought to be offended or not. She felt, briefly, as Philippe had said he did when Shirley read his mail; she told James that "love" was too private to be discussed in bed, and she offered a substitute word for it—say "mineral" or "Maurice." "Love" (or "Maurice") was easily damaged; it could not be helped. Other than "Maurice," everything had to be in primary colors, clear, and on the verge of burlesque. "If I can't laugh I don't want it," she said. He reminded her that two years ago she had said to him it had to be secret; it had to be violent; it had to be dark. She praised him for remembering. But he was accustomed to the tearful, tender, overwrought little German girls he picked up in the Latin Quarter who probably made the pretense at loving their only condition.

He woke Shirley early in the morning. He was expecting Rose. He said, "It is a pity I let you marry Philippe. It is obvious that you get on much better with me."

"You had better marry a young girl before you get much older."

"A young girl would bore me. I would have so much trouble with her mother. You know—if you marry a young girl the mother is there too." This was raving; a young girl was all he intended to marry. "Though one can be not young and still innocent. Take Renata—before Karel she had known only two men."

She sat up in bed with her elbows on her knees. "I won't discuss Renata. But James, do let me tell you something for your own good. It's something I've tried to explain to Philippe. It is about the only two men business. A woman will always say, 'It was never like this with anyone.' Oh, you needn't smile. I'm sure you have heard it." Without interrupting her, with gestures, he suggested that he wanted to make the bed. She got up, trailing a bedsheet. "I don't want to hurt your feelings but please believe me—what she means is, 'It is always like this.' What it mostly comes down to is being polite, you know. She forgets from one time to the next and then she remembers and says, 'It was never like this.' She'll say, 'It can't work for me unless I'm in love.' She's just forgotten. She's forgotten about the total stranger she met on the beach at Dubrovnik and how they both lied about who they were and where they came from. She will say, 'Only two other men before you.' I suppose it is because 'only one' would make it sound as though nobody wanted her, and any more than two makes her sound like a whore. Also, more than two men makes it hard to bring in the bit about 'It was never like this.' You'd begin wondering what her problem had been, exactly. Centuries of female rubbish is her problem, James. The menstruation mystique, the 'never like this' mystique, the business of 'only you' and of course those inevitable other two. James, if all the men with whom it could work perfectly were collected in the Place de la Concorde there'd be the biggest traffic jam since the Liberation of Paris. And James, they know it—all these women know it. Stop listening to them! Stop believing 'I can't unless...' and 'It won't work for me until...' and 'I have to be in love.' No wonder Freud said women couldn't be analyzed! Don't encourage emotional lying in young girls! Don't feed it with a phony climate! Let them be in love, but not with you and not for that reason." Amazed at herself, she added, "And by God, every word of this is true."

James, after a moment or two of dismay, took cover behind his

English face. "All this might apply to other men," he seemed to be saying, "but never to me." He disappeared without answering and presently she heard the shower running. By the bedside were two or three volumes of the simple pornography that, as far as she knew, was his only reading. He could not imagine any subjects more suited to prose than virginity, cruelty, initiation and the unwilling victims; and he could peruse dogged variants on these themes with the thoroughness of Philippe investigating lost Atlantis. Sometimes he said with a straight face that he read for the beauty of the style. No one knew why he kept most of his books in a laundry hamper. Rose believed that he was afraid of shocking his French acquaintances. The books apart, there was not much indication of his tastes. None of the furniture in this room belonged to him: the dressing table with a three-way mirror had been left behind by a previous tenant; a hassock covered in orange taffeta was believed to have been the gift of Madame Roux. The rest of the furniture looked as if the varnish on it had not yet dried. Upon the dressing table stood two Japanese dolls with wobbly heads, a tin of Guerlain's Jicky talcum—that would be Rose—and an ikon of the Virgin in a gilt frame. The Infant was disproportionately small—his head seemed no larger than a bell of the lilies he grasped.

She saw James in the mirror. He stood behind her, put his arms around her, and tried to help her do up the gilt buttons of her uniform.

"You look like a Red Cross girl in one of those old films," he said. "Like one of those American army nurses the Japs were so afraid of." He seemed to expect Shirley to say something about him. He was like Crystal Lily exclaiming "You have nice hair!" He now wore a new dressing gown, maroon and black, with a Noel Coward scarf. He had shaved, he had changed last night's bedclothes, rinsed last night's glasses, emptied Shirley's ashtray, and, politely, he wanted her to vanish. Rose was coming. He knew Shirley was a sensible person, with adequate troubles of her own, who would not want to create difficulties for him. Leaning forward as she fastened the last of the buttons, she saw that the ikon had been torn out of a magazine and, still ragged, slipped over a picture, the edges of which showed. His mother? His version of Geneviève?

"What was there before?"

"I was. But with the triple looking glass I see as much of myself as I want to." She was dawdling; he tried not to appear impatient.

"We aren't supposed to take these uniforms out of the store, but I always seem to have mine on me. James—how long is Philippe going to do this? When will he forgive me? How long can he stand his mother? When I call *Le Miroir* they pretend not to know where he is. They won't even say that he's sick or away or anything."

James removed the ikon. It had taken precedence over his own picture long enough. He glanced at Shirley then gazed full on at himself in the glass. "I'll see what I can find out," he said cautiously. He found the onslaught of the personal alarming. "I want to see him anyway. A matter of co-property that interests me."

"Do you think he'll speak to you?" It would have been tactless to suggest that Philippe found James unbearable.

"He will see me," said James, now smiling widely. He touched his temple and said to his reflection, "Brains, my dear fellow, brains."

In the middle of the day, from her living room, she heard James and Rose pause on the landing outside her door and confer in low whispers. They had probably been meaning to take her somewhere to lunch, but on catching the sound of a man speaking, they hesitated, then moved on.

On the blue sofa in Shirley's living room was a new stranger. His name was Gérald Ziff; he was an Alsatian. This was the first information he gave her. He sat with his feet wide apart, solidly planted, and drank scotch as if this were the outing of a lifetime. He had found Shirley with the greatest difficulty, he told her: Claudie had lost the address, but she had described the house; for proof, look at him! Here he was! But down in the courtyard were two, no, three staircases. No lights! No concierge! The shops were closed and empty. The mailboxes told him nothing; he could not even see Shirley's name.

"How did you find the mailboxes? For some reason I've never understood, they're in a dark little hallway behind Madame Roux's antique shop."

His mouth hung open—she would keep interrupting him! He had much to say and said it slowly. Offered a drink, he declared he did not object to drinking. He was not in training for anything but gave the impression he might be at any moment. Gérald's appearance—his thick shoes, the badge of an Alsatian football club on his jacket, his short hair, carved to a kind of peak, like a flattened dunce cap—spoke of him as active and plain and a promoter of fresh air and of healthy allegiances. Claudie had wanted to come with him to point out the house and introduce him to Shirley, he said. But at the last second her father had commanded her to walk the dog, help her mother in the kitchen, write a birthday letter to her old grandmother, and go to her room and stay there, all at once.

"Claudie has no room. She sleeps in the living room. So it is only a way of speaking. I keep out of women's business." Shirley wondered if he included Monsieur Maurel with the family's women.

"You could have found my address in the telephone book," said Shirley, before remembering that no one in Paris ever looked there and that she was still listed under "Higgins." Her number had been originally registered as belonging to "Tardy Antoine-M., Sculpture and Decoration." No one except Madame Roux knew anything about M. Tardy, who had lived here briefly years before. "Tardy" remained in the directory and on the downstairs mailbox through several tenancies until Madame Roux, who had a friend in the telephone administration, managed to have at least part of the listing changed. How this had been accomplished without the loss of the telephone was one of Madame Roux's closest secrets. The name now read, "Higgins S-M, Decoration." Even Philippe agreed that one should not attempt to have it changed to "Perrigny," let alone try to have "Decoration" removed. Telephone wires had been ripped out of the baseboard and the instrument borne away forever for less back-talk than that.

"We were not even sure of your name," said Gérald. His small blue eyes shone; he had proved he could do more than anyone expected.

The family must have taken it for granted he would fail. When he appeared at Shirley's door, saying "I have arrived to fetch you for lunch," she began explaining he had come to the wrong place; but after listening to her accent and staring hard at her hair and dress, he interrupted her: she was the American lady who had kindly brought Claudie home in a taxi after the poor child had fainted in the street. Shirley was surely the lady who had accepted Madame Maurel's invitation to lunch? *He* was the husband of Madame Ziff. Madame Ziff? Yes—Claudie's sister, Marie-Thérèse. Shirley's memory of them was a mill wheel; it rolled creakily. She recalled the girl, of course, and the long drive past the Renault works. In her mind she somehow blamed that family for the disappearance of Philippe. When the bell rang she had thought it was Philippe, and she had flung the door open with such delight on her face that Gérald might have thought, then and forever, that invitations such as these were almost too much of a favor. She understood that she conformed to a description Gérald had been given. He had scarcely seen her that other Sunday—only a glimpse as she turned to fly down the stairs. Later, looking down the stairwell, he had perceived the top of her head. Staring now, he checked an imaginary list. It made her uneasy —she supposed any scrutiny to be criticism. She preferred clothes that were large and vague and hid most of her imperfections. She still combed her hair as she had the day she arrived in Europe as Peter Higgins's bride.

Gérald seemed in no hurry to rush her back to the family. He was telling her about himself: he was interested in jazz, in Lionel Umptum and John Gorinar. There was not a soul with whom he could share this interest. His father-in-law...

"My husband is Philippe Perrigny. He writes the Bobby Crow jazz column. But that isn't all he does. You must have seen his name—he's with *Le Miroir*."

Gérald discarded the list his female relations had composed about Shirley and gazed at her very hard. "I read him. I used to, that is. He cares for the new jazz and Tale O'News Monk is too modern for me. I used to read *Le Miroir* too but it has become more of a left-wing paper now so I don't see it as often. My father-in-law... Shall I have the great pleasure of meeting Bobby Crow?"

"He's away just now. He's traveling. Otherwise he would be here, of course. I'm not often alone like this, I can assure you. At the moment he is writing a book about Goosey Gander."

Gérald sucked in his lip, stared all the more, and nodded hard. He seemed to have heard about the book too.

In the bedroom, changing her dress, brushing her hair, darkening her eyelashes, she was ashamed of herself for despising Gérald Ziff. He seemed to be a placid and innocent and totally unintelligent James, and she had mocked him, using Philippe. A truer self, detached from the deceitful creature before the mirror, said, "He is not writing anything that I know of, and he is not traveling. Either he is ill or he has left me for a time." She wanted to say to someone that her husband was a prisoner, kept by his mother as Picasso was said to be immured from strangers by his wife. She must be careful not to tell the strangers about it today at lunch. When she talked, Philippe was not her husband but part of a long story. Oh, what was this self-admonition, this shrinking from one's reflection? Shirley was warm, generous, brave even. Strangers sensed her qualities: the Maurels had committed the un-French act of inviting her, an unknown and undistinguished foreigner, to the most private of family meals, the Sunday lunch. She dropped her brush and dashed to the kitchen, where she pulled two bottles of wine out of a rack. She wrapped them in a paper bag saved by Philippe and folded away by him on a shelf under the sink. She was ready now and she talked and laughed as she preceded Gérald down the staircase. He jingled the keys to his Dauphine as if it were a windup toy. He did not offer to carry the paper bag and pretended not to see it. It was a hot sunny day; her street was empty. He got in the car first and leaned over to open the door.

"It is good that you are coming," he said almost secretly. "You understand—*they* have to get this over with too."

It was to Marie-Thérèse that Shirley delivered the wine. Claudie's sister wore shoes with thick, sponge-rubber soles, very like her husband's. She and Gérald looked as if they might stride out and away, over the street and across the vacant lot to be seen from the hall window. Shirley imagined the two of them, followed by a ribbon of snuffling children, marching against blowing papers and clouds of sawdust. Marie-Thérèse said, "How kind," aggressively, and stalked off clutching the two bottles. Abandoned in the entrance hall—for Gérald had vanished under his children as if buried alive, and Madame Maurel had not appeared at all—Shirley heard the bottles smacked down on a hard, tiled surface, and then, because she was listening for it, she heard the paper bag being folded and put away.

The family seemed to expect Claudie to look after the guest. Having embraced Shirley as though they were old friends, she stood posing in a doorway. She was dressed in skintight blue slacks and a striped jersey, and held a cigarette between thumb and forefinger, with the other three fingers straight in the air. The pose finished (was there an invisible photographer in the room?) she tossed her thick braid of hair and begged Shirley to come in and sit down. Claudie resembled youth in St. Tropez as it had been a few years earlier in the 1950's. At the same time, because of her boyish hands, her innocent complexion and thick figure, she reminded Shirley of the simple heroines of Russian country tales. Led by the great actress into a dismal low-ceilinged room, Shirley refused the offer of a white plastic chair set on insect legs that seemed too fragile to bear anyone. Three reproductions were hung at jumpy levels along one wall: a Dufy regatta, an Impressionist girl leaning on a window, and Van Gogh's *L'Arlésienne*. She was relieved to notice a plain leather armchair, a divan covered with a plaid blanket that evidently doubled as someone's bed, and a collection of photographs of children in First Communion costumes—for that was the room she had expected. Claudie flung herself down on the day bed. She seemed in union with the plastic-chair aspect of the room: the First Communion pictures were the domain of a rival. If the room had been a stage (and to Claudie it probably often was), the rival would have taken the armchair and she and Claudie would then have talked in alternating monologues until the audience finally grasped that the two were separated in thought, but joined in some kind of dreadful intention.

Claudie yawned like a cat, or like someone who has been told to pretend she yawns like one.

"How miserable you must be in this ugly room!" she said. "Once Papa was told about Maman's impulsive invitation, he commanded her to go through with it as a punishment and to prevent her from ever doing such a foolish thing again, but also to save face with you, because you are a foreigner. It was kind of you to understand that, and to have come. I must warn you that the food here is uneatable and my sister is very rude. You will go away in distress. How different it will seem from the joyous meal I had with you last Sunday!"

"*With* me?" Claudie had evidently decided to believe she had been Shirley's guest.

"You will never have to come back here after today," Claudie assured her. "And you can be certain they will not want to see you again. They will talk about you for days—my mother and sister will, not my father—going over everything you ate and wore and said. They are bitterly jealous of my friends and of anyone who loves me. But you and I will be far out of earshot of their conversation." The large hand, the strong wrist, described a gentle gesture. She and Shirley would be in Hawaii or Greece or Norway, she implied. "I want you to know my real world and my one true friend. I have already told him about you." She examined Shirley's clothes, as Gérald had done. Her look softened. "When I look at you it reassures me," she said. "Yes, I can tell you so quite frankly. Since I have met you I am no longer afraid of growing old."

The barking of the cretinous dog Bobby, and the screams of little boys who now rushed from all over the apartment to cluster in the hall, covered whatever answer Shirley might have wanted to make to this compliment. Rosenkavalier children, without their orchestral accompaniment, cried, "Papa! Papa! Papa!" Everyone was at the door now; Marie-Thérèse, with the sleeves of her honest blouse tucked back and her face tinged with an oven flush, rushed by the living room. Claudie rose, beckoning. They joined the crowd in the hall.

Monsieur Maurel came in and closed the door quietly behind him. He was a slight, thin-nosed man with a tight mouth and foul-tempered, intelligent eyes. His was a face that would never show pity for foolishness; he would fear nothing save one's seeming to be ridiculous. He carried a large box from a pastry shop. Surrounded by shrieking children, apparently suffering at the very sight of them, he closed his eyes. Claudie said poignantly, "Ah, little Papa!" He snapped his eyes open and said, "You! Go and put a skirt on." It seemed to Shirley that he had not received a welcome but an hysterical assault. This display of joy was perhaps the only way the family dared show violent feeling. He reminded her of a French comic actor, Louis de Funès, with his cunning, furious eyes glaring like an eagle's. She half-expected Monsieur Maurel to have the same view of himself, and she thought that the others, once the demonstration of enraged delight had died down, would drift off laughing. But it was not a joke: the homecoming of Papa—and why was he called Papa by his grandchildren?—was the most dramatic event that could happen to any of them; and yet, she thought, it must have been happening all the time.

It was Shirley who took the pastry box away from him, for even Marie-Thérèse seemed to have lost her presence of mind. She was not aware then that her gesture would brand her a creature of no upbringing. She believed, as she did of most people, that the poor man was shy and she was eager to make the first move, to put him at ease in his own home. She told her name: no one had remembered to introduce them. When Marie-Thérèse had relieved Shirley of the pastry box he shook hands. After that he did not look at Shirley again. Drawing a matchbox toy out of his pocket, he called one of the children: "Alain!" A pale child came forward, accepted the toy, and embraced the giver. Shielding his new treasure so no one could see it, the pale child faded back into the ranks. He was thoughtfully watched by all the others.

"Madame has brought us wine," said Maman.

Marie-Thérèse nodded twice, as if tolling the fate of the wine. Gérald looked moon-faced and optimistic, probably because they had been summoned to the dining room. Shirley counted five children, all of them boys: they sat at a wicker table on worn nursery chairs from which pictures of ducks were flaking away. Squabbling in low voices, the little boys glanced at their elders. The very sight of Papa made them hold still, and they were quite obviously afraid of their mother. Claudie had changed, was now wearing a blue dress with a large piqué collar, and had pinned up her braid. She was metamorphosed into the perfect secretary until she sat down heavily with her elbows on the table and suddenly looked Russian again. She really is a healthy piece, Shirley thought, and wondered what James would have made of her (he who proclaimed Renata innocent). Another Red Cross nurse? Claudie certainly seemed strong enough to drag the wounded off a battlefield. Korea came to mind, followed by Algiers, Verdun and Borodino. Like a stream of colors, battles ran together into one and became green and stagnant. At eight, Shirley had lain on her stomach on the floor to pore over pictures of Yugoslav partisans in *Life*. They were part of childhood, like Mary Poppins. Shirley ordered the partisans (who were her vassals) to march the Team-Brownings over a cliff and into a boiling sea. She heard her father remark that in partisan bands sexual intercourse between men and women was punished by death. He did not say what sexual intercourse consisted of, but Shirley could guess, though she had already discovered other names for it. She wondered now, thinking of James, of Rose, of Renata, if a permanent state of armed resistance might not be a form of salvation for everyone; at least it would cut out brooding, talk and idleness. As for "punished by death," why that would settle the question. It was plain, and probably safer than the subtle risk of loving.

Claudie had a curious way of pointing; like a child making a revolver out of his fist. Shooting down the assembled children she said, "Alsatian nursery chairs — Gérald's dowry. Better than my sister, who had no dowry at all, eh Gérald? Maman! My friend has brought us good wine, so you can take that Algerian beaujolais away."

"Yes, Madame has brought wine," said Gérald, as he might have said, "She has brought her own salt and pepper."

Five scratched leather-bottomed chairs had been pushed up to the table by Maman and Marie-Thérèse. There should have been six. Maman's solution to the crisis was to stand, counting "One, two, three, four, five" over and over. "There ought to be *six*. When we are alone we have just *three* chairs," she explained to Shirley, "except when my mother-in-law is with us, then we have four. Alain has his own little chair."

"Surely you must be six sometimes?" Shirley said.

"Never," said Claudie. "Today is the first time."

"Yes, sometimes, when Mémé is here and I am here and Marie-Thérèse is here too," said Gérald. He had found the sixth chair in a bedroom.

"Sometimes, when my mother-in-law, our dear Mémé, lives with us," began Maman, "we use the sixth chair quite often." She trailed off, wondering what she had wanted to say. "But now she is with her cousins in Lyon." Her face cleared. That must have been all she had been trying to remember—where her mother-in-law was.

Everyone sat down. Shirley had a clean napkin, still damp from a recent ironing; the others unfolded a napkin personal to each, identified by a ring or a special knot.

"This is all for you," Claudie murmured, as a large dish of hors d'oeuvres was passed along to her.

"What, the whole thing?" It still had not occurred to her that everything said here was serious.

"No, not the whole thing," said Gérald. "One slice of ham, two halves of hard-boiled egg," and he paused, silently estimating.

"You forgot to count the radishes," said Claudie.

"Papa has closed his eyes," said Marie-Thérèse.

Everyone looked at the head of the family. Papa's face was a death mask.

"Egg?" said Gérald to Shirley, urging her on. "You like eggs. You ate fried eggs when you and Claudie went to that restaurant." This was to show how good his memory was and how important he considered Shirley.

"Leave our guest in peace," said Madame Maurel. "Our guest will think we count the food in this house."

"We do," said Claudie. "Ask Gérald. He hates coming here."

"Our guest will think we quarrel," said Maman.

The dish was passed along. Everyone except Claudie took ham, egg, tomato salad, radishes and a pickle. Claudie, perhaps copying Shirley, had only a small slice of ham on her plate. "What diet are you pretending to be on now?" Marie-Thérèse asked her sister. She shrugged, admonishing herself. "Our guest will think we watch what everyone eats."

"Gérald does," said Claudie.

"This is intolerable," said Marie-Thérèse. "Papa, I beg you, I plead with you, open your eyes. Gérald is too polite to help himself until you have taken what you want."

Papa returned to life. Without a glance at any of the family, he transferred one slice of tomato and five radishes to his plate. "The butter," he said. Maman and Marie-Thérèse jumped up at the same time, but a clamor and quarrel at the children's table diverted them. Marie-Thérèse walked slowly toward the children and dealt out four sharp slaps. She had her hand raised over the fifth child, Alain, when Papa's eyes turned to her. Although her back was to her father, she lowered her hand. Maman, clutching the brooch at her throat, expelled her caught breath and sat down.

Shirley whispered, "The butter!"

The child who had been spared howled louder than anyone. "Come here, Alain," said Papa, and the palest and frailest of the five, the blond boy with expressionless hazel eyes, climbed on his grandfather's knee. "Dear little one," said Maman without conviction. Marie-Thérèse strode out of the room. She had a manner of walking that made her shoes sound angry. But when she returned bearing a roasted chicken carved up on a mattress of watercress, she looked calm and bitter again. Gérald beamed, as if he enjoyed more than anything hearing four children giving tongue. Papa broke off a piece of dry bread, looked for butter, shrugged, and stuffed the dry morsel in Alain's mouth. He picked up his glass, which was empty.

"The wine," he said.

Shirley found that she was comparing this family with the

Perrignys and this dining room with her mother-in-law's. At Madame Perrigny's table, generosity about food, if not of mind and spirit, was the rule. The Perrigny habit of discretion would have prevented a visitor from ever knowing how pinched and mean the Perrignys' private thoughts could be: Shirley could not have imagined open bickering. There would have been plenty of butter, excellent wine, twice the amount of chicken, the very whitest Viennois bread, and none of this jumping up and down, for nothing would have been forgotten. Here the windows were smeared and streaked. Voices, either complaining or protesting, evoked the faintest echo, as if they were raised not in a room but in an abandoned factory. Madame Perrigny's ramparts were her curtains—one layer of starched white net, then the lined, faded, disinfected, impeccable, dark green draperies. The Maurels had no curtains at all. Sunlight slanted across the Maurels' grayish panes, as it did over the sparkling Perrigny windows—here, at last, was a similarity: both families ate their meals in sunless rooms. Shirley looked around her. She saw on a low table pushed in a corner a wooden souvenir bear with a clothesbrush between its paws and a length of folded chintz. Perhaps the Maurels had taken the curtains down to wash the windows; but no—there were no curtain rods and the edge of the chintz was unhemmed and ragged. She caught an ironic look from Claudie and bent myopically over her empty plate. This blank staring of hers was a habit carried over from a time when she had been too vain to wear glasses. Philippe had cured her by teasing and saying, "One day you will hit your plate with the end of your nose." The world before Philippe and clear-sightedness had been a dark sky in which faces moved like planets. Trees were observed as if in rain, dark as if rain were covering them. Seeing created obligations: because she could now count every pebble in a handful, she felt as if she had to count them. In the old world she had identified people as infants do, by their scent and their voices. In the new, she had to look at people and see what they were like.

Lunch was now completely sidetracked because of a difference of opinion between Marie-Thérèse and her mother. Were the french-fried potatoes ready (Madame Maurel said they were) or still pallid and underdone?

"Bring them anyway," said Gérald.

"And spend the rest of the day digesting them?" asked his wife, introducing a brief reminder of the Perrignys.

"Do you find it difficult to be married to a Frenchman?" said Claudie to Shirley, sweetly, perhaps meaning this for Gérald and Papa.

The family stopped nagging and seemed suspended. Shirley knew the importance of such questions here. The difficulty was not in finding the right answer so much as in wondering why anyone should feel obliged to ask. She thought carefully and said, "All the people I have ever liked have had tuberculosis. I mean that when I become fond of anyone I usually find out that this person at one time or other was consumptive. So, quite naturally, after Philippe and I were married, I said, 'Did you ever have tuberculosis?' He seemed very upset and said, 'Who could have told you?' It is very difficult to get any information out of him about anything, but in this case he seemed to retreat into a private room and shut the door and stop his ears. Well, finally it came out that to the Perrignys this is such a shameful disease, such an affliction of the poor, that no middle-class person will ever admit to having had it, and it is called by another name—it is known as 'having a little pulmonary accident.' He said he'd had his little accident during the war, and that it was a bad time and that the sanatorium was full of miserable people. He said, 'It was the sort of place where they give you coffee in bowls.' Now this is the difficulty you were asking me about—it is things like having coffee in bowls or not. Because when my friends come to Paris the first thing they try to find and buy are those bowls, and they'll insist on drinking out of them so as to seem French. I would never have guessed that the mark of a good or a bad sanatorium had to do with cups and bowls. How could I explain to Philippe that I drank out of a bowl because *I* thought it was the French thing to do?

And why did he never tell me he wanted a cup? He took the conversation about tuberculosis as a roundabout way of making a point. I suppose it must be a *class* point. I don't know."

She had thought she was giving a simple answer of the kind advised by Mrs. Cat Castle, but the looks and the silence that followed made her realize she had taken a meaningless, impertinent question and turned it into a problem. She saw that her unshy reference to the disease was astonishing to the Maurels. They were obliged to put it down to a lack of education in the civilities. Also, she had confused them. Having established Philippe as a possible slum product, she had then attributed to him the woes and anxieties of a middle-class snob. About the bowls, no one could decide (once the Maurels began to speak again) if Philippe's stand was a good thing. At least it was unexpected.

"*We* use bowls," said Claudie. "Don't we, Maman? But then we've always had them and we never throw anything out."

Monsieur Maurel astonished everyone by remarking, "My uncle, with whom I lived for a time, never used anything for breakfast except large Sèvres cups. They were beautiful."

If a statue had spoken up the family would not have shown more fascination and alarm; all but Maman, who, at the word "uncle," looked as if she had plenty to say but was biting it back. It was she who changed the subject. "Our guest kindly brought this wine," she said, beginning all over again.

He gave it the merest glance. The child on his lap slid down and stood nearby, still sucking on the piece of bread his grandfather had fed him. Shirley wondered if the little boy were toothless; he did look senile. Papa now stared at Shirley, who, having now put on her glasses, could see him perfectly. She smiled as if returning a smile.

The chicken was cooling on its watercress: Gérald, with signals and grimaces, tried to prod Shirley into taking notice. Marie-Thérèse pushed the bottle an inch so that it stood on the round plastic doily intended for it.

"Did you think there would be nothing to drink in this house?" said Papa.

Maman watched helplessly as Claudie and Gérald, tired of waiting for Shirley, speared into the chicken with their own forks.

"I didn't bring the wine for myself," Shirley said. "I brought it for you. If you don't want it don't drink it." Her voice was as friendly as her intention had been.

"I saw a second bottle in the kitchen," said Maman. "Madame was too kind. Gérald has opened them both." She was a born tattler and informer. She fed Papa's wrath with twigs of news, hoping he would notice her and respect her.

"Wine should be exposed to air so as to oxidize," said Gérald.

"I don't like any of it," said Marie-Thérèse, softly, looking down at her plate.

Again deceived by language, Shirley thought she spoke of the wine, and she said, "Well, pour it down the sink then. I don't care."

Papa at once got up from the table with the bottle in his hand. Maman dabbed at her eyes with a napkin. Claudie helped herself to watercress and ate nonchalantly, with her head on one side, as if showing an audience how to eat imaginary food. Marie-Thérèse cut up chicken on her own plate and spooned the pieces to smaller plates for the children.

"Our guest has not been looked after," said Maman, choking. "Look after her, please," but Claudie and Gérald had taken the best of everything.

Papa had not departed in order to commit suicide, as his wife's tears suggested. He returned, still with the bottle, saying angrily, "Cork." Shirley did not know if he wanted to cork the bottle again, or if he had seen bits floating and had gone to take them out. He did not sit down; he said, "Madame will excuse me," and this time left the house. Shirley heard the door of the apartment closing, not slamming. She remembered what Maman had said to her on the staircase about Papa's quarreling with Claudie. She guessed that many meals probably ended like this. She was overwhelmed at having been addressed by Papa in the third person with such respect. It made up for being hungry. Gérald, all at once full of courage, poured wine, bellowed for bread, demanded the second bottle. He snapped orders at the children, he was sarcastic with Claudie, and announced that he was ready at any moment to meet Shirley's husband, the famous critic.

"She is *my* friend," said Claudie. "Not Gérald's!"

"Gérald can drive Madame home," said Marie-Thérèse. "Then he can ask Madame all the questions he likes about her husband." She spoke of Gérald as if he belonged at the children's table.

"We have not finished our meal!" said Maman. "There is the cheese, and Marie-Thérèse's apple tart, and Papa's ten coffee éclairs."

"If he brought ten, there's one short," said Gérald, looking at Claudie.

"I meant when *your* meal was finished," said Marie-Thérèse to her mother. Marie-Thérèse had the white brow and stained eyelids of someone whose childhood had been spent in bed. She had the persistent vitality of a child who has fought for life. None of her sons resembled her. They were square and blond and rather sly, like the Team-Brownings. Marie-Thérèse and Claudie did not resemble each other either, though something of their mother was in them both. Papa was the foreigner here. He was the father in authority, but Gérald might have been the actual father of both girls, had he been old enough.

"I wish my husband had not gone off that way," said Maman as Shirley came into the kitchen carrying a stack of plates. No one had asked her to help—indeed, there had been protests, but the alternative to helping was conversation with Claudie.

Shirley said, "Oh, my family is peculiar too."

Marie-Thérèse, who, like Shirley, was helping to clear the two tables, stood still, translating the remark into a private meaning in her mind. "So that is how we seem, now," she said.

"But my husband had nothing to eat, only radishes. And hardly any breakfast." Maman seemed afraid of her elder daughter. She lifted pale, anxious eyes to meet Shirley's for the first time that day.

"He went out early this morning, quite angry. We were so glad to see him back. And with ten éclairs!"

"He isn't hungry," Shirley said. "Even if he is, you shouldn't worry. It's only blackmail. He wants you to worry. He has probably gone to a restaurant."

"That is what Claudie did last Sunday," said Maman. "She quarreled with Papa and I slapped her. You know how necessary it is to slap a girl. Papa told her to walk the dog—so she says—and she walked too far and fainted. Then you found her and saw to it that she was given food."

"What is the matter with my family?" said Marie-Thérèse, hating everyone. "Why is everyone in restaurants? First Claudie, then Papa. No wonder foreigners think we are greedy. What kind of people spend all their time in public places? Vagabonds, homeless, new-rich..."

Before she finished Shirley had picked up her purse from a table in the hall and was trying to unlatch the front door. She was surprised when they ran after her, so upset and embarrassed. It seemed clear to Shirley that this hopeless party was over: she could not understand why they began asking each other menacingly, who, exactly, had caused "our guest" to run away? "Gérald, oh, where is Gérald?" cried his mother-in-law, as if his presence had ever mattered. Maman turned to Claudie saying, "Our guest will think..."

"Nothing," Shirley assured them. "I won't think anything. I just feel that now, this minute, we have all had enough." She ran down the stairs. Claudie called after her: "You will be hearing from me! I'm sorry about my family. I regret... regret... *regret*..."

Later she thought she had run all the way home. Although it was a bright afternoon, she recalled having run through the dark. She must have found a taxi or jumped aboard a bus. Without shutting the door of the flat behind her, she went straight to the telephone with the intention of calling for help. She would send Philippe a telegram. Help could not be had by talking into a dead line, but no one in his family would leave a telegram unread. Telegrams mean money spent. One does not simply let them lie. They may contain bad news about someone else. She was halfway to the telephone, having dropped her purse and shed her shoes, when she thought she heard him. She called his name. The telephone was not on the floor or on a chair, where she usually left it, trailing its cord like a snare, but neatly centered on a table. It looked cleaned and polished. He must have been here; perhaps he had called his mother, cautiously, saying, "I couldn't settle anything, finally. She was out." He had emptied one ashtray. In the boxroom, the tiered trays on his desk were empty and one typewriter had disappeared.

Suddenly she wanted to complain to someone. Talking to James was useless. What Shirley wanted was the friend Madame Roux had once been; a listener who was not forever dancing to her own piping, like Renata, and who did not present the mysteries and difficulties of intimately known men. Even when Madame Roux sat at the back of her shop watching the door for customers you knew she was attending. Shirley longed for the old Saturday afternoons before Philippe or when she had been between jobs. She and Madame Roux would sit drinking out of cracked cups, smoking Shirley's Gitanes and Madame Roux's Pall Malls, tearing Shirley's life to confetti only to put it back together much better than before... She missed the smoke, and the street seen through a rainy window, and Madame Roux and her sharp common sense. She was homesick for a dark January just before whatever was right between them had gone wrong, before Madame Roux felt the need to choose between Philippe and Shirley—as if Shirley minded sharing. She could have preferred Philippe but still liked me, Shirley thought.

The snow on the cobbles in the courtyard melted and froze to thin ice. The cups of coffee they held kept their hands warm. Shirley's first mistake had been talking about her marriage. First it was a joke; then it was serious; then Madame Roux turned to Philippe. It had happened in that order.

"Now he's being patient with me because I leave the towels on the floor," Shirley had said, giving an imitation of someone quietly outraged.

"You both wash too much," said Madame Roux, who seemed to know everything. "No one in this house had a hot water bill like yours. That may be what is affecting your nerves. If I bathed as often as you do, first my skin would become spongy, then it would detach itself in long strips. I thought when you had a shower put in that it would bring down your water bill, but I see it has not."

"He won't use it. It wets his hair."

She expected Madame Roux to laugh, as she used to. As long as she laughed Shirley was able to play the role of the hopelessly absentminded wife of a middle-class Frenchman. Sometimes she scarcely gave Philippe time to get out of the house before running down with a new fantasy. In her stories she always put herself in the wrong, but Philippe, seen as a perpetual victim, soon became absurd. Madame Roux began to respond by tightening her mouth and looking past Shirley, out the window.

Madame Roux snapped to, all at once practical. "You don't want him bald, do you? One shower too many and his hair will rot."

"Mine hasn't, and look at Renata's! Anyway it's not only that I leave towels all over the place. I think it has something to do with Philippe's being bored at *Le Miroir*. He's starting to cover the same stories over and over. There *is* some new television thing that interests him, but it will be just once a month. He'll be interviewing people to see their effect on France or else the reverse—I couldn't have been listening properly when he explained. Do you know what I think? I think he'd like to be free to write a novel about the Algerian War."

This brought them both to the verge of uncontrollable laughter: Shirley had so often smuggled whole sections of Geneviève's *A Life Within a Life* down to the shop, and they had so often laughed themselves weak over Charles, Bertrand and Flavia, that the very words "write a novel" were enough to set them off. Madame Roux was the first to become serious again: "If Philippe is bored, that's not your business." She still had the power to astonish. "Your only business is to see that he gets off to work whether he likes it or not."

"I don't even do that properly. He wakes *me* up. He makes the coffee. Sometimes I don't even hear him leaving. He used to work at home. He doesn't any more."

"You should be glad he is away all day instead of being underfoot."

"I should be out looking for a better job," said Shirley. "That part-time store thing is no good."

"You don't need a better job. Let him support you. You've supplied the apartment. The furniture is yours. All he did was move in. When you work, you are taking something away from a girl who may need it more than you. If you did not want to be married, you should not have chased after Philippe."

"Madame Roux! You know I didn't!"

"Marriage is made in bed," said Madame Roux sternly, as if she had invented it.

"If that were true there'd be nothing the matter with ours," said Shirley, for Madame Roux knew everything, even that.

"Then you're even more ungrateful than I had thought," said Madame Roux. "Thousands of girls would gladly be in your place, and they wouldn't complain as you do." This was to remind Shirley of the want of delicacy she had shown in marrying a Frenchman. The girls should have picketed the mairie, Shirley thought. Unfair! Unfair! Madame Roux leaned over the low table and asked the most personal question of all: "Wouldn't it have been the same with your first husband? Be honest. Think."

"I can't tell. We spoke the same language." Pete, who did not exist, stood in past time with heavy light around him. He grasped someone's bicycle. She could not see his mouth or his eyes. In a dream that frightened her Pete said, without seeming to speak, that some other person had died. She had thought, I have been married two years; then it was four; then six; but always she was thinking "married to Pete," not to Philippe. Pete had never been older than twenty-one. If she lived enough, one day she would be older than his mother. She said, "I don't know how it would have been. I don't know. When Philippe and I talk English he's at a disadvantage, and when it's French I'm never sure. I understand every word, but do I understand what French means? I might know every word in a sentence and still not add up the meaning. And then, with Pete..." She would not have lived in a place partly furnished by strangers. The curtains would have been taken down, the carpets rolled and tied with string and put in the basement for moths to feed on. Here you built a life around other people's leavings—your family's, or people you had never seen but whose traces you might find in provincial museums. You built around a past of glass cases, shabby lighting, a foul-smelling guardian saying "It is forbidden." No one could start from scratch until every room had been bombed flat as far as the horizon; and even then a residue in the mind would never be bombed away. She thought of Hervé, Philippe's friend, who filled his new married life with nylon washable velvet, with plastic tablecloths, and declared, "All this is new, and so am I."

She thought this but did not say it. What she had said was enough and she knew now what it must have sounded like when it was told back to Philippe; for Madame Roux, like James, could never explain what a story was *about*. As for Philippe's wanting to write about Algeria, all he had remarked was that someone should, for he and Hervé had been in a war they had not believed in and that was not officially a war at all. They were not veterans and not entitled to pensions. Privilege, a token income, seats in the Métro, a certain amount of nostalgia and boasting, were allowed for veterans of both world wars, the survivors of Indo-China, the old soldiers of the Resistance. But the combatants of Algeria seemed like bad weather. They were not a useful memory. "We haven't had our novelist," he said to Shirley. She glimpsed his restlessness; it was the diamond flash of a window across the Seine. The window swung outward, a branch moved; someone lives in that house, has opened the window; the sun is warming that person's arm. One day she and Philippe would grow silent and stout and she would stop looking for any meaning in these flashes. He said, "No one has come along to say that we were young or that our lives were interrupted or that we were unforgettable." They were, in fact, already forgotten. Did he want to be that one who would say it? When she read his name in *Le Miroir* she thought that if she had never known him she would have imagined him sharp and voluble and disappointed. She did not share his life, not in the way she had expected to, but she could see it, she could watch him. Of course he was happy! He had suddenly wanted to be married and had met Shirley, who was free. He had wished for a wife unlike his mother, and in that, God knew, he had been gratified. When he spoke of his mother he was respectful: he described her first crippling arthritic pains and how she would not have a doctor but simply accepted suffering with the words, "My mother and grandmother were the same." He recalled the delicious meals of his childhood and how he had been cautioned and made afraid of eating; he and Colette imagined their own stomachs awash with queer acids, poisonous and green. He remembered Thursday afternoons with Colette in a gravelly little square, marooned by streets he and his sister were not allowed to cross. They had played without toys and without getting dust on their clothes. Sad or happy memories? He did not say. "Beware of *parpaillots*," said Madame Perrigny one Sunday afternoon, having slumbered in her chair after lunch. She slept, frowning lightly, as if she had closed her eyes to search for a name or a date in her memory. What did it mean? What were *parpaillots*? Nothing, said Philippe. It had a meaning, but none to worry over. His godfather had written a book about the Council of Trent and the manuscript, presented as a gift to Philippe on his tenth birthday, was still in the house. His mother read bits of it sometimes and must have gone to sleep dreaming. *Parpaillots* had something to do with that—with the Council of Trent. Of course he had happy memories; of course he was happy now. He was not poor by French standards, and he was considered fortunate by, for example, Hervé. In Hervé's eyes he apparently earned money by doing nothing. His name was seen. His face gleamed on television sometimes. He could ring up other favored persons and say who he was, and they would at once write "Perrigny" in their appointment books. To Hervé, a technician in an electronics laboratory at the Science Faculty, his life was the life of a god. Philippe had a blinding headache at five o'clock every day. It was not because of eyestrain; it had nothing to do with sinus; one doctor said it might be the result of drinking strong coffee. No one really knew why at five o'clock someone invisible pressed a pair of thumbs between Philippe's eyebrows. He never complained. He let aspirin dissolve in water and drank the water slowly. He said he would not have been taken on at *Le Miroir* if his godfather had not been a close friend of one of the magazine's principal shareholders. This was a formal kind of self-effacement, but Shirley wondered if it were true or not true, and if there was anyone she could trust. All this Shirley had told, yes, told to the arch-traitor and enemy, Madame Roux, and Madame Roux had repeated it back to him. Madame Roux was rat, serpent, lizard, spider, bitch, vixen, roach and louse; all the same, Shirley missed her.

9

Montreal, June 17th, 1963

DEAREST GIRL:

Last Sunday the Russians sent a girl your age into space. It makes me wonder about the long-range value of education as I'm sure Valentina never had anything like your advantages. Better a woman than that poor little dog.

I want you to post me by first-class surface mail a concise history of Indo-China from 1887 to the present day with MAPS. I want it for Vincent, our janitor's son, who is learning French now but finding his textbooks dull and boring. I told him I would get him something worthy of his attention from my daughter in Paris. I have asked Vincent what he is interested in. He does not know but does not want to "stick around here," thus giving the green light to geography as an interest. I will give him my Harrap's. He is fourteen but has never been taught how to read a map or use a dictionary. They will never send Vincent into space.

Montreal, June 21st, 1963

Cat Castle still in Paris but says nothing about you. She thinks it is going to rain the whole summer. You have not mentioned this. "Light filtering from a gray transparent sky" does not describe any sort of Weather, at least not to me. Nor would I care for it as an attempt at verse.

Montreal, June 29th, 1963

Cat has seen the Moscow Theatre of Satire in Paris but did not see you among the "frumpy provincial-looking audience." She saw *The Baths* by Maiakovsky and some other thing all in Russian. It was "heavy going." Daughter Phyllis worried lest "Mum make some foolish sunset marriage now."

Have been reading some new material recently come to light, a vindication of the Peterloo Massacre. You are the age Effie Gray was when she up and left. Thank God I was always available for questioning, should you have needed it, and no one can say you got married in the dark, at least not the first time. When Cat married Ernie Castle she sent her mother a telegram from Lake Louise a couple of days later and Mrs. Pryor hot-footed it up there and took Cat home and explained to her in the train what she should have told her before. Cat had nice thick hair. She wore those peek-a-boo shirtwaists long before anybody, but with not much to show.

Montreal, July 3rd, 1963

I want you to send me a book called the ANNEE TERRIBLE BY VICTOR HUGO. This is a book of POEMS about the Franco-Prussian War 1870–71. Do not send unless the print is large and there is an ENGLISH TRANSLATION on facing page for each page of French. You will say that no such book exists, but I shall answer, "Have you looked?" There is no logical reason for this book not to exist as I describe it.

Who are these "new friends"? Who is this child? When you type do not then scribble all over the typing.

Montreal, July 10th, 1963

Instead of coming to stay with me in August, as invited,

Cat is going to Three Rivers with some dentist's son she met on a train. Cat is not always clear even in English, and they are French-Canadians. She must be out of her mind. Cat's French? Laughable. Daughter Phyllis "trembles to think." Daughter Phyllis was and still is a dim little body, in my opinion. Cat has been in Italy, Greece, Turkey, Austria, Bavaria, Scotland, England, and France, and if she can't be understood when she says "pass the salt" in Three Rivers then I just don't know.

Montreal, July 16th, 1963

Re your questions concerning Cat's marriage to Ernie. Cat's one idea was to get off the prairies. Her one wish was to live in a place where she would never again see a grain elevator. After about a year Ernie made her live in some town where the only thing in sight was a grain elevator, and when Cat would do something the other ladies didn't like, such as play ball on a Sunday (in her own yard), they made her feel it. Ernie was away a lot and she met some doctor. She already had Howard, or was it Kenny, on the way, so nothing came of the doctor. The world knew but Ernie didn't. She was the first woman to smoke cigarettes out on the street, and the first to go back to college every now and then, when it suited her, leaving Ernie with Howard, Kenny, Phyllis, and finally foolish little Nelson. Ernie settled all he could on the children because he thought she was unreliable. Destroy this letter.

By now Shirley had forgotten Renata. The source of her summer troubles had been supplanted by Claudie and the Maurels. Waiting for Philippe to make a sign of forgiveness had become part of living, just as their living together had been her life. Messages from Shirley to Philippe continued to appear, on and off, in the personal column of the Paris *Herald-Tribune*, but as it was a notorious mailbox for homosexuals she supposed that Philippe would consider the two names a coincidence; in any case, she doubted if Madame Perrigny was a subscriber or if she even knew that such a paper existed. The Maurel family were still trying to overtake their first failed invitation. Shirley had now sat down to four meals in their dining room, each a disaster. The Maurels quarreled so violently that no one save Gérald had time to swallow. Only Shirley seemed to be distressed by it; to the Maurels, normal conversation was either a whine or a scream. Except for Papa, who never looked at her, and Marie-Thérèse, who mistrusted Shirley with all her heart, Shirley had become everyone's tutelary saint. It was not in spite of her being foreign, but because of it. She would walk straight through their lives, and they knew that one day they would never have to think about her again. She was a stranger who carried absolution from either remorse or recollections. It was to Shirley that Claudie confided her anxiety over Alain. He was a deplorable little monkey. When addressed, he would tilt his head to one side, screw up his mouth, hold his hands as if his wrists were wax, and roll from one foot to the other. Maman spoke to him in the third person with a honeyed insistence that was close to dislike: "Does he want his steak cut in little, little bits?" He was too lazy to feed himself and had never been encouraged to do so. He opened his mouth, sucked each mouthful listlessly, and swallowed as much as possible whole. His hazel eyes were empty and bright as glass; but when he was harassed and frightened by Marie-Thérèse's children, his eyes whitened and he seemed blind. Left alone, he would stand dreaming and staring and masturbating. Maman or Marie-Thérèse were forever snatching his hand and slapping it scarlet. If one woman slapped, the other expressed pity, their directives and instructions, always in contradiction, fell like a melting flurry—nothing reached him. Sobbing, he would again clutch at the too small, too tight, babyish pants they made him wear. Claudie treated him as if he were a man she had met in a café. When he said something stupid she would shriek a special, high-pitched laugh she kept for the family. She seemed to think he was twenty-five and ironic. He could not decipher the alphabet or count to fifteen. He knew who Charles Aznavour was and had some notion concerning the Infant Jesus, but had never been read to. Enquiring, Shirley was told he would be given books when he was old enough not to leave fingerprints all over them, and that no one had time for reading.

Was it Claudie or Shirley who first decided the child should be taken away? "He ought to leave Maman but not me," said Claudie, "because he loves me physically." Shirley thought this was reason enough for his going, though Claudie seemed to look on it as the only justification for his remaining where he was. Shirley discovered that he had no bed of his own. At one time he had slept with his great grandmother, Mémé, then with Claudie. Sometimes, if Papa was away on a business trip, Alain would move in with Maman.

"That part is quite normal," Claudie explained. "He thinks Maman is his mother."

"Who does he think *you* are?"

"Another mother."

Shirley felt as if she and she alone had to rebuild a demolished house. She tried to make Claudie understand that Alain should not be sleeping with several generations of women.

"Speak to Maman," said Claudie morosely.

"Why don't you speak to her? He *is* yours, and what you women are doing is disastrous." Shirley went back to Early Church doctrine: "Do you know about Freud?"

Claudie gave a look as if to say she had known about Freud in several previous incarnations and did not need a reminder. "Maman will listen to you," she said.

Shirley too thought Madame Maurel would listen, but she doubted if she would act. Once, interceding on Claudie's behalf over some harsh rule Papa had laid down, Shirley had learned that Madame Maurel was proud of the difficulties of her marriage and willing to discuss them. They had sat primly in the living room while Madame Maurel described Papa's behavior. Many men do not like being spoken to in the morning, but Monsieur Maurel would not tolerate conversation even after his breakfast. It annoyed him to have to say "good-bye" as he left the house. When Maman had been as young as Claudie was now, she had got into the habit of weeping in the morning and saying that he did not love her. One day he dressed and departed and then let her know he would be staying with his favorite uncle, a lawyer and bachelor, for a few days. Papa remained with the uncle on and on. Maman dined with them every evening. Her place at their table faced a gold-framed painting of Vesuvius erupting all over a party of revellers, and when she started to dream about this painting she knew she was sliding into a way of life chosen by Papa. Papa and his wealthy uncle began to speak of their summer in Biarritz and of sending Maman to Divonne-les-Bains to take the nervous-breakdown cure. She poured coffee in the uncle's drawing room, sitting under a marble statue of a naked woman who held a lamp in her arms. The uncle laughed at some joke about marble buttocks with Maman there in the room—she still a bride and an eminently neglected one. She poured their coffee and passed cups for the last time. She did not return to her confessor, who had been promoting nothing except prayer and patience, but spoke this time to her own father. In one conversation with the bachelor uncle her father obtained Papa's return. Maman now learned that she was wealthy, quite as rich as the uncle. She had known that her dowry included a pharmacy on the rue La Boëtie, and urban property in Lyon and in Paris, but these were simply male holdings slipping from one tutor to another. As a married woman she was not allowed a bank account of her own; she could not pawn anything worth more than ten dollars; in both her civil and her religious weddings, words had been addressed to her to remind her of her subservient position, her duty. Now her father dinned into her head that she was rich, rich, and she got up from the interview understanding, at last, that money is power. It had not changed their relationship on the surface: Papa remained irascible, and she was just as morbidly afraid of spending as when she had thought herself helpless and poor. It was Papa who squandered on pastries and on dinkytoys; it was

Maman who had invested in this apartment. She feared him, she humored him, and he was rude and indifferent to her, but what did it matter. Her father had bought him for her and had purchased the very best. He was an engineer, which was an elite profession in France. Good profession, good family, no money, foul temper—oh, the best of husbands. Listening to her, Shirley had to suppress certain Canadian memories, such as the story about engineers shambling up to get their degrees, knees folded, knuckles grazing the floor.

By the time Madame Maurel had ended this ramble, Shirley was so far from the point (Claudie) that there was no hope of getting back. She wondered why Madame Maurel insisted so much on Papa's financial extravagance, the high cost of everything, and how poor they were even though they were rich; then she remembered one subject no one had ever touched on—Shirley's first meeting with Claudie and the money Shirley had paid that Sunday in the restaurant.

Papa's attempt to live with his uncle recalled to Shirley Philippe's return to his mother, but Shirley did not possess Madame Maurel's means of getting him back.

"Even a patient person can hate his wife sometimes," Shirley said. "I can imagine that. But surely only death can interfere with..."

"What?"

"Well, love," said Shirley, embarrassed at bringing up the word in this room. "Love has nothing to do with money. If it has, then I'm wrong about everything. If it were true, I'd be so wrong I'd have to start all my life over."

"Maman is bad for Alain," Claudie said. "Yesterday he came into the bathroom as I was having my bath. He looked at me for a long time and he said, 'Not pretty,' and went out. Now, I am particularly lovely in my bath, and if he had been brought up correctly he would have recognized it. He may have been using 'pretty' in a moral sense, meaning that it is not good to be naked. You must not forget that the Alsatian my sister married is a Protestant. Perhaps my mother has been contaminated, and Alain through her. For Alain's sake I ought to be fighting the Protestant mentality. I'd like to know what he says to Maman when he has a bath with *her*."

"He shouldn't be having baths with his grandmother..."

"He thinks she is his mother," Claudie explained again.

"...and he shouldn't sleep with her, because when he does he is replacing Papa."

"How else can he grow up?" said Claudie, slightly puzzled now.

"He must go away from here," Shirley must have said in desperation.

Not only were his future attitudes to women in question, but his personal habits were lamentable. His pot was carried into any room he chose, at any hour; he whiled away much of the day by sitting on it, gazing now into space, now at a comic book the pages of which were turned for him by Mémé, when she was around. He seemed unable to put on his own pants, and since the women of the family were apt to forget about them, he wandered around the apartment displaying a red circle on a bare bottom, like a Chinese insult.

In spite of three attentive generations of women, it was obvious he was lonely and bored. When he was given a toy he took it apart; when it was ruined he said he had nothing to do. Because he was destructive, the toys his grandfather gave him were put on a high shelf in a kitchen dresser "for later on." That left him with nothing but the pot until June, when the family—after much bickering and changing of plans—acquired television. The set went out of order almost at once because of Alain's fiddling with the knobs. No one scolded him. The cost of repairs immediately became part of the household expenses, while a dinkytoy with its wheels off made them feel bankrupt. One day Alain climbed up on a chair and tugged at the glass door behind which his toys were kept, visible but out of reach. The wood frame had been newly painted; the door stuck. As he tugged, half the dresser came crashing down. His chair fell sideways so that he was not badly hurt, save for a scraped bruise over an eye, but the fall knocked the wind out of his lungs. He took seconds drawing breath and expelled the breath in a howl. Women came running from everywhere. Maman and Mémé screamed at each other, while Marie-Thérèse, very white, piled broken dishes. She seemed to be adding up the losses, for her lips moved. Claudie stood in the hallway muttering, "He's all right, he's all right."

Papa said, "Alain is not to have any dessert."

Picking up a cue from the women, the child screamed, "My head is bleeding!"

"Put something on the cut," Shirley said to Marie-Thérèse, the sanest of the family. Calling "Hot water!" "Alcohol!" "Cotton!" the cavalcade of grieving women bore him away to the bathroom.

Shirley turned to Papa and said, "He might have been killed." She was shaking.

"I know. That is why he must be taught not to climb on furniture."

"Why don't they keep his toys where he can get at them? You never punish him normally, so why shout about dessert?"

"He has broken half the dishes," said Papa, meaning the chipped, coarse, brown china they used at breakfast. "Do you want me to congratulate him?"

They sounded married. Without speaking, without having looked at each other, they had gone widely around courtship and arrived. "I am told that you enjoy giving advice," he said. "Now I have heard an example of it. You have no children, at least none that we know of. Are you qualified to have an opinion about Alain? Are you competent?"

"Yes, I think I am."

"Have you loved anyone?"

"Is this a real question?"

"Yes. Tell me."

"If I've loved... My God, so many people. A Czech, but he went back to his own country. Another man, sort of like you. He rented houses in Cassis for a summer with his wife and children and godmothers and grandmothers. His wife was only supposed to care about the children, but that turned out not to be true. I wanted to spend that summer somewhere around Cassis but he was frightened. He said, 'Can't you see that I've got all these children and grandmothers and godmothers around?' I remember another man who wanted to take me to Luxembourg because he had to go there on business, and after we had been there and it did nothing but rain, he said to me rather hurriedly, as we were saying good-bye at an airport, 'Now darling that was your birthday present for next year.'"

"Is that all?"

"I'm thinking." She was thinking that Philippe had asked the same questions after they were lovers. Monsieur Maurel wanted to know everything *before*. He was old. Like Mrs. Castle gobbling éclairs in Pons, he knew about time and waste and that only the core of a situation mattered. She and Philippe still had time: they must have—how, otherwise, could they stand this separation? "I'm thinking back to another one. Ages ago. He was too old for me. He drank and he would ring up in the middle of the night. My mother would answer. She didn't like all that phoning. He married a pretentious girl, his idea of someone innocent. She was frightened by his drinking and that gave him an excuse to pity her, so I think they got along."

"You find the conversation amusing?" said Monsieur Maurel.

"Yes, in a way. I'm sorry. Is it serious? Well, you mean *love*, don't you? Oh, why isn't there a French word for 'like'?" She said the word in English, which made him blink, and she thought, He really *does* look like that comedian Louis de Funès; I don't dare ask if they're related. "Now if it were *like*, I could say I had affection for a Greek I know. I can't think of anything else to tell you. Not here in your kitchen."

"I would like to ask who had loved you. I thought you were married?"

"My husband loved me," she said, "but he abandoned me without any warning."

"Why did you come here today?" he said. "What interests you about my daughter and my wife? Could you not confine your friendship with Claudie to restaurants and cinemas? As a family we must bore you. We are not good company. I have seen how you translate every word we say before your mind can take it in. We have the worst table in Paris, so it can't be the food that tempts you. Why do you keep coming back? Is it because you want me to make love to you?"

"Probably," she said.

"I have no time for you," he said. "Not even an hour."

She went on speaking to him after he had left the room.

She picked up Alain's chair, she swept the floor, and she said to herself, You think you've insulted me. A sexual slight is a slap in the face, to you. But all you are afraid of is having to take your clothes off. Like James you probably need something, but you don't dare tell me what it is. Where did you imagine it *could* happen? I wonder. In my flat during your lunch hour? No—that would be under Philippe's roof, and if we were found out you would be involved. That is called adultery in the conjugal domicile and it is very, oh, very serious. You were trained by your rich old uncle and so what you dream of, I should guess, would be one of those "luxurious furnished studios" near the Bois de Boulogne. The concierge is elegant; he gives the man the key but never looks the woman in the face. If he were on the rack he couldn't identify her. It would be so much more comfortable than anything you've ever had at home—the marvelous bed and the spotless bathroom and the soft towels and the delicious meals around the clock. You would pretend to be scornful. How you would sneer and how you would admire the waiter out of an old Lubitsch movie, the bogus luxury! I can see the thick looped curtains, the pale carpet. Let me invent a detail for you—miniature flags waving over *langouste en mayonnaise*, a tribute to the mingling of nations. "I have no time for you." Imagine having made up a situation just because you had a good exit line. Imagine thinking, imagine *saying* it! Oh, poor little engineer! Poor Papa!

Soon after this, Claudie told Shirley that she was in love and might at any minute depart for foreign places with the lover. She could not tell his name or reveal their plan. Shirley would meet him soon. They would require her help. Meanwhile, Alain's future must be established. Shirley agreed. That scene in the kitchen had been lamentable. Without Claudie (not that she had ever been much use to him) Alain would be the sole object of a tormented grandfather whose spoiling had something unpleasant about it, and of an insect-minded grandmother who secretly loathed him. Shirley examined her address book as if she were a nineteenth-century aristocrat searching through the Gotha for a sound alliance, and went straight through without any luck whatever until she came to the V's, where "Van Tong" arrested her. Chinese? No, Hubert Van Tong was an unfrocked Belgian priest who had been living for some years with a sculptress from Vancouver; the sculptress's mother and Mrs. Norrington had been old university friends, but now each disapproved very much of the other's daughter. The sculptress, whose name was Virginia, no, it was Felicity, no, Honor, Honor it was, had abandoned two children of her own the day she received a grant for study abroad. She had often expressed remorse during the seven years since she had last seen them and might welcome starting over with Alain, who so evidently needed someone. Honor was said to have been a good mother; anyone who had known her before her flight to Europe always added to her qualities, "and she was so *marvelous* with those *children*!" The Van Tongs lived two hours by train from Paris in a charming town covered with roses. Hubert was a kind, quiet man who had the habit of saying, "Yes, I agree," which would be a change from Papa, Shirley wrote and was at once invited to bring Claudie to lunch. Behind the gray façade of an ordinary village house Shirley and Claudie found a courtyard filled with white geraniums. Claudie spent the day with most of her clothes off lolling in the little garden and admiring the studio, which contained Alain's future foster mother's welding equipment. Cats and doves, killers and victims, were the pets of the house. Pig iron and used bicycle parts spilled out of the studio to the court. It looked to Shirley like debris after an accident: she thought of hillsides strewn with women's shoes, ripped handbags, combs. "The kind of unexpected ingredient you find in the soup in Belgium," said Van Tong genially. He and Honor would be charmed to have Alain at least as a summer guest. They seemed to think he would be no more bother than one of the cats. Claudie put on her clothes unwillingly and embraced her new, intimate friends as if they were her family and she were emigrating. On the way back to Paris she remarked, "Alain will grow up surrounded by such good taste." Shirley had not considered that. She imagined Alain carrying his little pot out to the garden and vacantly watching cats leap at doves.

All at once, as if she met him, Claudie said, "What do you think of Philippe's new program?"

"What program?"

"On TV. It's only for the summer, but Gérald has found out from a man he knows that if it goes well they will keep it on. Does *he* like it?"

"Very much."

They were alone in a red plush compartment. Shirley had paid for first-class travel. Claudie sighed, for this was bliss to her, and said, "You lead such separate, mysterious lives. You each seem to have your own friends. I suppose you talk in the privacy of the night?"

"Yes, that's it."

"Do his friends meet you?"

"Not often."

"It sounds to me like the ideal marriage," Claudie said. "Gérald thinks so too, but not Maman."

"Claudie, you have no right to discuss my husband," said Shirley. Presently she said, "What does your father think?"

Claudie laughed and said, "We shall see." There was nothing but candor in her answering look.

Papa had not yet come in. The chintz curtain that was tacked across the dining-room window at night lay folded on a table. Shirley had discovered that no one could agree with anyone else about the dining-room curtains, and so this temporary system had become a permanent arrangement. Marie-Thérèse's crepe soles squeaked on the floor, but the passage of her shoes from floor to carpet and carpet to linoleum were all she had to declare. She and Gérald had been told about Claudie's secret; that was why they were here, and why they had gone to the unheard-of expense of hiring a baby-sitter for the youngest child. They had brought the great-grandmother, who was back from Lyon and staying with them. Nothing about the Ziffs so much as hinted at what they thought and felt. Gérald stood near the table, waiting, like a horse, and Claudie lay sprawled reading a paperback life of Jung. Alain and the four Ziff boys played in a bedroom, supervised by whimpering old Mémé. Claudie laughed loudly and immoderately at some light-hearted passage in the boyhood of Jung. It was a high-pitched and deliberately irritating laugh, but her mother's voice, talking quietly to her older sister—a counterpoint in every way—was the only reaction. Leaving Claudie to her merriment. Shirley began doing whatever seemed needed in the kitchen, and thought, Even if that isn't the way they want their bread cut, at least I have done it. After a time, feeling ignored, Claudie joined them. She gave Shirley a look of high amusement and said, "You look like a maiden aunt," and Shirley indeed felt old and thin. Claudie was quicker and more efficient than any of them, than even calm Marie-Thérèse, or Maman, who dropped and chipped whatever she touched. Claudie was showing what she could do when she chose. Shirley thought, Here we are, four women, preparing a meal that won't even be very good, trying to be on time for a bad-tempered man.

Was it true that he kept Maman on a tight food allowance, as she had suggested? What about Maman's income? They were to start with a vegetable broth, the liquid in which carrots and leeks had boiled, reduced with a handful of vermicelli. The vegetables, in a pool of liquid, were set aside, keeping warm. Little medallion veal steaks would follow, and green salad with the dark streaks Philippe and his family would never eat, believing snails had been spreading snail poison. Cheese, applesauce. Twelve-degree red ink wine, sold by the liter. The first meal Shirley had ever eaten here seemed like a banquet. She supposed she must be one of the family now.

"Claudie, pay attention!" said Marie-Thérèse. "Your friend has cut her hand with the breadknife."

In a quick look, Shirley tried to find the slight edge of exchange they had begun the day Alain had fallen off his chair; but Marie-Thérèse seemed to dread the idea that any conversation could ever take place between them. Maman looked at Shirley's hand, at the globe of dark blood. Claudie said, "Something has made you nervous, Shirley," and took the knife.

Papa was home! The great-grandmother instantly appeared and moaned some sort of senile warning as Claudie turned on the hall light. Mémé had only recently been cured of her habit of replacing with forty-watt bulbs anything stronger: Papa could not stand the sight of his wife squinting and frowning over her sewing, as if she were trying to pick ants out of the stitches. Marie-Thérèse's children gathered in the hall in a condition of subdued chaos, glancing anxiously at their mother, who frightened them very much. Maman touched the little dove pin at her throat for comfort. This heart-clutching fear—she has it five evenings a week all her life, Shirley thought. Gérald appeared from the dining room. His face was a study in perplexity, distress and physical want. The door opened. "Papa! Papa! Papa!" screamed the children. Monsieur Maurel closed his eyes.

Claudie said calmly, "Madame Perrigny has friends who want to invite Alain for the rest of the summer. They live in a healthy country place and they like children."

Shirley, sitting next to Papa, was trying to talk to him as if she had never met him before, and he was answering as if it was no effort for him to imagine he never had. The others were gripped in discussion. Shirley described to Papa a television program she had never seen (Philippe's) and how Philippe felt about it. He seemed to be listening; his eyes went from her face to his plate, but like Shirley, he was attending to something quite different.

"Completely out of the question," Papa said.

"What would it cost?"

"Nothing," said Claudie.

"They must be after something."

"Is it only for the summer?"

"Maman could have a holiday."

"A rest—at last."

"What about the Family Allowance?"

"Are they French?"

"Haven't they any children of their own, poor things?"

"Do they own their house?"

"Do they own any other property?"

"Any heirs? Godchildren?"

"Would Alain pick up a Belgian accent?"

"They know of course we would be doing them a favor? He is not a ward of the State! It would be intolerable to have them think such a thing."

"The air would be better for him."

"The air of Paris gives you cancer."

"Of the larynx."

"Of the lungs."

"How many acres? How many rooms in their château? Their villa, then. What do you mean by house?"

"A house with a garden is a villa, Claudie. Don't be stupid."

"They must be told he is allergic to nearly everything."

"Are you perfectly sure they are Catholics?"

"What do you mean, Claudie, by another form of life around the place? Oh, doves. How charming."

"Alain is going to play with doves!"

"I suppose they saw a picture of Alain and fell in love with him. Which photo did you show them, Claudie?"

"We must visit him every weekend."

"It is only for six weeks," Shirley put in.

"Alain, your little cousins will envy you."

"What about the Family Allowance?"

"It is such a small sum, it would be insulting of us to offer it."

"Maman should send flowers."

"Why? They should send them to her."

"It would be a gesture—chocolates."

"If they have a garden they don't want flowers. As for chocolates."

"Maman must write a charming letter."

"*What about the family allowance?*"

Originally it had been turned over to Claudie. Then Papa instructed his wife to keep it, because Claudie either lost the money or spent it on herself or bought Alain a monstrous woolly monkey that frightened him so he went blue in the face. It would be mortally insulting to offer money to these cultivated, wealthy people in their Burgundian château.

"After all, they want Alain for their own pleasure."

"If they went to a public charity and asked for a child they'd be given a miserable orphan."

"With alcoholic parents."

"Parents in prison."

Alain looked from face to face. Papa had left the table and stood by the uncurtained window.

"They bottle their own wine?" asked Gérald. "Vineyards?"

"Where? In Burgundy?"

"Probably in Burgundy. The best vineyards in Burgundy have been bought by Belgians."

"That is true. In fact there is a new generation of children in Burgundy completely blond. On account of the Belgian blood, you see. All these Belgians."

"They buy wine in bulk at a cooperative," said Shirley, but her voice was lost. "And they bottle it. That's all."

She understood Claudie's desire to get away. Even the distant sound of traffic suggested other, richer lives. They were marooned around a table. Papa had left the circle and now he spoke quietly from the window. His back was to them and they did not hear the first words. Gérald's voice was still heavily going on about the Belgians in Burgundy. First Shirley, then the others heard: "... for Claudie to grow up. Then it was Alain. When he grows up, I shall be too old. If he goes, I can leave now. If he stays, I stay." Now he turned and looked at them.

A cry of "Papa!" and Claudie leaped, it seemed, for his throat but at the last second changed her mind and flung her arms around his neck. He faced the family with great Claudie clinging and sobbing. He sought Shirley's eyes. She understood: this scene is played to me. She tried to put into her answering look, I give up—you win. He *had* won. That was the end of the project. Claudie never mentioned it again, and she left the apologies and explanations for the Van Tongs up to Shirley.

10

SHIRLEY played back the scene in the Maurels' kitchen, this time giving herself one or two good lines.

"As a token of friendship and particular esteem," she said, "I will let you decide how you shall be cooked. Would you like to be fried in oil or would you prefer to be cooked in the stewpan with tomato sauce?"

All her private dialogues were furnished with scraps of prose recited out of context, like the disparate chairs, carpets and lamps adrift in her apartment. She carried her notions of conversation into active life and felt as if she had been invited to act in a play without having been told the name of it. No one had ever mentioned who the author was or if the action was supposed to be sad or hilarious. She came on stage wondering whether the plot was gently falling apart or rushing onward toward a solution. Cues went unheeded and unrecognized, and she annoyed the other players by bringing in lines from any other piece she happened to recall.

Supposing she *had* asked Monsieur Maurel if he wanted to be fried in oil? Even if he had remembered anything at all about *Pinocchio* he would certainly have been startled at her suddenly declaiming in English. He could never have guessed how shy and uncertain she was in French. It was true that French literature had once been her major subject, but here again a mistake had been made, for the authors she had been taught to consider important had turned out to be despised in Paris, at least by Philippe's generation. Colette and Giraudoux were neither read nor mentioned, Gide seemed to have been all but forgotten, and Camus was more admired abroad. Philippe had confused her by saying kindly that, like all foreigners, she was fifteen to twenty years out of date, and then by praising *Gone with the Wind* (all that a novel should be) and *The Grapes of Wrath* (appreciated even by Hitler as portraying the real America). Shirley had never dared tell him how close she had once felt to a Giraudoux novel about a shipwrecked girl—another Shirley, perhaps—who, alone on her deserted island, tried to let herself perish of sunstroke and by drowning and even, by recalling everything base and vile in the world, of indignity. But death had no use for her, and finally she was given the promise that she would one day buy trick spiders and imitation grasshoppers and exploding cigars for her children in a shop close to the Place de la Madeleine. "*J'étais sauvée*," said the girl simply, and Shirley believed her. The only uncertainty in Shirley's mind was exactly where the promise had come from. "God," said Giraudoux carelessly, but Shirley supposed he had said that for want of vocabulary.

What similar, lunatic assurance could uphold her now? The summer was a tightrope. Somehow or other she had to reach the other side. She smiled in the dark in James's bed and put all her trust in the city that exists in memory, children who do not exist at all, and in the cheerful hoax. I have always been saved, she said to herself, but then remembered the tortured evenings when Philippe had made her meet his friends, how she had been daunted by the wave of hostility that rose to greet the stranger in Paris. Nothing seemed to be considered rude or preposterous if it was said to someone like her. "We wanted to give you beans and jam for dinner to make you feel at home, but my wife refuses to do American cooking"—that was how Hervé, Philippe's best friend, had welcomed her. Another of Philippe's friends had told her contemptuously that he had been given whipped cream with roast beef in Washington; had interviewed a chef in California who had never tasted asparagus and thought it was a weed; had talked to a painter in Chicago who had never heard of Braque. Attempting to reply was like fighting out of quicksand. This particular friend's American adventures had been collected in a widely selling book, which in itself was considered a positive answer. She was ashamed to remember now that she had minded, had nagged back, had let herself be hurt. The question of asparagus and Braque had been one of her rare disagreements with Philippe; they had discussed it for some reason even on their wedding day. It remained in her mind as their most passionate exchange. They had been married for less than an hour, they were in a café on the Place St. Sulpice, Shirley was pregnant, and the words "whipped cream and roast beef" made her throat sting with nausea. Why had she let herself be defeated, forgetting she was destined to be saved?

On the morning of Whitsunday, sitting on the edge of her bed reading her mother's letter, she had applied names to her conduct—deceitful, filthy, careless, damaging, corrupt. True? If true, then she might as well lay her head on a rock and die of sunstroke. In Berlin, she remembered, she had forgotten her password, but death had entered and then left her, and it would have been shameful to have remembered, as magic, "*J'étais sauvée.*"

Now followed a brief summer season of parties. The Maurels were part of Shirley's life, though they may not have known it. She thought that two worlds, theirs and James's, should be made to overlap. The Maurels wanted airing, contact with a livelier universe, while the Mediterranean contingent kept complaining that they never met anyone French. They were asked to meet in Shirley's living room, candle-lit for the occasion, one Sunday at six o'clock. Even Papa had come. Perfectly at his ease, he treated the women with unexpected charm and gallantry, and talked nothing but common sense to the men. He did not address a word to any member of his own family, of course, and to Shirley he was only just polite. She knew that he watched her and that it was for his approval that she had dressed. There was a complicity between them, as though they were slightly hostile lovers. It was now merely a question of where and when. Warned by Claudie that her family expected the party to replace a meal, Shirley had summoned her Scandinavian caterer, dropped after the disaster with her sister- and mother-in-law. Gérald stationed himself at the table on which the cold supper was laid and remained standing there with his mouth full of herring and bread and butter until his wife led him away. As for the rest of the family, unlike the Perrignys, they would try anything new providing they did not have to live with it, pay for it, or be reminded of it too often. The party went well: the Greeks thought they were better than the Maurels because they were more modern, and at least *looked* richer, while the Maurels knew *they* were superior because they were not foreign. This assumption of consequence made everyone cordial. Later the Maurels continued to ask about the Greeks, remembering their names and following whatever Shirley could reveal about their lives with interest. They did not wish to know them any better, but they accepted them as people they might hear about from time to time. "How is James?" Maman would ask, rather coyly. He had told Madame Maurel about the Greek evzone doll made into a lamp. The bulb under the skirt produced a comical effect when lighted. Gérald was interested in the idea, but Marie-Thérèse would not have had it in the house. Alone of the family, Marie-Thérèse suspected Shirley and seemed to wonder what Shirley wanted with them all.

Presently, when James gave a farewell party because his sisters and brothers-in-law were leaving Paris, he casually invited the Maurels and the Ziffs. Here they drew the line: enough was enough. Claudie was permitted to go, but on condition she spend the night in Shirley's apartment. Her father did not want her to cross Paris alone at a dangerous hour. In spite of his conversation with Shirley he still seemed to think that her flat was the safest place in Paris. As a substitute for Papa, Maman, Gérald and Marie-Thérèse, and so that James would not be disappointed, Shirley summoned Renata. She gave Claudie only as much information as seemed needed to keep Claudie from asking questions: Renata was twenty-five, she was a painter of portraits of rich women — a true vocation that had manifested itself when she was still very young—and now she earned a fat living in a milieu notorious for getting things free. That in itself showed she was remarkable. She was closely attached to her mother, who lived in America, and with whom she kept up a tense exchange of letters beginning, "Your brave and gallant attitude..." She was also very pretty and supremely elegant. This last was contradicted by Renata's arriving dressed in a Victorian orphan's uniform and with her long hair strained back. She wore no makeup and seemed pale and severe. She began speaking at once about her suicide attempt, taking it for granted Claudie would have been told of it, and was obviously gratified at the girl's excitement and awe. She did not ask where Philippe was. Renata and Shirley gave no sign of having ever known much about each other. Their forced closeness and its climax had given them the need to start over as acquaintances. The two visitors sat on Shirley's bed while she dressed. Claudie had bought for this occasion new underclothes and a new toothbrush. She told Renata that she expected the party to change her life.

Renata took Claudie's broad hand and read her fortune. "A tragedy is behind you," she announced. "You have come through the worst. You are in love, but you will meet someone more suited to you later on. I see two, no, *three* marriages. Perhaps one child, not more. Your first lover will always remain the love of your life. But he is married to someone else."

"That could apply to anyone," Shirley remarked. She could see that Claudie was dazzled and wondering if the change had already begun. She stared at her palm and then at Renata.

Bored with Claudie, Renata walked around the room. She pushed Shirley away from the mirror gently, and released her hair. The Victorian orphan had been a mood, nothing more. From the bathroom she called, "How does Philippe see to shave in this light?" and "You're so sloppy, Shirley, yet there's nothing personal in your house. This is like a room in a hotel waiting for the next lot of strangers."

"We can't all have lived-in bathrooms."

Renata wandered back and said, "You both look splendid"—this because she now looked so much better.

They walked upstairs, slightly edgy and solemn, although they were only going to a party. Claudie said, "I've never been up here before. What is all this?"

"A leftover from the Algerian War," said Shirley. "The man who lived in that apartment had his door blown in by a bomb."

"Why?" said Claudie.

"I don't know. The war was still on. The man had to move out."

"What had he done?"

"I keep telling you—I don't know. He must have done something. Madame Roux thought he had. She hated the Algerians. She was all for the paratroops. I wasn't for anybody."

"I was for the FLN, of course," said Renata with a contempt Shirley could not explain to herself—for who or what was the object? Shirley? Ben Bella? The French? "Philippe wrote some marvelous things in *Le Miroir* about his own experiences in the army. That was how they came to hire him, I'm told. It was probably his apartment the fascists were after. They made a mistake and blew up the wrong one."

"I didn't know him then. He didn't live here."

"Shirley, how can you be married to a man like Philippe and not understand anything?"

"He never asked me what I knew." Women had starved so that Shirley might vote; a girl in Algeria, a patriot, had been horribly mutilated with a broken bottle by laughing young men who were proud of their European culture. But revolution belonged to her mother; to Philippe; it was a night without signposts in which you were lost. How can Renata take sides when she is always on the way to a party? Claudie had been listening closely: anything to do with Philippe seemed to rivet her attention. Shirley, looking up, caught sight of two dim faces drawing back from the stairwell. "I keep seeing strange men on this staircase," she said. "I wonder if they're left over from that winter when all the flats were bombed?"

"It's only that couple next door to James," said Renata. "Some old maid and her brother. If you would only remember to wear your glasses!"

"That couple wouldn't be here now. They go away every summer."

"Then they've sublet. Shirley, stop fussing." She said to Claudie, "Shirley likes everything as dramatic and complicated as possible. You should hear her—'Orange juice destroys all the calcium in your system.' 'The air in Paris is polluted and we will all die of pneumonia.' Now it's 'Someone is watching me on the stairs.' Never listen to Shirley."

"Oh, but I do listen," Claudie cried. "I have never listened as much to anyone." When the others laughed she seemed bewildered.

"It's quite true about the orange juice," Shirley remarked. "I heard someone explain about it at a meeting Philippe took me to."

"Try to make a good impression on James, Claudie," said Renata. "He's looking for a wife. He has tried all of us, Shirley included. He would love to take someone unknown and exotic back to Greece. She will have to be young—you are. She should have a dowry. I'm certain you will have. And she ought to be virgin, or nearly. Are you, or nearly?"

"I sometimes feel as if I am still waiting," said Claudie, as if hoping that would do.

"That's no answer. How many men have you had in your life?"

"Only two," said Claudie, "and I hated it both times. One I loved but he was, well, married. The second was to get over the first one, like taking a spoonful of jam after castor oil."

"You'll do for James," said Renata.

Shirley instantly saw Claudie married to James. She saw a house, a white corridor, a room, green light along the wall. This beautiful light came from a window screened by broad-leaved vines. No, the vine was really a fig tree. Its leaves pressed the shutters back against the wall. The windows to this house were open forever. She saw at the end of the hall another white room, a dark, tiled floor and white armchairs. Here were assembled James's family and his friends, who were much superior to the foolish friends he had collected in Paris. They drank from blue glasses in which ice cubes tapped and floated. Shirley was there too, but all she could see of herself was her own wrist and a watch with a heavy strap. The watch was Pete's. She had worn it for a few days after his death and then she had given it to his mother. Mrs. Higgins had died too; what had become of that watch?

There was always a flaw in a prophetic vision, some detail that wandered on like an unwanted actor. She remembered the innocent opinion she and Pete had shared about Mediterranean life and how they had stood outside the vine-covered terraces of bars and seen the foreign women with their mysterious sunglasses and their thin brown arms.

From James's flat came the sound of a record. "*Donne tes seize ans.*" There seemed something immoral to Shirley in that song sung by a middle-aged man. But it was a favorite of James, who said, "He can't very well sing '*donne tes trente ans*,' can he?" James was wearing a Merrie England gilt-buttoned blazer and a cool, camel-like English expression. Still, he seemed to her lavish and Oriental, in keeping with her picture of the green-shadowed room.

During the evening Claudie suddenly turned to Shirley and said, "This is my life."

"Oh, Claudie, no. It would be an imbecile life, not worth caring about." She understood that Claudie was working up to some sort of daydream as uninformed as her own.

Renata remarked without lowering her voice, "They all had colored blood. Look at the whites of their eyes. Aphrodite isn't a real blonde. She had about half an inch of pure kink at the roots. James tried to sell me an apartment on the avenue Foch. Who was the real blonde handing drinks around?"

"Rose," said Shirley. She and Claudie were saying goodbye to Renata on the landing outside Shirley's door. Shirley was certain that James upstairs could hear every word.

"She didn't seem to belong to that crowd."

"She does because of James."

"His sisters are horribly flashy."

"They might not seem flashy in their own background."

Renata was dissatisfied with Rose or Shirley or the evening. Had she been undervalued? Had James seen her rich and not beautiful? "When Philippe comes in he'll be surprised to find Claudie in bed with you, won't he?"

"She'll be on the couch in the living room." So. James had not gossiped: no one knew.

"Claudie," said Renata, "finish that thing you were telling me about your fascinating father. Does Shirley know him?"

"About as well as I know your mother," said Shirley. "Look it's late and we're all very tired. Are you sure you don't want to come in, Renata, or do you want to go on talking on the landing?"

"I don't want to delay you two a minute longer. I could easily give Claudie a lift."

"My father wants me to stay with Shirley," said Claudie. "What I started to tell you was that my mother is rich, my father is not rich, and my father's mother is poor. Maman gives her our old clothes."

"We'll see each other again," said Renata. "I want to hear it all. Remember what I said—try to marry James, and never listen to Shirley."

Shirley knew that someone had been in the apartment. She could not have sworn that any particular object had been removed or displaced; she felt only the haunting and the intrusion. Philippe still possessed a key and could lend it to strangers. These strangers could enter whenever they wanted to. They might kill me one day, she thought. She remembered the two faces on the stairs.

She straightened up—she had been preparing Claudie's bed—and said brusquely, "I heard you telling everyone you were leaving home. Don't leave home unless you have a job."

"I thought your husband might help me," said Claudie. She stood in the middle of the room in her new nightdress with her hair over her shoulders. Shirley, frowning like a worried parent, remembered little Alain and Claudie in the bathtub and longed to snap, "Not pretty," but she knew Claudie would take that to be more Protestant depreciation of her beauty. "Gérald has spoken to him," Claudie said.

"What do you mean?"

"Gérald has spoken to your husband. He was in his office. Philippe is not traveling. He has come back."

"Why the devil did Gérald call him? Who asked him to?"

"It was about his jazz column. Gérald introduced himself as a friend of yours."

"And asked some favor? He had no right to do that. Damn him."

"You told Gérald he could."

"I never thought he'd be so stupid."

"Your husband said he doesn't do the jazz thing now, so he had no reason for seeing Gérald." Claudie paused and said, "He said he hadn't been doing it for at least six months. Did you know?" Shirley said nothing. "He might find some interesting work for me," said Claudie, but with less assurance this time.

"He doesn't hire and fire. Please go to bed."

"Oh, if you only knew how I envy you and how I long to live your life!" Claudie cried, and flung her arms around Shirley.

The telephone rang. James was alone. Rose had left him. He had insomnia. Shirley imagined how it would be, up there among the dead remains of the party.

"I'm too tired," she said. "Anyway Claudie's here." Before he could say "Bring her," she said, "She's asleep. And I can't leave her. She's afraid of the dark."

11

WHEN, finally, Shirley's presence no longer worked the magic with which James had once credited it, he moved his television from the living room to the foot of the bed. He sat watching, hoping for some sort of unexpected electronical stimulus, while Shirley read. She reread *Apropos of Dolores, Lolly Willowes, Mrs. Dalloway*, a part of *Anna Karenina*, part of the *Confessions of Felix Krull*, and all of *Persuasion*. She had to remember to take her book away in the morning, for anything other than *The Whip Angels* or the old Thesaurus James used to prop open the kitchen window would have made Rose wonder what went on late at night. When, as sometimes happened, Shirley forgot her book downstairs, she read the Thesaurus. It must have been in the apartment through several tenancies. James said he knew nothing about it.

"James, did you know that Peter Mark Roget was also the author of the *Bridgewater Treatise on Animal and Vegetable Physiology*? I'll bet you didn't."

One night on television they saw Philippe. She had been slow to grasp that he wanted nothing more to do with her, that "he has left me" was not a phrase invented to make people laugh at parties. She plagued James for news about him: "Did you see him? Did you really go to his office?"

"Yes, but we didn't discuss you. He doesn't know..."

"That I sleep up here? I should think not."

"If he did know it could only be because you talk to everybody," said James, as if he were hinting at something for her own good.

"Oh, I never see Renata now. I haven't seen her since your party, and now she's away. I don't know if she said she was going to Norway or Gibraltar but it was one of the two. I don't talk to anyone except you. Madame Roux pretends she's never met me."

"I *have* seen him," said James. "On a matter of co-property."

"He doesn't own anything. At least I don't think so. People always turn out to own more than you think they do. By the way, no one ever answered the *Herald-Tribune* ads."

"Well, I can tell you he will be away for some weeks. First he goes to Brittany…"

"He's been there. He's done the bit about the artichoke glut on the market. What he really ought to do is a three-part piece on Colette's liver."

"Then he goes to London to see why England can never, never improve or be in the Common Market"—here Anglophile James sounded solemn, newly convinced—"and then to Algeria to report on one year of peace. Is peace good or bad? Philippe will tell us."

"I've heard he doesn't do the jazz thing anymore. That means he doesn't need it. He has his own television setup—so they tell me. He's going up in the world, James? Better off without me? Is that it?"

"If you would look at the screen instead of shouting in my ear," James said, "you would see."

"He seems well," she said, after a moment. "Who's the old party with him? He looks like a flamingo."

"A famous American psychiatrist. Shirley, I wish you would not talk just now."

What struck her about Philippe was his newness. He was freshly minted. She could recognize his face but not his expression. She remembered his voice but not his clothes, and his professional manner daunted her. The program was one of a series comparing modern life in several countries with that of France, to the repeated detriment of the former. "America's a pushover for something like this," she remarked.

"I plead for silence," said James tensely. He seemed fascinated by Philippe.

The psychiatrist moves his mouth too much, she thought. He

hisses. I don't like his narrow eyes. What are these spots like pilot lights all around his glasses, sliding like beads? Why does he put his hand up over his face? Trouble with digestion. Two cruel lines between his eyebrows. And his accent: he's not an American. He's some transplant from the Danube. Ungrateful old bastard.

"In New York apartments all the furniture goes into the wall," said Dr. Karl Peter Callavari between two modest hiccoughs. "That is why in America women leave their husbands. There are no worldly goods to be considered. The beds, the tables, the chests of drawers, can be pulled up into the walls. She gathers up her personal clothing and makes a parcel and so departs."

"You can't pack a Murphy bed," Shirley agreed.

"Please cease speaking," said James.

Philippe addressed them: "Though none of us has ever seen the built-in furniture Dr. Callavari describes, or the heartless architecture that enables mothers to abandon their small children without regret..."

"And increases the racial problem," the doctor interrupted. "Yes, increases it. For as some move out others move in, which is not the case in Europe."

Why does Philippe bite his forefinger? He usen't to. The light that goes around and around the doctor's glasses gets him just under the eyelashes. Dear Philippe—I am sitting here naked, just with my glasses on. When the doctor meanders Philippe turns his head; he looks indifferent. But he is probably seeing himself too. His voice is good. He never says too much. "Isn't he attractive?" the Maurels are saying to each other. "Why did he choose Mrs. Higgins, do you suppose?" He really is attractive. God, I'm his *wife*.

"Dr. Callavari has put into words..."

In accented English the doctor suddenly uttered, "I may be called a Communist for saying this, but..."

James said urgently, "Tell me quickly something about Philippe—he used to give you sleeping pills. And then?"

"The American laundry problem," said Philippe, hurrying them back to French.

"Yes?" said the doctor, bright but unprepared.

"Is it the custom to keep dirty clothes on the floor and clean clothes on a chair in the parlor?"

After blinking and hiccoughing only twice, the doctor said calmly, "It is very often the custom."

Shirley suddenly remembered she owed James six hundred new francs and had owed them since the Sunday of Philippe's disappearance. She turned to tell him she had thought of this and said instead, "No."

"Philippe can't see us," James said.

"You wish he could, you mean."

"No one can see, it is only pretending."

"That's what they say about God," said Shirley. "I'm not sure about that, either. Anyway, nothing doing."

"It is a shame to waste this," James said.

Philippe turned around and looked straight into the camera with a look intended for her. What did it mean? How young he looks, she thought. No, I'm wrong. How old! Oh, what an old young man! No, he was not looking at her, he was looking at nothing. He looked as the dead do in dreams, and she knew too much about that.

"You're quite right in thinking you ought to kick me out," she said to James. "And I am aware that as a result of this mishap we must part." She mimicked him slightly, felt sorry, and said to herself, it doesn't matter. No more remorse. She looked up "remorse" in Roget's, but the page was torn across. "Failure" was suitable, but unkind where James was concerned. "I've found it," she said to him. "It's under 'adversity.' I've found why Philippe is sitting there talking rubbish with a total stranger instead of being home with me, and why I'm here with you when you'd be better off with Crystal Lily. Listen. 'one's star is on the wane; one's luck turns (fails); the game is up; one's doom is sealed; the ground crumbles under one's feet; *sic transit gloria mundi; tant va la cruche à l'eau qu'à la fin elle se casse.*'"

12

SOMETIMES she thought that Philippe's look had not been of the dead. "Trust me—I am conscious of all that happens," he might have wanted to say. Once she thought she saw him standing in Madame Roux's shop. Madame Roux folded her arms and hugged herself and laughed. Behind the pair was a wall of cracked and spotted mirrors. They seemed like twin owners of an enterprise that never could fail.

The bell behind the door jingled as gaily as if Shirley were someone welcome. Madame Roux, fatter even than she had been in June, smiled for a customer and changed nothing except the quality of the smile when she saw that the intruder was her former friend. The man with her had vanished.

"I was about to drop this letter in your mailbox," said Madame Roux. "Your friend left it with me. Not Miss Renata—your French friend. Yes, French," she continued thoughtfully. "You lunch at their house every Sunday; so she says. You know them so well that I cannot understand why they haven't your telephone number. Your friend looked in the directory, but apparently you had given them the wrong name. She was amused when I told her your name was Higgins."

"You know why it is Higgins in the book," Shirley said. She was astonished to see that her hand shook.

"You once told me you couldn't make the change from Higgins in your mind," said Madame Roux. She raised her tone slightly, as though she wanted someone else to hear this. "You said that 'Perrigny' seemed to you a kind of false identity."

"Higgins is only a name in a telephone book now. My name is Perrigny. I made the change."

"Perhaps too late," said Madame Roux.

"Philippe!" Shirley cried, pushing by, rattling a tray of chipped and grimy saucers. The space behind the bead curtain was empty, though cups and a full ashtray sat on the secret table. Perhaps he had slipped out the back entrance, past the storeroom. She would find him upstairs, neatly butting out a Virginia cigarette, waiting to ask, "Where were you that Saturday?" What came to her lips was a curious plaint: "My father never treated my mother this way."

"He is not here, and has never been since he left this house," said Madame Roux. "I have had a guest, yes. It was someone who had something private to say to me about a sale of property. I'm surprised you don't count the ends in the ashtray. You were never shy about going through Philippe's pockets."

Shirley let go of the bead curtain, which fell with a sound of pebbles rolling. "Something must be wrong with me," she said. "I get so tired at work now. I want to lie down on the floor and shut my eyes. I'm on my feet the whole day, and people aren't always pleasant."

"You have been in Paris too long," said Madame Roux. "Too long away from home." Large, bossy, motherly, she edged Shirley to the door. "You don't need to work. Leave work for girls who have no choice. Why don't you take a holiday in Switzerland? Or Spain?"

"I've never done that," Shirley said. "Just gone. I went to places with Philippe when he was working. He was nice about that. We went to Berlin and to Le Mans and Toulouse. He didn't have to take me with him. None of the others ever took their wives. They were glad to get away from them."

"You won't go to Switzerland, you won't go to Spain," said Madame Roux, as if Shirley had refused the universe. "I wonder why you don't go home? I mean home to your mother, to your own way of life." She opened the door, stopping the bell with one hand. "You look like a beaten dog, you know," she said. "You used to be so bright and strong, so sure of yourself."

"I've told you, I'm tired. I can't just go home, as you say. I'm too old. I'm going to be twenty-seven. You don't go home at that age, not where I come from. Besides, it's not my home any more. I live *here*. I have a house and furniture and ... and a husband and all that. I'm not a tourist. I'm not somebody who keeps moving on. I'm somebody's wife."

The message was from Claudie. They met in the brasserie where they had spoken for the first time. Claudie's closest friend sat next to her on the red leather banquette, and Shirley faced them on an uncomfortable chair. The friend was presented as someone with an important but undefined literary heritage. It was not clear whether he wrote or was descended from someone who had. "Proust," said Claudie carelessly. When the boy laughed she pretended she had meant something enigmatic. "Shirley, I have left them," she said. "I have left my family forever. I have my own room in a hotel."

"What are you living on?"

Claudie waved her hand. "What does that matter? I shall never sleep on a couch in a parlor again. It is what you wanted for me, isn't it?"

"Have you found a job?"

"All in good time," said the boy. "It is agreed that Claudie and I do not support each other." Was this irrelevant? He did not seem to think so. He was dark and delicate; he reminded Shirley of the Japanese dolls on the dressing table in James's bedroom. He earned the equivalent of two dollars a day doing consumer research, he said, perhaps giving the reason why he could not support Claudie. He did not explain what the work consisted of. Shirley supposed that he knocked on doors. His father, a nose-and-throat specialist, made him an inadequate allowance. Young Proust worked for the sake of dignity and to pay for his own cigarettes. "'Families, I hate you,'" he quoted. Claudie nodded her approval. He was expected to be home every Sunday for luncheon with the family. If he missed a Sunday, his pocket money was held up. "I have never cost my father one centime in cigarettes," he said. That settled, he began questioning Shirley. "I want your opinion about certain Anglo-Saxon authors."

Shirley, accustomed to this, knew that she would not have heard of any of them, but Claudie stared at her so anxiously that it was evident Shirley's prestige hung on the replies.

"Richard Debendock?" said the young man severely. "Greta Winterhalter?"

She could only gaze her approval, as though hypnotized. She had forgotten to wear her glasses. The shadeless lighting made their faces gleam like plates. Voiceless approbation seemed to be all that was wanted of her. Claudie, satisfied, began describing her hotel room (it overlooked a street populated by no one but prostitutes) and Marie-Thérèse's rage and shame when she had come to see where Claudie lived now and had looked out the window.

"Munter Brooke," came the piping interrogation. "Juan Alexis Bell? Valentine Purse?"

Shirley wondered if he would be offended were she to ask him to write the names down. She remembered Philippe and the jazz musicians, and how long it had taken her to discover who everyone really was.

"Shirley, I am in great trouble," said Claudie. "I think I might be pregnant."

"Would you mind writing *that* down?"

"There has been only one valid thinker in America since Locke Abrams," said the young man, "though Walter Jarvis Crispin has his adherents."

Claudie held the boy's fragile hand and announced their secret, important plan: they were going to the Middle East as volunteers in refugee camps. A Swiss organization would pay their passage from Marseille to Lebanon. Should the refugees turn out to be ungrateful and unrewarding, should the experience lack the spiritual returns they were after, why, they would then apply for permission to live in one of the Israeli kibbutzim reserved for zealous foreigners. Claudie glanced at the boy for confirmation. She was so much larger than he was; he could have danced on the palm of her hand.

"I'd like to say two things," said Shirley. "Can anyone at this table hear me? First, isn't there some unexpected trouble women can have? When men say they're in trouble it can be one of a hundred things. With women, 'trouble' means 'I am in love' or 'I am not in love' or 'I am pregnant.' The second thing is, you can't go to Israel if something goes wrong in Lebanon. You have to make up your mind now where you want to go and what you want to do."

The young man began to explain about his family: they were Jews converted to Catholicism in Portugal in the sixteenth century. He lived in two worlds. He would be equally at home in a refugee camp or a kibbutz. The American author Mallet Blick...

"We shall need a ring," said Claudie. "No, Shirley—you can't give me that... it's your wedding ring. The other, the turquoise. How kind you are!"

In a mountain village in Italy where everyone had gone to sleep except Shirley and Peter Higgins, a black cat walked along the path. Three long shadows, theirs and the cat's, walked before them, thrown by a pale village lantern and a bright moon. Where the street ended the three came upon a field—a lake in the moonlight—and behind it were indigo mountains.

"You are the only person who can explain my situation to Papa," said Claudie. "He respects you."

"But he knows your situation. The whole family has been to see where you live. So you said."

"All except Papa. He pretends he hasn't noticed I've left home."

"What do you want me to tell him? That you're getting married?"

"No, she doesn't want to get married," said the young man.

"Oh, then it's money. It's only money Claudie wants." Dismissing her brief memory of a field and mountains (so wounding that it could not be memory, she must have dreamed it) she said, "I've had enough brandy and I suppose you've had enough fruit juice. I'd better pay."

"She always finds reasons for paying," said Claudie, more and more proud of her.

"Claudie, that sounds like Renata. I think you have been seeing Renata and that she has been telling you a lot of rubbish."

"No," said Claudie. "You are the only person I listen to. Renata told me that Poland is the place for abortions, but there is all the bother of getting there and then trying to explain what you mean. Renata says they have the French culture, but still. My father will give you all the money you ask for, providing it is for me and you do the asking. I used to be the favorite, you know. I was always the favorite. They approved of my sister but they loved me. Now they despise me because I am poor and they hate me because I will not live in a cage."

"I absolutely refuse to say you are pregnant in order to get money for you."

"But it isn't only that, Shirley. There is the problem of Alain."

"We have already had Alain as a problem."

"I do need money," said Claudie anxiously, as if she had forgotten why.

"Keep Alain. Take Alain with you."

"Yes, do take him," said Marcel Proust in a thin voice. It was plain that Shirley was not proving to be as useful or sensible as he had expected.

Claudie placed her large white hand on the table and said, "Look at my ring." It was not Shirley's turquoise band, but a ring made of silver paper, a cigarette-paper ring. She was trying to bring him to a state of remembrance and guilt.

The boy ignored the ring. He said to Shirley, "I'm told that your husband is a celebrated critic. What is his name?"

She was not astonished to be the wife of a celebrated critic. She remembered where she might have seen Claudie's friend before: in the Select, choosing Germans for that war movie. If it hadn't been Marcel Proust it was someone very like him.

She would go to Monsieur Maurel. She would say, "Go and fetch Claudie and take her home. She isn't fit to be on her own. I gave her the wrong advice. It would have been good advice where I come from, but it doesn't make sense here."

"What is the name of your father's office?" she said.

"No one is allowed to call his office. He would murder any of us, even—no, *particularly* Maman. Did you get a letter from Maman? Perhaps she forgot a stamp on it. She often forgets. Maman thinks we still haven't given you a good meal, and she wants to try again. My family never entertain, but when they start with someone they can't stop. They always do something wrong because we are used to just being by ourselves, with a cousin or my grandmother sometimes. They are determined to go on inviting you until they finally get it right."

"She may stop going," said Marcel practically.

"Poor darling," said Claudie. "You've never been asked, have you? Not even once."

"She may have had enough of your family," he said coldly, with a slightly feminine sneer.

"No, she hasn't had enough yet," said Claudie. "She will save me and Alain. Shirley, promise me..."

"I'll see your father," Shirley said. "Somebody has to." As they stood up to leave she thought she noticed Marcel pocketing the change she had left for the waiter. It can't be, she thought. I'm blind and I've had too much brandy. He bored me and she made me feel nervous and I went on drinking.

Just then she saw someone she knew. Shirley's friend, a young woman wearing a belted raincoat, recognized her in the same instant and moved toward her. Shirley could not see her face—the other person was still across the room. She could distinguish nothing except the outline of someone familiar. It was not Mrs. Castle but someone much as Mrs. Castle must have been like when she married Ernie so as to get off the prairies. She was flooded with happiness, with relief, at seeing a person who knew her, who would not make mistakes with her name or ask for more than she could give. She walked toward the woman from home, unable to remember her old friend's name, but confident it would come back to her during the first words of conversation. This friend was tactful and kind. Their identities would be established at once. Shirley would say to her, "Don't leave me alone with these terrible people." The woman smiled, as sure of Shirley as Shirley was of her. Claudie's hand, which she violently tried to shrug away, prevented Shirley from walking into a large mirror.

Rain had rinsed the boulevard St. Germain. They emerged into a bright, moist, summer night. She was escorted, upheld, by Claudie and by Marcel Proust.

"It is the first time I have ever seen a woman drunk," said Claudie.

"Your friend is an original," he said. "She will certainly introduce you to a new world. But she lacks grandeur."

Shirley heard this in the way that a drugged patient, waking too soon, catches sound before he can make any sense of it.

The next day was suddenly and violently hot. From the living-room window she saw a tarry street and men walking with their jackets over their arms, like Americans. Feeling sick and unclean, she dragged herself across the city. She was an hour late and was once again dressed in the store uniform she had been told not to take home. The man who sacked her looked like a policeman, or like one of the stone-faced shabby functionaries in the office where foreigners queued to have their residence cards renewed. He wore a grubby shirt and a soiled tie, and seemed wretched and underslept. Although the façade of the store had been brought up to date for the new prosperity of the 1960's, his office was as full of string-tied dossiers as a provincial notary's. In an atmosphere of old age, dust and melancholy, she was told she could go. It was her own fault, he said to her. She had so often been forgiven! Her failings had been overlooked until now because of her good nature and her ability to cope with the Anglo-Saxon dialects—American, Australian or what have you. Nevertheless, he continued, there had been an obstinacy, a blind spot, about wearing the uniform. It was store property and—as if this were what really worried him—the uniform was not a *feminine* costume. "I have often been disappointed in people," her executioner remarked.

She understood that he had defended her until now and she had let him down. She was sorry. She wanted to tell him that she did not think harshly of him, but now he was handing her a check in lieu of notice. They did not want her around a minute longer. In another envelope was the cash deposit she had paid for the uniform before they had entrusted her with it: but the uniform was still on her back. Could she be relied on to go home, change, and return with the uniform in a cardboard box? He may have been clairvoyant; he must have known how it would be: how she would intend to come back, and how the uniform would be flung on the bed, then tossed in a cupboard; how her mind would click each time she saw it, and how finally she would not see it at all.

Wanting to be fair and, above all, to make him happier, she said, "It might be better if I bought some clothes now, in the store. Then I could change on the spot and leave the uniform with you."

"I am going to do you a great favor," he said, worn out with her. "I am going to keep you on the staff until noon so that you can have the employees' reduction of eleven percent. Please realize what I am doing for you."

She wandered off in the enormous store. "I don't work here," she explained to some north of England accents who wanted to buy a gallon of Chanel 5. After going upstairs and down on the escalator, she became hot and tired; finally, seeing a sign in the basement saying "This way to the Métro," she went home. She felt as if she had been sent out of school with a sealed note for her mother—uneasy, apprehensive, and glad to be free.

She had to pass an examination on Balzac. The title of the novel selected was *L'Album de Médecine Légale*, which she had never heard of. She had not studied for years and knew she would fail. Papers were passed around the silent room. Just as she knew the beating of her heart would destroy her, she knew she was dreaming. She could not have described the examination, even if there had been anyone here to listen. Her father had been cranky about revelations. "You can tell me what you dream if you give me a quarter," he would say, holding out a long hand. "If it has an unusually interesting plot I'll accept fifteen cents. If you aren't anywhere in the dream I'll settle for a nickel." Aged seven, she slid out of her chair at the breakfast table and fetched her pocket money, thus earning the right to complete attention. Her father pocketed the quarter, which was alarming of him. She could not always spend her money so unproductively. She learned that the easiest way of disposing of dreams was to forget about them.

She lay prone on the couch in the living room. Her hand, swollen with pins and needles, rested on the floor. The telephone rang in the dead afternoon. That was what had startled her—not something in the other world of the dream. She said to the telephone, "Philippe?" but the listener, on identifying her voice, had learned all he wanted. She heard a click, followed by a humming conversation of ghosts.

They are trying to frighten me, she thought. They are trying to kill me with fear. Then, across a new, sudden silence came an unmistakably Canadian voice. She said, "Mother?" The booming noise that followed was surely the waves of the sea.

"It's Cat Castle."

"Oh, Mrs. Castle—where are you? Has something happened to Mother?"

"I'm here in the airport. I'm on my way—on my way home."

"Can't I see you? Is there time? Which airport—Orly?"

Waves flooded the Orly telephone booth. Mrs. Castle surfaced and said, "Oh boy, French phones. How're you getting on?"

"All right. I wish I could see you."

"Does your mother say anything new about her cancer? Shirl! There's about ten people waiting for this phone. Not that they'll be able to hear anything once they get it."

"Don't hang up. Please, can't I come? Where are you? Mrs. Castle, listen—Philippe has left me and I've lost my job."

"I don't hear. He did what? So he finally got mad at you, eh? What'd he do that for?"

"I don't know. I read his mail. I wanted to be loved more."

"Louder, child."

"I wanted to be *loved more*."

"You're old enough to be smarter than that," Mrs. Castle cried, before she drowned.

Panic, confusion and sleeping in the afternoon were not the way to live a life. It was the moment for the summing-up Philippe believed in. In the desk he had said would be her working place, without saying what she was to do there other than write letters to her mother, were six of the thick, lined scribblers school children used. Six meant that he had six times encouraged her to collect her thoughts. She had taken this to mean that he wanted her to write the past in one column and the future in another and cross out each step of living as Mrs. Castle had done in Pons. Shirley's most recent plans for the future were dated April 12th:

1. Farm for sale in Nonville (S et M). Visit.
2. Herald Trib—do I owe them or do they owe me? Ask.
3. Coffee stains on carpet. What to do.
4. Renata's birthday. When?
5. File Mother's letters by dates.
6. Window boxes. Plants. Where buy earth. Ask.
10. Thyme, laurel, parsley, nutmeg, jello, sultana cookies.
11. Take all old handbags to place where they fix them. Ask Renata.
12. Change all lampshades. Measure them first. Buy tape measure.
13. Start radish and walnut diet.
14. Address book—bring up to date.
15. Separate summer and winter clothes. Decide what weather is going to be, and which to wear and which to put away.
16. Research for Philippe—"What use is a Festival?"
17. Who was Lord Arthur Savile? Ask.
18. De Beers, Western Holding, British Petrol, Shell, Courtauld, Dunlop, Canadian Pacific, Gillette, Xerox, US Steel. Find out.

When Philippe saw what she had written he said it was not what he had meant. She supposed, then, that he wanted in her a feminine variant of himself. Why, then, had he married *her*?

Madame Roux, stubbing out a cigarette, leaning forward, had

said, "No matter who he is, regardless of what he is after, marry him. You can settle any misunderstanding later. If he thinks you are rich, let him think it. Once you are married you will never be alone on a Sunday again."

It would have been cruel to answer, "I never am." Madame Roux was evoking Sundays of sour good weather and empty streets. She was speaking about deserted Sunday gardens in Saint-Maur, the suburb to which she returned every night and which she praised so bitterly. She loved rainy weekends—she had said so—with the lights on at four o'clock and the white winking of television in every living room, for then she was not alone on her street. She was urging Shirley to escape from weekends of tisane: from Sunday fantasies in which husbands and lovers merged into the one rapist she had never been lucky enough to meet; from Sundays of not washing and not combing her hair. When she said, "Marry him," she meant, "I would."

Shirley's hand swept across the page, over the dead list, and all at once she thought of Rose O'Hara. She saw her long face, her soft, piled-up hair; she guessed at Rose's secrets. Next time I see Rose I'll talk to her, she decided. I'll tell her about Philippe and Madame Roux and I'll tell her things even she doesn't know about James. I'll tell her about Claudie and her glue-pot of a family. I'll be Renata, and Rose can be me. But she knew that where James was concerned she was unlikely to "tell." In that case there was no point in telling Rose anything. How much more useful it might be to separate her summer and winter clothes! She saw a heap of clothing on her bed: sweaters in plastic cases, unmatched stockings knotted together, coats she could not wear because the buttons had been removed at the cleaners and were in the pockets, wrapped in brown paper envelopes. More than half the garments she owned were useless because some part of them had gone astray. Here was a green silk dress with seven tiny buttonholes at the back of the neck, and five of the buttons missing. Buttons would have to be specially made. Somewhere in Paris existed a shop where they would match the silk—perhaps take a sliver from the hem. Would it not be simpler to give the dress away to Renata, thus transferring the problem? No, she remembered; the errand is everything. If I conquer the errand I subdue life. I shall take a bus or a taxi to this shop after finding out where it is, if such a shop exists. In the meantime, the dress will be hanging in a non-season, between the summer and the winter clothes. One day the shop will ring me and say the buttons are ready. I shall cross Paris once again and collect the buttons and sew them on, providing I have found thread the same shade of green. That is what growing older is about; that is what the movement of time means. My mother is a button-matcher; so is Mrs. Castle, so are Rose, Renata, Papa and Maman Maurel, certainly Marie-Thérèse and Philippe. Pete? I don't know. Yes, I do know. Pete too. Also, Madame Roux; probably Sutton McGrath, Marcel Proust, Geneviève, Colette and Madame Perrigny. Everybody except Claudie and me, and Claudie thinks I am. She wants to be like me. I wanted to be like Philippe, and Claudie would like to be me. All right, Mother, Mrs. Castle: I start a new life. I become thrifty and careful. I sum up the past and so make a future possible. Both are imaginary, but never mind. I am plain. I give examples of what I mean. I am plausible and I keep it short.

She drew a line through the dead list from corner to corner and on the page that followed wrote, "How It Happened," but crossed that out too, remembering the way Mrs. Castle had proceeded in Pons. She lettered, "WHY P. LEFT ME AND HOW I LOST MY JOB." She had been standing, bending over the table, as she used to when reading Philippe's personal mail. Now she sat down, imitating him, even to his way of looking at a pen as if there were bound to be something the matter with it.

"Four explanations," she wrote.

"One, where I was on the Saturday night.

"Two, about James.

"Three, Pete—one or two things.

"Four, how I happened to write my mother a personal letter."

Feeling that some exergual phrase was needed to lend meaning to her explanations, she added, out of memory: "The possession of the signs of sexual privilege is the important thing, not the quality nor the enjoyment of them" (*Lucky Jim*). It did not measure up to a quotation from Kant or Dostoievski or Claude Levi-Strauss, but all the same it accounted for a great many actions she could remember, and might even be the complete answer to Mrs. Castle's question, "Why are you always in such a hurry to get married, I wonder?" It was the dead period of daylight, midafternoon—the time of day when she always felt slightly nauseated. She thought she might as well begin with:

1. WHERE I WAS ON THE SATURDAY

This is where I was on the Saturday you waited all night for me. First you thought I had gone to a party, then I suppose you thought I was with a man. All I had to do was creep into the room where Renata was sleeping it off and call you. All I had to say was, "Renata's tried to scare me." I could have added, "Please come and get me," and you would have come. I think so. Instead I sat by myself in Renata's kitchen looking at a few books I found in her john. Don't ask me why I didn't walk out of a mess that wasn't my making. It seemed to me I had no choice.

She's painted flowers, orange, red, orange-yellow, all over her kitchen. She hasn't put a shade or anything over the bulb on the ceiling, and when you're tired the room seems to whirl round and round, and if you're shortsighted like me, it hurts your eyes and makes you feel sick.

It was the Saturday of the holiday weekend and I think Renata and I were the only people in the building. The kitchen was cold as a cellar. I had my raincoat, and I had wrapped an anorak of Renata's round my legs. My purse had already been ransacked for what it might hold in the way of entertainment. What I had found was a piece of paper covered with your handwriting. I was obliged to tear it up later, for reasons I'll explain. (I feel as if I had all the time in the world.) What you had written was more or less this:

THE PLAYS OF TOFOLU GROUPE

I met Mr. Groupe and he had nothing to say. He had nothing to say because he was numb with brandy, can't understand five words of French, and does not, in any case, seem given to human speech. This means I have no interview and nothing to write. Nevertheless, I want to mention something about Mr. Groupe's work, and its effect on young playwrights everywhere in the world.

Thanks to Tofolu Groupe we no longer know what it means to be bored. The word has been eliminated. The chill, blank misery that overcomes us at a play, an exhibition of paintings, or a film, we take to be normal response to any of these events. Absence of tedium is spreading to every walk of life. On all sides one now hears "I am never bored," as if this boast were a token of enlightenment instead of the sign of a cloudy and ignorant mind. The major problem of our generation is not a breakdown of communication, as Mr. Groupe would have us think, but that there is too bloody much of it. (These were not your exact words, Philippe, and I have certainly lost something in translating them, but the idea is close.) Owing to the ease of travel, the teaching of languages, psychology, and sociology to underdeveloped students, the growing number of spiteful, nervous amateurs eager to analyze the conduct of their loved ones and broadcast their conclusions, we now understand all too well, and grasp all too quickly, what the other person is driving at. The source of present-day problems in France, as in Mr. Groupe's Ireland, is *complete comprehension*. We are at the point of no return, where a happy friendship, a cloudless sexual union, can be achieved only with someone whose language one never can and would never wish to know.

This, Philippe, you had stroked out with a blue pencil, followed by:

TOFOLU GROUPE: THE SOUNDLESS CRY

What animal does Tofolu Groupe resemble—could it be the llama, silent and aristocratic and ba? Released from the prison of order and the servitude of logic we are in the domain of ba. We recall that the theater of Tofolu Groupe leads us to the edge of the cliff. Groping for the shabby security of language as we have known it, we ba and ba in vain. Before us in emptiness—the inexistence of love and friendship, the vacuum of ba and ba and ba. Vertigo seizes both mind and body. We peer over the edge. Who will hold us back? Ba.

I spread this on the kitchen table. I squinted because of the ferocious light and underneath what you had written I added, "Honestly, Philippe, the first draft is better. If I were you, I wouldn't call it 'The Soundless Cry,' because you've already called something else that, I forget what, I think your piece on the declining Hungarian birth rate."

As soon as I had scribbled my comment I realized I could not slip this back among the papers on your desk. I had taken it by accident. I was looking for letters from Geneviève, to tell you the truth. I know she is only a friend, but I wouldn't be looking for letters if you were sleeping with her. I mean that—I would feel that something had happened and it was none of my business. You see, what goes on between you is much more puzzling. I don't get it. Why should she tell you about how her husband does or doesn't, and where and how and how often? Why should you then inquire in an exquisite prose poem if it is physical or moral revulsion she feels? How do you know she feels any at all? Kindly explain moral revulsion (Ba).

Why did I take this particular piece of paper? To write a shopping list or take down a message for you. I do this often, though I know you've given me notebooks of all sizes, some with perforated pages, some for making lists, and I know you keep a tumbler full of pens and pencils for me next to the telephone, hoping I won't take something of yours and then lose it. You've put a slate and pencil in the kitchen, and a goddamn notebook even in the bathroom. I know, I know. I carry the pens and pencils away to the wrong places, and one day I find everything all together—say, in a drawer of that chest in the hall, where early in the morning with a towel wrapped around me, I've so often written what passes for a laundry list. Everything in one drawer—all the pens and the slate and the little books and thick scribblers, like this one, where I am setting down every plausible thing I can think of.

As for the draft of your interview with Tofolu Groupe, I tore it up and flushed it away. Once I had written on it, it was no good to you, and I knew my comments were always stupid. You've told me so many times not to take your things—your sweaters, your comb, above all, the stuff on your desk.

After I'd got rid of T. Groupe I had nothing to do, so I started cutting my hair a bit with Renata's nail scissors. The operation was well under way before I remembered I had sworn to you I'd stop hacking at my hair once and for all and let it grow.

Part of the problem is that you have the habit now of saying "What's wrong?" before I've even had time to know if anything isn't right. I am not complaining, just pointing it out. You also said once, "You've done this before often enough—you ought to know what you're doing." I replied, but *as a joke*, "My father did it differently."

It wasn't true at the beginning (what you keep questioning about) but I think this winter it became true. It was such a cold winter—I feel we're still in it. The canals and rivers froze and there were no fresh vegetables in Paris. I saw a picture of a market stall in the morning paper and under the picture was written, "The dreaded rutabaga has again made its appearance..." When people talk to me about the Occupation of Paris they mention the dreaded rutabaga, so I took a magnifying glass to the picture, and what do you suppose I found? Turnips! Swedes! So *that* is the dreaded rutabaga! For future hard winters let me advise you: don't dread the Swede—learn how to cook it. You need pepper, butter. No butter—yes, of course. In a really hard winter there's no butter.

I prefer dark to daylight or any kind of light.

I've never understood the movies where people meet for the first time and then there's a cut to a shot of them in bed. The girl always looks rather swoony and grateful, though all she may have to be grateful to is some hairy little monkey wearing a St. Christopher medal and smoking a Gauloise. Nobody in movies ever runs out of cigarettes or has to look for parking space. When a girl is leaving her husband she never has to go down to the basement to look for a suitcase. There will be a brand new one right there. She will open any drawer at random and find in it, beautifully folded, every stitch she needs for running away. She packs without looking. I like to think that when she opens the suitcase she finds nothing but tablecloths. I wonder if people in real life think they're above reproach? I suppose they do. They've found out they can get away with murder.

I could hear Renata breathing—snoring, it was. I was distressed for her, knowing how she would have hated knowing there was a witness to this or to anything that made her seem vulnerable. By now fatigue, boredom and worry had made me hungry. It was the starvation point of the middle of the night, when you begin to feel cold and shivery and to long for something like onion soup. Renata's kitchen never held much in the way of comfort. All I could find was a bottle of French vodka, two-thirds empty, and a small wedge of Port du Salut cheese. The cheese looked new; I thought I had better save it for Renata. The doctor had said I was to give her milk to drink when she woke up. There was none in the house but cheese seemed close enough. Her refrigerator contained cold rice in a Fortnum and Mason pudding bowl, two hard-boiled eggs with cracked shells, a jar of Elizabeth Arden cleansing cream, a diaphragm in a box of gardenia talcum powder, twelve pairs of stockings, and a carton of Benson and Hedges. No pot, no pills in Paris: as Renata says, we are a generation behind in the City of Light, and we live the way our mothers did, on drink and diaphragms. I shut the refrigerator door and went back to the books. One was a paperback about torture in Algeria, the second a book of poems, and finally a novel by some friend of Renata's. I leafed through the least harassing of the three, wishing she would wake up or else that Karel Brock would arrive to replace me as a Renata-sitter. I was afraid to leave her, for I thought that if she came to and found herself deserted she might start all over again with her suicide, this time more competently. I imagined her stumbling barefoot out here to her kitchen and seeing on her felt bulletin boards the overlapping views of brutality and pain she cuts out of newspapers and tacks up there to gaze on during breakfast. She seems to like that everyday street scene of police tearing into a crowd. The picture is usually taken from high up, from the top of a building perhaps, and the crowd streaks off to three corners of the photograph.

The worst punishment I can imagine must be solitary confinement with nothing for entertainment except news of the world. I'd rather race spiders, though they scare me, or write limericks on my fingernails. My only nightmare (if you hate dreams just skip this) has to do with normal people turning into animals. I am with one, two, three, men. All at once I notice a change in their expressions; their eyes are like dogs', then wolves'. I think that if I go on speaking I can force them to be normal again, but my words are incoherent to them and they take my voice to be a threat. They can't understand what I am saying. They can't listen or reason. They are unpredictable and cruel. They can't help it. They can only hide or attack. In the dream I am not attacked. Are you surprised? I am the rescuer. I am a rescue party. Yes, I save someone, anyone, even you sometimes. It is summer in a city along a river. I walk in the streets with the victim, saved now, but no good to anyone. He is saved, but useless, a zombie. This dream is not worth a cent, and my father would not have heard about it for under a thousand dollars.

The novel by Renata's friend was about a plane accident. This plane has to land on a mountain peak in a snowstorm, and the crew and passengers, guided by a large black poodle, make their way to a mysterious Austrian ski lodge. This is adversity, and because of adversity the real character of every passenger is shown for what it is. The ski lodge is owned by an actor who says he has been expecting them. The actor is a neo-Nazi. The pilot of the plane is Mephistopheles, and the air hostess is Margareta. A passenger named Dr. Clark is Faust. The poodle assumes a sinister attitude on page 102 and tells the neo-Nazi that his wife is secretly the daughter of a famous rabbi and magician. A misprint in the book made it "rabbit" but the next page had it right.

Around three o'clock in the morning I heard a rat at the door. I sprang up to let the rat in. It was Renata's faithful and beloved companion, Karel Brock. He stood panting (six flights, no elevator after midnight) with his hand over his heart.

"Don't make so much noise," I think I said. "She's sleeping it off."

Karel came in and unwound yards of scarf. He looked (but only about the neck) as if he had been to school in Scotland, England, Ireland, Wales or New Zealand. Karel tries to show through his clothes that he's an artist, but sure of his footing, not a bum. He had on a putty-colored cap, a short belted coat, black pants and a black sweater, and soft leather boots. He has shaved his new little beard. Karel has short hair, not long. He looked fierce on account of the boots and because his haircut seemed so military. He appeared bold enough to knock me down and walk over my dead body into the other room, where Renata lay sleeping. But he just—no, this doesn't interest you. He barely glanced into the studio part of the flat. Renata's bed looked like Juliet's tomb. The studio has a glass roof by way of a ceiling. Even on a starless night there is always a certain amount of light. The sky is never black. You discover that if you ever sleep outside or under glass. Sometimes at Renata's, through the glass and dead leaves and dirt, you can see pigeons—the shape of their feet.

"Who's been here?" said Karel.

"A doctor from next door. I got his number from the police. He wasn't too happy about it. He said just to let her sleep and give her some milk when she woke up. He didn't want to be mixed up with her or with me."

I had also called the Poison Bureau. You call the ordinary police and they say, "Oh, you want the Poison People." But the Poison People never turned up. They just said to keep in touch. They didn't think it was all that serious from my description. I said she had taken a kind of super-aspirin. She had ground them down to powder because that was the way Marilyn did it last summer. Renata always thought she looked a bit like her, though she pretended she didn't. She'd say, "Oh, so-and-so said I looked like Marilyn, what a ridiculous thing to say." Actually, although Renata was about ten years younger, she seemed older than Marilyn. Something about her mouth or her eyes. She had ground the pills down with the back of a spoon and had put a few more in the coffee grinder. I found powder all over the place. I tasted it. It was like salt mixed with baking soda. I know the flavor because my mother didn't believe in toothpaste. She thought toothpaste contained what she called chemicals. My mother didn't know what "chemical" meant, but I had to do my teeth with salt and soda until I got married and left home.

You once asked me if I had ever had a girl. I told you no. Then you said, "Well, how about Renata?" Still no. Then you said, "Do you think Renata..." and so on. I said, "I wouldn't know. Anyway I don't want her, and she doesn't need me." I thought that was a good answer, but when you kept coming back to the question I realized you wanted Renata, or Renata and me together, but wouldn't say so. Renata might have said yes, I might have said no, but at least I'd have known what you were after.

I've already told you what Karel was wearing. I had kept my raincoat on, but I parted it to show him my black dress. You know those tarts in fur coats up behind the place du Châtelet? I felt I had made the same gesture with the same intention. Karel didn't know what to answer so he just sneered. He'd rather sneer than speak. He's twenty-two, so he couldn't have been an officer in the Waffen-SS or fought under Rommel. He was never the last living hero in a burning house. Nobody has ever invited him to confess his crimes. He hasn't committed any that I know of, unless neglect is a crime. He's not even European. He's really just North American, like Renata, like me. It's probably because he's been deprived of his true vocations that he twists his mouth before speaking. When he does speak, the scorn he can't help feeling pitches his voice higher than I think he would like.

I decided that Karel might be sneering at the way I looked. I said to him, "Miss Brooks had that kind of beauty which seems to be thrown into relief by poor dress!" As you know, I have the habit of quotations from my mother. I didn't know they were quotations until I started reading. I thought they were our family language. "At a village of La Mancha, whose name I do not wish to remember..." was how we interrupted long stories. "They threatened its life with a railway share" also had a family meaning; so did "I sit and wait for bouillabaisse," pronounced, *chez nous*, bully-base. I was hoping Karel would find me more interesting than I was feeling. I didn't want him to fall in love with me; I was just letting him know that irony wasn't required from the likes of him. I could supply it myself. In fact, I left an escape for myself in every direction.

But he wasn't even looking at me. He sat down in the kitchen and pulled toward him the plate of cheese I was keeping for Renata and began to eat like an animal, as if he had to guard his food. I saw him plainly as a stray, a cur. I stood with my back against the refrigerator and talked to him, with some idea of making him speak and bringing him back to a human form. As you know, I had run out of our apartment (yours and mine) without money or cigarettes. All I had were two Métro tickets and the reading matter I've already told you about. I got the hard-boiled eggs out and gave them to Karel. He peeled them carefully so that nothing was lost—none of the white came away with the shell. His mother must have told him once how that was done.

"We were great wasters at home, always throwing food away," I started babbling. "My father had an idea about vitamins dying. He said that one hundred and forty seconds after you slice a tomato, all the Vitamin C fades away. We ate fast on that account. Anything left over went right in the garbage, unless my mother was quick."

This just made Karel look desperately around for something more to eat. I found half a dozen black olives in a jar covered with mold. He refused the olives, though I could have washed them, and he flung open one of the books as if he were about to slap it senseless. He chanted, "'Myrtil...Sylvandre...Rosalinde...Chloris!' Oh, for Christ's sake..." He flipped back the cover and read out, "'Renata

Maguire, Paris, September 1960.' It's been kicking round since then. The cover's torn. She's never read it. She wouldn't know where to start."

"She wouldn't go out and buy a book if she wasn't going to read it," I said. "Renata only buys whatever she needs."

"Some guy gave it to her. Or someone like you."

"What do you mean, like me?"

He had started reading again in a high, mocking voice: "'*Là! Je me tue à vos genoux!*' You *like* this?" He couldn't just leave the book alone.

"I don't like any poems, actually. They're too insistent. It's like someone pushing on a door."

I sat down near him then, because I was so cold. I pulled a stool over by his chair and sat very close. I tried telepathy: I willed him to offer me money so I could call a taxi and go home. I didn't know how to ask him, because I didn't like him enough.

He said, "What do you mean, pushing on a door? To keep it shut, or what?"

"I don't know. I shouldn't have said it. It was dumb."

He surprised me by saying, "You're all right, Shirley, but why do you demote yourself all the time?"

"Demote?" I said. "I thought at first you said *devote*. Either way it would apply. I couldn't leave Renata, that's all. I'm not devoted. I thought she shouldn't be left alone. She'll change after this, won't she? She won't be the same person."

My hand lay on his knee, palm up. I was hoping, hoping, hoping he'd offer to lend me money.

He said, "Renata's the hardest bitch who ever lived. You'll say to her two weeks, three weeks, from now, 'Poor kid, what a lousy time you had,' and she'll say to you, 'What time? When?' When she told me about this, I said, 'It's none of my business.' She said, 'Do you have any money? Are you ever likely to?' What was money in it? She's got more than I have. She knew what she was doing. She said, 'Oh, I'll be looked after. All my life I've attracted people who want to look after me.' She meant you, Shirley, or somebody like you.

"Actually, the first doctor she went to wouldn't do anything. He wouldn't even sit down—he stood up to show it wasn't a consultation. But he was interested in her. He listened to the whole story. He said, 'Make him pay. Make the young man pay.' He was excited by her, though he seemed to think he was minding his own business."

Karel stared at my mouth and at my hand. The first realization is less of an event than in those movies I was mentioning earlier. I just said, "No, I'm too tired." Anyway, where? The kitchen table?

He said, "You sound like you'd been married for years."

"I have been, and the best part of my life is used up, and it hasn't been the best." It was my age I was speaking about.

"*You* should have taken Renata's pills, if that's how you feel."

"I'm not crazy," I said. "Though I'm not saying Renata might be. I don't like scaring people, and I don't scare myself."

Renata called us in a voice that let us know she had been awake and listening for minutes. She lay under a white lace coverlet she had bought at the flea market. Her hands and cheeks were apricot-colored—she had been skiing only two weeks before. She held her hands together lightly, like a child praying, and she managed to look as if she had been sacrificed. Karel got down on his knees, which was where she wanted him. He tilted his head to one side and immediately became sentimental. That movement of the head seems to release a cloud of confusion in the brain. I've noticed it before, not only with him. He muttered about her eyes, her hands, her courage, her talent as a painter of women's portraits, and finally, desperately almost, her long yellow hair.

"What did you do it for?" he kept saying. "Was it over me? Because you hated me?" He sounded so hopeful. Hate me, he seemed to be begging, and see what a Father Bear I'll become.

"Oh, yes," breathed the victim, smiling. "I thought you had been *cruel*."

As that was the most flattering thing Renata had ever said to Karel, I could tell she still had some use for him.

"I guessed the whole thing might be my fault," he said. He was pleased.

The room was whitening now. Renata's eyes were small and glittering, and she mocked him. Yes, but she wanted to keep him too. She switched on a little lamp beside her bed, though we could see as much as we wanted to see of each other, I thought. In the new white light Renata's were the only eyes that didn't narrow and blink. The edges of the room were still in shadow. I noticed a sleeping fox that turned out to be a pile of ski boots. Next, I remember, she and Karel started talking French. It's not their common language; Karel hardly knows any at all. As for Renata, you once said her French sounded like someone emerging from shock. But, you know, people will swallow any amount of absurdity so long as it's in another language—any other. Karel and Renata haven't invented French, but they've invented a way of being together.

I stood at the foot of the bed, looking down at them, and I said, "All you're trying to say is, he wasn't around when he should have been."

Karel, a kneeling gnat, pretended I wasn't in the room.

"As an experience, it was transcendent," Renata remarked.

I don't think Karel would have cared for that kind of language coming from me, but it sounded marvelous to him in French. After waiting a decent time for something to follow, I said, "It wasn't transcendent. Oh, it's been a real mess, I'll grant you that, but it doesn't go further. I should know."

"Of course she knows," said Renata without looking at me. "She absorbed it for me, so that I felt nothing except cold and pain, which you can have from indigestion. The whole experience was Shirley's. She wanted it. She followed me, watched me, she soaked up everything I could have felt. All the while pretending she was looking after me, pretending I needed her. She had time for me because all her time goes outside her own life. She hasn't a life. She'd rather live mine, or yours."

"Not Karel's," I said.

That was just Renata talking. I was used to her. I remembered her saying to me, "Only uneducated girls have problems like this. I don't understand it." When she asked me to help her I rang up five friends and said my Spanish maid was in trouble, married man, and I got five addresses one after the other. I don't think I was trying to live Renata's life.

Karel was edging up on the bed the way a pet dog will do. So far she hadn't said "Down!" or "Go away." They finally lay face to face, Renata under the counterpane, Karel with his boots on it. An eye fixed to the glass roof would have seen two seahorses; but no one ever watches from that direction. Only Renata's portraits, stacked around the edges of the room, were looking on. I could see one lopped head after another; then as the light rose I saw their throats and shoulders. She gives her sitters small ears, a long neck and an empty expression, and that seems to be what they like. They say to her, "Keep the likeness very simple," which to them means unwinding one's chignon and letting it trail along the birch tree they know Renata will provide as a throat. Renata is something of a fashion now. She goes to a lot of parties.

I sat down on the foot of the bed. I considered asking Renata to lend me the equivalent of two dollars, but she would have considered this an improper interruption.

I'm forgetful by nature, as you were the first person after my mother to point out. Perhaps because of that I long for perfect truth. I'm not sure that I've heard it spoken. I long for the dumb plain policeman writing "p-r-i-m-r-o-s-e must mean primrose" in his notebook. Not the spy, or the tricky detective—I don't long for him at all.

Renata said to Karel, "I breathed slowly, as I was told to do. I heard the doctor and Shirley talking about the Berlin Wall. The doctor had been to look at it during the Easter weekend. Shirley went to see it on her honeymoon. She had a miscarriage on that same honeymoon, and she seemed to think the doctor would enjoy hearing about it while he was busy with me. Shirley was something like thirteen months pregnant when Philippe finally married her. Poor Philippe. He drove her half across Europe in a Deux-Chevaux just to look at the Wall."

A great many people believe you married me because I was eighty-six days pregnant. Madame Roux says you married me for the apartment. Yes, you are supposed to have fallen in love with a bedroom, living room, box-room used as an office, windowless kitchen, entrance hall, and unheated bathroom with splendid view. Others say you simply thought it was time. No one has yet said that you married me because you couldn't think of your life any other way.

It is true that the doctor talked about bullfights and music festivals. He had been to Salzburg for the Mozart, and to Bayreuth for the Wagner, and to Holland for some other thing. Nevertheless, he said that now, in 1963, for sheer drama and historical excitement, nothing could beat the Wall. He said that in another year or two it will be covered with ivy and election posters, and that the time to see it is now. Then he said that Renata could rest for an hour and that I was to wait in a small room where his wife kept her collection of tropical shells under glass, and padlocked. I waited two hours. I had nothing to read and only the shells to look at. Like you, I am quickly bored. We have that in common. Unlike me, however, you still believe in the entertainment value of a well-stocked memory. I made an inventory of mine and discovered I knew this:

The gestation period of a mouse is 21 days. Of an elephant, 640.

If you see a toad jump from right to left, you will soon be surprised.

If it rains on your seventeenth birthday, marry as late in life as possible, and never on the eve of a holiday.

You can tell a man's character by the way he wears out his shoes.

The smell of camphor will make you feeble-minded.

A sapphire brooch in the shape of a clover means that the person wearing it has a stingy nature.

If yellow is your favorite color you will be in poor health all your life.

If you drink mint tea every day for a month you will succeed in business.

It is unlucky to send a bouquet with fewer than four kinds of flowers in it.

The eyes of adulterous men are not the same color. Bald men are liars. A man afflicted with gout will write one poem and send it to several women.

Renata slept peacefully during those two hours in the doctor's parlor. She woke up and saw a picture of John XXIII, and then a plastic basin decorated with a pattern of cornflowers. Later she said *I* had said, "If you're sick use the basin. The basin, not the floor." Just as she was telling this again, Karel began to breathe deeply. He was asleep. She gave a kick under the bedclothes, and he snapped to. I was lying across the foot of the bed now, leaning on one elbow.

"As I was explaining," Renata said crossly, "it was now quite dark. The window panes were colored yellow and blue, which made the room look serene and moonlit. Shirley bent over me with her pussy-cat tragic face. She said, 'I think they want us out of here,' and from the way she said 'us' I knew she would be in my story forever, and that I would have to depend on her for my memories."

Philippe, when I first knew Renata her favorite piece of reading was *The Trial of Joan of Arc*, because of the Duke of Alençon's testimony about Joan: "*Je vis ses seins, qui étaient beaux.*"

"Like mine," Renata would say, showing them.

After that she became obsessed with a French translation of *The Dybbuk*. She was entranced by the idea of mystical possession. She said to me, "How can you say, '*Je me souviens de moi-même à travers tes pensées*' in English?"

Well, you can't.

I wondered at the time how she intended to use the phrase—what she was saving it up for.

The doctor made me buy the pills for her. Two glass tubes. He said, "The blue ones, these, she must take every day until the tube is empty. The white things are in case she can't sleep. She is not to take too many. They aren't made of sugar."

He charged six thousand francs for her pills and another five because of Renata's long sleep. He said he wasn't running a hotel.

Karel kept yawning and dropping off. Once Renata pinched him. I don't know if he heard her say: "We came here and I went to bed with my clothes on. I heard Shirley answering the phone and saying, 'Oh, she's all right.' How did she know I was? She said to me, 'Rat-face called,' or perhaps 'rat's fate.' She meant you, Karel. *Karel!* Wake up! Shirley had taken it over, even to blaming you. I swallowed one of the blue pills and two more of the white. Shirley had those sunglasses of hers, so as to watch me from safety."

The fact is that I'm blind without them. I had on the sunglasses because I had broken the others.

Renata turned away from Karel and lay on her back. I saw what Karel couldn't: she had finished with the story, and in a moment or two he wouldn't be wanted anymore. His part of it was over before mine.

What Renata didn't tell, and what I'm telling you now, was how she called me the next day (THE SATURDAY) and why I dressed for a party; how I left you for her, because she needed me: how, when I got to her, she looked at me without love and said, "It's as much your doing as mine. You approved all the way." She sipped the tea I made her and looked at me. She said, "Why do you get away with everything? Everybody says Philippe made a mistake, but you're getting away with it."

If it is any help to either one of us, I shall always be ready to say it was a mistake for you and not for me. I was told about justice and responsibility quite often, but no one told me how my information could be applied.

She seemed stupid and sleepy suddenly. I think she said, "Will you stay until Karel comes?" Then she began that snoring, and I found the crumbs of powder. I could have gone away, pulled the door shut behind me, and shoved the key under the mat for the next party-goer to find. I could have come home and said to you, "Renata has killed herself, by the way." I had to remind myself that sane people live their whole lives like stones on a beach, rolling a little this way and that, and I thought I had better begin finding out how it was done. A careful stone. In the night, after the doctor had been there, and the police had taken information but given me none, I sat in her kitchen and tried to imagine why Renata should be brought back to life. I thought of reasons I could apply to stones, beginning with Divine Intention, but you know that any Intention has been given up. The experiment went wrong—it is boring. I thought about fear of the dark. I thought Renata might have waited to learn more about the microbes that live without oxygen and that will certainly be the start of a richer form of life; but I refused all belief in the value of suffering and I always will. I despise it. So my thinking about Renata had to stop there. Anyway, it was only a kind of aspirin.

Now—Karel, Renata, me. Karel seemed to feel she might like him better if he became constructive. He said, "I hope Shirley was smart enough not to talk to the police?"

"She couldn't," said Renata. "For one thing, she was my accomplice. *She* found the doctor for me."

She pushed his hand away from her face. Renata likes her dramas short.

From the pile of ski boots in a corner a shadow moved and floated toward the doorway. Renata sat up, her hair on her shoulders and her eyes opened wide. I don't know if you know it, but the only thing that can frighten her is rats. Why, then, does she live in a house full of rats, on a ratty street?

I said, "It wasn't anything, darling. It was just a little thing about the size of a hamster."

Karel rolled over and said casually, "Oh, it's a rat." He looked around for something to throw at it.

After that the three of us went to sleep.

I can't think of anything else about that night that would interest you.

I wish we could talk, but we can't talk unless you come back here. Perhaps you are dreading the conversation. We could decide beforehand which subjects to avoid. The only questions you've asked me have been: Who? When? How often? This way or that way? With Frenchmen? With Asians? With blacks? With ski instructors, taxi drivers, teachers, civil engineers? With politicians? Married, single, girls, boys?

I don't care for the life in cities. That's all I'd like to talk about. I am sick of chance encounters. I'd start off by saying it's a lousy way to live.

2. ABOUT JAMES

James noticed me long before I saw him. He would send me notes full of praise and anticipated pleasure. He'd leave the notes under the door. I thought he was the rather fat man who had his front door blown in by the OAS last year. Then he said who he was and where he lived. I went up to his flat. I didn't know you then. When he answered my ring he looked like a black fox. I think he is an architect in his own country, but his real interest is women. His sole activity seems to be the pursuit of women, and like all men of that kind he is supremely silly. The *difference* between James and other men like him is that sometimes he is funny and sometimes he is kind.

James worries about the purity of young girls. He can't bear to think of anyone touching a young girl. He is afraid about being impotent. He thinks he owes me something. Why?

James would not miss me if I moved away, but he would be sorry for a long time if he heard I had died.

3. PETE, ONE OR TWO THINGS

Well, as you know, he died. There was an English clergyman in the Italian town where it happened who tried to do all he could for me. I was tired and I didn't always know what people were asking me. The clergyman lent me a pencil and I wrote:

PETER HIGGINS
CALGARY 1935—ITALY 1956

There was room for more on the stone. The clergyman said, "Is there nothing else, child?" He meant, "Wasn't he someone's husband, someone's son?" But I felt that Pete had renounced us, left us behind. "Husband of..." seemed presumptuous—we had been married such a little time. I can't say I was thinking it then, the day I decided. I am thinking years later now. His mother has died since and no one will ever ask me about him, or wonder what he was like. If I had to describe him I couldn't tell much. His mother knew some things and I knew some. Even put together the information we had would not describe a man. She had the complete knowledge that puts parents at a loss finally: she knew all about him except his opinion of her and how he was with me. He didn't know all about her. How could he? She was a grown person with the habit of secrets before he was even conscious of her. He only knew what he could expect of her. She said later that she and Pete had been friends. How can you be someone's friend when you have had twenty years' authority over him and he has never had one second's authority over you?

He didn't look like his mother. He looked like me. In Italy on our wedding trip, we were mistaken for sister and brother. Our height, our glasses, our myopic stares, our assurance, our sloppy, comfortable clothes, made us seem related and somehow unplaceable. Only a North American could have guessed what our families were, what our education amounted to, and where he had got the money to spend on traveling. Most of the time we were just pie-faces, like the tourists in ads. The tourists are always clean and the Europeans are peasants or chefs or postmen. They smile, they look at strangers fondly. It isn't true. In real life Pete and I were grubby and the others clean, and no one smiled.

We didn't seem to be married: we made love in hotels, in strange beds; we ate our meals in cheap, bright little restaurants; we seemed to be prolonging the clandestine quality of love before. It was still a game, but now we had infinite time. I became bold, and I dismissed the universe. "It was a dirty little experiment," I would tell him, "and we were given up long ago." You know about my mother. To be able to say "we were given up" shows how far I had come. Pete's assurance was natural, but mine was recent. It had grown out of love. He was more interested in his parents than in God. There was a glorious treason in all our conversations. Pete wondered about his parents, but I felt safer belittling Creation. In her atheistic way, my mother had let me know quite a lot about the strength of the righteous; I still thought the skies would fall if I said too much.

What struck me about these secret exchanges was how we judged our parents from a distance now, as if they were people we had known on a visit. The idea that Pete and I could be natural siblings crossed my mind. What if both of us were adopted? We came from different parts of Canada, but we were only children and neither of us looked like our so-called parents. I used to watch him as if I were trying to trap him in mannerisms I could claim. I saw my own habit of sprawling, of spreading maps and newspapers on the ground. He had a vast appetite for bread and pastries and sweet desserts. He was easily drunk and easily sick. Yes, we were alike. We talked in hotel rooms while we drank the drink of the place, the grappa or wine or whatever we were given, prone across the bed, the bottle and glasses and the ashtray on the floor. We agreed to live openly, without secrets, though neither of us knew what a secret was. I admired him as I could never have admired myself. I remembered how my mother had said that one treeless, sunless day real life would overtake me, and then I would realize how spoiled and silly I had always been.

The longest time he and I spent together in one place was three days, in a village up behind the Ligurian coast. One night we walked the length of the village with a black cat leading the way. He said the cat would bring us luck. When we came to the end of the village street I knew that the only success of my life, my sole achievement, would be this marriage. The night before he died I dreamed he brought me the plans of a house. I saw the white lines on the blue paper, and he showed me the sunny Italian-style loggia that would be built. "It is not quite what we want," he said, "but better than anything we have now." "But we can't afford it, we haven't got the capital," I cried, and I panicked and woke: woke safe, in a room the details of which were dawn, window, sky, first birds of morning. Pete was still sleeping, still in the dark.

We packed and took a bus down to a town on the coast. We were to catch the express to Nice, then Paris, then home. This last Italian town of our journey was nothing—just a black beach with sand like soot, and houses shut up because it was the middle of the afternoon. We left our luggage at the station, with a porter looking after it, and we drifted through empty, baking streets, using up the rest of a roll of film. By now we must have had hundreds of pictures of each other in market squares, next to oleanders, cut in two by broomstick shade, or backed up, squinting, against scaly noonday shutters. Pete photographed a hotel with a cat on the step, in honor of the cat up in the village, and a policeman and a souvenir stand, as if he had never seen such things in Canada—as if they were monuments. I never once heard him say anything was ugly or dull; if it was, what were we doing with it? I think he was one of the people who could say, truthfully, "I am never bored." We were often stared at. We were out of our own background and did not fit into the new. That day I was eyed more than he was. I was watched by men talking in dark doorways, leaning against the façades of those inhospitable little shops. I was traveling in shorts and a shirt and rope-soled shoes. I sensed that this costume was resented but I didn't know why. There was nothing indecent about my clothes. They were very like Pete's. That baffled resentment—I'd seen it before. I remembered my mother holding a copy of *Vogue* at the end of a stiff, sunburned arm. I was about twelve, I suppose: it was the year when, without warning, skirts dropped to the ankle. "Honestly, Mrs. Norrington," said the neighbor who had brought the magazine. "Did you ever see anything like it?"

"No, never," said my mother, "and I, for one, shall not be stampeded." Her finger stabbed the page, smote the wide-eyed model. It was the Last Judgment, the Final Word.

Pete may not have noticed the men. He was always on the lookout for something to photograph or something to do, and sometimes he missed people's faces. On the steep street that led back to the railway station, he took a careful picture of a bakery and he bought a crescent-shaped bread with a soft, pale crust. He broke off a piece of the bread and ate it there on the street. He wasn't hungry; it was a question of using time. Now the closed shutters broke out in the afternoon and a girl appeared—girls with thick hair, smelling of jasmine and honeysuckle. They strolled hand in hand, in light stockings and clean white shoes. Their dresses—blue, lemon, the palest peach—bloomed over rustling petticoats. At home I'd have called them cheap and made a face at their cheap perfume, but here in their own place they were enravishing. I thought Pete would look at them and at me and compare, but all he remarked was, "How do they stand those clothes on a day like this?" So real life, the gray noon with no limits, had not yet begun. I distrusted real life because I knew nothing about it. It was the middle-aged world without feeling, where no one was loved.

He tossed away the bread he hadn't eaten, and laid his hands on a white Lambretta propped against the curb. He pulled it upright, examining it. He committed two crimes in a second: wasted bread, and touched an adored mechanical object belonging to someone else. I know these are crimes now, when it is no use knowing. The steering of the Lambretta was locked. He saw a bicycle then, and thought it belonged to an old man who was sitting on a kitchen chair out on the pavement. "This all right with you?" Pete pointed to the bike, then himself, then down the hill. He tried to show with a swoop of his hand that he would come right back. The pantomime also meant that there was still time before we had to be on the train, that up at the station there was nothing to do, that eating bread, taking pictures of shops, riding a bike downhill and walking it back were all doing, using up your life; yes, it was a matter of living.

The idling old man Pete had spoken to bared his gums. Pete must have taken this for a smile. Later, the old man, who was not the owner of the bike or of anything except the fat, sick dog at his feet, said he had shouted "Thief!" but I never heard him. Pete tossed me his camera and I saw him glide, then rush away, past the girls who smelled of jasmine, past the bakery, down to the corner, where a policeman in white, under a parasol, spread out one arm and flexed the other and blew hard on a whistle. Pete was standing, as if he were trying to coast to a stop. I saw things that were meaningless now—for instance that the sun was sifted through leaves, that there were trees we hadn't noticed. Under the leaves he seemed underwater. A black car, a submarine with Belgian plates, parked at an angle in front of a change office, stirred to life. I saw sunlight deflected from six points on the paint and chrome. My view became discomposed, as if the sea were suddenly black and opaque and had splashed up over the policeman and the road, and I screamed, "He's going to open the door!" Everyone said later I was mistaken, for why would the Belgian have started the motor, pulled out, and *then* flung open the door? I saw him do it, and I saw him drive away. No one had taken his number.

Strangers made Pete kneel and then stand, and they dusted the bicycle. They forced him to walk—where? Nobody wanted him. Into a pharmacy finally. He said to the policeman, "Don't touch my elbow," in a parrot's voice. The pharmacist said, "He can't stay here," because Pete was vomiting, but weakly—a weak coughing, like a baby's. I was in a crowd of about twenty people, with two cameras round my neck. In kind somebody's living room, Pete was placed on a couch with a cushion under his head and another under his dangling arm. The toothless old man turned up now, panting, with his waddling dog, and cried that we had a common thief before us, and everyone listened and marveled until the old man spat on the carpet and was turned out.

When I touched Pete, timidly, trying to wipe his face with a crumpled Kleenex (all I had), he thought I was one of the strangers. His mouth was a purple color, as if he had been in icy water. His eyes looked at me, but he was not looking out.

"Ambulance," said a doctor who had been fetched by the immaculate policeman. He spoke loudly and slowly, because he was dealing with idiots.

"Yes," I heard someone say, in English. "We must have an ambulance."

Now everyone inspected me. I was plainly responsible for something. For walking around the streets in shorts? Wasting bread? I was conscious of my sweaty hair, my bare legs, my lack of Italian—my nakedness—and I began explaining the true error of the day: "The train has gone, and all our things are on it. Our luggage. We've been staying up in that village—oh, what's the name of it, now? Where they make the white wine. I can't remember, no, I can't remember where we've been. I could find it, I could take you there. I've just forgotten what it's called. We were down here waiting for the train. To Nice. We had lots of time. The porter said he'd put our things on the train for us. He said he would meet us at the place where you show your ticket. I guess for an extra tip. The train must have gone by now. My purse is in the duffel bag up at the... I'll look in my husband's wallet. Of course that is my husband! Our passports must be on the train, too. Our traveler's cheques are in our luggage, his and mine. We were just walking round taking pictures instead of sitting up there in the station. Anyway, there was no place to sit—only the bar, and it was smelly and dark."

No one believed a word of this, of course. Would you give your clothes, your passport, your traveler's cheques to a porter? A man you had never seen in your life before? A bandit disguised as a porter, with a stolen cap on his head?

"You could not have taken that train without showing your passport," a careful foreign voice objected.

"What are you two, anyway?" said a man from the change office down the street, in a tough, old-fashioned movie-American accent. He was puffy-eyed and small, but he seemed superior to us because he wore a spotlessly clean shirt. Pete, on the sofa, looked as if he had been poisoned or stepped on. "What are you?" the man from the change office said again. "Students? Americans? No? What, then? Swedes?"

I saw what the doctor had been trying to screen from me: a statue's marble eye.

The tourist who spoke the careful foreign English then said, "Be careful of the pillows."

"What? What?" screamed the put-upon person who owned them.

"Blood is coming out of his ears," said the tourist, halting between words. "That is a bad sign." He seemed to search his memory for a better English word. "An unfortunate sign," he said, and put a hand over his mouth.

The real owner of the bicycle could not have Pete fined, as he wanted to. It was too late. The man from the change office was fined instead: he should have had the Belgian's name and passport number because he had done business with him. He cursed my life and Pete's death. The doctor said casually, "I hope you are not superstitious. A malediction has no power unless you are afraid of it." What I remember of the night was a vague consular person who said in the hospital corridor, "Why the hell didn't he use the brake?"

I sent his mother and father a cable. They flew over from Calgary as soon as they got it. They made flawless arrangements by telephone and knew exactly what to bring. They had a sunny room looking onto rusty palms and a strip of beach about a mile from where the accident had been. I sat against one of the windows and told them what I thought I remembered. I looked at the white walls, the white satin bedspreads, at Mrs. Higgins's impeccable dressing case, and finally down at my hands.

They had not understood until now that ten days had gone by since Pete's death.

"What have you been doing, dear, all alone?" Mrs. Higgins said to me gently.

I said, "Just waiting, once I'd cabled you." They seemed to be expecting more. "I've been to the movies." From this room we could hear the shrieks of children playing on the sand.

"Are they orphans?" asked Mrs. Higgins. They were little girls, dressed alike, with soft pink sun hats covering their heads.

"It seems to be a kind of summer camp," I said. "I was wondering about them too."

"It would make an attractive picture," said Pete's mother after a pause. "The blue sea and the nuns and all those bright hats. It would look nice in a dining room."

They were too sick to reproach me. My excuse for not having told them about the accident sooner was that I hadn't thought of them, but they didn't ask me for it. I remember saying, "I don't want to go back home just yet," which must have hurt them, because it meant I was already in the future. "I have a girl friend in the embassy in Paris. I can stay with her." I scarcely moved my lips. They had to strain to hear. I held still, looking down at my fingers. I was very brown, sun streaks in my hair, more graceful than at my wedding, where I knew they had found me maladroit—a great lump of a Campfire Girl. That was how I had seen myself in my father-in-law's eyes. Extremes of shock had brought me near some ideal they had of prettiness. I appeared now much more the kind of girl they'd have wanted as Pete's wife.

So they had come for nothing. They were not to see him or bury him, or fetch home his bride. All I had to show them was a still unlabeled grave.

When I dared look at them, I saw their way of being was not Pete's. Neither had his soft selective stare. Mr. Higgins's eyes were a fanatic blue. He was thin and sunburned and unused to nonsense. Summer and winter he traveled with his wife in climates that were bad for her skin. She had the fair, papery coloring that requires constant vigilance. All this I knew because Pete had told me.

They saw his grave at the best time of day, in the late afternoon, with the light at a slant. The cemetery was in a valley between two plaster towns. A flash of the sea was visible, a corner of ultramarine. They saw a stone wall covered with roses, pink and white and near-white, open, without secrets. The hiss of traffic on the road came to us, softer than rain; then true rain came down and we ran to our waiting taxi through a summer storm. Later they saw the station where Pete had left our luggage but had never come back. Like Pete—as Pete had intended to, rather—they were traveling to Nice.

Under a glass shelter before the station I paused and said, "That was where it happened, down there." I pointed with my white glove. I was not as elegant as Mrs. Higgins, but I was not a source of embarrassment either. I wore gloves, stockings, shoes.

The steep street under rain was black as oil. Everything was reflected upside down. The neon signs of the change office and the pharmacy swam deeply in the pavement.

"I'd like to thank the people who were so kind," said Mrs. Higgins. "Is there time? Shirley, I suppose you got their names?"

"Nobody was kind," I said.

"Shirley! We've met the doctor and the minister, but you said there was a policeman and a Dutch gentleman and a lady—you were in this lady's living room."

"They were all there, but no one was kind."

"The bike's paid for?" asked Mrs. Higgins suddenly.

"Yes. I paid. And I paid for having the sofa cushions cleaned."

What sofa cushions? What was I talking about? They seemed petrified, under the glass shelter, out of the rain. They could not take their eyes away from the place I had said was *there*. They never blamed me, never by a word or a hidden meaning. I had explained more than once how the porter that day had not put our bags on the train after all but had stood waiting at the customs barrier, wondering what had become of us. I told them how I had found everything intact—passports and cheques and maps and sweaters and shoes. They could not grasp the importance of it. They knew that Pete had chosen me and gone away with me, and they never saw him again. An unreliable guide had taken them to a foreign graveyard and told them, without evidence, that now he was there.

"I still don't see how anyone could have thought Pete was stealing," said his mother. "What would Pete have wanted with someone's old bike?"

They were flying home from Nice. They loathed Italy now, and they had a special aversion to the sunny room where I had described

Pete's death. We three sat in the restaurant at the airport, and they spoke quietly, considerately, because some people at the table next to ours were listening to a football match on a portable radio.

I closed my hand into a fist and let it rest on the table. I imagined myself at home, saying to my mother, "All right, real life has begun. What's your next prophecy?"

I was not flying with them. I was seeing them off. Mrs. Higgins sat poised and prepared in her linen coat, with her large handbag, and her cosmetics and airsickness tablets in her dressing case, and her diamond maple leaf so she wouldn't be mistaken for an American, and her passport ready to be shown to anyone. Pale gloves lay folded over the clasp of the dressing case. "You'll want to go to your own people, I know," she said. "But you have a home with us. You mustn't forget it." She paused. I said nothing, and so she continued, "What are you going to do, dear? I mean, after you have visited your friend in Paris. You mustn't be lonely."

I muttered whatever seemed sensible. "I'll have to get a job. I've never had one and I don't know anything much. I can't even type—not properly." Again they gave me this queer impression of expecting something more. What did they want? "Pete said it was no good learning anything if you couldn't type. He said it was the only useful thing he could do."

In the eyes of his parents was the same wound. I had told them something about him they hadn't known.

"Well, I understand," said his mother presently. "At least, I think I do."

They imagine I want to be near the grave, I supposed. They think that's why I'm staying on the same side of the world. Pete and I had been waiting for a train; now I had taken it without him. I was waiting again. Even if I were to visit the cemetery every day, he would never speak. His last words had not been for me but to a policeman. He would have said something to me, surely, if everyone hadn't been in such a hurry to get him out of the way. His mind was quenched, and his body out of sight. "You don't love with your soul," I had cried to the old clergyman at the funeral—an offensive remark, judging from the look on his face as he turned it aside. Now I was careful. The destination of a soul was of no interest. The death of a voice—now that was real. The Dutchman suddenly covering his mouth was horror, and a broken elbow was true pain. But I was careful; I kept this to myself.

"You're our daughter now," Pete's father said. "I don't think I want you to have to worry about a job. Not yet." Mr. Higgins happened to know my exact status. He knew my father had not left us well off, and my mother had given everything *she* owned to a sect that did not believe in blood transfusions. She expected the end of the world and would not eat an egg unless she had first met the hen. That was Mr. Higgins's view.

"Shirley must work if that's what she wants to do," Mrs. Higgins said softly.

"I do want to!" I imagined myself that day in a river of people pouring into subways.

"I'm fixing something up for you just the same," said Mr. Higgins hurriedly, as if he would not be interrupted by women.

Mrs. Higgins allowed her pale forehead to wrinkle, under her beige veil. Was it not better to struggle and to work? she asked. Wasn't that real life? Would it not keep Shirley busy, take her mind off her loss, her disappointment, her tragedy, if you like (though "tragedy" was not an acceptable way of looking at fate), if she had to think about her daily bread?

"The allowance I'm going to make her won't stop her from working," he said. "I was going to set something up for the kids anyway."

She seemed to approve, she had questioned him only out of some prudent system of ethics.

He said to me, "I always have to remember I could go any minute, just like that. I've got a heart." He tapped it, rapped his light suit. "Meantime you better start with this." He gave me the envelope that had been close to his heart until now. He seemed diffident, made ashamed by money and by death, but it was he and not his wife who had asked if there was a hope that Pete had left a child. No, I had told him. I had wondered too, but now I was sure. "Then Shirley is all we've got left," he had said to his wife, and I thought they seemed bankrupt, having nothing but me.

"If that's a check on the bank at home it might take too long to clear," said his wife. "After all Shirley's been through, she needs a fair-sized sum right away."

"She's had that, Betty," said Mr. Higgins, smiling.

I had lived this: three around a table, the smiling parents.

Pete had said, "They smile, they go on talking. You wonder what goes on."

"How you manage everything you do without a secretary with you all the time I just don't know," said his wife, all at once admiring him.

"You've been saying that for twenty-two years," he said.

"Twenty-three, now."

With this the conversation came to an end and they sat staring, puzzled, not overcome by life but suddenly lost to it, out of touch. The photograph Pete carried of his mother, which was in his wallet when he died, had been taken before her marriage, with a felt hat all to one side and an organdy collar and Ginger Rogers hair. It was easier to imagine Mr. Higgins young—a young Gary Cooper. My father-in-law's blue gaze rested on me now. Never in a million years would he have picked me as a daughter-in-law. I knew that: I understood. Pete was part of him, and Pete, with all the girls he had to choose from, had chosen me. When Mr. Higgins met my mother at the wedding, he thanked God, and was overheard being thankful, that the wedding was not in Calgary nor in Virginia, where his wife had relations. Remembering my mother that day, with her glasses on her nose and a strange borrowed hat on her head, and recalling Mr. Higgins's face, I thought of words that would keep me from laughing. I found at random, "threesome," "smother," "gambling," "habeas corpus," "sibling"...

"How is your mother, Shirley?" said Mrs. Higgins.

"I had a letter... She's working with a pendulum now."

"A pendulum?"

"Yes. A weight on a string, sort of. It makes a diagnosis whether you've got something wrong with your stomach, if it's an ulcer, or what. She can use it to tell when you're pregnant and if the baby will be a girl or a boy. It depends whether it swings north-south or east-west."

"Can the pendulum tell who the father is?" said Mr. Higgins.

"They are useful for people who are afraid of doctors," said Mrs. Higgins, and she fingered her neat gloves and smiled to herself. "Someone who won't hear the truth from a doctor will listen to any story from a woman with a pendulum or a piece of crystal."

"Or a stone that changes color," I said. "My mother had one of those. When our spaniel had mastoids it turned violet."

She caught in her breath then and glanced at me, but her husband, by a certain amount of angry fidgeting, made us change the subject. That was the only time she and I were close to each other—something to do with quirky female humor.

Mr. Higgins did not die of a heart attack, as he had confidently expected, but a few months after this Mrs. Higgins said to her maid in the kitchen, "I've got a terrible pain in my head. I'd better lie down." Pete's father wrote, "She knew what the matter was, but she never said. Typical." I inherited a legacy and some jewelry from her, and I have always wondered why. I had been careless about writing. I could not write the kind of letters she seemed to want. How could I write to someone I hardly knew about someone else who did not exist? Mr. Higgins married the widow of one of his closest friends, a woman six years older than he. They came to Europe for their wedding trip. I had the summer job I've just lost as interpreter in a department store. When my father-in-law saw me in a neat suit, with his name, Higgins, pinned to my jacket, he seemed to approve. He was the only person then who did not say I was wasting my life and my youth and ought to go home. The new Mrs. Higgins asked to be taken to an English-speaking hair-dresser, and there, under the roaring dryer, she yelled that Mr. Higgins may not have been Pete's father. Perhaps he had been, perhaps he hadn't, but one thing he was, and that was a saint. She came out from under the helmet and said in a normal voice, "Martin doesn't know I dye my hair." I wondered if he had always wanted this short, fox-colored woman. The new marriage might for years have been in the maquis of his mind, and of Mrs. Higgins's life. She may have known it as she sat in the airport that day, smiling to herself, touching her unstained gloves. Mr. Higgins had drawn up a new way of life, like a clean will with everyone he loved cut out. I was trying to draw up a will too, but I was patient, waiting, waiting for someone to tell me what to write. He spoke of Pete conventionally, in a sentimental way that forbade any feeling. Talking that way was easier for both of us. We were responsible for something—for surviving, perhaps. Once he turned to me and said defiantly, "Well, she and Pete are together now, aren't they? And didn't they leave us here?"

I forget him for months. I've kept nothing. I sent his mother all our Italian pictures and I gave her his camera with the last roll of film still in it. He never came back to me except in dreams, and then only after his mother died. There was a young girl with him. He said, "Everything I could feel has been killed." "But *I* am here," I cried. He never looked at me. The girl was not Mrs. Higgins, not even Mrs. Higgins disguised. In their private coldness he and the girl had eyes only for each other. She was someone belonging to me who had gone over to him. I knew I had lost two people, not one.

4. HOW I HAPPENED TO WRITE MY MOTHER A PERSONAL LETTER

I forgot my mother's birthday, and when I remembered it I cabled her a dozen red roses. My mother answered telling me not to waste money that way, but rather to send it to India. She said the roses brought to her door were obviously not the roses I had chosen in Paris. Now that Mr. Light has given up his business, the shop we always liked is full of artificial flowers from Hong Kong. A few dull, scentless blooms are kept in cold storage, but Mother does not think that is how flowers should be stored. Her birthday roses, delivered from Mr. Light's former place, were the color of dried blood, were congealed, and dropped their petals without ever having opened them. She thanked me for my impulsive concern and wondered if Mrs. Cat Castle had been at me, making me think I should cable flowers because Mother had a foot in the grave. She said Cat Castle was an old friend but a famous Cassandra and spreader of gloom.

Next time I wrote I sent her a bluebell. I picked it in Orsay on a Sunday, with you. You and I had been invited to lunch by your friend Hervé and his wife. They say they live "in the country" but it is really a fungus extension of Paris. Do you remember the Sunday traffic? The lights hung over the road like dead animals. At Orsay we parked between two cars like our own in front of a block of flats that looked like a hospital. "Our car is cleaner," you remarked. I know it is important if cars are clean or dusty. I suppose it must be. The entrance to the building was full of prams. We shouted into the crackling telephone system above the mailbox and even though Hervé wasn't expecting anyone except us, he made you yell your name three or four times. Hervé and his wife were new here. They used to live in a furnished room in a hotel, sneaking the milk and bread in, and cooking on an alcohol stove. Now they showed us the Venetian blinds, the wall-to-wall carpet in the bedroom, the garbage chute in the kitchen, and the bathroom with its real tub and real hot water. We were given a thimble of sweet port to drink, and I asked Hervé about his new job at the Science Faculty in Orsay, which was as new as their apartment. He turned his mouth down and looked at his wife, and they laughed with a bitter kind of meaning.

It wouldn't be such a bad job, he said, if he weren't dealing with fools and scholars. Did I know that the greatest discoveries and inventions had always been made by men who had no schooling? Nobel prize winners were fakes and parasites. I began to understand that Hervé's job was, perhaps, fetching sandwiches and coffee for the others, or going about with one of those mysterious keys and banging on the air conditioning or central heating.

You said to Hervé, "She isn't listening. Shirley never listens after the first ten words."

You smiled at me as if to say the remark had no edge to it.

You and Hervé were in Algeria, and you know something you will never say. When Renata sits next to a young man in the Métro, she finds herself wondering what he did in Algeria. She thinks of that young Algerian girl they raped with a bottle and she looks at the young man's hands and his calm reflection in the dark window and she wants to say, "Excuse me, but was it you?"

Now that both you and Hervé are married you never meet, except formally. Hervé's wife has a golden mustache and a gold heart on a chain. She gave us our lunch on a chrome-legged formica table dragged out of the kitchen. First we had canned sardines (to you and to Hervé and his wife, a delicacy; to me, a food of the unemployed) and then steaks, and chips out of a cellophane packet, quantities of very good bread, a Camembert, and a chocolate mousse. The mousse was what my mother calls "store pudding." I recognized the small plastic cups. You can see them at the grocer's on the same shelf as the yogurt.

"We are not bourgeois. We live like students," Hervé said. He loves his wife and seems proud of her.

"Shirley lives like a student too," you said. I wondered what you meant. Did you mean that you sometimes opened a door, looked in on my prolonged, youthful squalor and shut the door again? You and I were married. We lived in the same rooms.

"When we have children we shall have to stop being children too," said Hervé's wife. "But now we want to be young."

They didn't seem young: they might have been your age, twenty-nine or thirty. They had, as you have, a revulsive distaste for the furniture they had grown up with, but I thought that their children—for whose sakes they intended to be larger than life one day—might have an opinion about the chrome-legged table. You and Hervé discussed "the American economic takeover in France," of which you know a lot, and Hervé, who did most of the talking, nothing whatever. You didn't seem bored. I wondered, looking around the living room, noticing the absence of books and of lamps, where and what they read. I have suspected for some time now that you are the person who buys all the books sold in Paris. You and Hervé were still talking, outside now, on the balcony in comfortable chairs. I was in the kitchen, helping his wife scrape the plates and put the bread away. When I realized what had happened and that we were in exile I put down the butter dish I was holding and without a word to her came out to join you on the balcony. I was determined to find the place that belonged to me in this conversation. I said, "What do you mean when you say the Americans are *in* here—you mean they're running for mayor?"

"She says," you translated, "that reading *Le Monde* has changed her life."

"Naturally," said Hervé, and for the first time since our wedding day, when he had kept staring as though waiting for me to explode, he looked straight into my face.

After his wife had given us coffee we walked around the new university buildings and saw what remained of a grove of trees. The paths were broken by pools and lakes, where bulldozers had backed and turned. "Walk carefully," Hervé said to his wife. She and I, picking our way along the rims of craters, seemed in timid pursuit of the men. Suddenly I saw a lake of blue. The blond girl clutched her golden heart and turned at the same moment. For a second only, the new, sweet fragrance that rose from the blue lake was a secret between us. Until then, the low color tone of the suburb, the washed out sandiness of the afternoon, had made me wonder if there was a filter in my mind now as well as a weakness in my eyes. Often I have mistaken crumpled cigarette packs for flowers, but this color was true and the scent was real, and as I crouched down the better to see and touch I believed that you had led me outside the city after all.

Hervé's wife, kneeling, began to pick. Her cheeks were flushed; she seemed feverish, almost pretty. But her face was sober and sad, as if these flowers would be taken from her, as so much else had been. I broke off one moist stem. I heard your friend say to his wife, "Get all you can, for once." So that was what their life was about.

The next day I found the damp flower, still blue, in the pocket of my leather coat, and I thrust it inside a letter I had written my mother. I didn't especially want her to identify it for me: I thought that when she saw it she would know everything—that I had been away and had seen something growing.

When I write to my mother I am in the dark, screaming for a light or a drink of water—for attention from the bright staying-up world downstairs. I wrote to her because I had heard, that Sunday, for the first time, "Poor Philippe." I've heard it since, but that was the first time. Hervé said it, muttering to his wife. Something about your being married to me. Poor Philippe, married to a wife who can't even pick bluebells! That might have been all he meant. Hervé's wife gave me some of hers to take home, but as she did so she was smiling at you. I kept the bluebells in water three days alive and four days dead, and then you left me.

The instant my letter to my mother was in the mail I wanted to send a cable saying "DON'T READ LETTER," but I knew the disdain this would provoke. My mother thinks she is a free-thinker and free in every way, but at heart she believes in standing by decisions, even if you were drunk or drugged or tortured or twelve years of age when you made them.

My handwriting saved her. It gave her an excuse to say she hadn't heard my voice. Not for all the world would she have acknowledged that kind of cry. She said I had asked about *Endymion non-scriptus*, and now I believe her.

One other thing: I am not incompetent. I seem so, but I'm not. A first impression is always wrong: so is the second, third and twentieth. I really wish you would come back.

Someone whistled in the courtyard. The Australian, Sutton McGrath, practiced his guitar against a record of "Sweet Lorraine." "John Gorinar, John Gorinar," said Gérald Ziff over and over in Shirley's memory like a light blinking red-white, red-white, until finally a card with a translation of the name appeared and she cried, "Of course, *Django*!" She read what she had written so far:

WHY P. LEFT ME AND HOW I LOST MY JOB

1. Where I was on the Saturday.
2. About James.
3. Pete, one or two things.
4. How I happened to write my mother a personal letter.

"The possession of the signs of sexual privilege is the important thing, not the quality nor the enjoyment of them" (*Lucky Jim*).

End of July 1963: I think Philippe has left me and I know I have lost my job.

It seemed to be all she had to say. The past, detached from her, floated away like a balloon. When she opened her windows she heard the music of summer and recurring chances. If she had not been in Paris but in a different climate she might have heard birds as well. In Italy she had lain awake at dawn keeping her ear tuned to a single pitch—it was the only way to know what you were listening for. The sky was a shell; thin blue silk stretched from horizon to zenith. Behind the shell and the silk sang the unseen birds. Someone had told her that the Italians killed everything on the wing, that no birds sang. Mr. Higgins must have said that. He had been in Italy during a war. Yes, it was Mr. Higgins who said you never heard a bird singing there: the Italians had caught them in nets and eaten every one. She stood barefoot at a window and saw a giant cherry tree with a ladder against the trunk. This is the morning of the day of the end of the world.

Philippe returned, and they played a scene composed by Geneviève.

"What I hate is the destruction," he said, looking past her head.

"So it is settled!" she cried. She was lovely at that moment. She wore a long blond wig and a bright satin trouser suit with maribou around the ankles. She turned to the audience, briefly touched with despair at what the next day would be like. She sat with her arms over the arm of a chair and held out a glass for him to fill. He was holding an authentic bottle of Irish whiskey, and he was dressed like any reporter on a morning daily, entirely in cashmere.

"You are like someone who has been ill," he said. "When you are very ill you think you will change and the world will be a different place after you have recovered. Then you find you are the same, but weaker, and everyone else is the same, but busier."

Philippe discovered Shirley drinking absinthe and playing the guitar. He had been a prisoner of the Boche from 1914 to 1918, and seemed thinner and darker than before. The shadow of the starched lace curtain was printed over his face. Picking up his pack and helmet from the dining-room table, he said, "Do not expect to change, but try to be different next time, or another time." She wore a stiff collar and a ribbon bow; she had bobbed and frizzed her hair. She clasped her fingers, elbows out, palms facing the floor. "Your life is not my business now," he said, glancing at the guitar, which lay on a cushion.

She peeped up at him: "I didn't understand. I was so young. I thought you were going to start over. I thought you had come back."

"Take you back?" he said, as if repeating what she had said. "I'm not that elegant."

Philippe was discomposed, but only for a moment, when he discovered that the unknown expert on the question was his wife. A microphone, like Hervé's wife's locket, hung around her neck.

"All decisions are moral decisions," said Philippe, beginning the interview.

"Oh, Philippe—no one watching this will know what you're talking about. Having friends and making stupid mistakes has nothing to do with decisions; it only has to do with what you know from day to day."

"What you learn," he said through teeth and pipe.

"Well, what knowledge you can have."

"That is just Anglo-Saxon," he said. "Waiting to be informed."

The program announcer, *la speakerine*, a girl chosen to satisfy the tastes of every class, region and political party, and who seemed a smiling cross-mixture of cat and cow, erased her smile long enough to say, "Monsieur Perrigny has settled the question."

Because of the heat wave she lived behind closed shutters. A white electric fan blew straight on her forehead. She waited for someone to come to her and wondered if she had been forgotten. Someone did come. Marie-Thérèse arrived at the door. Her costume this hot day was an unfashionably long dress shaken out of a winter trunk and hastily pressed, and instead of the green felt beret, a round straw hat of the kind known as a Breton sailor. She did not apologize for having dropped in without any warning, though it was unconventional behavior for her. She had been shopping at the Bon Marché department store; with unusual and almost unnerving familiarity she showed her purchases—shirts, jerseys, bathing trunks and sandals, solid and cheap. She was taking her four little boys to Dinard for the month of August. Gérald, poor Gérald, would not be able to have any holidays at all this year. He would remain in Paris alone, missing his family, living on cold ham and canned tuna fish.

"What a pretty apartment," said Marie-Thérèse, looking around. "What attractive windows! What a charming blue sofa! How do you keep it so clean? Of course, without children..."

She went on that way until Shirley said, "Sit on the sofa if you want to. It's a rock. I'm warning you. My mother-in-law gave it to Philippe. He sleeps there when he comes in late and doesn't want to bother me." It was as easy to invent as to wear out one's memory. "My husband's health is not good," she went on gravely. "He has a misplaced heart. It has slipped a little to one side. Sometimes he has to sleep on a hard bed."

Marie-Thérèse did not seem to think this was an unusual affliction. She accepted the story, faintly smiling, waiting for Shirley to sit down too. She was not like Renata, who would have kicked off her shoes and made for the most comfortable armchair. Marie-Thérèse looked carefully around her, then chose the only unpleasant seat in the room. "I took a chance on your being home at this hour," she said. "I was nearby and I had your address. You do work, don't you?"

"Not today," said Shirley, as if imitating someone else's discretion. She sat like her mother-in-law, like a widow by Vuillard, like someone with her life's savings sewn up in her corsets. She thought that Philippe, who had wished her reasonable, judicious and prudent, should have been here now. Like Marie-Thérèse, she was in one of last summer's dresses. The two had in common an appearance of shabbiness and improvisation, and both were survivors of a heatwave in which Shirley had imagined herself alone. A bunch of sweetpeas—blue, pink, yellow—had also outlived the worst of the weather. The fan, pivoting, sent some of Philippe's leftover papers drifting onto the carpet.

Marie-Thérèse sat with her hands folded and her parcels on the floor beside her. She had come to visit the young woman Shirley had seen walking out of the mirror.

"Shall I make some coffee?" Renata had always needed it.

"At this time of day? No wonder American women are so nervous."

"The Finns aren't nervous, and they drink coffee all day." Shirley rushed on, "If you say you don't like Camembert here, everybody says, 'Oh, I suppose you have better cheese in Canada.' I get sick of it. It so happens I hate Camembert, it smells of wet babies." She was immediately out of breath. Other than James, who seldom counted for conversation, Marie-Thérèse was the first person she had talked to for several days.

"I have never eaten any cheese that was not French. I do not exclude other cheeses. It is merely a matter of my possibilities. It is not a choice." Marie-Thérèse was surprisingly gentle away from the others. "What do you think of Claudie's latest?" she said.

With a little care Shirley could have answered, "Latest what? Cheese? Job? Pregnancy? Political opinion?" She put her hands flat on her cheeks. She had drunk a glass of wine for breakfast because

Renata had once said it was a sound thing to do. Wine burned up the wrong kind of energy and left you with just the amount you needed for a useful day. The wine burned like a spoonful of acid. She felt a headache, a light tap between the eyes. She scraped a knuckle over her forehead, looking at the light of day reflected in a mirror beyond Marie-Thérèse's head. She said that Marie-Thérèse—she supposed—wanted to stop the so-called marriage. Well, there was no marriage yet, though there easily could be. Why shouldn't Claudie be married to Marcel Proust and go and live in the Middle East? Did it sound less intelligent than anything Marie-Thérèse, or her mother, or Shirley herself had ever done? Claudie might be married in the suburb of Boulogne-Billancourt, where the Maurels lived. That was the most convenient way of getting a man and a woman together, so why the fuss? She would have her family around her, with little Alain dressed in a blue sailor suit.

Shirley had married Philippe in the mairie of the sixth arrondissement, on the place St. Sulpice, with the square cold and dead below the windows, and tramps slumbering on the benches and pigeons like lumps of lead thrown across the sky. Hervé and Renata had been the witnesses. Then they had all four gone to a café on the square and sat next to a goldfish tank, and argued about roast beef, asparagus and Braque. Philippe and Shirley might easily have walked a few steps more and been married again in the Église St. Sulpice. Why not? Shirley had been a widow, not a divorcée (as everyone seemed to imagine). Philippe was a Roman Catholic. Had he wanted a civil marriage in order to be free to divorce her? People in love have an unlimited capacity for shocking each other. He may well have had just such an escape clause in mind. Supposing you stay away from home all night? You might be ill, or dead, yet the first words that could come into the mind of Gérald, who is waiting, might be, "I am free," just as if your disaster were a defiling piece of evidence. This evidence comes into his hands and so degrades and damages his idea of you that he is saved from his feelings. Nothing is so startling as the speed and decision with which a man will suddenly cut his losses. You think he is like you, struggling in the current, and all at once he is safe on shore. He could swim perfectly well all along —he was only pretending. Shirley declared: "Never give him time to think, and take good care not to let him find out he can live twenty-four hours without you." Shirley would not have minded a church marriage. Secretly she had probably wanted it. Her mother's ardent letters on the matter ("Tell me plainly—have you *turned*?") only made her laugh. But Philippe had never suggested such a thing, which meant, probably, that the wife after Shirley would be the real one. With Shirley he was in transit from his mother's life to a life of his own. But their marriage was a fact; it had taken place. It was all down on the paper somewhere. *That* was the tap between the eyes.

"Who do you mean by Marcel Proust?" said Marie-Thérèse, keeping out of this wild diversion the one remark that interested her.

"He's really Jean-Luc something. I just call him Marcel because he's small and delicate and he says he's a part of some literary family." Marie-Thérèse frowned slightly, as though trying to separate this "Marcel" from so many others. Shirley said, "Jean-Luc is the boy Claudie wants to marry, though I doubt if he wants to marry her, or ever will. I'm sure he doesn't, in fact." She felt deflated and humble after her riotous speech.

"Where is Claudie?" Marie-Thérèse looked around as if Claudie, large and grinning and sure of herself, might step out from behind a curtain.

"Claudie's in her hotel. She doesn't live *here*." Shirley laughed suddenly; "Did she really let you think she was leaving home for me?"

"She has left our father's house," said Marie-Thérèse, making it sound as if her father were in himself a property to be inherited over and over. Without any change in her manner she said, "Madame, Claudie is very much my father's daughter. It would not do for you to become involved. You would be caught between two stones. They both have cold hearts, but his at least goes with a kind of cold judgment; Claudie has no mind and no feelings. My parents had to take Alain, whom she had more or less abandoned. It would be a mistake for her to have another child."

"Tell her that," said Shirley.

"Alain is a great worry," said Marie Thérèse.

"Marcel might adopt him," said Shirley, giving herself over to the idle, speculative chatter she and Renata had enjoyed. The future was a series of guesses, none of them attached to anything real.

"Proust, you said?" said Marie-Thérèse, trying for logic again.

"It's a joke. I thought you knew about him. I didn't understand at first that you were fishing. It's only a joke. Why didn't you just say you wanted information? I could have told you at once that I hadn't any."

"*Proust*! She doesn't even know what it means," said Marie-Thérèse almost fondly. "She has a few set speeches. Did she ever tell you she had dreamed of a rose tree decaying? Did she ever use the phrase 'the dark corners of a woman's life'?"

"I think she did, yes. I think it was Claudie. Or else it was my other friend, Renata."

"Silly little animal," said Marie-Thérèse.

"I thought it was out of some old Ingmar Bergman movie."

"No, it was something I once said. Claudie used to listen to conversations. You would find her behind a sofa and say, 'What are you doing there?' She would answer, 'I'm pretending to be a doll,' and she would become stiff and frozen, like one of those porcelain dolls with real eyelashes. I noticed one in the window of the antique shop downstairs." She looked straight at Shirley with her pale eyes, yet she might have been looking at anything else—a fan, a chair. "Did you ever see the piece of lead that made the eyes open and close? I thought real eyes were like that, and that there was that Y-shaped lead piece inside our heads. When I was small I thought this. Claudie hid and listened for years. She remembered every secret conversation I ever had with my father. When she repeats anything it is not to spread calumnies. No, she repeats true stories, but with Claudie as the principal character."

Shirley wanted to say, Look here, did you ever really say 'the dark corners of a woman's life' to Monsieur Maurel, or to anyone? You couldn't have—you were the only member of the family I respected! She said, "I promise you that Claudie did not leave on my advice. My only advice was that she should look for a job. My only mistake was in letting her meet a friend of mine named Renata. Pretending to be a china doll is nowhere near what Renata is capable of, and I could see that Claudie was taken in. Now what I want to know is, What are you doing without your husband, your mother or your children? I didn't know you ever *could* be alone."

"I am free today," said Marie-Thérèse. "The three older boys have been asked to the house of a school friend—something I do not approve of—and the little one is with my mother, and Gérald has a business lunch." She made a thin line of her mouth. She wanted all her men at home, where she could control them.

Oh, what does she want? Shirley wondered. Why doesn't she say she knows where Claudie is? She has been there.

"Here we are in thin dresses," said Marie-Thérèse, still meandering. "And Paris is so unsettled—tomorrow we may be wearing our coats and sweaters again. But you are so competent and organized, I am sure nothing can surprise you. You must be ready for every change. You were not astonished to see me, for example. You accept everything as it happens. If someone came to my door, I would ask who it was through the closed door, or I would be very still and hold my breath and wait for the intruder to go away. I think of the person at the door as a man with a little suitcase, which he will open and then try to sell me laces and bits of embroidery which I don't want and can't afford. This man has only one arm, he has no home, and he has an incurable illness. I am always afraid of this man. I always have been. I am afraid of the blind. I buy the soap that the blind make, but I give it to my grandmother. I am afraid to use it. I am afraid it could be unlucky. Supposing I opened the door one day and someone came in and talked as if answering questions, when no questions had been asked? But you accept all this."

"I don't want to seem rude, but I've heard it before," said Shirley. "I never expected it from you, though. I've already heard people try one subject after another without getting to the point. That's why I'm not surprised. When you live the way I have, everything seems natural."

"What is the way you live?"

After a few moments Shirley said, "I know a lot of people, but I don't depend on anyone. I wish you could see the view in that mirror—your profile, the sweetpeas and the light from the window."

"The way you live would never do for Claudie. She will never be independent, though she likes saying she knows people too. Once she showed me her address book and said, 'I could see a different person every day for five months if I wanted to.' But she will never be independent."

"You've never let her. You've never let her learn anything."

"At home, there is a large wardrobe the top shelves of which are filled with the textbooks of courses Claudie began and gave up. We had to let her try subjects that could be taught to someone who hadn't finished school. She tried typing and Spanish and sewing and bookbinding, but nothing lasted. Maman would have forced her to stick to something, but Papa always gave in."

"He wants it that way," said Shirley. "The dependent daughter. She'll never marry anyone."

"It would be a blessing for us if some man did marry her, but a catastrophe for him."

Shirley did not know if Marie-Thérèse meant a catastrophe for Papa or for the husband.

Now rain blackened the street. The mirror was darkened. In a cold, sudden draft a door banged.

Shirley thought, I was hoping someone would remember me, but it was only Marie-Thérèse. I can't spend a summer this way. A summer is as long as a lifetime. What will become of me now?

"I was wondering," she said. "What will become of Claudie?"

"I have been wondering for ten years," said Marie-Thérèse. "I was eight when she was born." Here came a new pause. She seemed to be looking for a topic, but gave it up. She cast one more clear look about, and then, seeing the cloudburst, stopped and gathered up her parcels. She made a last attempt: "When you invited Claudie to leave home and live with you..."

"Did I?" Shirley was standing. "Claudie's never lived here. The only people from that family who have come here without invitation are Gérald and you. The two I know least. The Flying Ziffs. I may have thought Claudie should leave home, but I doubt if I said so. I wouldn't want her here. What would I do with her? I haven't said a word—I promise you that. Claudie does the talking, just as you've been doing. Though I did put in quite a long bit about my wedding, I must admit. I wouldn't interfere with your father, not unless Claudie asked me to." She remembered that Claudie had asked something.

"I must tell you one more thing," said Marie-Thérèse, hugging her parcels, cold in the draft. "It is our mother who is afraid of losing Claudie, not Papa. She is bound to, one day, and she will lose her stupidly, because anything to do with Claudie has to be stupid. Whatever happens, I pray there will not be any outsiders involved, and no scandal."

"Your family doesn't seem to have any friends, so there can hardly be any scandal."

Marie-Thérèse stared, then smiled. "It is like a dream, having this conversation outside my own family."

"If we were both dreaming it could hardly be sillier, I know."

"I dreamed I saw myself sleeping," said Marie-Thérèse, unaware she now owed Shirley a quarter, to be accepted in her late father's name. "I was ugly. I saw myself with my ugly pointed ears."

"Oh, poor Marie-Thérèse!" Shirley cried, hurt by the picture the other woman had of herself.

Marie-Thérèse turned away. She had not liked being called "poor," and seemed to fear that Shirley might touch her.

"Let's have lunch together," Shirley said, for now she was looking at Marie-Thérèse—looking at *her*, and not at her effect on the mirror. She saw her as pale and thin-skinned, and so unlucky with her questions that led nowhere. "I've been living on *vin rosé* and breakfasts, and finally even the marmalade ran out. You don't have to go home. You just said so."

"I never care what I eat, or even if I do," said Marie-Thérèse, which seemed a cold way of accepting. "I never go out. You will have to decide everything. Only foreigners know where restaurants are in Paris."

Shirley thought, I don't even care how that was meant. Her attention was fixed on the pretty gilt-framed mirror in the hall, Renata's wedding present. Am I all right? she asked the mirror. Am I fit to be seen? Her face bore an unexpected resemblance to her mother's. She remembered the anxious energy she had put into getting ready on the day Gérald had come for her—how carefully she had dressed for an unknown family who were half hoping she would not turn up. My purse, my cigarettes, my money, no, not my gloves; gloves make you look foreign here. Am I ready? Am I wearing shoes? My hair, my wedding ring, my smile—are they handicaps or will they help me?

Madame Roux, caught in the act of placing an authentic 1914 bidet (now a plantstand) in the window, opened her mouth as the two went by. It was a wide sign of astonishment, as in a silent film.

"It is because we look so respectable," Shirley explained.

But Marie-Thérèse, in the bitter voice of someone recalling a dim, old injustice, was speaking about food: "Around Strasbourg, where Gérald was born, they have so much food that they play games with it. At Christmas the *charcuteries* are decorated with Nativity scenes made out of garlic sausage and potato salad. The Infant Jesus is a dill pickle, a radish and toothpicks. A normally built woman can eat a dozen snails, pike tart, foie gras in aspic, a haystack of *choucroute*, Munster cheese, and apple pudding, and then, for digestion, a pear weighing half a pound. She will also have bread and beer, or white wine, and then coffee. They are particular about their coffee. When I met Gérald I asked him how coffee was made in Alsace. He said that it was easy: one bought the best, and used a lot of it. Imagine! What I've described might be a luncheon. At five o'clock this same woman will drink thick hot chocolate with little croissants stuffed with almond paste, or a piece of pastry rolled around apples, raisins and walnuts. That will keep her peaceful until dinnertime. Dinner will be a heavy soup of pork, potatoes, leeks. Then she will have potato salad and a cold breaded pork chop, and perhaps some of the apple pudding left over from lunch, if something else hasn't been made in the meantime—perhaps plum tart. In spite of all that food, their eyes are bright and the whites very clear. They get fat, their busts are imposing, but their skin is like peach down. These women are calmer, less complicated than we are. The sky is cleaner than in Paris. The air seems unpolluted. The stars in the heavens spell f-o-o-d. Until he married me, Gérald had never sat down to a meal where there were fewer than six people, and with less food than could feed sixteen."

And then he married this frugal daughter of Paris, who was enjoying her cold description of meals she would have thought it immoral to prepare. Shirley said, almost absently, "I wonder why we all got married so young?"

"My mother must have told you. No? Did she tell you that when I married Gérald she lost part of herself? It's a thing she tells sometimes. It is from our mother that Claudie has her taste for phrases."

"I've never had a real conversation with your mother. We haven't often been alone."

Marie-Thérèse said very lightly, "She talks as if she had seen you often. No matter. I was tied to her skirts. She made me too religious. Oh, it is of no importance now. I was afraid I might become a nun, and so I married. I was afraid I would feel I had to be a nun. My mother's best girlhood friend, whom we called Aunt Françoise, was a nun. Whenever Maman took me to visit her I felt that she wanted to give me away as a present to her old friend. Each of them had a brooch with two gold doves on a little branch. They had exchanged them when they were young girls. I think the two girls were supposed to be those doves. When Maman married Papa, Aunt Françoise sent hers back to Maman, like someone turning in the Legion of Honor. That's the story I've heard. It made Maman feel she had done something wrong in getting married. Later, Maman may have regretted being married because Papa was hard to understand. Hard for *her* to understand. I've never found him difficult. He seems indifferent now, but I can remember... It doesn't matter. Maman would sit in Aunt Françoise's convent parlor with me beside her and weep and weep. Aunt Françoise—I still called her that, though she had another name in religion—seemed cool and triumphant. She laid her hand on my head and said she could see the bridal veil. Maman stopped crying at once, saying 'Do you?' with so much joy, as if with those words Aunt Françoise had forgiven her for having had me. After Claudie came, I was so out of favor that I would have done anything to please Maman. But not that, not become a nun. I couldn't promise that, even at nine, at ten. I didn't want that veil. It was the other veil I wanted, the real bridal veil, and I shut myself off from Maman deliberately, so that she couldn't get at my affections. I already knew I would keep my affection for my children. I still did not know who my husband would be; I had no idea about him. I cut myself off from Maman abruptly, without explaining. And I was so young! She may have suffered. Until I was eight years old she had fed me with a spoon. I never learned to use my hands. I sat with my hands on the table and she fed me. From time to time I must have refused to swallow, the way Alain does now. That was a long time ago. I was seventeen when I met Gérald. A year later I went to Papa and said 'It will be Gérald or no one.' He and Gérald dined alone— the first and last time they ever had a conversation. They never speak—did you notice? There is no anger between them, but what can they say? Papa told him there would not be a marriage settlement, not one centime. But Gérald still wanted me and he has never reproached me. Never."

Shirley briefly compared the cloister with having Gérald as a husband. There should have been a third chance. Marie-Thérèse's voice created transparent pictures; the noise of the traffic on the boulevard Saint Germain slipped through the account of a life—part of a life. Shirley saw them as she saw cars starting and stopping and one taxi sliding like an eel around a corner past a red light.

"She had fed me with a spoon," said Marie-Thérèse, "and I hated eating. It bored me. Yes, I was like Alain. You see, she is doing it all over again. She is doing to Alain what she did to me. I would open my mouth, like a little bird..."

Over her voice, through the traffic, slid a third picture: Alain opening his bird mouth and Papa slipping into it a morsel of bread.

"One day my mother seemed nervous and tired and she said, 'I am having another child, and if you don't feed yourself you will die.' That was how I began to eat. When they took me to the clinic to look at Claudie I thought she was hideous, black as a monkey. I knew even then Maman would have the hold on her she's had on me, that she would tie her up, and that it would take another form. I didn't hate the dark baby, but I must have decided then to have only blond children. By the time Claudie was two or three she was fair as a Scandinavian, but I still see her ugly and dark."

I congratulate you, Shirley said to herself. That serve was more than adequate. As you will see, I know the rules: confidence for confidence, mine will be equal to yours. That is how we avoid blackmail at the end of the game. No one will need to say, "Don't say I said it." You limit your play to food and money, and you bring in your mother. My turn, now—what would you like to know? If only I knew what you were after! But that is the one thing you can't tell. I wasn't jealous of a younger sister; I never had one. My father? Not interesting—an old man. Are you wondering about Philippe? You have seen him on television and you say to yourself now, "With all of France and Navarre to choose from, why Shirley Higgins?" "Never wonder, Louisa..." (C. Dickens) is the way we will head this. You may be asking yourself how we met. When I first came to France I used to wonder how people met at all. They seemed so separate, so uninvolved with each other that I wondered they could testify at trials— how they recognized each other at all, let alone knew anyone's name.

The first time I saw him was at a party Renata had taken me to, and the second was by accident, in the street. I was carrying a basket of groceries—to be exact, scotch and salted peanuts. I was holding an umbrella. At the party he had been the bewildered Frenchman, charming and polite, wondering what he was doing there with all those drunks. It was the first time he had ever seen pretty, respectable, drunken girls. We sat next to each other on the floor and I poured all my life out, except the part that mattered. When we met in the street a week later he fell in step beside me. I may have recognized him first—yes, I probably waved my umbrella and smiled the wide, dumb welcome that makes us seem like children to them. We discussed straight away in the rain whether the Hitler movement had really been black magic. It was the big topic that season. His information was a best-selling book about all kinds of magic, and mine came from Renata. As I listened to Philippe talking, I realized she had read the same book. When we came to the door of the courtyard (Madame Roux meanwhile peering, pop-eyed and avid, over her fortune of wigless dolls and soup tureens) I saw him through fogged-up glasses. I had been expecting a miracle for some time.

"You are wearing a wedding ring," he remarked.

"I am a widow."

"A young widow."

"I don't know. I'm twenty-five."

"Young widows don't exist any more," he said. "They belong to the 1914 war."

Whenever I did not know why something had been said, I thought it was because I did not understand French well enough or else that I was stupid. I translated us both from the beginning into characters out of books, but they were children's books he had never heard of. Under the umbrella, I was Jo, and he was Professor Bhaer. A few days later, when he turned up to fetch me for dinner, by appointment, I had forgotten all about him. I lived a small, dogged life then. I didn't depend on anyone in particular and I knew a lot of people. He said, "Shall I come back a little later?" I was wearing a hideous Mexican shift Renata had passed on to me. I was drinking rye and water and eating my supper, a peanut-butter sandwich. "I have never been in an American apartment before," he said, looking around. The rooms were different then. He brought the desks and the shelves and the wine rack and the blue sofa later on. What we called "the box-room" later had nothing in it but an ironing board and a picture frame. There were no proper cupboards. My clothes were everywhere. I kept a flashlight for weeks in the bathroom because I didn't know where the fusebox was.

"The furniture is French, I guess," I said, as though I hadn't seen it before. "I've hardly ever been in a real French apartment, so that makes us even. I took this over from another girl. I'm not American. I'm Canadian."

"Then *you* are French," he said politely.

"With my accent? I could hardly speak a word until I came here. Now I do pretty well, don't you think? Or haven't you heard me? People here are always saying, 'You must be Maria Chapdelaine.' Sometimes I just say yes, to make things easier. I get her mixed up with that other one, Madeleine something, who saved I don't know which place from the Iroquois."

I sat down, facing him, tugging the shift down over my knees. I was cold with shame, not over my appearance, but because of the gnawed sandwich, which I tried to hide under a crumpled paper napkin in an ashtray. All I could think of to say next was, "Make you a sandwich?"

"*Le Miroir*, where I work, published a series of nine articles on the Canadian question," said polite Philippe.

"Oh, the question. I don't know all that much. Just what people keep telling me. No, that's not fair. I know a little, but when I try to explain I keep having to start from zero every time, and it wears me out. I saw the things in *Le Miroir*. I didn't read them; I just looked at the pictures to see if there was anyone I knew. I thought they were kind of melodramatic. You don't know how dull and stubborn people can be. These articles—weren't they called 'The Scream' or something?"

"'The Silent Cry.' That was the name of the series." He sat on the edge of a chair as if he were waiting for news of some kind. I see him there and I remember your saying, "It will be Gérald or no one." He can grow old, fret about his digestion, lose his hair, he still will be that one. We had met before, but now we looked. Presently he said, "I wrote the articles. I wrote the first two, which were in the form of a general essay, and I wrote the summing up. The others were a matter of editing." Then he quoted in the elegant beautiful French he speaks, "'It is a silent cry, torn from the lungs piercing as pain, rending the firmament.' Surely that sounds like your country, as the situation is now?"

"I don't always get the meaning in French. Not awfully well. I'm sorry. I'm certain you know much more than I do. Were you the one who went all over the place with a notebook asking for the Museum of Roman Antiquities? Because there isn't one, you see. So there was no reason, just because some person couldn't direct you to a place that doesn't exist, for writing, 'Once again centuries of European culture and tradition were trampled underfoot!'"

"I was not there," he said. "I worked from information supplied."

"By the guy with the notebook?"

"By a girl named Geneviève Deschranes."

Instant jealousy was what the name provoked: the name, and the way he said it. I said, "So you screamed at a distance?" I was suddenly conscious of my voice, my way of speaking. I felt ludicrous, ungraceful—barbarous. "I'd better get dressed," I said. "I haven't even offered you a drink. Do you want one? Everything is in the kitchen."

When we went out three quarters of an hour later I left a light burning. I had hastily made my bedroom and the bathroom neat; I knew we would be coming back. He hadn't said a word and I hadn't either, but I knew. We went by the Hotel Montalembert—where we are now—and I said, "I always salute the Montalembert and the Pont-Royal, because it was in one or the other that Fabrice took a room for Linda."

"Who are they?"

"Don't you know *The Pursuit of Love*? It was part of my folklore too. When I was eleven or twelve, and still riddled with idiot thoughts about Parisian behavior, I had no time for love stories that didn't end with betrayal or dying. I swore I would never settle for anything less."

"I do not know them," he said severely. He must have thought I was describing close friends. He seemed suspicious, just as I had been of the horrible Geneviève and her notebook.

I began reciting the meeting in the railway station, how Linda, sitting on her luggage in her mink coat, said, "*Je suis la fille d'un lord anglais*," but Philippe merely looked darker, and sorry he had ever met me. Whenever I thought I was exercising a talent for irony he thought I was being intolerably arch. We went on being at cross-purposes for a long time, in that sense. What we were not in any contradiction about was our desire to get the ritual public dinner over with and get to bed. Rain came down on us like stones, like that cloudburst a little earlier this morning. Two girls dashed out of the Montalembert to a taxi. I thought, as always, that I looked a mess. I felt humble at the sight of their pale dresses, their light fragile shoes; they were like girls I had seen in Italy once. They were charmed: rain fell all around them without deflating their hair or splashing their clothes.

"It's something wished for them at their christening," I said, and Philippe did not reply, having sensed by now that I was nervous. His knowledge of it made me panic but instead of keeping quiet I went on: "Later, Fabrice threw Linda's mink coat in a wastebasket and brought her sables. That's a French lover for you. But maybe you have to have the mink ready to be thrown away first. I mean, would you give sables to a girl who just had an old raincoat to get rid of?"

He opened the door of a restaurant in one of the streets running down to the Seine, murmuring something about being certain Americans never went here. Neither then nor later could I persuade him that I was anything else. I was—by voice, dress, manner and speech—immutable. We hung up our wet coats and squeezed past the bar. The owner of the restaurant, whose name was Aristide, and who knew me well, greeted Philippe by his name and pretended he had not seen me. I was thankful, for I wanted Philippe to think he had shown me a place foreigners had never heard of, though it was now in most of the guidebooks. I did not tell him that Aristide and Suzanne had been my friends once, and how hardworking they had seemed—how worthy of my help and affection. At first they had been so poor that they bought food for one meal at a time, calculating, as a computer would have done for them, what people were likely to order, or even if anyone was likely to turn up. Sometimes they were still washing dishes at three in the morning, and I sat with them, drinking their Armagnac and cautioning them against tuberculosis and nervous breakdowns. I brought customers to them, and their success, finally, was a little bit mine. (This is the place: Suzanne is the blonde behind the bar.) I saw that Philippe glanced back at the zinc counter which was half covered with cakes and fruit tarts and a great bowl of strawberries and a crock of pears in syrup. He was looking at the food, not at Suzanne. As for Suzanne, she was measuring with her eye the amount of cream spooned over a plate of strawberries by a new, small, sleek waiter. She looked up and saw me looking, but took no notice of me. One day I must have done something displeasing to them. They stopped making me welcome. Around the same time, the prices rose and the cream thinned. First I mourned them, then I forgot all about them. When I stopped coming here they simply stopped being real people. I could no more say when the friendship ended than fix the exact moment of falling asleep. When I saw them again I was merely astonished that anyone I forgot could still go on existing.

"The owner is very commercial," said Philippe, meaning this as a compliment. He was praising Aristide's social gifts, his manner of making customers feel important and secure.

We were wedged at the end of a long table, face to face, next to a cold radiator. Being new to each other, we looked around for some source of conversation. We examined a painting composed of lacquer and burned matches without speaking. Neither knew how the other felt, and each was afraid of being taken for a Philistine. A small notice above our table explained that the picture was part of the restaurant's private collection, and that a prize for the best painting of the season would soon be established and a jury selected and made known. I wanted to tell Philippe that this had been my idea too, that I had said it to them as a joke, but Philippe at once began to talk about something more interesting. He said, "Your gesture with the sandwich was so touching…your trying to hide it. Did you think I wasn't going to give you anything to eat?"

"I was just suddenly hungry," I lied. "I sometimes skip meals, and then..."

We were wasting time. He said, "I do too. I was brought up to think far too much about food. I know there are people who do not let a day go by without counting out meat and eggs and butter and bread, and I suppose they are normal—probably. A long drive in the country that has no point to it but a long, slow meal is my idea of hell. But that isn't at all what I want to say to you. What is a young, pretty widow doing in a foreign country? Why, at the party where I met her, was she wearing dark glasses? Does she hide behind them? Her hair is true chestnut, and it would be striking if it were longer. Why does she cut it as if she were leaving for military service? All these rude questions have a reason, and you are certainly as conscious of it as I am. Otherwise you would not have bothered to see me again. I have another question—I hope not the last. Between the time I met you and today, I have been asking other questions about you. Your friends tell me that you give everything away. Why do you give everything away? It sounds like a kind of imbalance. Has anyone ever tried to stop you?"

I *was* off-balance and I began trying for a sentence in French: "About the glasses, I just don't see all that well...They aren't just sunglasses, and I lost the others, the real ones."

"Who is responsible for you?" he said, holding the menu. "Is anyone?"

Now at that point I still didn't know what his name was. I had been told, but I'd forgotten. He stared at me as if he had to have an answer before he could deal with the waiter.

The answer that came to mind was, "At my age?" but "No one who can stop me giving everything away," was what I said. This had a double sense in English. It meant, also, giving away the end of a story, revealing the point too soon.

This conversation and the knowledge of what it was really about had cut my appetite, but not Philippe's: he ate a large slice of pâté with bread and butter, sole in cream, and strawberries, as if he had all the rest of his life to consider me. He spooned two strawberries on to my plate and insisted I taste them; I wondered if he had been raised to think that women need to be coaxed. It seemed to me an extraordinary physical gesture, as if we were already lovers. I didn't sense then that we could not be friends. I don't know why, but we never became friends. I smoked while he ate tranquilly, and then we talked about each other. As we spoke I was sweeping away forever a Yugoslav who was translating the correspondence of Gide into Croat, and a lesser figure, an American Fulbright scholar who couldn't choose between me and some lawyer down in Aix-en-Provence. His choice was made for him that evening without his knowing it, and his voice, saying "But honestly, I owe this guy such a lot," faded and was lost until now, as I re-create it for the sake of telling you this. My hand trembled slightly as I lifted it to my hair. (That was unusual, and that is why I remember it. My hand shook when Madame Roux handed me a letter from your sister not long ago, too.) My hair had been wet by the rain, and, yes, it must have been ugly. I wished I were of surpassing beauty, but not for myself—for Philippe.

To Marie-Thérèse Shirley said, "My husband brought me to this restaurant the first time we ever went anywhere together. He asked me if I would let my hair grow long, and I said I would. But I was impatient and would forget what I had promised."

Shifting the parcels on the chair beside her, Marie-Thérèse only said absently, "Claudie dries her hair with her head in the oven. The cost of the gas . . ." Looking up, she fixed her light eyes on Shirley in her curious unseeing way and said, "Do you know when I last ate in a restaurant? When Gérald's family was here for the baby's christening. They are Alsatians—great eaters." Shirley felt a brief astonished fright. Marie-Thérèse was probably so unused to speaking, so unrehearsed with her private stories, that she had to start from the beginning every time. "Yes, they make a cult of eating," she said. "We went to a restaurant where they could have the sort of food they are used to. I couldn't take anything more than tea for days afterward. It was the waste that sickened me. Nothing can cure me of the idea that food left over is wasted and that food eaten is also wasted in a way. Yes, the waste. All that money going into people. But being in a restaurant, here, with you, that is amusing. I am not conscious of waste. I am sure you eat in charming places every day. Your life must be charming. I envy you your charming life. Tell me, how does one go about finding a restaurant on a charming street?"

A current of air that had been chilled by rain rushed in every time the door was opened. The two shivered suddenly in their light dresses. Every other woman seemed appropriately dressed. The summer street was metamorphosed into autumn; should rain fall again, there would be a roof of umbrellas. Everyone else had been warned. Marie-Thérèse had become distant now, as if remembering how Shirley earlier had called her poor. They were not speaking in their true voices; their true voices must be lingering still on the street. The street and the day had been struck with their impression. They were not only here in the restaurant, but also on the corners of streets they had crossed. Like Shirley's parents, cycling with bluebells, they were immortal in the afternoon. She could have said to Marie-Thérèse, "I love you," but that would have frightened them both. "I shall get Claudie home to you," she said. "That's a promise." Marie-Thérèse accepted the promise, but nothing more; the summer day when she had eaten well, drunk good wine, and said what she wanted to someone who listened, was already as unreal as the nightmare in which she saw herself sleeping with such ugly ears.

13

ON A WALL in the courtyard a child had scrawled with chalk NAST DATTE FI HYBT, which meant, in code, that Philippe had come back to her. It was the final communication leading up to his return. Marie-Thérèse had been a messenger. Not for nothing had Shirley been led to choose that particular restaurant. She reviewed each prophetic phase of this day's weather: the morning as dry as grass, the wind, the rain, the cold, and now a shadow over the streets like the darkness of lilacs. She knew he would be there as she slid her key in the door. He was; he sat in the living room letting the telephone ring as if it would be spying for him to answer it now. Beside him, on the sofa, was a blue dufflebag, stuffed and laced tight. She frowned and said fiercely, "So you've come back!" He could not know that this was only the hellfire preacher in *Cold Comfort Farm* addressing his cringing flock. Once again, fatally this time, she had reflected their life in a joke he could never share, framed with a private folklore he knew nothing about.

> Dearest Mother,
>
> I saw Philippe a few minutes ago. He came to pick up one or two things and to talk about our divorce. It went quite well. He is always polite. We will divorce on grounds of "reciprocal wrongs." He was very generous about taking the blame for things I had never complained of or even thought about. If we had children this question of "reciprocal wrongs" would be useful, because you get to share their custody, being equally bad parents. As it is, for us it

just means it will be faster and cheaper. You can't divorce in August, there's no one around to divorce you, they are all taking their holidays then, but a man Philippe knows can pull some strings and have our divorce by October. We have to appear before someone and say we do not want a reconciliation, whether or not this is true. Apparently this person watches you closely and if there is the slightest hesitation he sends you home to think it over. Philippe hopes that for once I will remember where I am and what I am doing and not let my mind wander and that I won't say too much. I am to answer questions quietly and briefly with a calm, determined expression. Nor am I to show too much hostility. The judge is watching for hostility too. He wants determination and sadness.

Philippe has met a girl he likes. He thought it was right to tell me. I expected her to be a girl he already knew, but he seemed surprised I would think it. When we were together he never looked at anyone but me.

Please do not start believing and saying Philippe left me for some other person. It is not the case. The two things are separate. The new girl is new, new, new. He is not going to do anything headstrong and intends to wait at least a year.

I hope you can read my writing this time. Philippe has taken both typewriters. I have been leading up to this in my letters—at least I tried to.

He and I can't see each other again because of collusion.

I meant to ask him why he had married me, so that I could tell other people. But perhaps no one will ask me that any more now. I wanted to tell him that I was not sure why he had left me. I haven't behaved in any way that was not predictable from our first conversation. Well, I said nothing. I'm about as I always was, so please don't worry.

Shirley ended her letter there. She could have added, "He has done me one favor. He had me watched—yes, watched. So I wasn't paranoid when I kept seeing strange men on the stairs. He has what he calls 'evidence,' but as I am agreeing to everything and not making trouble nor asking for money, he is willing to go along on the grounds of reciprocal wrongs. What made him think I would ask him for money?" All that had been prophetic out of the day, finally, was something she had said to Marie-Thérèse about a man cutting his losses. Philippe had cut his as impulsively as he had gambled. She understood now why there could never be a trace of her exchange of stories with Marie-Thérèse. She saw her short life with Philippe pulled out of the ground and left dying. The threadlike roots tried to draw strength from thin air. She thought of the permanent shadows left on walls in Japan after the explosion. She and Philippe were without shadow. They were soundless; they had dissolved.

Her last conversation with James in Paris was all but drowned out by the radio which James kept on at top level, perhaps hoping it would prevent his having to listen to Shirley. He had turned in his rented television set, sold his Braun stereo speakers to Madame Roux at a price she considered a bargain and that James knew to be a profit for himself, and had kept nothing but a transistor he was taking back to Greece. For the fourth or the fifth time he explained, "You put the apartment in Philippe's name when you married him."

"It wasn't in anyone's name. There was never a lease."

"Philippe had a lease. Madame Roux gave him a lease."

"Why didn't he tell me?"

"He probably did and you forgot."

"How could Madame Roux give him a lease? She was only the go-between."

"Shirley, *she* was the landlady."

"Then why didn't she just come out and say so?" James sighed, and she said, "I know—it's like educating a horse. I feel like one of those white horses trying to waltz."

James said, "Madame Roux owns your apartment. I owned this one. I sold it to her. I tried to interest Philippe in buying yours, but it was too late. I was trying to protect you. Now she owns most of the building."

"How about the Australian? What does he own?'

"Which Australian?"

"Sutton McGrath. Remember, Madame Roux had everyone sign a petition about his guitar? He lives up on the sixth floor in one of the maids' rooms. Who owns it?"

"I have never met an Australian," said James, "but my guess would be that Madame Roux owns quite a lot of the sixth floor. She tried to sell me your apartment. I would have been your landlord." At this suggestion of intimacy between them he looked briefly toward the bedroom, but had already changed his mind even before she said, "No, please, let's straighten this out." He was on his way to Greece not for a holiday, but to live, to pick up a life abandoned for a five-year holiday. She was part of the holiday; so was Rose.

He began again. "You and Philippe are living apart, but you are living in his legal domicile."

"He can't put me out of my own home. Can he?"

"He won't, but he can."

"But I *found* it. It's *mine*. It's my home. He just moved in, and then he moved out."

"But in the meantime he had a lease in his name."

"I've paid rent. I paid after he left. He paid for June, but I paid for July, and I've paid in advance for August."

"He abandoned it, yes," said James. "Abandoned the conjugal domicile. But so did you. First you stayed with Renata and went around telling everyone; then you spent every night up here."

"But I hadn't abandoned anything! Oh, James, I just don't understand this way of thinking. James, you're a kind of friend of Madame Roux's, aren't you?"

"In business. For the rest she is a cow, and I was afraid she would be a pest, always watching from the shop window."

"She talked to you, though. She talked about Philippe and me."

"No more than you do, poor Shirley. You talked to her again the other day. I saw you."

"I just told her my mother isn't well and that if I suddenly turn up in Canada to see how she is it will make her suspicious. I felt like telling somebody and Madame Roux just happened to be there. I keep wondering—it's not my business, and yet it is—what you and she said to each other."

"We were talking one day when you came in, and I did go out the back door. We were talking about the sale of this place. She didn't want anyone to know, and she asked me to leave when the bell rang. Later on she told me it was only you, so I might have stayed."

"No, I meant when you talked to her before I married Philippe, when you were still pushing those affectionate notes under my door. What did she tell you then?"

"That you were charming. Now I must phone for a taxi. If you hadn't given up your car to Philippe you might have driven me to the airport."

"I won't drive a car, and I don't think I gave it up. I think it was cheaper to buy it in dollars or something, and I think he paid me in francs. I never took much notice of money. Madame Roux and I used to be friends. What did she tell you?"

"That you were charming," he said again, and smiled.

"Oh, *please* tell me. It would help me now."

"If you are hysterical I can't talk to you at all."

"I'll never say a word, I'll never repeat a thing, I'll never go back to her. I'll never hold it against you ... I swear."

"Just the ordinary things women say about each other," James said at last rather coldly. "That you were a whore who slept with anybody. She didn't believe you and Philippe were married at first."

"Did *you* think we weren't married?"

"I won't be cross-examined," said James.

"We've never talked before, except in bed. If this is the only conversation we can have I don't much like it." She was quiet as he dialed for his taxi, and when he had finished she said, "You're leaving. Claudie has left her family; she's in a crummy hotel. She wants to live my life and she seems to think that's the kind of place I would have chosen. Rose—where did you say Rose was? The Isle of Wight?

I've never heard of it. Renata—Renata has vanished. Karel's in Ibiza—he *would* be there. Philippe is going to a spa for his liver. Which is the liver one? He really did have hepatitis; he said so. I wish I could go somewhere in August and September. I don't want to sit here waiting for October and the reconciliation meeting where we're both going to say no."

James, watching for the taxi from the window, said without turning, "Come to Greece, if you think you would like it."

"And stay with you?"

"No, we can't in Athens. You would be with my mother."

"Would she want me? Wouldn't she think there was something between us?" He turned then, and for the first time since she had known him he looked embarrassed. She said kindly, "Your mother would know right away I wasn't a girl you were going to marry. Right?"

"Could you learn another language?" he said. "If you had to?"

"I learned French, sort of."

"Could you learn Greek?"

"You mean you want a Greek husband for me? You can't want to marry me yourself."

"Oh, I don't know," said James with a trace of Philippe's elegance. "I owe you something."

"I owe you more. You gave me company when I wanted it, and although it looked scandalous to Madame Roux, and it seemed incredible to Philippe, it wasn't complicated for me. Now you're offering me a refuge when I need it. You do mean it, don't you?"

"About coming to Greece? I mean *that*," he said, surprised, as if it were the easiest thing he had ever promised. "The taxi," he said, looking distractedly at his cases. She stood up; they moved to the door together.

"James," she said rapidly, "Why was it a secret about all the buying and selling of apartments? You'd have lost money if I had known? I talk too much? This is what people are like," she said, marveling. "All the creeping and rushing around, like little animals. I never hear or see any of it. You and Madame Roux, Madame Roux and Philippe. There's something I didn't tell you. Philippe had us watched."

"What else could he have done? He wanted his divorce."

"He could have talked to me—explained. Do you think I'd have hung on to him? Screamed and cried? Asked for money?"

"He had to protect himself," said James. "Supposing you were pregnant? By law he would still be the father. As soon as I saw his funny men I understood. I went to him at once and I said to him, 'Your funny men can stand there forever. But mutual grievances, my dear fellow, will get you the cheapest and quickest divorce.' Now what are you crying about? Would you have liked two funny men walking in at five in the morning? I saved us both, my dear," said James, meaning himself. "You must not cry. I understand that it is very sad for you to see me leaving, but you will come to Athens, and my mother is a very nice woman. Please sit down for a moment. The taxi can wait. You cannot go out of here crying. What made you cry?"

"It's all right. I've stopped."

"Perhaps it was Madame Roux? Philippe did not care for her. He thought she was tougher and stronger than you, for a time, and then he didn't understand you any more. Madame Roux thought she was stronger and tougher than Philippe, but she was only more cunning. He started off by telling her too much—unusual for a Frenchman. They don't say much to women as a rule." He smiled secretly; no woman existed to whom he would ever have told too much. This was about as much as he would ever say.

"Philippe talked to women sometimes, but not to me. It was my fault."

"He is with a stupid young girl now," said James. "Her name is Claire. She has golden hair down to her arse, and a nice nose. Her teeth were capped by the best dentist in Paris. You could still rescue him from this healthy young girl if you cared to. It would be an act of kindness."

"Oh, James, I've done so much of that. I don't know how any more. Think of Claudie alone in that hotel room, believing she's been saved from her family. Even when people say they want to be rescued they don't really. I can't help Philippe. He never really thought we were married. It was like being in transit between two flights or between two wars or something. It didn't count. He may have used me to get away from home, or just to be in love. He *did* love me, you know, and he wanted someone unlike his mother. But in the end he wanted someone like her too. Anyway, not like me."

"Now I must depart," said James, clearly irritated by this talk of love, which Shirley had laughed at from him. "How many men do you think you will marry? They will all remember you with nostalgia and regret."

"Oh. Thank you."

After a moment's silence, which was meant to let her know that his offer did not spring from impulsiveness, he said, "Come to Greece. Any time. Tomorrow. Stay until your divorce. If you want to marry again I can find you the person, and you will see that having known me was not a waste of time. I found my sisters husbands. I might even marry you myself." He expected her not to take this seriously. When he married it would be to an heiress and a virgin, like Philippe's new Claire.

"I have to look after Claudie before I leave," she said, "just that one thing. Then I'll come."

"As you like," he said. "But you are a fool, Shirley. All this looking after people. It's exactly what Philippe detested. Luckily I understand you."

"James, do you?"

"Oh, yes, very much. More than anyone I knew in Paris. Come to Greece. You'll see. You'll *hate* it!"

Clasping her hands to quiet them (she had been calm as long as she was passing almond cakes and pouring tea), Madame Maurel said to her guest, "When Claudie was fourteen she looked at boys. That was how it began. The dining-room table in the old apartment was near a window, and we had to pull it away from the wall so that we could all sit round it. Claudie would help when she was made to, but then she would always make an unnecessary trip around the table so as to look out of the window at men. It was during the first months of the Algerian War. There were more policemen on the streets and more conscripts about and Claudie liked to look at them. All the way around the table," said Madame Maurel, shaking her head. "We stopped that."

"How?" said Shirley.

"How do you stop a girl of fourteen doing anything? Slapped her face, screamed. Children forget scoldings but they remember blows. One day her father became furious because of the noise she was making. You see, Claudie would never cry out when she was hit, but she always had an impertinent answer to everything and she would suddenly scream for no reason. I had locked her in a room that day and she was kicking the door and insulting me. He went into the room where she was and shut the door behind him. He said something—I have never known what. She came out with him and she was pale, and for days everything disgusted her. Whatever he told her made her ill, but it stopped her. She never went near that window again."

"Something nasty in the woodshed."

"What?"

"I'm sorry. Now I've annoyed two people with one book."

"This is boring for you," said Maman.

"No, please go on. I can't talk to Claudie unless I have something new to say to her and I can't say anything unless I know what she has heard before."

"It was a difficult time," said Madame Maurel. "Marie-Thérèse hardly spoke a word to me in those days. Oh, wait until you have daughters!"

"Mine will be blessed with trick spiders and exploding cigars, as promised," said Shirley. "Whatever your husband said didn't have an eternal effect."

Maman sighed and said, "She did have a child, but only that one."

Shirley did not add to this, "She may be having another." She wondered how Monsieur Maurel would take the news. She thought of how quickly annoyed he was, as though his nerves lay like a network outside the skin. It must have been like living with an incurable toothache. She pitied him, though it was Maman and the others who suffered for Monsieur Maurel's aching tooth. "Claudie thinks you have not had a good life," she said. "She thinks you were a slave to your husband."

"Naturally I have been," said Maman composedly.

"She thinks he is egocentric, and spoiled..."

"Men are naturally selfish," Maman said.

"...and that everyone has been sacrificed to him." She wanted to go on but her French was giving out. She said, "Claudie just wanted to live like a normal person. She wanted to earn her living. She thought that unless she left you she would never learn anything except housework."

Maman glanced at the large Norman wardrobe standing out in the hall. On the top shelves were the textbooks of subjects Claudie had begun and let go: she had started Spanish, bookbinding, pottery, bee-keeping (fortune to be made supplying honey to bakers of *pain d'épices*), costume design and textile design. She had tried a dozen things, but nothing paid as well and took so little effort as living at home and quarreling with the family. No wonder Maman was distressed and suspicious at her having left!

Shirley said, "Every girl looks at her mother and wants to have a better life than she had."

Maman twisted the little pin at her throat. "Why should my daughter have a better life than mine?" she said. Shirley had forgotten why. "Do you know," said Maman shyly, "when Claudie brought us Alain, well, it was too bad, but we weren't the first decent family where such a thing had happened. As Alain was to think I was his mother, and had our name, we moved here to a new neighborhood and avoided a scandal. It didn't break me. But when Marie-Thérèse left I felt as if part of myself had gone. They lived with us, you know, until about a year ago."

"Papa and Gérald and children and Mémé and everybody. You all lived *here*?"

"Not in this apartment. First we had the flat just across the landing. We bought it when Alain was born. We had three bedrooms. We built an extra shower in the kitchen because Gérald insisted. Two of the children slept with their parents, and Claudie and Mémé together with two others, and Alain with us."

"But weren't you terribly crowded?"

"We didn't feel crowded. We understood each other. Claudie was difficult and Marie-Thérèse never looked at me, but we were a family. I could do anything I liked with Marie-Thérèse once. I raised her to be my ideal of a daughter. I *made* Marie-Thérèse. I made her into the daughter I wanted. Then she married that... that *Ziff* from Strasbourg." Maman looked weak, defiant and proud. She said, "Until she was seventeen she never made a remark in public without first looking at me to see if it was all right. My husband preferred Claudie, I am sorry to say. I was so unhappy when I knew Claudie was on the way! I had my one daughter and she was all I wanted. The reason Claudie is so large is that while I was expecting her I felt sick unless I was eating. I would sit down to a cup of hot chocolate and buttered bread and I would feel well again, for about half an hour. Then I'd have the nausea again. Marie-Thérèse was devoted. She would lie in bed beside me, stroking my face. She didn't know about babies and I didn't want to spoil her innocence, and she must have thought it strange, my being so blown up and fat and hungry and sick. Yes, my husband liked Claudie. Claudie is so... pretty..."

She went on rambling, putting bits of almond cake in her mouth, stirring sugar in her tea, and at last she said what Shirley was waiting to hear: "If you think anything can be done about Claudie, you had better see my husband. I shall never go to her," said Maman, weak Maman. "I wouldn't go to her if she were dying. Claudie will have to come to me. I don't care who brings her." Wondering why Shirley had looked away so suddenly, Maman turned too and saw the reproduction of the Dufy regatta. "Naturally, you would never see that on a wall in America," she remarked.

He did not sound surprised, hearing Shirley on the telephone. She thought again what poised voices most Frenchmen had and how well they spoke their language, never hesitating or stumbling. He told her to come to his office, where no member of the family had been admitted. It was in the rue d'Amsterdam in a building intended for shabby living. The offices seemed improvised; the stairs were filthy and dark. A secretary sat like a wet dog outside his door. Smeared windows near his desk looked across a court, over a large skylight, and into other offices. Shirley could see prison light shining on girls wearing nylon smocks. She sat down on the chair reserved for clients. There was nothing in the room to suggest the business of the place. Papa's firm exported every kind of electrical machine, Claudie had said, from coffee grinders to transformers, but Claudie may have been wrong.

He placed his hands flat on the desk—Claudie's gesture. He was self-contained, but his silence seemed almost excited. It must have been his tactic in business to let the other man commit himself. He knew why Shirley had come; in spite of the family's being forbidden to call the office, Maman had probably confirmed that Shirley was on her way.

"Well, I'm here for Claudie," Shirley said. "She's alone in a cheap hotel, she can't pay her bill, and the boy she was living with is leaving France. I *think*. I *think* that sums it up. She may be pregnant too. I don't know."

"Really? Claudie is indolent, lazy and dirty. I am astonished that she isn't pregnant every day of the week. What else have you come to say?"

"She wants to be forgiven. No, not so much forgiven as accepted by her family. Accepted as she is." He looked at her, nodding. "She doesn't think she should have another child. I won't help her get rid of it. I absolutely refuse to have anything to do with it because I have just helped another friend, and I ... at least, I have said I won't help. Because if she has to abandon this one as she did Alain ..." She felt as if the wheels of this conversation were sloughed in mud. That was because she did not know what she wanted to say. She was alone with Papa, therefore privileged. She had an audience, and what an audience! She had, all to herself, the ear of power. If only she were quick and clever she might have known what impression of her he had taken in a moment ago, when he relaxed suddenly and sat back in his chair.

"Yes, and so she abandoned Alain," he said. "What next?"

"Well, he hardly seems her child, does he? She has nothing to say about the way he is brought up."

"Is that what you came to my office to say?"

"No, although I do think it. I don't think Alain should still use a pot, for instance, or sleep with his grandmother and all that. Claudie isn't really ready for another baby."

"She hasn't asked me. If she does ask, she will hear. She has managed until now without asking anything."

"She is old enough to have a personal life," said Shirley, sounding prim.

"Exactly. She doesn't need my advice about how to carry it on."

"But what are we going to do? She's alone in a hotel on a street full of prostitutes. When I look out of her window and see them, I get the feeling that is how Claudie will end up. She left home for someone who doesn't want her. She isn't fit to live alone, though that is what she ought to be doing."

"I heard rumors around the house, echoes in the kitchen, that she was planning to take up residence abroad."

Shirley muttered, "They wanted to go to the Middle East and work with refugees." As she spoke she knew she was saying something idiotic, which no one had ever believed. She imagined refugees in Lebanon confiding their lives and destinies to Claudie. She came back to reality and said, "What would you do with another child?"

"I? Nothing. I shall have nothing whatever to do with another child."

"Claudie isn't fit to..." Now it was clear. She sat up straighter and became sure of herself. Yes, this was the way it was: because of the upbringing he had given Claudie, she was not fit to bring up anyone else. "She needs about eighty thousand francs. Please don't think I suggested it—I hate the whole business. And she owes the hotel too..."

"I hope you didn't suggest it, for your sake. You could be sent to prison."

This was the second time jail had been mentioned. People kept on asking for her help and then wanting to jail her for giving it.

"Someone has to do something," she said. "Someone should give her some money."

"Someone probably will."

"Do you think *I* should?"

"I haven't said I think anything. But I can see you are deeply interested in the matter, so interested that you haven't yet said what you have come to see me about."

"She might kill herself," said Shirley.

"Oh. Yes. How did she say she was going to do that?"

"Don't laugh, please. I have another friend who is a much tougher proposition than Claudie and even she tried. I could get the money for her. But it seems wrong from your point of view. Dishonorable."

Now he smiled, as if she had said something endearing. "There is also the father," he said.

She was about to answer, "You are the father," but of course he meant Jean-Luc. She had never considered Jean-Luc as a possible father, any more than Karel. Even Renata had not counted on Karel to help. He was expected to disappear until the problems were settled and the danger was past. "I don't know about him. His family has money, but he doesn't earn much. He seemed to be counting on this refugee job."

"I hear phrases at home, complete sentences sometimes, even when I am trying not to listen. I hear you thought it would be a good idea for my daughter to leave her son and her home and live with a jobless young man."

"I didn't know she *had* really left home until Marie-Thérèse told me! I didn't believe it. I don't really know this Jean-Luc. I've just met him once. I hardly know Claudie. To tell you the truth, I really don't know much about the situation."

The telephone on his desk rang. He picked it up, listened, and put it down without speaking. It had given him time to think over and sum up what had been said. "You have talked to her about freedom from her family, haven't you."

"She talked to me, mostly. I do think it is wrong for a girl her age to have to ask for pocket money. I think she should work."

"Yes," he said, and glanced out the window to the office across the court, where stenographers sat round-shouldered.

"That isn't work," said Shirley. "It's . . ." but she did not know the French for "drudgery." "I only meant I thought she should be able to support Alain."

"For the next twenty years? It would be agreeable."

"You don't believe any of it, do you?" Shirley said. "You don't think she had even the beginning of an idea." The sky could not be seen from this room, but the courtyard went black and she felt the approach of the summer storm. She knew she must stand up, shake hands, say good-bye and apologize for having disturbed him on a busy day. "Claudie tried to be free," she muttered.

"Free to do what?" he said. "To get money from her father to give to her lovers? To have a dirty life in a dirty hotel? What else did you offer her?"

"I don't lead a dirty life."

Now he was not facing Shirley, but, unknown to him, Shirley's mother. Behind her was still another person, a tall woman who had sat in her kitchen reading to the unemployed while they spread butter over toast. One day she would be frightening to men such as Monsieur Maurel. Tall as her grandmother, unshakeable as her mother, she spoke back at him out of a future. He sensed, though may not have remembered, what he had said; may then have heard something like "How dare you?" and sidestepped without actually retreating.

"A sad life, I meant," he said.

Sad! He should have been around last winter, any Saturday, with the telephone ringing, and James not understanding that she was married and that Philippe would never like him, and poor Gertrude telling about the man who was not likely to divorce his wife. He ought to have known Renata!

"No, not sad," she said, in this room equipped for nothing else but sadness though of course she could not be sure. "I've thought *you* were jealous sometimes. Something to do with Claudie."

He said, "Claudie is a concern, a charge, like an indigent parent. My intelligent daughter married a fool. As for my not wanting Claudie to work—do you know what *Arbeit Macht Frei* means? It was written over the gates of concentration camps. How did you meet Claudie?"

"She was sent to me by St. Joseph," Shirley said. "I had asked St. Joseph to send me someone who could change my life. Don't you think it is strange that I should have heard the same story twice a few weeks apart? That two girls should have come to me saying they were pregnant, and that this was catastrophic, and that they should ask me what could be done? Why the same story? Why me?"

"If you were interested in criminal justice, and made your profession follow your interest, you would keep hearing about murder," he said.

"What do you mean?" she asked, and said to herself, Why aren't people ever clear? Why don't they say what they mean?

"My father sounded quite amiable on the telephone," Claudie said. "I am grateful to you. August is approaching and the matter of the holidays had to be settled. Maman has taken a villa at Dinard. A month in Dinard should be good for me."

"Did your father tell you that this time if you come home it is to stay?"

"No. He has all of August to tell me that."

Claudie sat up in bed in her hotel room with her hair on her shoulders. She looked so like Renata when Renata had been frightened by the shadow of a rat that Shirley said, "Are you certain you want to go home? No one is forcing you. I just feel that your plans weren't quite ready...you should have been better prepared..." Her own voice sounded high and anxious; she wondered what her audience consisted of—if she intended someone other than Claudie to hear.

A magnifying mirror hung from a ribbon around Claudie's neck. Staring down into the glass she outlined the shape of her eyes. Her mouth was pulled to one side with the effort of concentrating, and it was a moment before she could answer: "I don't feel well, but I am not ill. Not at all. I'll outlive everyone." She pulled the mirror away, offered chocolates to Shirley, and had some herself. She had been reading some hitherto unpublished letters of Chekov in a thick little magazine that was unpleasant to touch. She had cut the pages with a comb; the bed was covered with paper crumbs. The magazine had been Marcel Proust's parting gift. "Jean-Luc really had meant to leave," said Claudie. "But what could I do without help, without money, without my parents' consent, and without being married? I can't tell from here whether it is a fine day," she went on, squinting at the window. "And don't tell me it has to be nice because it is Paris. Some streets are always gray."

A slim reddish creature—a cockroach?—moved along the base of the wall. Out of Shirley's capacity for forgetting crawled a live memory: Renata, and the plastic basin with the pattern of cornflowers.

"I hate Paris now," Shirley said. "All I can see are garages and banks and the whores down there, under your window. The smell of the bistro downstairs nearly made me vomit when I passed it just now. I've forgotten why I live here. I don't remember why I came."

"If my family could hear you they wouldn't believe it," said Claudie, beginning to pin up her hair. "They think you know what you are doing every minute. Do you remember when you first met Papa, and you took the box of pastries away from him as if it belonged to you? Their private name for you after that was 'the Roman general.'"

"Your mother called me that? And Marie-Thérèse?"

"Yes, all of them. It was envy, of course. I wish you were my mother."

"I was about six when you were born."

She could see into the windows of an apartment across the street. She seemed to be looking at miles of parquet flooring.

"Now what if my children's stories were collected into a book?" said Claudie, leaning back. "It would be an immediate bestseller. I could support Alain and have him taught languages. I could travel. I might have an operation on my nose. All the women in my family have ugly ears and noses. Do you know my story about the squirrels who live in a tunnel?"

"What kind of story is that?"

"One I wrote for children. I'm talking to you about my stories. These squirrels are in their burrow underground."

"You mean rabbits, don't you? Or foxes?"

"I've never seen a fox," said Claudie crossly. "The two baby squirrels belong to a doomed race. In the story the baby squirrels and their mother are sitting on a bench. The mother has chosen to die with the little ones..."

"What kind of death?"

"By order. It has been ordered, and all the little ones are doomed. The mother is sitting there waiting to die with them. It will not change anything. She is really very stupid. It is an obstinate animal decision, and she is sitting there in an obstinate animal way. Outside the door the father squirrel dances up and down and hammers on the door in a rage. His rage adds to the terror."

"What is he so angry about?"

"It isn't explained. It just adds to the terror."

"That's a charming story for children," Shirley said. "Perhaps you could have it filmed and shown at bedtime. The condemned babies, the ignorant sacrificial mother, and the father's anger creating a new fear... and, of course, there is the whole new idea about squirrels living underground."

"You know the club, the Orpailleur? You've seen their puppets?

Jean-Luc knew a man there who wanted to make a puppet play out of that story. But nothing came of it."

"I've never heard of the Orpailleur as a place for children's stories."

"No, perhaps not my stories. With whiskey at two thousand francs a glass, they would want everything clear. Perhaps I could write another ending. You know that my father is very ill, don't you? Did Marie-Thérèse tell you?"

"Who told you?"

"I read anything I find lying around. As you do, Shirley. We're alike. I know everything. Papa may be going to die, I think."

"It is not your father who is ill. It is my mother. The only person I mentioned it to in Paris is Madame Roux. So you've been there too, have you? Yes? And she told you I was a great reader, particularly of my husband's mail?"

"Have you ever made love with a dying man?" said Claudie, very frightened, waiting for Shirley to forget what she had said.

"Question for question," said Shirley. "Is Papa the father of Alain?"

Claudie stood on her feet now, arms akimbo. She was perfectly groomed and dressed from the top of her head to her waist. From under the bed, pulling the garments with one foot, she retrieved a pair of stockings and a garter belt. "I had a skirt somewhere," she said, looking for it. She suddenly flashed her most innocent smile. "I wanted so much to live like you, Shirley," she said. "My dream was to have money and love and never grow old. I wanted to be like you, happy. You are sitting on my skirt, I'm afraid. I shall have to ask you to give it to me. Chekov lost his virginity at thirteen. He had terrible parents too."

When her father came in she wept in his arms. Shirley buried her face in Chekov's letters. When she next looked, Claudie sat on the edge of the bed, pulling up her stockings. Shirley turned her back and she fixed her eyes on the windows across the street. It embarrassed her to be here with Papa while Claudie finished putting her clothes on. He stood, cold and impatient, with his arms folded; but when he came to stand behind Shirley, as if to see what she was seeing, the touch of his hand on her arm seemed a movement of pity.

All right, then, she thought. Settle my problems. Run my life. How much would it cost me? She gave up wondering. Claudie would know soon.

The two Maurels said good-bye as if this were Shirley's room. In an odd way she felt that it could be and that the tag ends were for her to tie together. She had been unable to bring order to her own kitchen the morning of Whitsunday, but within other people's lives she had automatic gestures of neatness.

She opened each of the drawers. Claudie had left behind a photograph of Alain. It was the picture that was to have been shown to the ex-priest and the sculptress. He sat on one ankle, in a classic children's studio pose, with his weight on an arm and a hand, and a light spot on his forehead, and looked dully into space. Around the edges of the frame, all but obliterating him, were pictures of people Claudie liked as well or better: Claudie herself, and Gérard Philippe as "Le Cid," and James Dean. The last two were dead. Face down was an old passport picture of Papa, with his tie knotted up under his chin. Change the hair and tie, and he was almost handsome; at any rate, he had once been young. He looked as if he might easily recite Wordsworth's "Ode to Duty," and he looked much like his elder daughter.

She found an empty bottle of Coty's Emeraude, faded and sweet, the neck of the bottle mossy with dust, and an advertisement torn out of a newspaper: a film director was looking for a girl of fifteen to play Madame de Sévigné's daughter. The film would be played in modern dress. Madame de Sévigné, a rich widow living in a suite at the Ritz ... The girl, her daughter, was to be pure, beautiful, talented, inexperienced and perverse.

Shirley left the door open behind her. When she came out to the street she had a foretaste of autumn. She imagined August and autumn, then winter, through the window of the empty room. The whores on the corner spread newspapers over their heads as the first drops of rain began to fall. The smell of frying from the dark bistro, which had been nauseating only a few hours before, now had its winter aspect and suggested shelter and warmth. She would leave Paris the day after tomorrow. When she came back in two months' time, the rain would have washed everything away.

14

IT RAINED through autumn and winter and through part of the next spring, and then one April Friday was suddenly, blindingly hot. Shirley looked in cafés she had known and saw nothing hut strangers. Gérald Ziff stopped, turned; she turned too. He waved at her. They looked at each other and smiled without speaking. The girl beside him was younger than Marie-Thérèse. She was tall and very thin with curly hair and freckles. She was a girl who would keep turning her ankles and slipping out of her shoes. Shirley wondered if he was spending August in Paris this year too.

He must have trusted Shirley, for he dared tell the family he had seen her. The next afternoon, as she knelt in the boxroom separating rubbish from the rubbish she was obliged to keep, and looking quickly through whatever Philippe had forgotten or left behind (his personal property was none of her business now), the telephone rang in the living room. When it persisted she answered it, ready to take a message for the new tenant of the apartment, Sutton McGrath. The listing in the book was still "Higgins S-M, Decoration" and might be for some time to come, but the telephone was now Mc-Grath's. Even the lock on the door had been changed. Madame Roux was guardian of the keys.

"Yes, I suppose I do sound surprised," she said to Madame Maurel. "I don't expect anyone to call me here. I don't live here now. Yes, eight months, nearly nine. No, not in Greece. I was in Greece for a few weeks. I have just come from there now. Yes, I can come to you, but not for a meal. I haven't time. Tomorrow, Saturday, in the afternoon."

She had to turn the key in every day to Madame Roux. Madame Roux would part the bead curtain wearing, as always, a smile for a customer. When she saw it was Shirley she did not efface the smile but let her eyes go dead. She held out her hand.

"Finished?"

"No, I'm afraid I shall have to come back tomorrow, and perhaps once after that."

"He is very patient," said Madame Roux. "He would have been within his rights to have had everything belonging to you put out in the courtyard."

"Was he within his rights to move into an apartment for which I was still paying rent? Never mind. It doesn't matter."

A hand parted the bead curtain; a blond head looked out. The guitar-playing McGrath said, "You can take your time, you know. I'm sorry about the mixup, but I do have a lease. I put your stuff in that little room; I thought it would make it easier for you."

"Yes, thank you. It does. You were wise to insist on a lease. I never thought of anything like that."

"I didn't insist on anything," he said. "Madame Roux had it ready for me. Didn't you?" He seemed uncertain.

"Did I not!" she said, opening the door and letting the bell ring. "And, oh, Mrs. Higgins, your mail. Some personal mail. I have kept it for you, as you have no mailbox now."

Shirley was careful to rip the unopened letters across before throwing them away; otherwise the garbage men were likely to fish them out of the cans and post them again, thinking they had been dropped there by mistake. Out of today's handful she kept only one. Every inch of the envelope was covered with forwarding addresses. It had been mailed in Canada in July and had been traveling to the wrong places ever since.

> Dear Shirl:
> A word to say I am safely in Three Rivers as you sounded frantic when we talked on the phone. Am staying with the family of the young man I told you about that I met on the

train coming up from Rome. Getting on pretty well but don't follow all the gabbling. The young man has won an award for the best TV play of the month. It is about some boy practicing self-abuse in a Jesuit school and all that goes through his mind—waves on beach, showers of plum blossom, sheep grazing, Hiroshima. The play does not tell why these thoughts occur. Probably had no mother. Hope all your worries are over, tho' they seldom are until the grave, ha ha.

Your old Friend
Cat Castle

The Norman wardrobe had been moved out of the Maurels' entrance hall and into the living room, and most of the furniture had been re-covered with Gordon Hunting tartan.

"Claudie's idea," said Maman. "She had great gifts as a decorator. She is now planning to work in that direction."

Maman's hair was half gray, as if she had achieved what she wanted finally and no longer felt any need to look young. The gray made her seem less fragile, more determined. Papa was dressed as if he had indulged in a shopping weekend in London. The new Anglomania Shirley had noticed in store windows and on the boulevards had overtaken even the Maurels. The tiered First Communion pictures were still in a corner, with a newcomer among them: a framed magazine cover showing the young widow and her two children under the printed words *"Hommage à Jackie Kennedy."* It was a family photograph, like the picture of Marie-Thérèse as a bride.

Maman said, "You are so thin!"

"I always was."

"Perhaps. But were you always so fair?" Maman looked accusing. Now that she had stopped dying her own hair she had become suspicious of everyone else.

"It was the sun in Greece. No, I wasn't there the whole winter. First I went to Canada. Last August. Yes, suddenly. I was sent for.

My mother died." All she could see in her mind was the picture someone had taken, and forced her to look at, of her mother in her coffin: her mother, who had never worn makeup, made foreign with lipstick and rouge. "I had to stay quite some time. There was so much to do. Everything had been ransacked or pillaged or given away. At the end, there was no one to stop her from giving everything away. Most of the gifts were made in her lifetime. By the time she died the pictures were out of their frames and stacked around the walls on the floor. Sometimes people she had given them to only took the frames. The rugs were rolled and tied with string. She had given away all the linen. She had embroidered linen from her own mother's trousseau that had never been used. Gone. She gave to anyone who came to the door. She gave my christening silver to the postman. It had my name on it. I might have wanted it for my own children ... but perhaps it's better not to hand anything on."

"But her fortune?" said Maman, clasping her hands.

"Bills, mostly. There was no money in my family. Did I behave as if there was? I didn't mean to. I don't believe my mother really left bills. She wasn't like that. All sorts of people came round claiming from me. I had no way of proving, one way or another. She never kept records and never wrote her own checks."

"But *you*—?" said Maman.

"Nothing, except her library. She left me her books. She tried to give them away too, but of course no one would have them. That's how they happened to come to me. I had to pay someone to cart them off. I only wanted my childhood books but they had vanished ages ago. I don't think she imagined she was doing anything *against* me. She may have had a motive, but it wasn't hostility or revenge. She knew I had something from my mother-in-law. By the way, I am Mrs. Higgins again. I was finally divorced for desertion. I suppose it was only fair. You don't keep your divorced husband's name in France. I didn't know until Philippe's lawyer sent me a registered letter threatening me with something."

Maman and Papa Maurel looked at each other, not covertly; it was not a sly exchange, but a bold, frank, long look. Shirley had never seen them look at each other before. Her words had brought out in them whatever they had in common—something to do with money, family, privacy, one's race. *How barbaric, how curious this is,* they were telling each other. *What an eccentric family she must have. How fortunate that nothing like that could happen to us. Nothing unusual will ever touch the Maurels.* The pain she had felt when she looked at the photographs began to recede. She wanted to tell them, "Of course I'm peculiar, but then I was born feet first." She saw a silhouette in the passage and then a girl of about fifteen came into the room. Her hair hung to within an inch of her shoulders. She was dressed in a short skirt and a tight pink sweater. As she sat down, Shirley saw the edge of a lace petticoat. The girl wore her high-heeled shoes awkwardly, as if she knew they were too grownup for her.

"Hello," said Claudie in a shy voice. She pressed Shirley's hand and sat down on a footstool, pulling her skirt to her knees with care, and then resting her chin on her hands. She looked up as if at three adults, and as though wondering what she herself would be like one day. While the others talked, she played with the ring Shirley had given her, a band set with turquoise and pearls. There was something so passive in her waxen young face that Shirley felt she was again seeing a picture of the rouged and powdered dead. It seemed to her she had seen traces of this effigy from the beginning. Yes, in the taxi, that first day. She remembered Claudie's face, and she recalled a drowned pigeon in the current of the Seine.

"My girl," her mother called her now, as if Claudie had found a relationship but lost her own name.

"I am looking for a job," said Claudie plaintively, "but everywhere I go, they tell me I am too young. When I say I have a child to support no one will believe me. I am so tired of it."

Papa almost smiled. "Ah, my girl," said Maman again. Claudie turned her head in the old way to see the effect on Shirley of what she had just said, and for a second Shirley saw a living face.

"The brasserie is closed, Claudie. They have built a great fence around it and they say there will be a supermarket on that corner."

Claudie looked as if she had never heard of a brasserie, that or any other, in her life.

"What about James?" said Maman.

"James is all right. He is with an architect in Athens. He really is an architect—at least, he is being one in Athens. I saw his sisters and Jo-Jo and Rex. They all have very large flats in very white buildings. James is at home, though he pretends he hates it and misses Paris. He bullies his married sisters." All eyes were on her face now, and she went on bravely. "I would never have fitted in. I couldn't have spent my life eating cakes and talking about movies, which is all there is for women. Or gossiping, and it isn't interesting gossip. The Parthenon is lighted up, but one can't live on that. There are foreigners, but they don't work. They are on the fringe. I couldn't live that way, *or* live like a Greek. James says he would rather be here but I'm not sure that it's true. He can always come back to Paris for holidays and be sentimental. But there was nothing for me, nothing at all."

"So you are not married and not engaged," said Maman with satisfaction. "Like our little Claudie. But Claudie has time."

"She seems to be giving herself time," said Shirley. "Wouldn't we all, if we knew how? It's true that I'm twenty-seven now, but Jane Austen could have been wrong."

No one asked who Miss Austen was. They were through with foreigners forever. Still, they were sorry when Shirley rose to leave, and they kissed her as if she were departing on a journey instead of having returned from one. Claudie's lips were cool and reluctant as a fastidious child's.

Papa saw Shirley out to the lift. He stood with his hand on the elevator button, as if he could make it climb faster. He said, without lowering his voice. "Claudie is fine now."

"My girl!" they heard Maman cry within the flat. "Where are you? What are you doing? Is Alain awake? Asleep?"

"She seems calm," said Shirley.

"Claudie is happy," said Papa, as if he had decided it that way once and for all. The pressure of his hand on hers as they parted was without meaning. He had never known her except as Claudie's disturbing, picked-up acquaintance. "They are all happy," he said. "All the women. You will be happy too one day. As happy as any of them. Be patient." He shut her away into the lift before she could ask him to say what he meant.

15

SHE HAD always known that sorting would be a waste of effort. There was nothing she wanted to keep. The Australian could have the ironing board, the box of tennis balls, her mother's letters, the mop with its skirt of furry dust, her raincoat, twenty or so coat hangers, two boxes of Christmas tree ornaments, a shoe carton holding a folded beach hat and a roll of scotch tape, a zippered, insulated picnic carryall, a Portuguese shopping basket, a plastic bottle for sprinkling clothes, a spray can of starch, a flashlight, a roll of velvet self-adhering wallpaper, a Chianti bottle wired for use as a lamp, a leather box containing loose coins from four or five countries, a stack of books, a bread board, a cheese board, a round tin box for storing Christmas cake, a painting of a rag doll signed Renata Maguire—that was all she cared to enumerate for today. Philippe had done some shedding too: he had left manuscript paper, clips, brown paper envelopes, a portable radio, espadrilles and a cache of *Le Miroir* tied with string; slipped under the string was a tag reading, "Articles 1961–2." Philippe might want those. As she picked the bundle up the string broke. "In this, the last spring of the long Algerian war..." she read. Would this war produce its author, its filmmaker? That must have been what Philippe had been asking when he wrote, "Creation is independent of reality, or, more explicitly, it finds its roots in time and events only to detach itself..." She remembered Madame Roux saying, "If I had a bath every day, my skin would detach itself in long strips." She continued reading "... progressively. A series of plastic events can only flow from spontaneous exigencies. Politics and creation..."

She thought, Darling Philippe, you can also write it backward; for instance "... creation and politics. Spontaneous exigencies flow from a series of plastic events. Ba." As she tried to knot the broken string she saw on the floor, apart and alone, the guidebook *The Peep of Day* which Mrs. Castle had given her in Pons. "He will sit upon a white throne," Shirley read, "and he will wear a crown upon his head, and everybody will stand round his throne. He will open some books, in which are written down all the wicked things that people have done. God has seen all the wrong things you have done. He can see in the dark as well as in the light, and knows all your bad thoughts. He will read everything out of his book before the angels that stand around. Yet God will forgive some people, because Christ died on the cross for them. Whom will he forgive?"

The answer that followed was not reassuring. "Dearest Girl," she found, on a single sheet of paper, folded and tucked between the end page and cover. "The sadly macerated and decomposed specimen you sent me for identification is without doubt *Endymion nutans* or *Endymion non-scriptus*, or *Scilla nutans* or *non-scriptus*." She remembered now that all but one page of this letter had been incorporated into Geneviève's novel. One day, owing to Shirley's carelessness, Philippe might be called on to praise in print a passage such as (French), "'Very well,' said Bertrand, and his shoulders were eloquent of his defeat. 'Who *is* the greatest anthropologist of our day?'"; immediately followed by (English), "Hope all this is not so as her trip is costing her children a lot of money."

This was no good either. Philippe's articles must be separated somehow or other from the dust mop and the can of starch. She saw herself turning the key over to Madame Roux and heard her own voice saying, "A man is coming to take everything away at ten o'clock on Tuesday morning. He will drive a bright yellow truck, and he will know exactly what to do." Madame Roux and Sutton McGrath would sit and wait for the yellow truck. They would run to the shop window whenever a car stopped, but all they would find would be the Japanese importer pretending to look at old teakettles and trying to discover if Madame Roux was wearing blue. Smiling now, she stepped back from a trodden sheet of yellow paper. She turned it over and saw, under a famous poem, a familiar hand:

> GOODSIDE'S GOODSIDE'S GANDER
>   WITHA WATHA WARES
> HOW SAD TO PUNCH A POOR OLD MAN!
>   AND THROW HIM DOWN THE STARE'S!

> "How to decipher this? How can it be applied? The rise of Africa? Fathers supplanted by their sons?"

Shirley knelt on the floor and spread this sheet of paper on a trunk. It was a trunk she had not yet opened and now quite happily knew she never would. She wrote, "Darling Philippe, I have finally come round to your way of thinking. G. Gander is without doubt concerned with loyalty, fidelity, passing the buck and the situation in Berlin." She wanted to add, "It is also what Ruskin missed," but who was Ruskin? She slipped the page inside one of the envelopes Philippe had abandoned and addressed it to him in care of his mother.

She posted the message about an hour later. It slipped through steel teeth concealed behind the mail slot and became an irretrievable error. The wind that April afternoon blew straight from Russia. She saw a blossoming pear tree in front of the Église des St. Pères. The gutters were full of cigarette butts and fallen chestnut flowers. When she lifted her sunglasses she noticed that the sky was an extraordinary color, on the frontier of white and blue. She supposed that they would see each other again in time, in dreams and recollections.

GREEN WATER, GREEN SKY

> Ay, now am I in Arden; the more
> fool I; when I was at home, I
> was in a better place: but
> travellers must be content.
>
> —WILLIAM SHAKESPEARE, *As You Like It*, Act II

I

THEY WENT off for the day and left him, in the slyest, sneakiest way you could imagine. Nothing of the betrayal to come showed on their faces that morning as they sat having breakfast with him, out on the hotel terrace, a few inches away from the Grand Canal. If he had been given something the right length, a broom, say, he could have stirred the hardly moving layer of morning muck, the orange halves, the pulpy melons, the rotting bits of lettuce, black under water, green above. Water lapped against the gondolas moored below the terrace. He remembered the sound, the soft, dull slapping, all his life. He heard them say at the table they would never come here in August again. They urged him to eat, and drew his attention to gondoliers. He refused everything they offered. It was all as usual, except that a few minutes after he was in an open boat, churning across to the Lido with Aunt Bonnie and Florence. Flor and Aunt Bonnie pushed along to the prow and sat down side by side on a bench, and Aunt Bonnie pulled George toward her, so he was half on her lap. You couldn't sit properly: her lap held a beach bag full of towels. The wind picked up Flor's long pony tail of hair and sent it across George's face. His cousin's hair smelled coppery and warm, like its color. He wouldn't have called it unpleasant. All the same, it was an outrage, and he started to whine: "Where are *they*?" but the wind blew so that you couldn't hear a thing.

He had been on the beach most of the morning before he planted himself in front of Aunt Bonnie in her deck chair and said, "Where've they gone? Are they coming here?"

Aunt Bonnie lowered the book she was reading and regarded

George with puckered, anxious face—in his memories, an old face, a frightened face. She sat under a series of disks, in dwindling perspective; first an enormous beach umbrella, all in stripes, then her own faded parasol, then a neutral-colored straw hat. She said, "Well, you know, it's like this, Georgie, they've gone off for the day. They wanted to have one little day on their own. You mustn't be selfish. They're only looking at old pictures. You'd rather be on the beach than looking at pictures..."

"I'd sooner be looking at pictures," George said.

"...so we brought you over to the beach," said Aunt Bonnie, not even listening. "You mustn't be so selfish all the time. Your mother never has a minute. This trip is no fun for her at all."

Oh, they had managed it beautifully. First they were out on the hot terrace, offering him gondoliers, then he was abandoned with Aunt Bonnie and Flor.

Even years later, when they talked about that day, and his parents wondered how they had found it in them to creep off that way, without warning or explanation; even when they were admitting it was quite the worst thing to do to a child; even then, there was an annoying taint of self-congratulation in their manner. He had been a willful, whiny, spoiled little boy, and some people, Aunt Bonnie for one, claimed that his parents were almost afraid of him. His Fairlie cousins had called him the Monster, while his mother's relatives, more serious and concerned, often said he was being badly prepared for the blows and thumps of life, and wouldn't thank his parents later on. As it happened, George had turned out well. At seventeen, he was a triumphant vindication for his parents of years of hell. Oh, Lord, what he had been at five, his mother liked to say, smiling, shaking her head. At seven! He had ruined their holiday in Venice that time, although they always took all the blame: they should never have gone off for the day, creeping away when his back was turned. It might have marked him for life. *There* was a frightening thought. Like any averted danger, they liked to bring it up. "Do you remember, George, that time in Venice with Bonnie and Flor?"

Of course he remembered. He still had six little cockleshells picked up on the Lido. He remembered the brilliant parasols, askew in the hot wind, and Flor, his cousin, thin, sunburned, fourteen, sitting straight in the center of a round shadow; she sat and scooped sand with her fingers and looked out on the calm sea. George might have drowned for all she cared. He stumped about on the sand by himself, tomato-pink, fair-haired, deeply injured, rather fat. The sea was so flat, so still, so thick with warmth you might have walked on it. He gathered shells: black, brown, cream-and-pink, with minutely scalloped rims. Aunt Bonnie carried them back to Venice for him in her pockets, and now six were left. They were in a shoebox along with a hundred or so other things he would never throw away. He had another remnant of Venice, a glass bead. It came from a necklace belonging to Flor. She bought it that day, at an open stall, just in front of the place where the boat came in from the Lido. The clock on the Piazza began clanging noon, and the air filled with pigeons and with iron sound. They were filing off the boat in orderly fashion when suddenly Flor darted away and came back with the necklace in her hands. Aunt Bonnie hadn't finished saying, "Oh, do you like those glass beads, Flor? Because if you do, I'd rather get you something decent..." The string of the necklace broke an instant later, the first time Flor pulled it on over her head. The glass beads rolled and bounded all over the paving; pigeons fluttered after them, thinking they were grains of corn. The necklace breaking, the hotly blowing wind, excited Flor. She unstrung the beads still in her hands and flung them after the others, making a wild upward movement with her palms. "Oh, stop it," her mother cried, for people were looking, and Flor did appear rather mad, with her hair flying and her dress blowing so that anybody could see the starched petticoat underneath, and the sunburned thighs. And poor little George, suddenly anxious about what strangers might think—this new, frantic little George ran here and there, picking up large lozenge-shaped beads from under people's feet. When he straightened up, hands full of treasure, he saw that Florence was angry, and enjoying herself, all at once. Her hands were still out, as if she wanted to give just anyone a push. But perhaps he imagined that, for she walked quietly beside him, back to the hotel, and told him, kindly, that he could keep all the beads.

He still had one of those beads. He used to roll it about his palm before exams. There were other times, the many times he said, "God, help me this once, and I'll never bother you again," and it was the bead he held on to, and perhaps addressed. It was a powerful charm; a piece of a day; a reminder that someone had once wished him dead but that he was still alive.

Oh, there was no doubt that Florence had wished him dead. After lunch that day he and Flor had hung over rickety wooden railings and watched a small cargo loading what seemed in his memory to be telephone poles; although he must have been mistaken. Flor leaned forward, resting on her thin brown arms. Their faces were nearly level. She turned and looked at him, half smiling, eyes half closed, as people turn and look at each other sunbathing, on hot sand, and he was giving the smile timorously back when he met her eyes, green as water, bright with dislike, and she said, "It would be easy to push someone in right here. I could push you in." He remembered the heavy green water closing out the sky and the weight of clouds. The clouds piled on the horizon moved forward and covered the lagoon. Once he had fallen in the pond at his grandmother's house—the Fairlie grandmother he and Florence had in common. He was sailing a boat and took one false step. The water in this pond was kept dirty for the sake of some dirt-loving mosquito-eating Argentine fish his grandmother cherished—grown fish the size of baby minnows. These darting minnow fish came around him as he lay in the pond, unmoving, and he felt the soft tap of their heads against his cheeks. The most oppressive part of the memory was that he had lain there, passive, with the mossy water over his mouth. He must have been on his back; there was a memory of sky. The gardener heard the splash and fished him out and he was perfectly fine; not on his back at all, but on his face, splashing and floundering.

He didn't think about this in Venice. It was much later when he placed the two memories one on the other, glass over glass. In Venice, he didn't reply: there wasn't time. There wasn't even time for rage or fear. Aunt Bonnie was waiting for them after her afternoon sleep. They were to find her in the Piazza, and feed the pigeons, and listen to the band. He stamped along on fat legs behind Flor, through heat like water, head down. They stopped and weighed themselves on a public scale that told them their fortunes as well as what they weighed. Their fortunes came down on colored cardboard rectangles. George's said, "Do not refuse any invitations this evening," and Flor's said that she must take better care of her liver, and that she would soon be seeing someone off by train. "Mama's waiting," Flor said, throwing her fortune away. She grabbed his arm and made him walk faster. When they came up to Aunt Bonnie, sitting with tea and a plate of little cakes, they were both flushed with heat, but neither of them complained. They were acting in unison, without having been told. They were doing everything to please Aunt Bonnie. George had an instinctive awareness that this aunt loved him, not because he was Georgie Fairlie and ought to be loved, but because he was a relative, Aunt Bonnie's brother's son. He understood that Flor must know her cousins; she mustn't become too strange. He was conscious of a quality of love that was a family and not a personal thing. Florence was playing up well too. Earlier, at lunch, out on the terrace of the hotel, when one of them said something funny the other laughed much harder than the joke deserved, and Aunt Bonnie laughed with a sad, grimacing pleasure that was painful to see. Her husband, Uncle Stanley, had been so dreadful to her, he had humiliated her so deeply that she couldn't live in America; she couldn't show her face. She was condemned to live abroad and bring Flor up in some harmful way: harmful for Flor, that is. That was what Aunt Bonnie told him, in a high wretched voice, and Flor listened, bent over her plate, flashing a glance sideways, now to her mother, now to George, to see how he was taking it. She listened as if she had never heard any of it before, although it must have been her daily fare. Flor was patient; she was patient even with George's stammer. He asked long riddles, stammering like mad if he thought a waiter might be listening, and his cousin was good about guessing the answers, even when he had left out some clue, or given the whole thing away by telling it backward. That laughter, that patience, was for Aunt Bonnie. George had never been separated from his parents before and had fugitive thoughts that they might never come back, but he still understood about Aunt Bonnie, without having been told. It was the first time he had been expected to do anything for anyone in his life.

To please Aunt Bonnie they stood on the edge of the Piazza, not too far away, because she would want to see them enjoying themselves. They shook grain out of newspaper cones and flung it around. Aunt Bonnie watched from her café table, and nodded, and smiled.

Without looking at George, Flor said, "You saw Stanley, didn't you?"

"He came on the boat," said George.

"Was she with him?" said Flor. "What's she like?"

He didn't hedge, as an older person might, and say, "What's who like?" or anything of the kind. He thrust one foot toward a fat, feeding pigeon—taking a stand. He said, "She brought us all different things. She brought me candy."

"I see," said Flor. "They came to see you off. That was loyal of your parents. That was nice." He didn't understand sarcasm. He went on scattering corn. "How old is she?" said Flor, after a time.

"Around thirty-three," said George solemnly, to whom "fifty-eight" or "thirty-one" might have meant much the same. He had heard said of his own mother that she was thirty-three.

"She couldn't even be my mother," said Flor contemptuously. "Mama's forty."

"What fun you're having," came Aunt Bonnie's wailing voice.

They bought new cones of grain and flung it out in an awful rite, in silence. The pigeons were too fat and lazy to fly. They waddled around George's feet, pecking and squabbling and pushing one another away.

"She took it all right," Flor suddenly began again, "until some damn fool went and told her the other one was younger and better looking. She was all right, at first. She even said to me, 'Your father is going to live with this other person. I'm sure she's perfectly sweet.'

She couldn't complain," said Flor. "She'd had this man around for ages, this doctor. So she couldn't complain. She used to take me to this doctor for sun lamps on my spine. She must have thought I was deaf and dumb and blind. The nurse of this doctor taught me to play gin rummy. Stanley never said anything and then all of a sudden he blew up and threw her out. Threw us *both* out," said Flor. "Threw her out of the house and she took me too." She was rather affected, telling this, although that was certainly not the word George would have used then. He mistrusted the toss of her head, and the glance she gave, seeing if he was impressed. The effect of this story was to increase his stolidness. He dropped corn one grain at a time, choosing his pigeons. "Nobody was loyal," said Flor. "You stinking Fairlies weren't loyal. You see him all the time. It doesn't matter. She's different now. She never looks at anyone." In George's memory it was here that Florence cried: "She'll never do anything any more. I'll always keep her with me." That wasn't affected. There was no toss of hair, but the same queer pushing attitude of hands he had seen after the necklace broke. She meant these words, they weren't intended for George. It was a solemn promise, a cry of despair, love and resentment so woven together that even Flor couldn't tell them apart.

The paper cones were empty again. This time they threw them away and went back to Aunt Bonnie's table. It was time to listen to the band. Flor ran to her mother and there, in front of everybody, all the strangers and waiters, flung her brown arms around Aunt Bonnie's neck. She cried, "Oh, you look so tired, you look so fed up! Do you hate this place?"

"Darling," said Aunt Bonnie, who had been crying, "it's only for you. You looked so sweet and pretty there with Georgie. I'm sure you hate me. You'll hate me one day. I'm sure I should bring you up some other way. I'm no good at this."

"I'll never hate you, I'll love you," Florence said angrily. "I hate Stanley, I hate George, I hate everybody, I love you."

They sat close so their cheeks were pressed and both of them talked at once and began laughing and crying, with an easiness of emotion, as if they did this a lot. They didn't care about the waiters and they had forgotten George, who stood apart, with an eddy of pigeons around his feet. He loathed his cousin and aunt. He was so embarrassed at what they were doing, he wanted to fly at them and punch them and make them stop. He was alone and ridiculous with pigeons. His parents had gone off for the day without him. They had sneaked off without saying goodbye. It came over him, the hollowness of having been left, the fury at having been made a fool. He dropped his hands to his sides and opened his mouth and howled and howled. His eyes were shut to crescents and his mouth a great cave. He was much too big to be crying this way.

"I've scared him," Florence said, from her mother's side. "I told him something silly, for a joke."

But he wasn't going to let her have the satisfaction of that, and he shut his mouth and opened it again to gasp: "It-wasn't-you," from the circle of waiters and his fluttering aunt, who had sped to take him in her arms. Flor thought he was being honorable, an honorable boy, and she looked at him in a perfect fury of contempt and then turned her back; until both of them were grown, she never really looked at him again. The look was enough to make him stop crying. He waited until his parents returned that evening, apprehensive in their guilt, then he staged the scene all over again, this time sure of the response. He wailed, "You left me all alone," to which Aunt Bonnie gave an accompanying wail, "My word of honor, he was good as gold," while his mother, rocking him, crooned, "I know, I know," to both.

Flor was dressed for dinner by then, in a dark blue dress. Her arms were bare, her pony-tail hair brushed, coppery, over one shoulder. George's mother stopped mooning over him long enough to stare, admiring—this particular public scene took place in the hotel bar; George was by now getting the hang of attracting and ignoring the public, although he didn't do it so well as Flor—and she exclaimed: "Flor, honey, do something tremendous. You're too pretty to waste."

"Whatever happens," Florence said, composedly, "I shall never marry a Fairlie. I've had enough family. Nothing would persuade me to marry a Fairlie and nothing would persuade me to marry George."

Why this should have made everyone laugh was beyond George: but it became a family expression, brought up, through the years, whenever George and Florence were made to meet. They met summers, two and three years apart, so that every time it was like meeting a different person. Florence paid no attention to him and they never spoke: although his parents never seemed to notice this. "Flor is sweet," his mother said once, "but she's not like a young girl at all. She's too grown up. I wish Bonnie would send her to college here."

"She wouldn't fit in any more," his father said. "Anyway, why come back here? She doesn't want to marry a Fairlie."

This reminded George's mother of Venice and she smiled. George was in love with the daughter of the man who owned the garage in the place where they went summers. His parents hadn't started worrying about Barbara Sim: not yet. They still thought it was young and touching and funny; young and funny like George's reply to Florence in the Venice hotel bar: "I'd sooner get nothing for Christmas for nineteen years than marry you."

They met summers: an unreal meeting in hot New York, one year when Bonnie decided to brave it out and then found it was August, nobody there. Once there was a meeting in England, in a hotel, and then somewhere else, on a blowy sandy beach. It was always hot and Aunt Bonnie had a new thing now, migraine headache. Then there was the last meeting, when Flor married a man called Bob Harris she had known in Cannes, and they came back to New York, not creeping this time, but with clatter and circumstance.

They met in an apartment someone had lent the Harris couple. It was full of dark wood and paintings of ships. "This stuff isn't just old," Bob Harris said. "It's period." George didn't hear this: it was repeated to him later on. Because Aunt Bonnie couldn't stand the air-conditioning, the windows were open, the room dense with heat and noise. Most of the people here were Fairlies. George counted eleven persons, including himself, who bore the Fairlie features *in toto*: white hair, white lashes, ruddy cheeks, and, in the case of the less fortunate, the big front teeth. They had come in from everywhere to see the bride. Once you were in the family, you were in to stay: death, divorce, scandal—nothing operated, nothing cut you away. Bob Harris was in it now too. He would fit in, sift down, find his place. Now that he was in there would be no criticism, not a flicker, not a glance. No one would recall that Bonnie had written from Cannes: "Well I don't know what's going to happen now but Florence has gone and married this Jew." When George's mother had read this bit aloud, she had taken on just a shade of Bonnie's whiny accent, that sacred Fairlie drawl, and it came out: "Flounce has gonen married..." Nothing else was hinted: nothing survived except their manner of saying "Bob Harris" all the time, as if it were all one word.

There were no Harrises in the room, although Harrises were known to exist. Harris *père* had given Florence a handsome wedding present, and someone had seen his name, quite dignified, on an advertisement for his wine-importing firm. Bob Harris ran the French end of the business: he lived in Paris. He was the same age as Florence, twenty-four. It was the good life. George heard all this and understood. He was part of this family, so much so that he understood their hints and suggestions, their stressed words, even when nothing important was said. It had all been settled for him in advance: his attitudes and perceptions had been decided for him before he was born. Perhaps because the room was so crowded and hot George began to sweat. He felt sweat breaking on his back and under his arms and was sure it showed through his clothes. Only, as it happened, no one was looking at him. They were much too interested in Florence, who was really a beauty now, straight and quiet, with the pretty coppery hair wound in a knot behind her head. They had all been told by Bonnie, separately, as a secret, that there was something wrong with Florence; she could never have children; she wasn't well. There was a high tide of noise and Aunt Bonnie's voice above them all. George and his parents had driven in from the country and come here late: everyone but Florence was loud and drunk. After a time George forgot what people might be thinking of him and he began covertly watching his cousin, from under his whitish lashes, looking for traces of illness, traces of love. He was seventeen that summer and always looking for things. He sat on a chair at right angles to the sofa on which Florence sat with his aunt. They were holding hands. He saw that every time Flor's husband came near her he brushed some part of her skin with the back of his hand; and that although Flor never looked at him she was aware of that faintly brushing foreign masculine hand. It was as though some projection of the two, as a couple, was quite apart and in another room, or simply invisible.

"She'll never do anything any more. I'll always keep her with me." This voice came at him, hurled out of the past, with the violence of his cousin's warm hair picked up by the wind and blown across his face.

"Georgie," said Florence, and she bent toward him, the first time she had said anything to him for years, "do you remember how hot it was in Venice when we were kids? I was just reminding Mama. Do you remember that?"

"But New York is *too* hot," said Aunt Bonnie, as if it were somebody's fault.

"Do you remember how green it was all the time?" Flor said to him. "Everything was so clear and green, green water, even the sky looked green to me."

He had been staring, but now he looked inadvertently into her eyes, dark-lashed, green as the lagoon had been—he thought he remembered it now. He couldn't reply. Bob Harris kept moving around, too hospitable, doing too much: at least it seemed so to George, who was sensitive to how people did things. He wanted Bob Harris to be above reproach.

"You were an awful little boy," Flor said to him, smiling. She bent toward him but still held her mother's hand. He had heard about his bratty childhood so often that he no longer minded hearing it. "You wanted so much watching," Flor said. "I think I wasn't a good nursemaid."

He said rather stiffly, "It was only one day."

"But what a day," she said, still smiling, still kind. "You used to run all over the place, like a little mouse. We could hardly keep up."

He said, "I don't remember any of that." His cured stammer returned: "I remember crying in the square."

"I think you cried a lot," said Flor.

"Only once."

The dialogue faltered. They remained in an attitude of conversation, as if posed. "George ought to come over to us in Paris next year," they heard Aunt Bonnie say. "He certainly must do that," Bob Harris chimed in. "He certainly must."

"You know I can't have children?" Florence said, looking George fully in the face. He mumbled a reply. She said, "It was nice of him to want to marry me, all the same."

"Flor," he said, "I've got this bead. It's lucky... no, take it... I swear, it brings luck..." It was out of his pocket and on his wet palm: clear, flawed, the treasure of Venice.

Flor looked at him with a half smile and puckered brows. "What is it, George?" she said clearly, as if to make him stop stammering.

He would have given anything not to have started this. "You know, you bought this string of beads? And it broke? When we came back from the beach? You bought this string of beads and broke it..."

"I'm not a person who breaks things," Flor said. "I don't remember that."

George said, "We came off the boat, you know? You went right over to this sort of booth."

"It's just that I'm not a person who breaks things," Flor said. "Of course, if you say it happened, it's true. I haven't much memory."

"I thought you sort of broke it on purpose," he said.

"Oh, George," said Flor, shaking her head, "now I know it can't be real. That just isn't me. It didn't happen."

He had kept it ten years. He had only to roll it in his hand or put his eye to the clear flawed glass and the air was full of pigeons and bells and the movement of Flor breaking something because she wanted something broken; perhaps because she was going to be with Aunt Bonnie for life. Sometimes it was as though Flor had never left his thoughts, even when he didn't think of her at all. Because of her, the twin pictures, love and resentment, were always there, one reflecting the other, water under sky. Everything had happened as he remembered; the day had taken place; it had taken its place in his life. He closed his hand because he thought he looked rather silly, sitting there, with a lozenge of glass on an open palm. Of course it had taken place: look at all these people tangled together, all the Fairlies, and Flor and Bonnie, and now Bob Harris was in it too. And what about his own parents? After that day in Venice they had sworn they would never leave him again, never, ever, and they had kept their word, so that their love for him was a structure, and he was inside. They might have resented it, sometimes. He had: sometimes he had. And now he was going to college and leaving them and maybe the next year he would take that invitation and go to Paris, and the inevitable disloyalty, the faithlessness, the casting-off, made him feel as if he were already at an imagined distance, and remorseful, and starting back.

Flor looked at his closed fist. "Why do people keep things?" she said.

"I don't know," said George. "I guess it proves you were somewhere."

She said, "I feel as if we hadn't ever been in the same place."

"George!" his mother cried from across the room. "Do you remember that time in Venice with Bonnie and Flor?"

"Do you want this?" he said quickly. "It's really yours."

"It wouldn't help me," said Florence. "We weren't ever in the same place. We don't need luck in the same way. We don't remember the same things."

2

BONNIE McCarthy opened a drawer of her dressing table and removed the hat her sister-in-law had sent from New York. It was a summer hat of soft, silken material in a pretty shade of blue: the half-melon hat her sister-in-law had begun to wear at fifteen and had gone on wearing, in various colors and textures, until her hair was gray. This particular melon was designed for travel. It could be folded until it took no more place in a suitcase than a closed fan. Bonnie pushed her lips forward in a pout. She held the hat between thumb and forefinger, considering it. She pulled it on her head, tugging with both hands. The frown, the pout, the obstinate gestures, were those of a child. It was a deliberate performance, and new: after years of struggling to remain adult in a grown-up world, she had found it unrewarding, and, in her private moments, allowed herself the blissful luxury of being someone else.

The hat was a failure. Framed by the chaste blue brim, she seemed slightly demented, a college girl aged overnight. After a long look in the triple mirror, Bonnie said aloud, "This just isn't a normal hat." She dropped it on the table, among the framed pictures and the pots of cream. None of the clothes from America seemed normal to her now, because they no longer came from a known place. She had left her country between the end of the war and the onslaught of the New Look (this is how history was fixed in her memory) and, although she had been back for visits, the American scene of her mind's eye was populated with girls in short skirts and broad-shouldered coats—the war silhouette, 1-85, or whatever it was called. Her recollection of such details was faultless, but she could not have said under which President peace had been signed. The nation at war was not a permanent landscape: Bonnie's New York, the real New York, was a distant, gleaming city in a lost decade. A lost Bonnie existed there, pretty and pert, outrageously admired. This was the Bonnie she sought to duplicate every time she looked in the glass—Bonnie tender-eyed, blurry with the sun of a perished afternoon; Bonnie in her wedding dress, authentically innocent, with a wreath of miniature roses straight across her brow. With time—she was at this moment fifty-two—a second, super-Bonnie had emerged. Super-Bonnie was a classic, middle-aged charmer. She might have been out of Kipling—a kind of American Mrs. Hauksbee, witty and thin, with those great rolling violet blue eyes. When she was feeling liverish or had had a bad night, she knew this was off the mark, and that she had left off being tender Bonnie without achieving the safety of Mrs. Hauksbee. Then she would think of the woman she could have been, if her life hadn't been destroyed: and if she went on thinking about it too much, she gave up and consoled herself by playing at being a little girl.

When Bonnie was still under forty, her husband had caught her out in a surpassingly silly affair—she had not in the least loved the lover—and had divorced her, so that her conception of herself was fragmented, unreconciled. There was Bonnie, sweet-faced, with miniature roses; wicked Mrs. Hauksbee, the stormy petrel of a regimental outpost; and, something near the truth, a lost, sallow, frightened Bonnie wandering from city to city in Europe, clutching her daughter by the hand. The dressing table was littered with these Bonnies, and with pictures of Florence, her daughter. There was Flor as a baby, holding a ball in starfish hands, and Flor on her pony, and Flor in Venice, squinting and bored. To one side, isolated, in curious juxtaposition, were two small likenesses. One was a tinted image of St. Teresa of the Infant Jesus. (Bonnie had no taste for obscure martyrs. The Little Flower, good enough for most Catholics, was good enough for her.) The Saint had little function in Bonnie's life, except to act as a timid anchor to Bonnie's ballooning notion of the infinite. The second picture was of Bob Harris, Bonnie's son-in-law. It had been taken on the beach at Cannes, two summers before. He wore tartan bathing trunks, and had on and about his person the equipment for underwater fishing—flippers, spear, goggles, breathing tube—and seemed to be a monster of a sort.

When she had done with the hat, Bonnie licked her forefingers and ran them along her eyebrows. She pulled her eyebrows apart and counted twenty times, but when she released the skin, the line between her eyes returned. "La première ride," she said sentimentally. She put on a wry, ironic look; Mrs. Hauksbee conceding the passage of time. When she left the dressing table and crossed the room she continued to wear the look, although she was already thinking about something else. She sat down at a writing table very like the dressing table she had just abandoned. Both were what her son-in-law called "important pieces." Both had green marble tops, bandy legs, drawers like bosoms, brass fittings, and were kin to the stranded objects, garnished with dying flowers in a vase, that fill the windows of antique shops on the left bank of the Seine.

Bonnie was easily wounded, but she had sharp, malicious instincts where other people were concerned. She seldom struck openly, fearing the direct return blow. The petty disorder of her dressing table, with its cheap clutter of bottles and pictures, was an oblique stab at Bob Harris, whose apartment this was, and who, as he had once confided to Bonnie, liked things nice.

She pulled toward her a sheet of white paper with her address in Paris printed across the top, and wrote the date, which was the fifteenth of July. She began: "My darling Polly and Stu—First about the hat. You sweethearts! I wore it today for the first time as it really hasn't been summer until now. I was so proud to say this is from my brother and his wife from New York. Well darlings I am sorry about George I must say I never did hear of anybody ever getting the whooping cough at his age but I can quite see you couldn't let him come over to Paris in that condition in June. Two years since we have seen that boy. Flor asks about him every day. You know those two were so crazy about each other when they were kids, it's a shame Flor was seven years older instead of the other way around. At least we would all be still the same family and would know who was marrying who. Well, nuff said."

So far this letter was nearly illegible. She joined the last letter of each word on to the start of the next. All the vowels, as well as the letters n, m, and w, resembled u's. There were strings of letters that might as well have been nununu. Now, her writing became elegant and clear, like the voice of someone trying on a new accent: "The thing with him coming over in August is this, that he would have to be alone with Florence. Bob Harris's father is coming over here this year, and Bob Harris is going with him to the Beaujolais country and the Champagne country and I don't know what all countries for their business, and they will be in these countries all of August. Now I have been invited to stay with a dear friend in Deauville for the entire month. Now as you know Flor is doing this business with a psychiatrist and she REFUSES to leave Paris. It wouldn't be any fun for Georgie because Flor never goes out and wouldn't know where to go even if she did. It seems to me Georgie should go to England first, because he wants to go there anyway, and he should come here around the end of August when I will be back, and Bob will be back, and we can take Georgie around. Just as you like, dears, but this does seem best."

Bonnie was in the habit of slipping little pieces of paper inside her letters to her sister-in-law. These scraps, about the size of a calling card, bore a minutely scrawled message which was what she really wanted to say, and why she was bothering to write a letter at all. She cut a small oblong out of a sheet of paper and wrote in tiny letters: "Polly, Flor is getting so queer, I don't know her any more. I'm afraid to leave her alone in August, but she pulls such tantrums if I say I'll stay that I'm giving in. Don't let Georgie come, he'd only be upset. She's at this doctor's place now, and *I don't even like the doctor.*"

It was three o'clock in the afternoon. Florence was walking with cautious steps along the Boulevard des Capucines when the sidewalk came up before her. It was like an earthquake, except that she knew there were no earthquakes here. It was like being drunk, except that she never drank any more. It was a soundless upheaval, and it had happened before. No one noticed the disturbance, or the fact that she had abruptly come to a halt. It was possible that she had become invisible. It would not have astonished her at all. Indeed, a fear that this might come about had caused her to buy, that summer, wide-skirted dresses in brilliant tones that (Bonnie said) made her look like a fortuneteller in a restaurant. All very well for Bonnie, who could be sure that she existed in black; who did not have to steal glimpses of herself in shop windows, an existence asserted in coral and red.

At this hour, at this time of year, the crowd around the Café de la Paix was American. It was a crowd as apart from Flor as if an invasion of strangers speaking Siamese had entered the city. But they were not Siamese: they were her own people, and they spoke the language she knew best, with the words she had been taught to use when, long ago, she had seen shapes and felt desires that had to be given names.

"...upon the beached verge of the salt flood..."

She did not say this. Her lips did not move; but she had the ringing impression of a faultless echo, as if the words had come to her in her own voice. They were words out of the old days, when she could still read, and relate every sentence to the sentence it followed. A vision, clear as a mirror, of a narrowing shore, an encroaching sea, was all that was left. It was all that remained of her reading, the great warehouse of stored phrases, the plugged casks filled with liquid words—a narrowing shore, a moving sea: that was all. And yet how she had read! She had read in hotel rooms, sprawled on the bed—drugged, drowned—while on the other side of the dark window rain fell on foreign streets. She had read on buses and on trains and in the waiting rooms of doctors and dressmakers, waiting for Bonnie. She had read with her husband across from her at the table and beside her in bed. (She had been reading a book, in a café, alone, the first time he had ever spoken to her. He had never forgotten it.) She had read through her girlhood and even love hadn't replaced the reading: only at times.

If Bonnie had been able to give some form to her own untidy life; if she had not uprooted Flor and brought her over here to live—one majestically wrong decision among a hundred indecisions—Flor would not, at this moment, have feared the movement of the pavement under her feet and watched herself in shop windows to make sure she was still there. She would not have imagined life as a brightly lighted stage with herself looking on. She would have depended less on words; she would have belonged to life. She told an imagined Bonnie, "It was always your fault. I might have been a person, but you made me a foreigner. It was always the same, even back home. I was the only Catholic girl at Miss Downland's. That was being foreign."

"What about the Catholic girls from Mexico?" said Bonnie, from among the crowd before the newspaper kiosk where Flor had paused to consult, blankly, the front page of the *Times*.

Trust Bonnie to put in a red herring like the Mexican girls at school; it didn't merit a reply. Still, the discovery that it had always been the same was worth noting. It was another clearing in the thicket that was Dr. Linnetti's favorite image: another path cleared, another fence down, light let through. She groped in her purse for the green notebook in which she recorded these discoveries, and she sat down on a vacant chair outside the café.

The table at which she had put herself was drawn up to its neighbor so that a party of four tourists could have plenty of room for their drinks, parcels, and pots of tea. One of the four had even pulled over an extra chair for her aching feet. Florence put her notebook on the edge of the table, pushing an ashtray to one side. The *vertige* she had felt on the street was receding. In her private language she called it "the little animal going to sleep." What was the good of an expression like Dr. Linnetti's "vertigo experienced in the presence of sharp lines and related objects"? The effort of lines to change their form (the heaving pavement), the nausea created by the sight of a double row of houses meeting at the horizon point, the triumph of the little fox, had begun being a torment when she was twelve, and had come to live abroad. In those days, Bonnie had put it down to faulty eyesight, via a troubled liver, and had proscribed whipped cream. Now that it was too late, Florence remembered and recognized the initial siege, the weakening of her forces so that the invader could take possession.

Accepting this, she had stopped believing in Dr. Linnetti's trees, clearings, and pools of light. She was beset, held. Nothing could help her but sleep and the dreams experienced in the gray terrain between oblivion and life—the country of gray hills and houses from which she was suddenly lifted and borne away. Coming into this landscape was the most difficult of all, for they were opposed to her reaching it—the doctor, her mother, her husband. Circumstances were needed, and they were coming soon. In two weeks it would be August, and she would be left alone. Between now and August was a delay filled with perils; her mother hesitating and quibbling, her husband trying to speak. (He no longer attempted to make love. He seemed to have a tenacious faith that one day Dr. Linnetti was going to return to him a new Flor, strangely matured, and more exciting than ever.) This period traversed, she saw herself in the heavy silence of August. She saw her image in her own bed in the silence of an August afternoon. By the dimming of light in the chinks of the shutters she would know when it was night; and, already grateful for this boon, she would think, Now it is all right if I sleep.

"Some people just don't care."

"Ask her what she wants to drink."

"Maybe she's after you, Ed Broadfoot, ha ha."

These were three of the four people on whom Flor had intruded. They thought she was French—foreign, at any rate: not American. She looked away from the notebook in which she had not yet started to write and she said, "I understand every word." A waiter stood over her. "*Madame désire?*" he said insultingly. In terror she scrawled: "Mex. girls wouldn't take baths," before she got up and fled—wholly visible—into the dark café. Inside, she was careful to find a place alone. She was the picture of prudence, now, watching the movements of her hands, the direction of her feet. She sat on the plush banquette with such exaggerated care that she had a sudden, lucid image of how silly she must seem, and this made her want to laugh.

She spread the notebook flat and began to write the letter to Dr. Linnetti, using a cheap ballpoint pen bought expressly for this. The letter was long, and changed frequently in tone, now curt and businesslike, when she gave financial reasons for ending their interviews, now timid and cajoling, so that Dr. Linnetti wouldn't be cross. Sometimes the letter was almost affectionate, for there were moments when she forgot Dr. Linnetti was a woman and was ready to pardon her; but then she remembered that this cheat was from a known tribe, subjected to the same indignities, the same aches and pains, practicing the same essential deceits. And here was this impostor presuming to help!—Dr. Linnetti, charming as a hippopotamus, elegant as the wife of a Soviet civil servant, emotional as a snail, intelligent—ah, there she has us, thought Flor. We shall never know. There are no clues.

"What help can you give me?" she wrote. "I have often been disgusted by the smell of your dresses and your rotten teeth. If in six months you have not been able to take your dresses to be cleaned, or yourself to a dentist, how can you help me? Can you convince me that I'm not going to be hit by a car when I step off the curb? Can you convince me that the sidewalk is a safe place to be? Let me put it another way," wrote Flor haughtily. Her face wore a distinctly haughty look. "Is your life so perfect? Is your husband happy? Are your children fond of you and well behaved? Are you so happy..." She did not know how to finish and started again: "Are you anything to me? When you go home to your husband and children do you wonder about me? Are we friends? Then why bother about me at all?" She had come to the last page in the notebook. She tore the pages containing the letter out and posted the letter from the mail desk in the café. She dropped the instrument of separation—the lethal pen—on the floor and kicked it out of sight. It was still too early to go home. They would guess she had missed her interview. There was nothing to do but walk around the three sides of the familiar triangle—Boulevard des Capucines, rue Scribe, rue Auber, the home of the homeless—until it was time to summon a taxi and be taken away.

Florence's husband left his office early. The movement of Paris was running down. The avenues were white and dusty, full of blowing flags and papers and torn posters, and under traffic signals there were busily aimless people, sore-footed, dressed for heat, trying to decide whether or not to cross that particular street; wondering whether Paris would be better once the street was crossed. The city's minute hand had begun to lag: in August it would stop. Bob Harris loved Paris, but then he loved anywhere. He had never been homesick in his life. He carried his birthright with him. He pushed into the cool of the courtyard of the ancient apartment house in which he lived (the last house in the world where a child played Czerny exercises on a summer's afternoon), waved to the concierge in her aquarium parlor, ascended in the perilous elevator, which had swinging doors, like a saloon, and let himself into the flat. "Let himself into" is too mild. He entered as he had once broken into Flor's and Bonnie's life. He was—and proud of it—a New York boy, all in summer tans today: like a café Liégeois, Bonnie had said at breakfast, but out of his hearing, of course. She was no fool. The sprawled old-fashioned Parisian apartment, the polished bellpull (a ring in a lion's mouth), the heavy doors and creamy, lofty ceilings, appealed to his idea of what Europe ought to be. The child's faltering piano notes, which followed him until he closed the door on them, belonged to the décor. He experienced a transient feeling of past and present fused—a secondhand, threadbare inkling of a world haunted by the belief that the best was outside one's scope or still to come. These perceptions, which came only when he was alone, when creaking or mournful or ghostly sounds emerged from the stairs and the elevator shaft and formed a single substance with the walls, curtains, and gray light from the court, he knew were only the lingering vapors of adolescent nostalgia—that fruitless, formless yearning for God knows what. It was not an ambience of mind he pursued. His office, which was off the Champs-Elysées, in a cake-shaped building of the thirties, was dauntingly new, like the lounge of a dazzling Italian airport building reduced in scale. The people he met in the course of business were sharp with figures, though apt to assume a monkish air of dedication because they were dealing in wine instead of, say, paper bags. There was nothing monkish about Bob: he knew about wine (that is, he knew about markets for wine); and he knew about money too.

Nothing is more reassuring to a European than the national who fits his national character: the waspish Frenchman, the jolly Hollander, the blunted Swiss, the sly Romanian—each of these paper dolls can find a niche. Bob Harris corresponded, superficially, to the French pattern for an American male—"un grand gosse"—and so he got on famously. He was the last person in the world to pose a problem. He was chatty, and cheerful, and he didn't much care what people did or what they were like so long as they were good-natured too. He frequented the red-interiored bars of the Eighth Arrondissement with cheerful friends—more or less Americans trying to raise money so as to start a newspaper in the Canary Islands, and apple-bosomed starlets with pinky-silver hair. Everyone wanted something from him, and everyone liked him very much. Florence's family, the indefatigable nicknamers, had called him the Seal, and he did have a seal's sleek head and soft eyes, and a circus seal's air of jauntily seeking applause. The more he was liked, and the more he was exploited, the more he was himself. It was only when he entered his darkened bedroom that he had to improvise an artificial way of thinking and behaving.

His wife's new habit of lying with the curtains drawn on the brightest days was more than a vague worry: it seemed to him wicked. If ever he had given a thought to the nature of sin, it would have taken that form: the shutting-out of light. Flor had stopped being cheerful; that was the very least you could say. Her sleeping was a longer journey each time over a greater distance. He did not know how to bring her back, or even if he wanted to, now. He had loved her; an inherent taste for exaggeration led him to believe he had worshiped her. She might have evaded him along another route, in drinking, or a crank religion, or playing bridge; it would have been the same betrayal. He was the only person she had trusted. The only journey she could make, in whatever direction, was away from him. Feeling came to him in blocks, compact. When he held on to one emotion there was no place for another. He had loved Flor: she had left him behind. It had happened quickly. She hadn't cried warning. He accepted what they told him—that Flor was sick and would get over it—but he could not escape the feeling that her flight was deliberate and that she could stop and turn back if she tried.

He might have profited by her absence, now, to go through her drawers, searching for drugs or diaries or letters—something that would indicate the reasons for change. But he touched nothing in the silent room that was not his own. Nothing remained of the person he had once seen in the far table of the dark café in Cannes, elbows on table, reading a book. She had looked up and before becoming aware that a man was watching her let him see on her drowned face everything he was prepared to pursue—passion, discipline, darkness. The secrets had been given up to Dr. Linnetti—"A sow in a Mother Hubbard," said Bonnie, who had met the lady. He felt obscurely cheated; more, the secrets now involved him as well. He would never pardon the intimacy exposed. Even her physical self had been transformed. He had prized her beauty. It had made her an object as cherished as anything he might buy. In museums he had come upon paintings of women—the luminous women of the Impressionists—in which some detail reminded him of Flor, the thick hair, the skin, the glance slipping away, and this had increased his sense of possession and love. She had destroyed this beauty, joyfully, willfully, as if to force him to value her on other terms. The wreckage was futile, a vandalism without cause. He could never understand and he was not sure that he ought to try.

His mother-in-law was in the drawing room, poised for discovery. She must have heard him come in, and, while he was having a shower and changing his clothes, composed her personal tableau. The afternoon light diffused through the thin curtains was just so. Bonnie was combed, made up, corseted, prepared for a thousand eyes. Her dress fitted without a wrinkle. She was ready to project her presence and create a mood with one intelligent phrase. She had been practicing having colored voices, thinking blue, violet, green, depending on the occasion. Her hands were apart, hovering over a bowl of asters—a bit of stage business she had just thought up.

If Bonnie had not been the mother of Flor, and guilty of a hundred assaults on his generosity and pride, he might have liked her. She was ludicrous, touching, aware she was putting on an act. But a natural relationship between them was hopeless. Too much had been hinted and said. She had wounded him too deeply. He had probably wounded her. She greeted the young man as if his being in his own apartment were a source of gay surprise, and he responded with his usual unblinking reverence, as if he were Chinese and she a revered but long-perished ancestor; at the same time, he could not stop grinning all over his face.

The effect of discovery was ruined. Bonnie had dressed and smiled and spoken in vain. Even the perfect lighting was a lost effect: the sun might just as well set, now, as far as Bonnie was concerned. She was only trying to look attractive and create a civilized, attractive atmosphere for them all, but nobody helped. He saw that she was once more offended, and was sorry. He offered her a drink, which she refused, explaining in a hurt voice that she was waiting for tea.

"Where's Flor?"

"*You* know," said Bonnie. On the merits of Dr. Linnetti they were in complete accord.

He sat down and opened the newspaper he had brought home. Bonnie gave a final poke at the flowers and sat down too, not so far away that it looked foolish, but leaving a distance so that he need not imagine for one second Bonnie expected him to *talk*. He looked at his paper and Bonnie thought her thoughts and waited for tea. She was nearly contented: it was a climate of mutual acceptance that had about it a sort of coziness: they might have been putting up with each other for years. The room seemed full of inherited furniture no one knew how to get rid of; yet they had taken the apartment as it was. They were trailing baggage out of a fabricated past. The furnishings had probably responded to Bob's need for a kind of buttery comfort; and the colors and textures reflected Bonnie's slightly lady-taste that ran to shot silk, pearly porcelain, and peacock green. Afloat on polished tables were the objects she had picked up on her travels, bibelots in silver and glass. There was a television set prudishly hidden away in a lacquered cabinet, and on the walls the paintings Bob had purchased. It was not a perfect room, but, as Bonnie often told her sister-in-law in her letters, it could have been so much worse. There was nothing in it of Flor.

When Flor came in a few minutes after this there was someone with her: a tall, round-faced young woman with blond hair, whose dress, voice, speech, and manner were so of a piece that she remained long afterward in Bob's memory as "The American," as though being American were exceptional or unique. Flor hung back. The visitor advanced into the room and smiled at them: "I'm Doris Fischer. I live down below. It's marvelous to find other Americans here."

"We met on the stairs," said Flor seriously.

"Met on the stairs, Flor? Met on the stairs?" Bonnie sounded fussed and overcontained, as if she might scream. Flor never spoke to strangers and, since spring, had given up even her closest friends. The two young women seemed about to reveal something: for an instant Bonnie had the crazy idea that one of the two had been involved in a fatal accident and that the other was about to describe it. That was how you became, living with Flor. Impossible, illogical pictures leaped upward in the mind and remained fixed, shining with more brilliance and clarity than the obvious facts. Later she realized that this expectation of disaster was owing to a quality in the newcomer. Doris Fischer, so assertive, so cheerfully sane, often took on the moody gestures of an Irish actress about to disclose that her father was a drunkard, her brother an anarchist, her mother a saint, et cetera. It gave a false start to her presence: any portentousness was usually owing to absent-mindedness or social unease, although that could be grave enough.

"We were both down there waiting for the elevator," said Doris, in her friendly, normal way. "It was stuck some place. You know how it never works in this building…" They had started to climb the stairs together, and she had spoken to Flor. That was all. It was quite ordinary, really.

In Flor's mind, this meeting was extraordinary in the full sense of the word. That any one should accost and speak to her assumed the proportions of fatality. She had been pinpointed, sought out, approached. In her amazement she grasped something that was not far wrong: she had been observed. Doris Fischer had been watching the comings and goings of these people for days, and had obtained from the concierge that they were American. Thoughts of simply presenting herself at their door had occurred and been rejected: wisely, too, for Bonnie would not have tolerated that. This spider role was contrary to Doris's nature. She was observing when she wanted to be involved, and keeping still when everything compelled her to cry, "Accept me!" She was a compatriot and lonely and the others might take her at that value, but Flor's perspective was not wholly askew. Doris was like a card suddenly turned out of the pack: "Beware of a fair-haired woman. She attaches herself like a limpet to the married rock." She would want them all, and all their secrets. She would fill the idleness of her days with their affairs. She would disgorge secrets of her own, and the net would be woven and tight and over their heads.

Everyone remained standing. The fairly mundane social occasion—the person who lived downstairs coming to call—was an event. Doris Fischer saw the husband and the mother as standing forms against the hot summer light. Her eyes were dazzled by the color in the room. The chandelier threw spectrums over peacock walls; blue silk curtains belled and collapsed. Doris thought the room itself perfectly terrible. Her own taste rotated on the blond-wood exports from sanitary Sweden; on wrought-iron in its several forms; on the creeping green plants that prosper in centrally heated rooms but die in the sun. Nothing in her background or her experience could make her respond to the cherished object or the depth of dark, polished wood. She saw there were modern paintings on the walls, and was relieved, for she disliked the past. Radiating confidence now, she stepped farther inside, pointed at the wall opposite, and accused something hanging there.

"It's very interesting," she said, in an agreeable but slightly aggressive voice. "What is it? I mean, who's it by?"

"It is by an Australian who is not yet recognized in his own country," said Bob. He often spoke in this formal manner, never slurring words, particularly when he was meeting someone new. He considered Doris's plain brown-and-white shoes, her plain shirtwaist dress of striped blue cotton, her short, fluffy hair. He was anything but aggressive. He smiled.

They all turned to the painting. Bonnie looked at a bright patch on the bright wall, and Doris at something a child of six might have done as well. Flor saw in the forms exploding with nothing to hold them together absolute proof that the universe was disintegrating and that it was vain and foolish to cry for help. Bob looked at a rising investment that, at the same time, gave him aesthetic pleasure; that was the way to wrap up life, to get the best of everything. Quite simply, he told the price he had paid for the painting last year, and the price it would fetch now that the artist was becoming known: not boasting, but showing that a taste for beauty paid—something like that.

Distress on the fringe of horror covered the faces of the three women, like a glaze, endowing them with a sudden, superficial resemblance. Florence's horror was habitual: it was almost her waking look. Bonnie suffered acutely at her son-in-law's trampling of taste. Doris, the most earnest, thought of how many children in vague, teeming, starving places could have been nourished with that sum of money. Doris stayed to tea; they kept her for dinner. She came from Pennsylvania but had lived in New York. She knew no one Bonnie knew, and Bob thought it typically wicked of his mother-in-law to have asked. They were all in a strange land and out of context. Divisions could be recognized; they needn't be stressed. Doris said that her husband was a cameraman. Sometimes she said "cameraman," sometimes "film technician," sometimes "special consultant." He was in Rome on a job, and would be there all summer. Doris had decided to stay in Paris and get to know the place; when Frank was working, she only got in his way. She was imprecise about the Roman job. A transferred thought hovered like an insect in the room: She's lying. Bonnie thought, He's gone off with a girl; Bob thought, They're broke. He's down there looking for work. Doris was clumsy and evasive, she was without charm or fantasy or style, but they insisted she stay. Flor could do with an American friend.

In honor of the meal, Doris went home and returned wearing some sort of finery. She looked like a social worker going to the movies with a girl friend, Bonnie thought. Unjust appraisal always made her kind: she all but took Doris in her arms. Doris was surprised at the meal, which was scanty and dull. She was accustomed to the food of her childhood, the hillocks of mashed potatoes, the gravy made with cream; she knew the diet of a later bohemia, spaghetti with wine and the bottles saved for candleholders. She could not decide if these well-to-do people were ascetic or plain stingy. Flor ate next to nothing. Doris looked at her over the table and saw a bodiless face between lighted candles—a thin face and thick, lusterless hair. They had lighted the candles without drawing the curtains, and, as the summer night had not yet descended, the room was neither dark nor light, which, for some reason, Doris found faintly disturbing. The dining room was Chinese: throughout the meal she was glared at by monsters. It was enough to put anybody off. Bonnie chattered and nervously rattled the little bell before her. Bob was all indifference and charm. He couldn't stop charming people; it was a reflex. But it didn't mean much, and Doris left him cold. She sensed this, and wished she could make him pay. She would have been distant and mysterious, but she had already talked too much about herself. She had given it all away first go. They had bantering jokes together, underneath which moved a river of recognition. Bonnie listened to them with a glued smile, and fell into a melancholy state of mind, wondering if she were to spend the rest of her life with moral, mental, social, and emotional inferiors. She thought these two were perfectly matched. Actually, they were alike, but not in a way that could draw them together. Neither Bob nor Doris had much feeling for the importance of time: either of them could have been persuaded that the world began the day he was born. It was not enough on which to base a friendship; in any case, Doris had decided she was chiefly interested in Flor. One day she would ask Flor if Bob really loved her, and if he had any intellectual interests other than painting, and what they talked about when they were alone, and if he was any good in bed. This was the relationship she was accustomed to and sorely missed: warm, womanly, with a rich exchange of marital secrets. She smiled at Flor, and Bonnie intercepted the smile and turned it toward herself.

"Florence is spending August in Paris," Bonnie said, with a curved, smiling, coral-colored voice. "True Parisians prefer the city then." Bob Harris looked at his mother-in-law and was visibly shaken by a private desire to laugh. His mother-in-law stopped being Mrs. Hauksbee and glared. It seemed to Doris good-humored enough, though exclusive. She wondered if Flor was pregnant, and if that was why Flor was so quiet.

That night, Bonnie got the invitation to Deauville out of the bottom tray of her jewelry case, where she kept letters, medical prescriptions, and the keys to lost and forgotten trunks. She scarcely knew the woman who had sent it. They had met at a party. The signature evoked a fugitive image: thin, dark, sardonic, French. She began saying to herself, I hardly know Gabrielle, but it was a case of affinity at first sight.

Gabrielle—the Frenchwoman—had rented a villa at Deauville. She was inviting a few people for the month of August, and she stated in her letter what Bonnie's share of costs would be. Bonnie was not offended. Possibly she had always wanted this. She sat at her dressing table, in her lace-and-satin slip, and read the letter. She wore horn-rimmed reading glasses, which gave her appearance an unexpected dimension. When she looked up, the mirror reflected her three ways. Her nose was pointed; underneath her chin hung a slack, soft little pouch. She saw clearly what Gabrielle was and who the other guest would be and that she had been selected to pay. She saw that she was no longer a young woman, and that she depended for nearly everything material on a son-in-law she had opposed and despised. She closed her eyes and put the edge of the letter between her teeth. She emptied her mind, as if emptying a bottle, and waited for inspiration. Inspiration came, as warm as milk, and told her that she had been born a Fairlie, that her husband had ill-used her, that her daughter had made a *mésalliance*, and possessed a heart as impierceable as a nutmeg, whereas Bonnie's heart was a big, floppy cushion in which her loved ones were forever sticking needles and pins. This daughter now bore the virus of a kind of moral cholera that threatened everyone. Inspiration counseled Bonnie to fly, and told her that her dingy aspirations might save her. She opened her eyes but did not look at herself in the glass, for she no longer knew which Bonnie she expected to see. She said aloud, in an exceedingly silly voice, "Well, everybody deserves a little fun."

Later, she said to Flor: "I won't feel so badly about leaving you, now that you've got this nice friend." She made this sound as casual as she could.

Flor gave no sign. She was cunning as a murderer: "If I seem too pleased, she'll be hurt, she won't go away." She imagined the hall filled with suitcases and someone coming up the stairs to carry them away.

Flor had given as her reason for spending August in Paris that Dr. Linnetti had deemed it essential. Even if she went away, she would have to continue paying for the three weekly appointments. She related the story, now firmly ensconced in modern mythology, of Dr. Freud's patients, and how they all went skiing at the same time every year, and all broke their legs in the same way, without warning, and how, as a result of his winter difficulties, a tradition of payment while on holiday had become established. If she left Dr. Linnetti in the lurch, Dr. Linnetti might resent her, and then where would they all be? "Morally, it stinks," said Bob. He threatened to go and see the doctor, but Flor knew he wouldn't. He had insisted on treating the whole thing as nothing at all, hoping it would become nothing, and he would not have committed a positive act. Bonnie now began talking about Flor's August in Paris quite gaily, as a settled event, which left Bob without an ally. He was perplexed. His father was expected from New York any day now. He could not leave his wife alone in Paris, he could not really take her with him on a long business trip, and he did not want his father to see what Flor, or their marriage, had become. He had depended on Bonnie, whose influence had seldom failed. After a time he understood about Deauville. Bonnie knew that he understood. She remembered the philosophy of self-sacrifice she had preached, and that still moped in a corner of their lives like a poor, molting bird. She would have smothered if she could this old projection of herself; but it remained, indestructible as the animal witness in a fairy tale. Bob ignored her now. He seemed to have turned his back. He continued to offer holiday pictures to Flor with accelerated enthusiasm: Spain, Portugal, Portofino, Lausanne, Scotland, gaudy as posters, and as unsubstantial, were revealed and whisked away. "I have to stay here," she said. He obtained nothing more.

Because of Bob's nagging, Bonnie became possessed with the fear that Flor might decide not to stay alone after all, and oblige Bonnie to take her to Deauville. This was hardly feasible, seeing how queer Flor had become. She was likely to say and do anything. She had always been a moody girl, with an unpredictable temper, but that was the personality that went with red hair. Then, too, she had been pretty: a pretty girl can get away with a lot. But, since spring, she had floated out of Bonnie's grasp: she dressed oddly, and looked a wraith. If she did queer things in front of these people at Deauville, Bonnie felt she wouldn't know where to hide from shame. If Flor and Doris Fischer became good friends, Flor might remain more easily in Paris, doing all the sensible things, chatting away to Dr. Linnetti, visiting couturiers with Doris, eating light lunches of omelet and fruit, and so forth. Diet was of great importance in mental equilibrium: you are what you eat. Friendship mattered, said Bonnie, not losing sight of Doris: friendship, rest, good food, relaxing books. In the autumn, Flor would be a different girl.

Flor heard and thought, I used to believe she was God.

Five days remained. Bonnie was rushed off her feet and wore an expression of frank despair. She had left essential duties such as hair, nails, massage, until the end, and every moment was crowded. Nevertheless, because of the importance of the Flor–Doris friendship, she accepted Doris's suggestion one day that they all three go for a walk. Doris liked wandering around Paris, but when she walked alone, she imagined North Africans were following her. Being fair, she was a prize. She might be seized, drugged, shipped to Casablanca, and obliged to work in a brothel. Even in New York, she had never taken a taxi without making certain the window could be lowered. This cherished fear apart, she was sensible enough.

The three women took a taxi to the Place de la Concorde one afternoon and walked to the Pont Neuf. They crossed to the Left Bank over the tip of the Ile de la Cité. It was a hot, transparent day; slumbering summer Paris; a milky sky, a perspective of bridges and shaking trees. Flor had let her long hair free and wore sandals on her feet. She seemed wild, yet urban, falsely contrived, like a gypsy in a musical play. Bonnie walked between the two girls and was shorter than both. She was conscious only of being shorter than Flor. It was curious, being suddenly smaller than the person over whom you had once exercised complete control. Bonnie's step was light: she had been careful to keep a young figure. Doris, the big blond, thought she looked beaky and thin, like a bird. A mean little bird, she amended. There was something about Bonnie she didn't like. Doris wore the dress they had come to consider her day-duty uniform: the neat, standard shirtmaker. Bonnie's little blue hat would have suited her well. Bonnie thought of this, and wondered how to offer it. Doris expressed from time to time her sense of well-being on this lovely day. She said she could hardly believe she was really alive and in Paris. It was like that feeling after a good meal, she said, sincerely, for the gratification of her digestion compared favorably with any pleasure she had known until now. Although neither Flor nor Bonnie answered, Bonnie had an instant's awareness that their reaction to Doris was the same: they needn't share a look, or the pressure of hands. Later, this was one of her most anguished memories. She forgot the time and the year and who was with them, remembering only that on a lost day, with her lost, loved, girl, there had existed a moment of unity while crossing a bridge.

Flor was letting herself see in high, embossed relief, changing the focus of her eyes, even though she knew this was dangerous. Human cunning was keeping the ruin of Paris concealed. The ivy below Notre Dame had swelled through the city's painted crust: it was the tender covering of a ruin. The invasion of strangers resembled the busloads of tourists arriving at Pompeii. They were disoriented and out of place. Recording with their cameras, they tried not to live the day but to fix a day not their own. It had so little to do with the present that something she had suspected became clear: there was no present here, and the strangers were perfectly correct to record, to stare, to giggle, to display the unease a healthy visitor feels in a hospital—the vague fear that a buried illness might emerge, obliging one to remain. Her heart had left its prison and was beating under her skin. The smell of her own hands was nauseating. Nobody knew.

When they reached the opposite shore, Bonnie decided the walk had gone on long enough. She began looking for a taxi. But Flor suddenly said she wanted to continue. The others fell in step; three women strolling by the Seine on a summer's day.

"There is a window with a horse in it," Florence said seriously. "I want to see that."

Bonnie hoped Doris hadn't heard. There was nothing she could do now. Her daughter's eyes were wide and anguished. Her lips moved. Bonnie continued to walk between the two young women so that any conversation would, as it were, sift through her.

"Didn't we walk along here when I was little?" said Flor.

Flor never spoke of the past. To have her go into it now was unsettling. It was also a matter of time and place. It was four o'clock, and Bonnie had a fitting with her dressmaker at five. She said, "Oh, honey, we never came to Paris until you were a big girl. You know that."

"I thought we used to come along here and look at the horse."

This was so bizarre, and yet Bonnie could not help giving Doris an anxious, pathetic glance, as if to say, "We used to do things together—we used to be friends." They were still on the Quai de Montebello when Flor made them cross the street and led them to a large corner window. Well, there was a stuffed horse. Flor wasn't so crazy after all.

An American woman, dressed rather like Doris, stood before the window, holding a child by the hand. Crouched on the pavement, camera to his eyes, was the husband, trying to get all of them in the picture—wife, child, horse. The boy wore a printed shirt that matched his father's, and his horn-rimmed glasses were the same, but smaller. He looked like the father reduced. Doris's delighted eyes signaled that this was funny, but Bonnie was too bothered with Flor to mind: Flor looked at the child, then at the horse, with a fixed, terrified stare. Her skin had thickened and paled. There was a film of sweat on her cheeks.

The child said, "Why's the horse there?" and the mother replied in a flat bored voice, "*I* dunno. He's dead."

"That's wrong," said Flor harshly. "He's guarding the store. At night he goes out and gallops along the river and he wears a white and red harness. You can see him in the parks at night after the gates are locked."

Doris, joining in what she imagined the play of a whimsical mind, said, "Ah, but if the gates are locked, how do you get in to see him?"

"There's a question!" cried Bonnie gaily.

She was not listening to her own voice. Everything was concentrated on getting Flor away, or getting the three open-mouthed tourists away from her.

"We did come here when I was little," said Flor, weeping, clasping her hands. "I remember this horse. I'm sure I remember. Even when I was playing in the grass at home I remembered it here." She saw the leafy tunnels of the Tuileries on an autumn day, and the galloping horse: she could not convey this picture, an image of torment, nostalgia, and unbearable pain.

"Oh, love," said her mother, and she was crying now too. There was something in this scene of the old days, when they had been emotional and close. But their closeness had been a trap, and each could now think, If it hadn't been for you, my life would have been different. If only you had gone out of my life at the right time.

Doris thought: Spoiled. Fuss over nothing. She also thought, I'm like a sister, one of the family. They say anything in front of me.

Perhaps this was true, because it seemed natural that Doris find a taxi, take them home, and put Flor to bed. She even ordered a nice cup of coffee all around, putting on a harmless comedy of efficiency before the cook. By now, after a few days, she might have known them for years. She came into their lives dragging her existence like a wet raincoat, and no one made a move to keep her out. She called them by their Christian names and had heard Bonnie's troubles and hinted at plenty of her own. Bob referred to her as Moonface because she was all circles, round face, round brown eyes. The first impression of American crispness had collapsed. Her hair often looked as if mice had been at it. The shirtmaker dresses were held together with pins. Dipping hems had been stitched with thread the wrong color. She carried foolish straw baskets with artificial flowers wound around the handle, and seemed to have chosen her clothes with three aims in mind: they mustn't cost much, they must look as if anybody could wear them, and they must be suitable for a girl of sixteen. She did not belong in their lives or in the Paris summer. She belonged to an unknown cindery city full of used-car lots. She sat by Flor's bed, hunched forward, hands around her knees. "I know how you feel in a way," she said. "Sometimes I feel so depressed I honestly don't like going out on the street. I feel as if it's written all over me that something's wrong. I get the idea that the mob will turn on me and pull me apart because I'm unhappy and unhappiness is catching." She seemed genial and lively enough, saying this. She was fresh from a different world, where generalized misery was possibly taken for granted. Bob said that Moonface was stupid, and Flor, for want of any opinion, had agreed, but could Flor be superior? She would have given anything to be a victor, one of that trampling mob.

There wasn't much to be had from Flor, and Doris turned to Bonnie instead. She would try every member of the family in turn, and only total failure would drive her away. Within the family, on whatever bankrupt terms, she was at least *somewhere*. She had been afraid of never knowing anyone in Paris: she spoke very little French, and had never wanted to come abroad. But it was not long before she understood that even though they had lived here for years, and used some French words in their private family language, they were not in touch with life in France. They had friends: Bob and Bonnie seemed to go about; but they were not in touch with life in the way Doris— so earnest, so sociologically minded—would have wanted. Still, she enjoyed the new intimacy with Bonnie. For the few days that remained, she had tea every day in Bonnie's bedroom. Bonnie was packing like a fury now. They would shut themselves up in the oyster-colored room, Bonnie dressed in a slip because a dress was a psychological obstacle when she had something to do, and gossip and pack. Doris sat on the floor: the chairs were laden with the dresses Bonnie was or was not going to take to Deauville. Bonnie was careful to avoid dropping the Deauville hostess's name, out of an inverted contempt for Doris, but Doris got the point very soon. She was not impressed. She suspected all forms of titled address, and thought Bonnie would have been a nicer and more sincere person if she had used her opportunities to cultivate college professors and their wives.

Bonnie didn't care what Doris thought. Everything was minimal compared with Flor's increasing queerness and her own headlong and cowardly flight. She talked about Flor, and how Flor was magnifying Bonnie's failings for Dr. Linnetti.

"All children hate their parents," said Doris, shrugging at this commonplace. She was sewing straps for Bonnie. She bit off a thread. There were subjects on which she permitted herself a superior tone. These people had means but were strictly uneducated. Only Bob had a degree. As far as Doris could make out, Flor had hardly even been to school. Doris was proud of her education—a bundle of notions she trundled before her like a pram containing twins. She could not have told you that the shortest distance between two points was a straight line, but she did know that "hostility" was the key word in human relations, and that a man with an abscessed tooth was only punishing himself.

"All I can say is I adored my mother," said Bonnie. "That's all I can say."

"You haven't faced it. Or else you don't remember."

Bonnie remembered other things: she remembered herself, Bonnie, at thirty-seven, her name dragged in the mud, vowing to Flor she would never look at a man again; swearing that Flor could count on her for the rest of her life. She had known in her heart it was a temporary promise and she had said, "I still have five good years." At forty-two, she thought, My life isn't finished. I still have five good years. And so it had been, the postponement of life five years at a time, until now Flor was married and in a dream, and Bonnie was fifty-two. She wanted Flor to hold off; to behave well; not to need help now, this very minute. She was pulled this way and that, now desperate for her own safety, now aghast with remorse and the stormy knowledge of failure. She left Doris sitting on the floor and went into her daughter's room. Flor was lying on the bed, wide-eyed, with a magazine. She kept a magazine at hand so that she could pretend to be reading in case someone came. None of them liked her habit of lying immobile in the semi-dark.

Bonnie sat down on the bed. She wanted to say, Flor, I've had a hell of a life. Your father was a Catholic. He made me be a Catholic and believe a lot of things and then he left off being one and divorced me. And that isn't everything, it's only a fragment. What she said was: "Darling, I'm not going to suggest you see a priest, because I know you wouldn't. But I do agree with Bob, I don't think Dr. Linnetti is any good. If you're going to stay here in August anyway you should see someone else. You know, I used to know a doctor..."

"I know," said Flor, loathing awakened.

But Bonnie hadn't meant that old, disastrous love affair. She had meant a perfectly serious professional man out in Neuilly. Flor's eyes alarmed her. She fingered the magazine between them and thought of the other doctor, the lover, and wondered how much Flor had seen in those days. Flor must have been eleven, twelve. She felt as though she had been staring in the sun, the room seemed so dark.

"You see," said Flor, "I'm perfectly all right and I don't need a priest. Mama. Listen. I'm all right. I'm slightly anemic. It makes me pale. Don't you remember, I was always a bit anemic?"

Flor had said what Bonnie wanted said.

"Oh, I know," said Flor's mother eagerly. "I remember! Oh, lambie, when you were small, the awful chopped raw liver mess you had to eat! You were anemic. Of course I remember now."

"It makes me tired," said Flor gently. "Then there's Doctor L., three times a week. That's tiring too. It just wears me out. And so, I lie down. August alone will be just wonderful. I'll lie down all the time. I'm *anemic*, Mama."

Bonnie's soft eager eyes were on her daughter. She would have cried at her, if she dared, Yes, tell me, make me believe this.

Now, that was the disarming thing about Flor. She could be so sensible, she could explain everything as though you were the nitwit. She could smile: "Don't *worry* about me," and you would think, Flor knows what she's doing. She's all right.

All the same, thought Bonnie, it was a pity that she was only twenty-six and had lost her looks.

Bob Harris had no division of purpose. He wanted Flor to go away from Paris for the next four weeks. Sometimes he said Cannes, because she liked the sea. He mentioned Deauville, but Bonnie pulled a long face. He knew there was more to it than getting through August, but that was all there was time for now. His father had arrived from New York. He was a mild old man, who had not wanted this marriage. He seemed to take up no space in the apartment, and he made everyone generous gifts. Bonnie tried to charm him, and failed. She tried to treat him like a joint parent, with foolish young people to consider, but that failed too. She gave up. She felt that disapproval of the match should be her own family's prerogative and that the Harrises were overstepping. The old man saw Flor, her silence, her absence, and believed she had a lover and that her pallor was owing to guilty thoughts. The young people had been married two years: it seemed to him a sad and wretched affair. There were no children and no talk of any. He thought, *I warned him*, but he held still: he did not want to cause the estrangement of his only son. His gentle sadness affected them all. He was thinly polite, and looked unwell. His skin had the bluish clarity of skimmed milk. Bonnie wanted to scream at him: I didn't want your son! She wondered why he felt he had to be so damned courtly. In her mind there was no social gap between a Jewish wine merchant and her ex-husband's old bootlegger of thirty years before.

Bonnie and her son-in-law were linked in one effort: keeping the old man from knowing the true state of affairs. Bonnie was always willing to unite when their common existence was threatened. She deplored the marriage and believed Flor might have made a better match, but most of the time she was grateful. She worshiped the Harris money: she would have washed all the Harris feet every day if that had been part of the deal. There had always been an unspoken, antagonistic agreement with Bob, which Flor had never understood. She never understood why Bob was nice to her mother. She guessed—that was at the start, when she was still curious and working things out—that it was Jewishness, respect for parents. But this was a subject from which he slid away. Evasion was seared into his personality. He had a characteristic sliding movement of head and body when conversation took a turn he didn't like. It was partly because of this that they had named him the Seal.

The façade they put up now was almost flawless: the old man may even have been deceived. In the effort, they were obliged to look at themselves, and these moments, near-horror, near-perfection, were unrehearsed. They dragged resisting Flor to parties, to restaurants, to the theater. At times Bob and Bonnie began to believe in the situation, and they would say, in amazement, "There, do you see how good life can be?" Flor seemed quite normal, except that she complained of being tired, but many women are like that. One day they made an excursion to Montparnasse: Bob bought pictures, and Bonnie had unearthed a young artist. She said he was Polish and full of genius. It was a bad outing: Bob was irritated because Bonnie had promised to help the young man without telling him first. The studio was like dozens more in Paris: there was a stove with last year's ashes, and the pictures he showed them were cold and stale. There was a flattering drawing of Bonnie tacked to the wall. The painter talked as if he owed his diction to an attentive study of old Charles Boyer films. He had a ripe-pear voice and a French accent.

"I don't like him," said Bob, when they were driving home. "He's nothing. He paints like a little girl. Anyway, he's a phony. What's that accent? He's just a New York boy."

"He has lived here for many years," said Bonnie, the bristling mother-bird.

"I may live here a lot longer but that won't change my voice," said Bob. "He's afraid. He's scared of being what he really is. If he talked naturally he wouldn't be Michel Colbert. Colbert. Colbert. What is that?"

"What is Harris?" said Bonnie, trembling.

Nothing was said, nothing was said about anything, and the silence beat about them like waves. The elevator in the building wasn't working again. Bonnie clutched at Flor as they climbed the stairs. "What have I gone and done?" she whispered heavily, pinching Flor's arm.

Flor had not been lying down a minute before her husband came in and slammed the door behind him. He stood over her and said, "Why the hell didn't you back me up?"

"I didn't listen," said Flor in terror. "I didn't speak."

"That's what I'm saying. What do you suppose my father thinks?"

He didn't go on with it. Too much had been taken away from him. He did not want to diminish what remained. Flor seemed frightened, looking up at him, curled on the bed like a child, and he was filled with pity for her and for them all. She had been dragged from her bed for the futile visit to the studio and now he had to drag her out again. She was a sick girl: he had to remember that. He sat on the bed with his back half turned and said gently, "We have to go out for dinner, you know?"

"Oh, no, no."

"It's my father and some of his friends," he said. "You know I have to be there. These people have invited us. Bonnie's coming." By this he meant that Bonnie understood the requirements of life.

"I'd rather not go."

He was so tired, yet he was someone who had never been tired. He thought, You shouldn't have to plead with your wife over such simple things. "It'll do you good," he said.

"I went to the studio," she said plaintively.

"People go two places in one day," he said. "It's not late. It's summer. It's still light outside. If you'd open those shutters you'd see." He had a fixed idea that she feared the dark.

Light and dark were outside the scope of her fears. She moved her head, unable to speak. He would have taken her hand only he never touched her now. In the spring, she had begun pleading with him to let her sleep. She had behaved like a prisoner roused for questioning. Tomorrow, she had promised, or in the morning. Any moment but now. He woke her one dawn and was humiliated at what they had become, remembering Cannes, the summer they had met. He couldn't discuss it. He never touched her again. He couldn't look at her now. Her hair, loose on the pillow, was a parody of Cannes. So were the shuttered windows.

Flor felt his presence. She had closed her eyes but held his image under the lids. He was half turned away. His back and the shape of his head were against the faint summer light that came in between the slats of the shutters. One hand was flat on the bed, and there was the memory of their hands side by side on the warm sand. When he had moved his hand to cover hers, there remained the imprint of his palm, and, because they were both instinctively superstitious, they had brushed this mold away.

He said in such a miserable voice, "Are you really all that tired?" that she wanted to help him.

She said, "I've already told you. I'm afraid."

He had heard of her fear of cars but couldn't believe it. He had never been afraid: he was the circus seal. They had always clapped and approved. He tried to assemble some of the practical causes of fear. "Are you afraid of the next war? I mean, do you think about the bombs and all that?"

Flor moved her head on the pillow. "It's nothing like that. I don't think about the war. I'm used to the idea, like everyone else." She tried again. "Remember once when we were out walking, remember under the bridge, the boy kicking the man? The man was lying down."

"What's the good of thinking about that?" he said. "Somebody's kicking somebody else all the time. You can't make yourself responsible for everything."

"Why didn't the man at least get up? His eyes were open."

He had been afraid she would say, Why didn't we help him? The incident had seemed even when they were witnessing it far away and grotesque. When you live in a foreign country you learn to mind your own business. But all this reasoning was left in the air. He knew she was making a vertiginous effort to turn back on her journey out. He said something he hadn't thought of until now. It seemed irrefutable: "We don't know what the man had done to him first." Perhaps she accepted this; it caused a silence. "I'm glad you're talking to me," he said humbly, even though he felt she had put him in the wrong.

"I'm afraid of things like that," said Flor.

"Nobody's going to pull you under a bridge and kick you." He looked at her curiously, for she had used a false voice; not as Bonnie sometimes did, but as if someone were actually speaking for her.

"Sometimes when I want to speak," she said in the same way, "something comes between my thoughts and the words." She loathed herself at this moment. She believed she gave off a rank smell. She was the sick redhead; the dying, quivering fox. "It's only being anemic," she said wildly. "The blood doesn't reach the brain."

On an impulse stronger than pride he had already taken her hand. This hand was warm and dry and belonged to someone known. He had loved her: he tried to reconstruct their past, not sentimentally, but as a living structure of hair, skin, breath. This effort surpassed his imagination and was actually repugnant. It seemed unhealthy. Still, remembering, he said, "I do love you," but he was thinking of the hot, faded summer in Cannes, and the white walls of his shuttered room on a blazing afternoon, and coming in with Flor from the beach. He saw the imprint of his fingers on her brown shoulder; he thought he tasted salt. Suddenly he felt as if he might vomit. His mouth was flooded with saliva. He thought, I'll go crazy with this. He was appalled at the tenderness of the wound. He remembered what it was to be sick with love.

"You'd better come out," he said. "It'll do you good. You'll see there's nothing to be afraid of." With these words he caused them to resume their new roles: the tiresome wife, the patient husband.

He had never insisted so much before; but too much had been taken away in his wife's retreat and he had been, without knowing it, building on what was left: money, and his own charm. He could not stop charming people. The concierge was minutes recovering from his greeting every day. These elements—the importance of business, his own attractive powers—pulled away like the sea and left him stranded and without his wife.

Flor's crisis had passed. The sharp-muzzled animal who inhabited her breast had gone to sleep. She looked at her husband and saw that whatever protected him had left him at that moment; he seemed pitiable and without confidence. She might have said, Forgive me, or even, Help me, and it might have been different between them, if not better, but Bonnie came in. She knocked and must have thought she heard an answer. Neither Bob nor Flor heard clearly what she said. The present rushed in with a clatter, for Bonnie threw the shutters apart with an exclamation of annoyance, and past love, that delicate goblet, was shattered on the spot.

Bob stood beside Bonnie. Between them, joined enemies again, they got Flor up and out. "I shall never forgive you," said Flor; but she rose, bathed, put up her hair. Their joint feeling—her and Bob's—was one of relief: there was no need to suffer too deeply after all. No present horror equaled the potential suffering of the past. Reliving the past, with full knowledge of what was to come, was a test too strong for their powers. It would have been too strong for anyone; they were not magical; they were only human beings.

Two days after this, on the fourth of August, everyone except Flor went away. The cook and the maid had already departed for Brittany, each weighted with a full, shabby suitcase. Bob and his father left by car in the morning. Bob was hearty and rather vulgar and distrait, saying goodbye. He patted Flor on the buttocks and kissed her mouth. This took place on the street. She had come down to see them loading the car—just like any young woman seeing vacationers off. She stood with her arms around her body, as if the day were cold. The old man, now totally convinced that Flor had a lover in Paris, did not look at her directly. In the afternoon, Bonnie took off from the Gare St. Lazare and Flor went there too. The station was so crowded that they had to fight their way to the train. Bonnie kept behaving as though it were all slick and usual and out of a page entitled "Doings of the International Smart Set": young Mrs. Robert Harris seeing her mother off for Deauville. Bonnie was beautifully dressed. She wore a public smile and gave her daughter a woman's kiss, embracing the air.

Flor saw the train out. She went home and got out of her clothes and into a nightgown covered with a pattern of butterflies. She had left a message for the cleaning woman, telling her not to come. She went from room to room and closed the shutters. Then she got into bed.

She slept without stirring until the next morning, when there was a ring at the door. Doris Fischer was there. She looked glossy and sunburned, and said she had caught a throat virus from the swimming pool in the Seine. She was hard, sunny reality; the opponent of dreams. She sat by Flor's bed and talked in disconnected sentences about people back in the States Flor had never seen. At noon, she went into the kitchen and heated soup, which they drank from cups. Then she went away. Flor lay still. She thought of the names of streets she had lived in and of hotel rooms in which she had spent the night. She leaned on her elbow and got her notebook from the table nearby. This was an invalid's gesture; the pale hand fretfully clutching the magic object. There were no blank pages. She had used them all in the letter. She looked at a page on which she had written this:

Maids dancing in Aunt Dottie Fairlie's kitchen.

Father Doyle: If you look in the mirror too much you will see the devil.

Granny's gardener

B. H.: The only thing I like about Christ is when he raised the little girl from the dead and said she should be given something to eat.

She turned the pages. None of these fragments led back or forward to anything and many called up no precise image at all. There was nothing to add, even if there had been space. The major discovery had been made that July afternoon before the Café de la Paix, and the words, "it was always this way," were the full solution. Even Dr. Linnetti would have conceded that.

She could not sleep unless her box of sleeping tablets was within sight. She placed the round box on the notebook and slept again. The next day, Doris returned. She sat by Flor's bed because Bonnie had gone and there was no one else. The traffic outside was muffled to a rustling of tissue paper, the room green-dark.

"What are those pill things for?" Doris said.

"Pains," said Flor. "My teeth ache. It's something that only happens in France and it's called *rage de dents*."

"I've got good big teeth and I've never had a filling," said Doris, showing them. "That's from the German side. I'm half Irish, half German. Florence, why don't you get up? If you lie there thinking you're sick you'll *get* sick."

"I know perfectly well I'm not sick," said Flor.

Doris thought she was on to something. "You know, of course," she said, fixing Flor sternly, "that this is a retreat from life."

For the first time since Doris had known her, Flor laughed. She laughed until Doris joined in too, good-natured, but slightly vexed, for she guessed she was being made fun of.

"Don't worry about me," said Flor, as lucidly as you pleased. "I'm a Victorian heroine."

"The trouble is," Doris said, "you've never had to face a concrete problem. Like mine. Like..." and she was away, divulging the affairs she had only hinted at until now. Her husband had left her, but only for the summer. He intended to return, and she knew she would take him back, and that should have been the end of it. That was the story, but Doris couldn't leave it alone. Behind the situation struggled memories and impulses she could neither relate nor control. Trying to bring order through speech, she sat by Flor's bed and told her about their life in New York, which had been so different. Names emerged: Beth and Howard, Peter and Jan, Bernie and Madge, Lina, who was brilliant, and Wolff and Louis, who always came to see them on Sundays, and lived in a stable or garage or something like that. They were prudently left-wing, and on speaking terms with a number of jazz musicians. They had among their friends Chinese, Javanese, Peruvians, and Syrians. They had a wonderful life. Then this year abroad things had happened and her husband, filming a documentary for television, had met a woman studying Egyptian at the Ecole du Louvre. "Don't laugh," said Doris miserably to Flor, who was not laughing at all.

Why did these things happen? Why was Doris alone in Paris, who had never been alone in her life? Why weren't they still in college or still in New York? Why was she nearly thirty and in a foreign place and everything a mess? "You tell me," Doris demanded.

Flor had no replies. She lay on the bed, in a butterfly-covered nightgown, and her dreams were broken by Doris's ring at the door. Doris occupied the chair beside her bed as if she had a right to it. She came every day. She opened cans of soup in the kitchen and she never washed the saucepan or the cups. She took clean dishes from the cupboard each time, and it was like the Mad Tea Party; although even there, eventually, it must have become impossible to move along. The dishes here would finally reach an end too, and she would have to do something—go home, or follow her husband, whether he wanted her around or not, or stay here and wash cups. Flor was not making the division between days and nights clearly, but she knew that Doris came most frequently in the afternoon. She told Flor that she woke up fairly optimistically each day, but that the afternoon was a desert and she couldn't cross it alone.

Then a disaster occurred: Flor's sleeping tablets disappeared. She took the bed apart and rolled back the carpet. Doris helped, unexpectedly silent. It was a disaster because without the pills in the room she was unable to sleep. Her desire for sleep and dreams took the shape of a boat. Every day it pulled away from shore but was forced to return. She had left the doorkey under the mat so that Doris could come in when she wanted, after a warning ring. She got up early one day and took the key inside. She heard a ring and didn't answer. The ring was repeated, and Doris knocked as well, but Flor lay still, her eyes closed. Once the imperative ring surprised her in the kitchen, where she was distractedly looking around for something to eat. There were empty cans everywhere, which Doris had opened for her, and dirty cups, and a spilled box of crackers. She found cornflakes and some sour milk in a jug and a sticky packet of dates. In a store cupboard there were more tins. She opened a tin of mushrooms and ate them with her fingers and went back to bed. This scene had the air of a robbery. It was midday, but the light was on; the kitchen was shuttered, like every other room. Flor's quest for food was stealthy and uncertain, partly because the kitchen was not her province and she seldom entered it. When Doris rang, she stood frozen, in her nightgown, her head thrown back, her heart beating in hard, painful, slow thumps. She had a transient fear that Doris possessed a miraculous key and could come in whenever she wanted to. She felt the warmth and weight of her thick hair. Her neck was damp with fear.

The ringing stopped. That afternoon she slept and half slept and had her first real dream, which was of floating, sailing, going away. It was pleasant, brightly lit, and faintly erotic. There emerged the face of a Russian she and her mother had once talked to in a hotel. She remembered that in the presence of a whirlwind you defied Satan and made the sign of the cross. She opened her eyes with interest and wonder. She had followed someone exorcising a number of rooms. She was not in the least frightened, but she was half out of bed.

The building was empty now. She heard the concierge cleaning on the stairs. In the daytime there was light through the shutters. She was happiest at night, but her plans were upset by the loss of the pills. Once her husband telephoned and she replied and spoke quite sensibly, although she could not remember afterward what she had said. She turned her room upside down again, but the pills were gone. Well, the pills might turn up. There were other things to be done: cupboards to be shut, drawers tidied, stockings put away. She knew she would be unable to lie in peace until everything was settled, and August was wearing away. Every day she did one useful thing. There were the gold sandals Bonnie wanted repaired: she had left them on a chest in the hall so that Flor would see them on her way out. These sandals did not belong in the hall. The need to find a place for the broken sandals drove her out of bed one afternoon. She carried the sandals all around the flat, from shuttered room to room. There was no sound from the street. In her mother's bedroom she forgot why she had come. She let the sandals fall on a chair; that was how Bonnie found them, one on the chair, one on the floor, with its severed strap like a snapped twig some inches away.

Once she had told Dr. Linnetti that her husband was her mother's lover. She had described in a composed voice the scene of discovery: he came home very late and instead of going into his own room went into Bonnie's. She knew it was he, for she knew his step, and the words this man used were his. She heard her mother whisper and her mother laugh. "Then," said Flor, "he tried to come to me, but I wouldn't have it. No, never again." A month later she said, "That wasn't true, about Bob and my mother." "I know," said Dr. Linnetti.

"How do you know?" said Flor, trembling, in Bonnie's room. "How do you know?"

She saw herself in a long glass, in the long loose butterfly-covered nightdress. She looked like a pale rose model in a fashion magazine, neat, sweet, a porcelain figure, intended to suggest that it suffices to be desirable—that the dream of love is preferable to love in life.

"You might cut your hair," said Bonnie.

"Yes," said Flor. "You'd love that, wouldn't you?"

Bonnie's windows were closed and the oyster-silk fringed curtains pulled together. But still light came into the room, the milky light of August, in which Flor, the dreamer, floated like a seed. Bonnie had not entirely removed herself to Deauville, for her scent clouded the room—the cat's-fur Spanish-servant-girl scent she bought for herself in expensive bottles. Flor moved out of the range of the looking glass and could no longer be witnessed. She opened a mothproof closet and looked at dresses without touching them. She looked at chocolates from Holland in a tin box. She looked desultorily for her pills. She forgot what she was doing here and returned to bed.

She knew that time was going by and the city was emptying, and still she hadn't achieved the dreams she desired. One day she opened the shutters of her bedroom and the summer afternoon fell on her white face and tangled hair. There was the feeling of summer ending; it had reached its peak and could only wane. Nostalgia came into the room—for the past, for the waning of a day, for a shadow through a blind, for the fear of autumn. It was a season not so much ending as already used up, like a love too long discussed or a desire deferred. An accumulation of shadows and seasons ending led back to some scene: maids dancing in Aunt Dottie's kitchen? She held the shutters out and apart with both hands, frozen, as if calling for aid. None came, and she drew in her thin arms and brought the shutters to.

She was interrupted by the concierge, who brought letters, and said, "Are you still not better?" She left unopened the letters from her husband because she knew he was not saying anything to her. She opened all the letters from Dr. Linnetti, those addressed to herself, and to her mother and her husband as well. She had long ago intercepted and destroyed the first letter to Bob: "Her hostility to me was expected..." (Oh, she had no pride!) "but she is in need of help." She gave the name of another doctor and said that this doctor was a man.

Flor had no time for doctors. She had to finish sewing a dress. She became brisk and busy and decided to make one dress of two, fastening the bodice of one to the skirt of the other. For two days she sewed this dress and in one took it apart. She unpicked it stitch by stitch and left the pieces on the floor. She was quite happy, humming, remembering the names of songs. She wandered into Bonnie's room. The mothproof closet was open, as she had left it. She took down a heavy brocaded cocktail dress and with Bonnie's nail scissors began picking the seams apart. There was a snowdrift of threads on the parquet. The carpet had been taken away. When she went back to bed, she could sleep, but she was sleeping fitfully. There were no dreams. It was days since she had looked into the notebook. The plants were dying without water and the kitchen light left burning night and day. For the first time in her memory she was frightened of the dark. When she awoke at night it was to a whirling world of darkness and she was frightened. Then she remembered that Bonnie had taken the prescription for the sleeping tablets and she found it easily in the jewel case, lower tray.

She dressed and went down the stairs, trembling like an invalid, holding the curving rail. The concierge put letters in her hand, saying something Flor could not hear. She went out into the empty city. The quarter was completely deserted and there was no one in the park. She saw from the fit of her dress that she had lost pounds. It was the last Sunday of August, and every pharmacy she came to was closed. The air was heavy and still. There was no variation in the color of the sky. It might have been nine in the morning or four in the afternoon. The city had perished and everyone in it died or gone away; she had perceived this on a July day, crossing the Pont Neuf. It was more than a fancy, it was true. The ruin was incomplete. The streets lacked the crevices in which would appear the hellebore, the lizards, the poppies, the ivy, the nesting birds. High up at one of the windows was a red geranium, the only color on the gray street. It flowered, abandoned, on its ledge, like the poppies and the cowslips whose seeds are carried by the wind and by birds to the highest point of a ruin.

There were no cars. She was able to cross every street. The only possible menace came from one of the letters the concierge had put in her hand. She came to a café filled with people, huddled together on the quiet avenue. She sat down and opened the letter. It was nearly impossible to read, but one sentence emerged with clarity: "I am writing to Dr. Linnetti and telling her I think it is *unprofessional* to say the least," and one page she read from the start to the end; "I want this man to see you. It is something entirely new. Everything we think of as mental comes from a different part of your body and it is only a matter of getting all these different parts under control. You have always been so strong-minded darling it should be easy for you. It is *not* that Swiss and *not* that Russian but someone quite new, and he had helped thousands. When he came into the room darling we all got to our feet, it was as if some unseen force was pulling us, and although he said very little every word counted. He is most attractive darling but of course above and outside all that. I asked him what he thought of The Box and he said it was all nonsense so you see darling he isn't a fake. When I explained about The Box and how you put a drop of blood on a bit of blotting paper and The Box makes a diagnosis he was absolutely horrified so you see love he isn't a fake at all. I remember how you were so scornful when The Box diagnosed my liver trouble (that all the doctors thought was heart) so it must be an assurance for you that he doesn't believe in it too. Darling he was so interested in hearing about you. I am going to ask Dr. Linnetti why you must pay even if away and why you must have sessions in August. He is coming to Paris and you must meet. He doesn't have fees or fixed hours, you come when you need him and you give what you can to his Foundation."

She became conscious of a sound, as a sound in the fabric of a dream. Florence looked away from Bonnie's letter and saw that this sound was real. At one of the café tables, a laughing couple were pretending to give a child away to a policeman. The policeman played his role well, swinging his cape, pretending to be fierce. "She is very naughty," said the mother, when she could stop laughing enough to speak, "and I think prison is the best solution." All the people in the café laughed, except Flor. They opened their mouths in the same way, eyes fixed on the policeman and the child. The child cried out that it would be good, now, but everyone was too excited to pay attention. The child gave one more promise and suddenly went white and stiff in the policeman's grasp. He gave her back to her parents, who sat her on a chair. "She'll be good now," the policeman said.

The closed face of Paris relaxed. This was Paris: this was France. Oh, it was not only France. Her mother's mother's gardener had broken the necks of goldfinches. "If you tell you saw, you'll get hit by lightning," he had said.

"It's because of things like that," said Florence earnestly, retracing her steps home, "I'm not afraid of bombs."

She unlocked the empty apartment and the element she recognized and needed but that had evaded her until now rushed forward to meet her, and she knew it was still August, that she was still alone, and there was still time. "I only need a long sleep," she said to the empty air. The unopened letters from Bob she put on the chest in the hall. Her advancing foot kicked something along and it was a trodden, folded letter that had been pushed under the door. It was dirty and had been walked on and was greasy with city dust. She carried this letter—three sheets folded one over the other—around the flat. She closed all the doors except the door of the kitchen and the door of her bedroom. The passage was a funnel. Her sleep had been a longer and longer journey away from shore. She lay down on the bed, having been careful to remove her shoes. The letter spoke to her in peaked handwriting. She had no idea who it was from.

"I have stupid ideas," said this pointed hand, "and you are right to have nothing to do with me. You are so beautiful and clever." It groveled on like this for lines. Who is the writer of this letter? Her husband loves her but has gone away with another woman. "The girl knows I know, and it doesn't work, we are all unhappy, he has his work, and I can't just make a life of my own as he suggests. I thought you would help me but why should you? You are right not to let anyone hang on your skirts. The important thing is that I have made a decision, because I understood when you locked me out that what is needed is not slow suffering or hanging on to someone else, but a solution. I went out on the street that day and wanted to die because you had locked me out and I realized that there was a solution for me and the solution was a decision and so now I am going home. I am not going *away* but going *home*. He can follow, or he can stay, or he can do what he likes, but I have made a decision and I have cabled my father and he is cabling the money and I am going home. I'm leaving on the sixteenth and I'll wait for you every evening, come down if you want to say goodbye. I won't bother you again. All I want to tell you is I hid your sleeping pills and now I know I had no right to do that, because every person's decision is his own. I know I was silly because you're young and pretty and have everything to live for and you wouldn't do what I was afraid you would. I can't even write the word. You may have been wanting those pills and I'm sorry. They're in the kitchen, inside the white tin box with 'Recipes' written on it. Don't be angry with my interference and please Florence come and say goodbye. Florence, another thing. Everybody makes someone else pay for something, I don't know why. If you are as awful to your mother as she says you are, you are making her pay, but then, Florence, your mother could turn around and say, 'Yes, but look at my parents,' and they could have done and said the same thing, so you see how pointless it is to fix any blame. I think my husband is making me pay, but I don't know what for or why. Everyone does it. We all pay and pay for someone else's troubles. All children eventually make their parents pay, and pay, and pay. That's the way I see it now, although I may come to change my mind when I have children of my own. Florence, come once and say goodbye."

She had no time and no desire to say, They have paid. At the edge of the sea, the Fox departed. She saw the animal head breaking the water and the fan-shaped ripples diminishing against the shore. She turned her back and left the sea behind. At last she was going in the right direction. She rode Chief, her pony, between an alley of trees. Chief was a devil: he daren't bolt, or rear, but he sometimes tried to catch her leg against a tree. Nearby somebody smiled. She held herself straight. She was perfect. Everyone smiled now. Everyone was pleased. She emerged in triumph from the little wood and came off Chief, her pony, and into her father's arms.

3

DREAMS of chaos were Wishart's meat; he was proud of their diversity, and of his trick of emerging from mortal danger unscathed. The slightest change in pace provoked a nightmare, so that it was no surprise to him when, falling asleep in his compartment a few seconds before the train arrived at Cannes, he had a dream that lasted hours about a sinking ferryboat outside the harbor. Millions of limp victims bowled elegantly out of the waves, water draining from their skin and hair. There were a few survivors, but neither they, nor the officials who had arrived in great haste, knew what to do next. They milled about on the rocky shore looking unsteady and pale. Even the victims seemed more drunk than dead. Out of this deplorable confusion Wishart strode, suitably dressed in a bathing costume. He shook his head gravely, but without pity, and moved out and away. As usual, he had foreseen the disaster, but failed to give warning. Explanations unrolled in his sleeping mind: "I never interfere. It was up to them to ask me. They knew I was there." His triumph was only on a moral level. He had no physical vanity at all. He observed with detachment his drooping bathing trunks, his skinny legs, his white freckled hands, his brushed-out fringe of graying hair. None of it humbled him. His body had never given him much concern.

He was pleased with the dream. No one was gifted with a subconscious quite like Wishart's, tirelessly creative, producing without effort any number of small visual poems in excellent taste. This one might have been a ballet, he decided, or, better still, because of the black and white groupings and the unmoving light, an experimental film, to be called simply and cryptically "Wishart's Dream." He could manipulate this name without conceit, for it was not his own. That is, it was not the name that had been gummed onto his personality some forty years before without thought or care: "Wishart" was selected, like all the pieces of his fabricated life. Even the way he looked was contrived, and if, on bad days, he resembled nothing so much as a failed actor afflicted with dreams, he accepted this resemblance, putting it down to artistic fatigue. He did not consider himself a failed anything. Success can only be measured in terms of distance traveled, and, in Wishart's case, it had been a long flight. No wonder he looked wearing, he would think, seeing his sagged face in the glass. He had lived one of society's most grueling roles, the escape from an English slum. He had been the sturdy boy with vision in his eyes—that picked-over literary bone. "Scramble, scrape, and scholarship" should have been written on his brow, and, inside balloons emerging from his brain, "a talent for accents," and "a genius for kicking the past from his shoes." He had other attributes, of course, but it wasn't necessary to crowd the image.

Wishart's journey was by no means unusual, but he had managed it better than nearly anyone. Most scramblers and scrapers take the inherited structure with them, patching and camouflaging as they can, but Wishart had knocked his flat. He had given himself a name, parents, and a class of his choice. Now, at forty-two, he passed as an English gentleman in America, where he lived, and as an awfully decent American when he went to England. He had little sense of humor where his affairs were concerned, no more than a designer of comic postcards can be funny about his art, but he did sometimes see it as a joke on life that the quirks and crotchets with which he was laced had grown out of an imaginary past. Having given himself a tall squire of a father, who adored horses and dogs, Wishart first simulated, then genuinely felt, a disgust and terror of the beasts. The phantom parent was a brandy swiller: Wishart wouldn't drink. Indeed, as created by his equally phantom son, the squire was impeccably *bien élevé* but rather a brute: he had not been wholly kind to Wishart, the moody, spindly boy. Wishart often regretted that he would never overtake the mighty Pa, in manliness, that is; he had already outrun him in brains. He said this to friends. The friends, seeing a clear-cut case, urged him to free himself from the shadow of Pa, and Wishart would promise to try. For a time he would try, as if the squire in his great boots had existed, as if there had been a moony Wishart in the garret reading Keats. Now that was surely a joke, or might have been, if only there had been someone to share it with. But Wishart had no witnesses. The only person out of the real past he remembered without disgust was a sister, Glad, who had become a servant at eleven and had taught him how to eat with a knife and fork. The joke was airtight; Wishart was safe. He had an innocent faith that the past, severed from him, could not persist in a life of its own.

At the beginning, in the old days, before he had been intelligent enough to settle for the squire and had hinted at something grand, he had often been the victim of sudden frights, when an element, hidden and threatening, had bubbled under his feet, and he had felt the soles of his shoes growing warm, so thin, so friable was the crust of his poor world. Nowadays, he moved in a gassy atmosphere of goodwill and feigned successes. He seemed invulnerable. Strangers meeting him for the first time often thought he must be celebrated, and wondered why they had never heard of him before. There was no earthly reason for anyone's having done so; he was a teacher of dramatics in a preparatory school, and once this was revealed, and the shoddiness of the school established, it required Wishart's most hypnotic gifts, his most persuasive monologue, to maintain the effect of his person. As a teacher he was barely adequate, and, if he had been an American, his American school would never have kept him. His British personality—sardonic, dry—replaced ability or even ambition. Privately, he believed he was wasted in a world of men and boys, and had never bothered giving them the full blaze of his Wishart creation; he saved it for a world of women. Like many spiteful, snobbish, fussy men, or a certain type of murderer, Wishart chose his friends among middle-aged solitary women. These women were widowed or divorced, and lived in places Wishart liked to visit. Every summer, then, shedding his working life, a shining Wishart took off for Europe, where he spent the summer alighting here and there, depending on the topography of his invitations. He lived on his hostesses, without shame. He was needed and liked: his invitations began arriving at Christmas. He knew that women who will fret over wasting the last bit of soap, or a torn postage stamp, or an unused return ticket, will pay without a murmur for the company of a man. Wishart was no hired companion—carrier of coats, fetcher of aspirin, walker of dachshunds. He considered it enough to be there, supplying gossip and a listening ear. Often Wishart's friends took it for granted he was homosexual, which was all to the good. He was the chosen minstrel, the symbolic male, who would never cause "trouble." He knew this: it was a galling thought. But he had never managed to correct it. He was much too busy keeping his personality in place so that it wouldn't slip or collapse even in his dreams. He had never found time for such an enervating activity as proving his virility, which might not only divert the movement of his ambitions, but could, indeed, take up an entire life. He had what he wanted, and it was enough: he had never desired a fleet of oil tankers. It sufficed him to be accepted here and there. His life would probably have been easier if he had not felt obliged to be something special on two continents; but he was compelled to return to England now, every year, and make them accept him. They accepted him as an American, but that was part of the buried joke. Sometimes he ventured a few risks, such as "we were most frightfully poor when I was a child," but he knew he still hadn't achieved the right tone. The most successful impostures are based on truth, but how poor is poor, and how closely should he approach this burning fact? (Particularly in England, where the whole structure could collapse for the sake of a vowel.) These were the trials that beset poor Wishart, and sometimes caused him to look like a failed actor who has had a bad dream.

He got down from the train, holding his artfully bashed-up suitcase, and saw, in the shadow of the station, Mrs. Bonnie McCarthy, his best American friend. She was his relay in the south of France, a point of refreshment between the nasal sculptress in London who had been his first hostess of the season and a Mrs. Sebastian in

Venice. It would have been sweet for Wishart at this moment if he could have summoned an observer from the past, a control to establish how far he had come. Supposing one of the populated waves of his dream had deposited sister Glad on shore? He saw her in cap and apron, a dour little girl, watching him being greeted by this woman who would not as much as have spat in their direction if she had known them in the old days. At this thought he felt a faint stir, like the rumor of an earthquake some distance away. But he knew he had nothing to fear and that the source of terror was in his own mistakes. It had been a mistake to remember Glad.

"Wishart," his friend said gravely, without breaking her pose. Leaning on a furled peach-colored parasol, she gave the appearance of living a minute of calm in the middle of a hounding social existence. She turned to him the soft, myopic eyes that had been admired when she was a girl. Her hair was cut in the year's fashion, like an inverted peony, and she seemed to Wishart beautifully dressed. She might have been waiting for something beyond Wishart and better than a friend, some elegant paradise he could not imagine, let alone attain. His admiration of her (charm, wealth, aspirations) flowed easily into admiration of himself: after all, he had achieved this friend. Almost tearful with self-felicitation, he forgot how often he and Bonnie had quarreled in the past. Their kiss of friendship outside the station was real.

"Did you get my telegram?" he said, beginning the nervous remarks that preceded and followed all his journeys. He had prepared his coming with a message: "Very depressed London like old blotting paper longing for sea sun you." This wire he had signed Baronne Putbus. (There was no address, so that Bonnie was unable to return a killing answer she would have signed Lysistrata.)

"I died," Bonnie said, looking with grave liquid eyes. "I just simply perished." After the nasal sculptress and her educated vowels, Bonnie's slight drawl fell gently on his ear. She continued to look at him gaily, without making a move, and he began to feel some unease in the face of so much bright expectancy. He suddenly thought, Good God, has she fallen in love? adding in much smaller print, with me? Accidents of that sort had happened in the past. Now, Wishart's personality being an object he used with discretion, when he was doubtful, or simply at rest, he became a sort of mirror. Reflected in this mirror, Bonnie McCarthy saw that she was still pretty and smart. Dear darling Wishart! He also gave back her own air of waiting. Each thought that the other must have received a piece of wonderful news. Wishart was not envious; he knew that the backwash of someone else's fortune can be very pleasant indeed, and he waited for Bonnie's good tidings to be revealed. Perhaps she had rented a villa, so that he would not have to stay in a hotel. That would be nice.

"The hotel isn't far," Bonnie said, stirring them into motion at last. "Do you want to walk a little, Wishart? It's a lovely, lovely day."

No villa, then; and if the hotel was nearby, no sense paying a porter. Carrying his suitcase, he followed her through the station and into the sudden heat of the Mediterranean day. Later, he would hate these streets, and the milling, sweating, sunburned crowd; he would hurry past the sour-milk smelling cafés with his hand over his nose. But now, at first sight, Cannes looked as it had sounded when he said the word in London, a composition in clear chalk colors, blue, yellow, white. Everything was intensely shaded or intensely bright, hard and yellow on the streets, or dark as velvet inside the bars. Bonnie seemed to be leading him somewhere. He supposed it had to do with her surprise.

"I hope you aren't cross because Florence isn't here," Bonnie said. "She was perishing to meet your train, but the poor baby had something in her eye. A grain of sand. She had to go to an oculist to have it taken out. You'll love seeing her now, Wishart. She's getting a style, you know? Everyone notices her. Somebody said to me on the beach—a total stranger—somebody said, Your daughter is like a Tanagra."

"Of which there are so many fakes."

Like many people who are too much concentrated on their own persons, Wishart sometimes believed he was invisible and could not be heard. He did not have a great opinion of his friend's intelligence, and may have thought that a slight obtuseness also affected her hearing. It was insensitive of her to mention Flor, now, just when Wishart was feeling so well. From the beginning, their friendship had been marred by the existence of Bonnie's daughter, a spoiled, sulky girl he had vainly tried to admire. He remembered her as a preener and head-tosser—that long tail of carrot hair! There was a wounding memory of her posturing on a beach and looking as though she had bitten a lemon every time Wishart opened his mouth. She had a jerky, resentful way of speaking and a detestable American voice. Wishart was an amusing mimic, and would have sacrificed any personality save his own for the sake of a story. Re-created by Wishart, Bonnie emerged sounding like Zasu Pitts. "And the daughter," he would say. "When she parts those perfect lips to speak. Oh!" And he would close his eyes in remembered pain. "But then she *is* perfect. Why should Aphrodite utter?" This way of going on was one of his few errors. He was not sure of his ground, had it all at second hand. Even as a pose it was out of date.

"There are literally millions of men chasing Flor," Bonnie said. "I've never seen anything like it. Every time we go to the beach or the casino..."

He realized with boredom—boredom that was like having a dry biscuit stuffed in one's mouth—that they were going to talk about Venus-Flor. "She worships me," Bonnie used to tell him. "That girl simply worships me." But as far as Wishart could tell, it had always been Flor on the altar with Mama at her feet.

"I'm surprised she hasn't offered you a son-in-law," he said, knowing that this praise of Flor was leading up to a complaint. "But I suppose she is still too young."

"Oh, she isn't," Bonnie cried, standing still. "Wishart, that girl is twenty-four. I don't know what men want from women now. I don't even know what Flor wants. We've been here since the tenth of June, and do you know what she's picked up? A teeny little fellow from Turkey. I swear, he's not five three. When we go out, the three of us, I could die. I don't understand it, why she only likes the wrong kind. Only likes, did I say? I should have said only *attracts*. They're awful.

They don't even propose. She hasn't even got the satisfaction of turning them down. I don't understand it and that's all I can say. Why, I had literally hundreds of proposals, and not from little Turkeys. I stuck to my own kind."

He wanted to say, Yes, but you were among your own kind. The girl is a floater, like me. He sensed that Bonnie's disappointment in what she called her own kind had affected her desires for Flor. Her own kind had betrayed her; she had told him so. That was why she lived in Europe. Outside her own kind was a vast population of men in suspenders standing up to carve the Sunday roast. That took care of Americans. They walked on, slowly. A store window they passed revealed the drawn, dried expression that added years to Wishart's age but removed him from competition and torment. He found time to admire the image, and was further comforted by Bonnie's next, astonishing words:

"Someone like you, Wishart, would be good for Flor. I mean someone older, a person I can trust. You know what I mean, an Englishman who's been in America, who's had the best of both."

He knew that she could not be proposing him as a husband for Florence, but he could have loved her forever for the confirmation of the gentleman he had glimpsed in the window, the sardonic Englishman in America, the awfully decent American in England. He slipped his hand under her elbow; it was almost a caress. They reached the Croisette, crossed over to the sea side, and Bonnie put up her parasol. Wishart's ballooning good humor hung suspended as he looked down at the beaches, the larvae bodies, the rows of chairs. Every beach carried its own social stamp, as distinct as the strings of greasy flags, the raked, pullulating sand, the squalid little bar that marked the so-called students' beach, and the mauve and yellow awnings, the plastic mattresses of the beach that was a point of reunion for Parisian homosexuals. Wishart's gaze, uninterested, was about to slide over this beach when Bonnie arrested him by saying, "This is where we bathe, Wishart, dear." He turned his head so suddenly that her parasol hit him in the eye, which made him think of her falsehood about Flor and the grain of sand. He looked with real suspicion now at the sand, probably treacherous with broken bottles, and at the sea, which, though blue and sparkling, was probably full of germs. Even the sky was violated: across the face of it an airplane was writing the name of a drink.

Bonnie has fallen into that one, he thought: Queen Bee of a pansy court.

"Oh, my sweet heaven," Bonnie said, unaware of Wishart's busy brain. She stood still, clutching Wishart by the arm, and said it again: "Sweet heaven. Well, there she is. There's Flor. But that's not the Turk from Turkey. Now, Wishart, her mother is to have a treat. She's got a new one. Oh my sweet heaven Wishart where does she find them?"

"I expect she meets them in trains."

From that distance he could admire Bonnie's girl, thin and motionless, with brown skin and dark red hair. She leaned on the low wall, looking down at the sea, braced on her arms, as tense as if this decision over a beach was to decide the course of her life.

"She does have extraordinary coloring," he said, as generously as he could.

"She gets it from me," said Bonnie, shortly, as if she had never noticed her own hair was brown.

The man with Florence was stocky and dark. He wore sneakers, tartan swimming trunks of ample cut, a gold waterproof watch, a gold medal on a chain, and a Swedish university cap some sizes too small. He carried a net bag full of diving equipment. His chest was bare.

"Well, I don't know," Bonnie said. "I just don't know."

By a common silent decision the two rejected the beach and turned and came toward Bonnie. They gave an impression as harsh and unpoetical as the day. The sun had burned all expression from their faces, smooth brown masks in which their eyes, his brown, hers green, shone like colored glass. Even though he had never dared allow himself close relations, Wishart was aware of their existence to a high degree. He could detect an intimate situation from a glance, or a quality of silence. It was one more of his gifts, but he could have been happier without it. Pushed by forces he had not summoned or invented, he had at these moments a victim's face—puzzled, wounded, bloodless, coarse. The gap between the two couples closed. Bonnie had taken on a dreamy, vacant air; she was not planning to help.

"This is Bob Harris," Florence said. "He's from New York."

"I guessed that," Bonnie said.

It was plain to Wishart that the new man, now sincerely shaking hands all around, had no idea that Mrs. McCarthy might want to demolish him. Perhaps it seemed suitable, almost proper, that he should meet Flor's mother now. Wishart's anguished guess had been in order: after days of what had seemed to Bob interminable pursuit, Florence had come to his room. He stayed in one of the sugary palaces on the Croisette: the room was too noisy, too bright, and it was Flor, in the end, who seemed most at ease, adjusting the blind so that slats of shade covered the walls, placing her clothes neatly on a chair. She seemed to him exclusive, a prize, even though the evidence was that they were both summer rats. He had met her in a café one afternoon. He saw his own shadow on her table and himself, furtive, ratlike, looking for trouble. But he was already forgetting this, and his slight disappointment in her, and in the untender afternoon. He was forming an evasive figure who was only partly Flor; he remembered a half-darkened room and a secret relation on another level of the day. He noticed that Flor kissed her mother anxiously, as if they had been parted for days, or as though he had taken Flor to another country. The affection between the two women pleased him. His own mother, having died, had elevated the notion of motherhood. He liked people who got on with their parents and suspected those who did not.

Wishart permitted Bob to pump his hand up and down, as if to show that he recognized good manners when he saw them. Flor's sullen "Hullo Wishart" had been worse than a snub. He decided that Bob was no problem where he was concerned: his shrewdness was not the variety likely to threaten Wishart, and he would take up Flor's time, leaving Bonnie free to listen to Wishart's chat. He did not desire Bonnie to himself as a lover might, but he did want to get on with his anecdotes without continual interruptions.

Every day after that the four met on Bonnie's beach and lunched in a restaurant Bonnie liked. If Wishart had disapproved of the beach, it was nothing to his opinion of the restaurant, which was full of Bonnie's new friends. Wine—Algerian pink—came out of a barrel, there were paper flags stuck in the butter, the waiters were insolent and barefoot, the menu written on a slate and full of obscene puns. Everyone knew everyone, and Wishart could have murdered Bonnie. He was appalled at her thinking he could possibly like the place, but remembered that her attitude was the result of years of neuter camaraderie. It didn't matter: on the tenth of July he was expected in Venice. It was not a pattern of life.

It seemed to Wishart that Bonnie was becoming silly with age. She had developed a piercing laugh, and the affected drawl was becoming real. Her baiting of Bob Harris was too direct to be funny, and her antagonism was forming a bond between them—the last thing on earth she wanted. Bob had the habit of many Americans of constantly repeating the name of the person he was talking to. Bonnie retaliated by calling him Bob Harris in full, every time she spoke to him, and this, combined with her slightly artificial voice, made him ask, "Is that a southern accent you've got, Mrs. McCarthy?"

"Well, it just might be, Bob Harris," Bonnie cried, putting one on. But it was a movie accent; she did it badly, and it got on Wishart's nerves. "Well, that's a nice breeze that's just come up," she would say, trailing the vowels. "We're certainly a nice little party, aren't we? It's nice being four." Nice being four? Nice for Wishart, the adored, the sought-after, Europe's troubadour? He closed his eyes and thought of Mrs. Sebastian, Venice, shuttered room, green canals. Then Florence burst out with something. Only Wishart guessed that these cheeky outbursts, fit for a child of twelve, were innocent attempts to converse. Because of the way her mother had dragged her around, because she had never been part of a fixed society, she didn't know how people talked; she had none of the coins of light exchange. She said in an excited voice, "The Fox, the Ape, the Bumblebee, were all at odds, being three, and then the Goose came out the door, and stayed the odds by making four. We're like that. Mama's a lovely bumblebee and I'm fox-colored." This left Wishart the vexing choice between being a goose and an ape, and he was the more distressed to hear Bob say placidly that it wasn't the first time he had been called a big ape. All at once it seemed to him preferable to be an ape than a goose.

"Have you got many friends in Paris, Bob Harris?" said Bonnie, as if she hadn't seen Wishart's face pucker and shrink.

"Last year I had to send out one hundred and sixty-nine Christmas cards," said Bob simply. "I don't mean cards for the firm."

"The Bambino of the Eiffel Tower? Something real Parisian?" Even as Bonnie was bringing this out Wishart knew it was wrong. Bob looked down, with a smile. He seemed to feel sorry for Mrs. McCarthy, who didn't know about the cards people sent now, nondenominational, either funny or artistic, depending on your friends.

Alone with Wishart, Bonnie was the person he liked. When they laughed together on the beach it was like the old days when she had seemed so superior, enchanting, and bright. They lived out the fantasy essential to Wishart; he might have been back in London saying and thinking "Cannes." They had worked out their code of intimate jokes for the season: they called Bonnie's young friends *les fleurs et couronnes*, and they made fun of French jargon with its nervous emphasis on "moderne" and "dynamique." When Bonnie called Wishart *un homme du vingtième siècle, moderne et dynamique*, they were convulsed. Flor and Bob, a little apart, regarded them soberly, as if they were a pair of chattering squirrels.

"Wishart is one of Mama's best friends," said Flor, apologizing for this elderly foolishness. "I've never liked him. I think he thinks they're like Oberon and Titania, you know, all malice and showing off. Wishart would love to have wings and power and have people do as he says. He's always seemed wormy to me. Have you noticed that my mother pays for everything?"

In point of fact, Bob paid for everything now. He expected to: it was as essential to his nature as it was to Wishart's to giggle and sneer. To amuse Bonnie, he had sneered about Bob. "Wishart doesn't like the way I look because Wishart would like to look like nothing at all. The hell with him," he said placidly. He really was awfully pleased with himself: lying on her back on the sand, Flor shaded her eyes to see him properly. He was turned away. He seemed casual, indifferent, but she knew that he stayed on in Cannes because of her. His holiday was over, and his father, business and family-minded, was waiting for him in Paris. The discovery of Flor had disturbed him. Until now he had liked much younger girls with straight hair and mild, anxious eyes; girls who were photographed in the living room wearing printed silk and their mother's pearls. His ideal was the image of some minor Germanic princess, whose nickname might be Mousie, who seems to wear the same costume, the same hair, and the same air of patient supplication until a husband can be found. This picture, into which he had tried to fit so many women, now proved accommodating: the hair became red, the features hardened, the hands were thin and brown. She stared at him with less hopeless distress. At last the bland young woman became Flor, and he did not remember having held in his mind's eye any face but hers, just as he would never expect to look in the mirror one morning and see any face except his own.

These two people seemed to Wishart common objects, washed together by a tide of mutual mindlessness and simple desire. To oblige Bonnie, he pretended to see in Flor a courted darling, and Bob one of a chain of victims. "Bob is just a deep, creative boy looking for a girl with a tragic sense of life," he said to Bonnie, who laughed herself to tears, for, having tried to trap Bob into saying "stateside" and "drapes," and having failed, she needed new confirmation of his absurdity. The conversation of the pair, devoid of humor, was repeated by anyone close enough to hear. "Do you know what they're talking about *now*?" was a new opening for discussion, amazement, and, finally, helpless laughter.

"They're on birds today," Wishart said, with a deliberately solemn face.

"Birds?"

"Birds." They collapsed, heaving with laughter, as if in a fit. The *fleurs et couronnes*, out of sympathy, joined in.

"Do you know what bothered me most when I first came over here?" Wishart had heard Flor say. "We were in England then, and I didn't recognize a single tree or a single bird. They looked different, and the birds had different songs. A robin wasn't a robin any more. It was terrible. It frightened me more than anything. And they were so drab. Everything was brown and gray. There aren't any red-winged blackbirds, you know, nothing with a bright flash."

"Aren't there?" The urban boy tried to sound surprised. Wishart sympathized. The only quality he shared with Bob was ignorance of nature.

"Didn't you know? That's what's missing here, in everything. There's color enough, but you don't know how I miss it, the bright flash."

He saw the sun flash off a speedboat and everywhere he looked he saw color and light. The cars moving along the Croisette were color enough.

"Will you always live here now?" said Flor. "Will you never live at home again?"

"It depends on my father. I came over to learn, and I'm practically running the whole Paris end. It's something."

"Do you like business?"

"Do you mean do I wish I was an actor or something?" He gave her a resentful look and the shadow of their first possible difference fell over the exchange.

"My father never did anything much," she said. Her eyes were closed and she talked into the sun. The sun bleached her words. Any revelation was just talk. "Now they say he drinks quite a lot. But that's none of my business. He married a really dull thing, they say. He and Mama are Catholics so they don't believe in their own divorce. At least, Mama doesn't. I suppose he thinks he shouldn't be living with his second wife. If he still believes."

"How about you?"

"I'd believe anything I thought would do me or Mama any good."

This seemed to him insufficient. He expected women to be religious. He gave any amount of money to nuns.

These dialogues, which Wishart heard from a distance while seeming to concentrate on his tan, and which he found so dull and discouraging that the pair seemed mentally deficient, were attempts to furnish the past. Flor was perplexed by their separate pasts. She saw Bob rather as Bonnie did, but with a natural loyalty that was almost as strong as a family tie. She believed she was objective, detached; then she discovered he had come down to Cannes from Paris with a Swedish girl, the student from whom he had inherited the cap. Knowing that "student" in Europe is a generous term, covering a boundless field of age as well as activity, she experienced the hopeless jealousy a woman feels for someone she believes inferior to herself. It was impossible for Bonnie's daughter to achieve this inferiority; she saw the man already lost. The girl and Bob had lived together, in his room, where Flor now went afternoons while Bonnie was having her rest. Flor's imagination constructed a spiteful picture of a girl being cute and Swedish and larking about in his pajamas. Secretly flattered, he said no, she was rather sickly and quiet. Her name was Eve. She was traveling on a bus. Cards arrived bearing the sticky imprint of her lips: a disgusting practice. Trembling with feigned indifference, Flor grabbed the hat and threw it out the window. It landed on the balcony of the room below.

Bob kept the cap, but he gave up his hotel and moved into Flor's. The new room was better. It was quiet, dark, and contained no memories. It was in the basement, with a window high on the wall. The walls were white. There was sand everywhere, in the cracked red tiles of the floor, in the chinks of the decaying armchair, caked to the rope soles of their shoes. It seemed to Flor that here the grit of sand and salt came into their lives, and their existence as a couple began. When the shutters were opened, late in the afternoon, they let in the peppery scent of geraniums and the view of a raked gravel path. There must have been a four-season mimosa nearby; the wind sent minute yellow pompoms against the sill, and often a gust of sweetish perfume came in with the dying afternoon.

Flor had not mentioned the change to Bonnie, but, inevitably, Bonnie met her enemy at the desk, amiable and arrogant, collecting his key. "Has that boy been here all along?" she cried in despair. She insisted on seeing his room. She didn't know what she expected to find, but, as she told Wishart, she had a right to know. Bob invited her formally. She came with Flor one afternoon, both dressed in white, with skirts like lampshades, Bonnie on waves of "Femme." He saw for the first time that the two were alike and perhaps inseparable; they had a private casual way of speaking and laughed at the same things. It was like seeing a college friend in his own background, set against his parents, his sisters, his mother's taste in books. He offered Bonnie peanuts out of a tin, brandy in a toothbrush glass. He saw everything about her except that she was attractive, and here their difference of age was in the way. Bob and Florence avoided sitting on the lumpy bed, strewn with newspapers and photographs. That was Bonnie's answer. They knew she knew: Bonnie left in triumph, with an air she soon had cause to change. Now that Bonnie knew, the lovers spent more time together. They no longer slipped away during Bonnie's rest: they met when they chose and stayed away as long as they liked. If they kept a pretense of secrecy, it was because to Bob a façade of decency was needed. He had not completely lost sight of the beseeching princess into whose outline Flor had disappeared.

When he and Flor were apart, he found reason to doubt. She had told him the birds of Europe were not like the birds at home, but what about human beings? She never mentioned them. The breath of life for him was contained in relations, in his friendships, in which he did not distinguish between the random and the intense. All his relationships were of the same quality. She had told him that this room was like a place she had imagined. The only difference was that her imagined room was spangled, bright, perfectly silent, and full of mirrors. Years after this, he could say to himself, Cannes, and evoke a season of his life, with all the sounds, smells, light and dark that the season had contained; but he never remembered accurately how it had started or what it had been like. Their intimacy came first, then love, and some unclouded moments. Like most lovers, he believed that the beginning was made up of these moments only, and he would remember Flor's silent, mirrored room, and believe it was their room at Cannes, and that he had lived in it too.

One afternoon at the beginning of July, they fell asleep in this room, the real room, and when Flor woke it was dark. She knew it had begun to rain by the quickening in the air. She got up quietly and opened the shutters. A car came into the hotel drive: a bar of light swept across the ceiling and walls. She thought that what she felt now came because of the passage of light: it was a concrete sensation of happiness, as if happiness could be felt, lifted, carried around. She had not experienced anything of the kind before. She was in a watery world of perceptions, where impulses, doubts, intentions, detached from their roots, rise to the surface and expand. The difference between Bob and herself was that he had no attachments to the past. This was what caused him to seem inferior in her mother's view of life. He had told them freely that his father was self-educated and that his mother's parents were illiterate. There were no family records more than a generation old. Florence had been taught to draw her support from continuity and the past. Now she saw that the chain of fathers and daughters and mothers and sons had been powerless as a charm; in trouble, mistrusting her own capacity to think or move or enjoy living, she was alone. She saw that being positive of even a few things, that she was American, or pretty, or Christian, or Bonnie's girl, had not helped. Bob Harris didn't know his mother's maiden name, and his father's father had come out of a Polish ghetto, but he was not specifically less American than Florence, nor less proud. He was if anything more assertive and sure. She closed the shutters and came toward him, quietly, so that he would not wake and misinterpret her drawing near. Lacking an emotional country, it might be possible to consider another person one's home. She pressed her face against his unmoving arm, accepting everything imperfect, as one accepts a faulty but beloved country, or the language in which one's thoughts are formed. It was the most dangerous of ideas, this "only you can save me," but her need to think it was so overwhelming that she wondered if this was what men, in the past, had been trying to say when they had talked about love.

The rainstorm that afternoon was not enough. Everyone agreed more rain was needed. Rain was wanted to wash the sand, clean the sea, cool their tempers, rinse the hot roofs of the bathing cabins along the beach. When Wishart thought "Cannes" now it was not light, dark, and blueness, but sand, and cigarette butts, and smears of oil. At night the heat and noise of traffic kept him awake. He lay patient and motionless with opened owl eyes. He and Bonnie compared headaches at breakfast: Bonnie's was like something swelling inside the brain, a cluster of balloons, while Wishart's was external, a leather band.

He could not understand what Bonnie was doing in this place; she had been so fastidious, rejecting a resort when it became too popular, seeming to him to have secret mysterious friends and places to go to. He still believed she would not be here, fighting through mobs of sweating strangers every time she wanted a slopped cup of coffee or a few inches of sand, if there had not been a reason—if she had not been expecting something real.

After a time he realized that Bonnie was not waiting for anything to happen, and that the air of expectancy that day had been false. If she had expected anything then, she must have believed it would come through him. She talked now of the futility of travel; she abandoned the Venus image of Flor, and said that Flor was cold and shallow and had broken her heart. There was no explanation for it, except that Flor was not fulfilling Bonnie's hopes and plans. Self-pity followed: she said that she, Bonnie, would spend the rest of her life like a bit of old paper on the beach, cast up, beaten by waves, and so forth. She didn't care what rubbish she talked and she no longer tried to be gay. Once she said, "It's no good, Wishart, she's never been a woman. How can she feel what I feel? She's never even had her periods. We've done everything, hormones, God knows what all. I took her to Zurich. She was so passive, she didn't seem to know it was important. Sometimes I think she's dumb. She has these men—I don't know how far she goes. I think she's innocent. Yes, I really do. I don't want to think too much. It's nauseating when you start to think of your own daughter that way. But she's cold. I know she's cold. That's why we have no contact now. That's why we have no contact any more. I've never stopped being a woman. Thank God for it. If I haven't married again it hasn't been because I haven't men after me. Wishart! It's tragic for me to see that girl. I'm fifty and I'm still a woman, and she's twenty-four and a piece of ice."

He was lying beside her on the sand. He pulled his straw hat over his face, perfectly appalled. It was a pure reaction, unplanned. If he let his thoughts move without restraint into the world of women, he discovered an area dimly lighted and faintly disgusting, like a kitchen in a slum. It was a world of migraines, miscarriage, disorder, and tears.

Another day, complaining of how miserable her life had been in Europe, she said, "I stopped noticing when the seasons changed. Someone would say that the trees were in bud. I hadn't even noticed that the leaves were gone. I stopped noticing everything around me, I was so concentrated on Flor."

She talked to him about money, which was new. When he discovered she was poor, she dwindled to nothing, for then she had nothing to make her different or better than anyone else. She had always been careful over pennies, but he had believed it was the passionate stinginess of the rich. But she was no better than Wishart; she was dependent on bounty too. "I get no income at all, except from my brothers. And Stanley isn't required to support me, although he should, as I've had the burden of the child. And Flor's money is tied up in some crazy way until she's thirty. My father tied it up that way because of my divorce, he never trusted me again. Believe me, he paid for it. I never sent him as much as a postcard from that day until the day he died. Family, Wishart! God! Lovely people, but when it comes to m-o-n-e-y," she said, spelling it out. "Flor's allowance from Stanley was only until her majority and now he hardly sends her anything at all, he forgets, he isn't made to do anything. She'll have to wait now until he dies. They say the way he's living now there won't be anything left. Wishart, my brain clangs like a cash register when I think about it. I never used to worry at all but now I can't stop."

"You thought she would be married by the time her allowance from Stanley stopped." No tone could make this less odious. He thought he had gone too far, and was blaming her for having started it, when she relieved him by being simply angry.

"Do you think it's easy? Marriage proposals don't grow on trees. I can't understand it. I had so many."

This was the beginning of the conversation they had had on the Croisette. It showed how worn their friendship had become. It was used down to the threads, they had no tolerance for each other any more, and nothing new to give. They were more intimate than they needed to be; he blamed her. *He* had tried to keep it bright. Once Bob had asked why Bonnie lived in Europe, and Wishart had replied, "Bonnie had Flor and then, worn out with childbearing, retired to a permanently sunny beach." This was a flattering version of Bonnie's divorce and flight from home. "Don't you listen," Bonnie said, immensely pleased. (She was pleased on another count: they were sitting on the outer edge of a café, and Bob was repeatedly jostled by the passing crowd. He had once said he liked people and didn't mind noise, and Bonnie saw to it that he had a basinful of both when it could be managed.) Wishart wanted their holiday to go on being as it had sounded when he said, in London, "I am going to Cannes to stay with a delightful American friend." The American friend now questioned Wishart about his plans. He perceived with horror that she was waiting for a suggestion from him. He might have been flattered by Bonnie's clinging to him, but in friendship he was like a lover who can adore only in pursuit. In a few days, he would be in Venice with Mrs. Sebastian—blessed Mrs. Sebastian, authentically rich. Snubbing Bonnie, he talked Venice to the *fleurs et couronnes*. Rejected by Wishart, abandoned by Flor, Bonnie took on a new expression; even more than Wishart, she looked like the failed comedian afflicted with dreams. He knew it, and was pleased, as if in handing over a disease he had reduced its malignant powers.

Then, in time to bump him off his high horse, Wishart received a letter from Mrs. Sebastian putting him off until August. There were no apologies and no explanations. She simply told him not to come. He remembered then that she was cold and vulgar, and that she drank too much, and that, although she was a hefty piece, her nickname was Peewee and she insisted on being given it; she was avaricious and had made Wishart pay her for a bottle of DDT and a spray one summer when the mosquitoes were killing him. He remembered that in American terms Bonnie was someone and Mrs. Sebastian nothing at all. Bonnie became generous, decent, elegant, and essential to Wishart's life. He turned to her as if he had been away; but as far as she was concerned he *had* been away, and he had lost ground. He regretted now that he had failed to worship Venus-Flor, and had not taken seriously Bonnie's earnest preoccupation with Bob Harris, the one from Turkey, and all the sots and lumpkins who had gone before. The dark glasses that seemed to condense the long curve of the beach into a miniature image were averted now. Even a diminished penitent Wishart could not find his own reflection.

For her part, Bonnie was finding her withering Marchbanks tedious. His pursy prejudice no longer seemed delicious humor. He made the mistake of telling her a long name-studded story of school politics and someone trying to get his job. It established him in reality—a master afraid for his grubby post—and reality was not what Bonnie demanded. She had enough reality on her hands: in the autumn that girl would be twenty-five.

Wishart tried to get back on their old plane. "Distract her," he said lazily. "Move on. Divert her with culture. Inspect the cathedrals and museums. Take her to the Musée de l'Homme."

"You don't meet any men in museums," said Bonnie, as if this were a sore point. "Anyway, what's the good? She only comes to life for slobs." After a moment she said quietly, "Don't you see, that's not what I want for Flor. I don't want her to marry just anybody. It may sound funny to you, but I don't even want an American. They've always let me down. My own brothers... but I don't want to go into it again. I want a European, but not a Latin, and one who has lived in the States and has had the best of both. I want someone much older than Flor, because she needs that, and someone I can trust. That's what I want for my girl and that's what I meant when I said proposals don't grow on trees. Neither do men." But what did Wishart know about men? He was a woman-haunter, woman's best friend. She put on her sunglasses in order to hide her exasperation with him, because he was a man, but not the right person.

Her expression was perfectly blank. There was no doubt now, no other way of interpreting it. In spite of his recent indifference to her, she had not changed her mind. Wishart was being offered Flor.

He had never been foolish enough to dream of a useful marriage. He knew that his choice one season might damn him the next. He had thought occasionally of a charming but ignorant peasant child, whom he could train; he had the town boy's blurry vision of country people. Unfortunately, he had never met anyone of the kind. Certainly, his peasant bride, who was expected to combine with her exceptional beauty the fact that she wouldn't object to cleaning his shoes, was not Flor.

This was not the moment for false steps. He saw himself back in America with a lame-brained but perfect wife. Preposterous ideas made him say in imagined conversations, The mother was a charmer, I married the daughter.

He forgot the dangers, Bonnie as a mother-in-law. A secret hope unfurled and spread. He got up and in a blind determined way began to walk across the beach. Not far away the lovers lay on the sand, facing each other, half asleep. Flor's arm was under her head, straight up. He saw Bob's back, burned nearly black, and Flor's face. They were so close that their breath must have mingled. Flor's beauty decreased, became less standard; he would not have called her a Venus now. Their intimacy seemed to Wishart established; it contained an implicit allegiance, like a family tie, with all the antagonism that might suggest as well. They came together. Wishart saw that Flor remained outside the kiss. Two laurels with one root: where had he heard that? Each was a missing part of the other's character, and the whole, in the kiss, should have been unflawed.

Flor wondered what it was like for a man to kiss her and remembered words from men she had not loved. It was a narcissism so shameful that she opened her eyes and saw Wishart. He was the insect enemy met in an underground tunnel, the small, scratching watcher, the boneless witness of an insect universe: a tiny, scuttling universe that contained her mother, the pop-eyed Corsican proprietor of this beach, the *fleurs et couronnes*, her mother's procession of very best most intimate friends—before Wishart, a bestial countess to whom Flor, as a girl, had been instructed to be nice. In a spasm of terror that Bob mistook for abandonment, she clung to him; he was outside this universe and from a better place.

Wishart returned to Bonnie and sank down beside her on the sand, adjusting his bony legs as if they were collapsible umbrellas. If he continued in error it was Bonnie's fault, for she went on again about men, the right man, and Flor. The wind dropped: Cannes settled into the stagnant afternoon. The *fleurs et couronnes* were down from their naps and chattering like budgerigars. Bonnie had been polishing her sunglasses on the edge of a towel. She stopped, holding them, staring. "Last night I dreamed my daughter was a mermaid," she said. "What does it mean? Wishart, you know all about those things. What does it mean?"

"*Ravissant*," said one of her court. "I see the blue sea, and the grottoes, everything coral and blue. Coral green and coral blue."

"There is no such thing as coral blue," said Wishart mechanically.

"And Florence, *la belle Florence*, floating and drifting, the bright hair spread like..."

"She sang and she floated, she floated and sang," took up a minor figure who resembled a guppy. At a look from Bonnie he gave a great gasp and shut up.

"It was nothing like that at all," said Bonnie snappily. "It was an ugly fish tail, like a carp's. It was just like a carp's and the whole thing was a great handicap. The girl simply couldn't walk. She lay there on the ground and couldn't do a thing. Everybody stared at us. It was a perfectly hopeless dream and I woke up in a state of *great distress*."

Wishart had been so disturbed by the kiss that moved into blankness. He could not form a coherent thought. What interested him, finally, was the confirmation for Flor as a *poseuse*. How conceited she had been, lying there, exploring her own sensations as idly as tourists turning sand from one hand into the other. He recalled the expression in her eyes—shrewd, ratty eyes, he thought, not the eyes of a goddess—and he knew that she feared and loathed him and might catch him out. "It won't do," he said to Bonnie, or "It wouldn't do, a marriage with Flor." He heard the words, "she has a crack across the brain," but was never certain if he had said them aloud. Bonnie turned her pink, shadowed face to him in purest amazement. She noticed that Wishart's eyes were so perturbed and desperate that they were almost beyond emotion, without feeling, like those of a bird. Then she looked up to the sky, where the plane was endlessly and silently writing the name of a drink. She said, "I wish he would write something for us, something useful."

His mistake had been greater than the gaffe about Flor. Everything trembled and changed; even the color of the sky seemed extraordinary. Wishart was fixed and paralyzed in this new landscape, wondering if he was doing or saying anything strange, unable to see or stop himself. It was years since he had been the victim of such a fright. He had believed that Bonnie accepted him at his value. He had believed that the exact miniature he saw in her sunglasses was the Wishart she accepted, the gentleman he had glimpsed in the store window that first day. He had thought that the inflection of a voice, the use of some words, established them as a kind. But Bonnie had never believed in it. She had never considered him anything but jumped-up. He remembered now that she had never let him know her family back home, had never suggested he meet her brothers.

When Bonnie dared look again Wishart was picking his way into the sea. He was wearing his hat. He did not mind looking foolish and believed eccentricity added to his stature. After standing for a time, knee-deep, looking with the expression of a brooding camel first at the horizon and then back to shore, he began to pick his way out again. The water was too dirty for swimming, even if the other bathers had left him room. "Large colored balls were being flung over my head and some things against it," he composed, describing for future audiences the summer at Cannes. "The shrieking children of butchers were being taught to swim."

Farther along the beach Bob Harris carried two bottles of beer, crowned with inverted glasses, down to Flor. Bonnie watched without emotion. Their figures were motionless, to be printed against her memory, arrested in heat and the insupportable noise.

Everyone around Bonnie was asleep. The sirocco, unsteady, pulled her parasol about on the sand. Sitting, knees bent, she clasped her own white feet. There was not a blemish on them; the toes were straight, the heels rosy. She had tended her feet like twin infants, setting an example for Flor. Once, exasperated by Flor's neglect, she had gone down on her knees and taken Flor's feet on her lap and shown her how it ought to be done. She had creamed and manicured and pumiced while Flor, listless, surreptitiously trying to get on with a book, said, "Oh, Mama, I can do it." "But you won't, honey. You simply don't take care of yourself unless I'm there." She had polished and tended her little idol, and for whom? For a Turk not sixty-three inches high. For Bob Harris in tartan trunks. It was no use; the minutes and hours had passed too quickly. She was perplexed by the truth that had bothered her all her life, that there was no distance between time and events. Everything raced to a point beyond her reach and sight. Everyone slid out of her grasp: her husband, her daughter, her friends. She let herself fall back. Her field of vision closed in and from the left came the first, swimming molecules of pain.

Wishart, coming out of the teeming sea, making a detour to avoid being caught up and battered in a volley-ball game, came up to Bonnie unobserved. Patting his yellowed skin with a towel he watched the evolution of his friend's attack. Her face was half in sun. She twisted to find the shadow of the rolling parasol. Bitter, withdrawn, he was already pulling about himself the rags of imaginary Wishart: the squire father, Mrs. Sebastian rolling in money above the Grand Canal. Bonnie believed she was really dying this time, and wondered if Flor could see.

Flor said, "I think Mama has one of her headaches."

"You two watch each other, don't you?" He had asked why she said "Mama" and had been told it was a habit of the Fairlies, her mother's family. She said it as she might have explained, "Everybody in our family has used the same toothbrush since nineteen twelve."

A haze had gone over the sky. She finished her beer, spread her striped beach-towel a little away from him, and lay still. He had told her that his father had telephoned from Paris, and that this time it was an order. He was leaving soon, perhaps the next day. This was July. The summer, a fruit already emptied by wasps, still hung to its tree. He was leaving. When he had gone, she would hear the question, the ghost voice that speaks to every traveler, Why did you come to this place? Until now, she had known: she was somewhere or other with her mother because her mother could not settle down, because every rented flat and villa was a horrible parody of home, or the home she ought to have given Flor. When he had gone, she would know without illusion that she was in Cannes in a rotting season, the rot was reality, and there was no hope in the mirrored room.

"Are you coming to Paris later on?" His father was waiting; he spoke with a sense of urgency, like someone trying to ring off, holding the receiver, eyes wandering around the room.

"I don't know. I don't know where we'll go from here, or how long Mama will stay. She and Wishart always finish with a fight, and Mama loses her head, and we go rushing off. All our relations at home think we have such a glamorous life. Did you ever go out in the morning and find a spider's web spangled with dew?" she said suddenly. "You'll never find that here. It's either too hot and dry, or it rains so much the spider drowns. At my grandmother's place, you know, summers, I used to ride, oh, early, early in the morning, with my cousins. All my cousins were boys." Her voice was lost as she turned her head away.

"Flor, why don't you go home?"

"I can't leave my mother, and she won't go. Maybe I don't dare. She used to need me. Maybe now I need her. What would I do at home? My grandmother is dead. I haven't got a home. I know I sound as if I feel sorry for myself, but I haven't got anything."

"You've got your mother," he said. "There's me."

Now it was here, the circumstance that Bonnie had loathed and desired. He moved closer and spoke with his lips to her ear, playing with her hair, as if they were alone on the beach or in his room. He remembered the basement room as if they would never be in it again. He remembered her long hair, the wrinkled sheets, the blanket thrown back because of the heat. It was the prophetic instant, the compression of feeling that occurs in childhood and in dreams. Wishart passed by: his shadow fell over their feet. They were obliged to look up and see his onion skin and pickled eyes. They were polite. No one could have said that they had agreed to change the movement of four lives, and had diverted the hopes, desires, and ambitions of Bonnie and of Bob's father, guides whose direction had suddenly failed.

Wishart went back to his hotel. It was the hour when people who lived in *pensions* began to straggle up from the sea. Whole families got in Wishart's way. They were badly sunburned, smelled of Ambre Solaire and Skol, and looked as if they couldn't stand one another's company another day. Wishart bathed and changed. He walked to the post office and then to the station to see about a bus. He was drily forgiving when people stepped on his feet, but looked like someone who will never accept an apology again. He sent a telegram to an American couple he knew who had a house near Grasse. He had planned to skip them this year; the husband disliked him. (The only kind of husband Wishart felt easy with was the mere morsel, the half-digested scrap.) But he could not stay on with Bonnie now, and Mrs. Sebastian had put him off. He put his full horror of Cannes into a heartrending message that began "Very depressed" but he did not sign a funny name for fear of making the husband cross. He signed his own name and pocketed the change and went off to the station. This time he and Bonnie were parting without a quarrel.

That night there was a full moon. Bonnie woke up suddenly as if she had become conscious of a thief in the room; but it was only Flor, wearing the torn bathrobe she had owned since she was fourteen, and that Bonnie never managed to throw away. She was holding a glass of water in her hand, and looking down at her sleeping mother. "Flor, is anything wrong?"

"I was thirsty." She put the glass on the night table and sank down beside her mother on the floor.

"That Wishart," said Bonnie, now fully awake, and beginning to stroke Flor's hair. "He really takes himself for something."

"What is he taking himself for?"

Bonnie stroked her daughter's hair, thinking, My mermaid, my prize. The carp had vanished from the dream, leaving an iridescent Flor. No one was good enough for Florence. That was the meaning of the dream. "Your hair is so stiff, honey, it's full of salt. I wish you'd wear a bathing cap. Flor, have you got a fever or something?" She wants to tell me something, Bonnie thought. Let it be anything except about that boy. Let it be anything but that.

At dawn, Wishart, who had been awake most of the night, buckled his suitcase. No porter was around at that hour. He walked to the station in streets where there was still no suggestion of the terrible day. The southern scent, the thin distillation of lemons and geraniums, descended from the hills. Then heat began to tremble; Vespas raced along the port; the white-legged grub tourists came down from the early train. Wishart thought of his new hostess, academic, a husk; she chose the country behind Grasse because of the shades of Gide and Saint-Ex; ghosts who would keep away from her if they knew what was good for them. He climbed into the bus and sat down among working men who had jobs in Grasse, and the sea dropped behind him as he was borne away.

In the rocking bus his head dropped. He knew that he was in a bus and traveling to Grasse, but he saw Glad, aged twelve, going off at dawn with her lunch wrapped in an apron. What about the dirty, snotty baby boy who hung on her dress, whose fingers she had to pry loose one at a time only to have the hand clamp shut again, tighter than before? Could this be Wishart, clinging, whining, crying, "Stay with me"? But Wishart was awake and not to be trapped. He took good care not to dream, and when the bus drew in at Grasse, under the trees, and he saw his new straw-thin hostess (chignon, espadrilles, peasant garden hat) he did not look like a failed actor assailed with nightmares, but a smooth and pleasant schoolmaster whose sleep is so deep that he never dreams at all.

4

For all the reaction he was getting he might as well have been alone. When he spoke, no one replied. So far, no one had said, "How thoughtful of you, George," although it was he who had chosen the table in the bar, where they could be quiet and alone, instead of the crowded dining room. Dinner was over. The waiter leaned on the bar, adding up the check, counting, as though he couldn't believe the total, the bottles of wine and rounds of brandy. The bartender read a spread-out newspaper. George's Aunt Bonnie was pushing herself into a bolero of monkey fur; she had irritably waved away his offers of help. There was a third person at the table, his aunt's son-in-law, Bob Harris. Harris couldn't see Aunt Bonnie's struggles: his elbows were on the table, his face behind his hands. George observed, as part of a still-suspended opinion, that Harris wore two rings, one that was modern and gold and matched his cuff links, and a small onyx, squeezed onto the little finger of his left hand. It looked like a woman's ring. Perhaps it had belonged to Harris's wife.

"It's f-funny," George began again. He was trying to say that there was a funny light over the Louvre, as if beams of warm, theatrical color were being played from somewhere behind—from the rue de Rivoli, for instance. The windows of the Left Bank bar where they had dined gave on this sight, which was nothing more than the last blaze of day. George had been looking for themes of conversation and he was now trying this. Nobody cared.

"This dinner is on me," said George, despairingly, to Harris's still hidden face.

At that moment the waiter sprang to help George's aunt. Twisting, craning, waving her thin arms, she wrestled with the bolero. Now it was inside out. The waiter removed it, shook it, guided Aunt Bonnie's groping hands. "*Merci*. Now what did you want, Georgie dear?" But by now it was night. Nothing remained except a vanishing saffron cloud.

Harris sat back with his hands on the table, smiling faintly, so full of himself, so smooth, that George wondered if the grieving movement had not been something dreamt. Often in his childhood he had been assured that a dramatic moment clearly seen and heard had never taken place. Harris nodded at the waiter: "There's your bill," and the waiter bent over George with the check folded on a plate, and a pencil so that he could sign. Harris seemed to enjoy using English expressions such as "bill." The dark clothes he wore gave him a grave, foreign air, and he appeared older than his age, which was twenty-six or seven. He had a dark, soft face, and might have been a Greek or a Persian educated in England, if one took the sum of his face, his manner, his rings, and his clothes. In a letter home Aunt Bonnie had said that her son-in-law looked like a suburban gangster. To George, Harris was neither foreign nor gangster, nor suburban, nor entirely respectable. He was familiar in a distinctly American way, but he was not the kind of American George had been brought up to know well. In strange Paris, he was as complete in familiarity as someone from George's own world might have been, although different in quality—urban, sharp. He watched George's troubles without offering to help. George was grateful for that. The spurt of assurance that made him demand a table in the bar, and insist dinner be served there, had damped out. His stammer was back. He was not sure of his French. For a minute he had been decisive, representing the male element in Aunt Bonnie's family. The minute ended, he was George again, with everything being George implied, at least to himself. He had to explain to this waiter that he was not staying at the hotel. That he therefore couldn't sign the bill. That he wanted to pay with a traveler's check and be given his change in francs. He brought it off as if he had been entertaining in foreign restaurants all his life, and Harris helped by keeping out; not so Aunt Bonnie, who screamed, "We're not really going to let this little boy pay for that meal?"

Poor Aunt Bonnie had put herself in a costume so grotesque that anything she had to say was dimmed. Her clothes must have come out of a trunk: they smelled of camphor and the dark—the fur, the sagging dress of black chiffon, the ropes of amber and jet, her pointed satin shoes, the purse with its chain handle and amber clasp. Her hair seemed to George dyed. He could not remember if his aunt had been wearing this head of hair when he had seen her two years before. The space between his having been seventeen, and at home, and being nineteen, and abroad, could not be measured by any system known to him; not even by the changes in people he knew.

Aunt Bonnie dabbed at her lipstick with an embroidered handkerchief. "You're a real Fairlie, George," she said. "That was a nice meal." In spite of her grief she had eaten melon, chicken, salad, cheese, and ice cream. She had refused everyone's cigarettes, sending out for a brand of her own, and had complained about the wines. Sometimes she let her head hang as if her neck had snapped, then she would suddenly look, and speak, and glance at George with his father's blue eyes. As for Harris, he simply behaved as if he were alone.

George didn't notice when Harris left the table, so easily did he slide away, until Aunt Bonnie put her powdered face next to his and said, "He's gone to take care of the bill and get your check back for you. Now, don't say a word when he comes back. Don't thank him. He likes doing these things. George, I don't know what I would do now without Bob. He was so awfully nice to her. He was just so nice to her all the time. Florence could be trying. Oh, yes, she was an angel itself, but she could be trying too. I know you don't think so, you only saw the good side, she loved you so. But that boy was married to her, he had to live with her, just as I had to live with her, and he was just nice to her all the time."

"*You* didn't have to live with her," George said. It was the kind of statement that went out of his mouth before it was through his mind; it was just an intention, not even a thought. He looked at his aunt in perfect dismay, as though she had said something strange; but Aunt Bonnie said amiably, "Why darling, Flor and I were so close, you know. She'd have been miserable without me, always worried. And I'd have worried about her. It wouldn't have been fair to Bob, leaving him with this worried girl on his hands. I mattered terribly in their marriage, dear. I used to think of myself as a kind of lightning rod."

"Nobody, *nobody* ever gets the better of Bonnie," George's father had once said. "She's sweet, she's helpless, she's had some stinking deals. But nobody ever gets the better of her. This Harris had better be tough." They hadn't known much about Harris then, except that Aunt Bonnie didn't like him. Florence met him on a beach or in a hotel and married him straightaway. She didn't care what people said and she wiped out with one gesture all the care and love and planning—but those were Aunt Bonnie's words. She had been mournful, poor Aunt Bonnie, with her only girl gone to waste; she never saw it as anything less.

Aunt Bonnie seemed to have forgotten her old objections now. "Flor loved him," she crooned. "Yes, she did. He was so nice to her, you see. Flor had a lot of love in her." Abruptly she changed her tone, became matter-of-fact: "Bob went out to see her today, without me. They don't let us see her together, *I* don't know why. He said she was as loving as could be. She didn't know his name or anything but she put her head on his shoulder and stroked his face and she made him eat little pieces of bread from her tray. You see, even now she's full of love." Then Aunt Bonnie drew back and cried, "I was just saying, I wish Georgie knew someone in Paris more fun than us. He's not having a good time, he says."

Harris had returned and stood by the table. George's reflexes were slow. The falsehood, the outrage, the impertinence of his aunt made him stammer in his mind. As if he would have complained; as if, to these stricken people dressed in mock mourning, he could have complained. He wished Harris would look at him so that he could signal it wasn't true.

"We could do something later," Harris said in a neutral voice. "Whatever he wants."

"Do," said Aunt Bonnie warmly. "Oh, do. Florence would want you to be having fun."

The stupidity of the remark did not make it less cruel. George put himself in Harris's place and felt sick. He took refuge in contemplating the walls of the bar, which were papered with maps of Paris. He tried to find the names of streets. When he came back to his aunt and Harris again he saw they were looking away from each other. They seemed bewildered. Each was the witness of the other's suffering and that must have been terrible to bear. Harris probably wasn't taking in half the foolish things she said. He looked like a man who had come into a known station only to find all the trains going to the wrong places or leaving at impossible times: endlessly patient, he was waiting for the schedules to be rearranged.

"I'll g-go pay the check," said George, for something to say.

"You already have," said Harris. "Don't you remember?"

"Georgie thought *you'd* gone to pay it when you sneaked away like that," Aunt Bonnie said. She got up and scraped together her scarf, purse, fan, and gloves and tottered toward the door. She walked like a crone; she seemed to have made up her mind to be old and tactless, and dress like the Mad Woman of Chaillot. "I want to walk home," she said from the door. "I want to walk all the way home. You boys can come back after and pick up the car. I want to walk the way Florence used to walk. Florence loved the Paris night."

The night Florence had loved met them with the noise of traffic. The Seine was oily and still. This was the end of summer and the city seemed depleted by the season just endured; the heart of the city was emptied by the number of strangers on the streets, the motion of cars and boats, the prying search-lights on the monuments, the pressure of hands, feet, cameras, eyes. George had instantly felt it when he arrived from London that afternoon. If London could be described as too thick, Paris was too thin. He was glad this ruined holiday was over. He was glad he would soon be going home and no longer obliged to think and compare and consider the very quality of the air he took in.

"Lovely!" cried Aunt Bonnie, turning her sharp nose up to the sky. She gave an arm to each of the men. George took the fan and gloves, Harris the scarf and purse. He seemed at ease; but George felt as if he were carrying twenty fans and eighty pairs of gloves. He thought of the White Rabbit, whom he suspected he resembled. His aunt pattered across the street, George stumbled, and only Harris managed a normal walk. They stopped on the Seine side of the Quai Voltaire and the men waited for orders. The whole thing had got into Aunt Bonnie's hands. "I want to go along the quais," she decreed, "and over to the right bank on the Pont de l'Alma, and up the Avenue Montaigne, and home. It's a long walk, but Georgie should see Paris."

George waited for Harris to object; it seemed to him an insanely long walk. But Harris nodded his head and they went on again—the oddest trio you could imagine, George thought, unused to oddity. Nothing had prepared him for this situation, in which he kept trying to find his feet. "George is so lucky," his mother had once said. "He's had all the good disadvantages." His training was planned for the social rather than the human collapse. His shed youth now seemed a piling-up of hallucinations, things heard and seen that were untrue or of no use to him. He was a tall person with large hands and feet, light blue eyes, and pale brows, lashes, and hair. His expression was earnest and kind. He had the voice and manner of his father's family and he wore the family face; it was an undistinguished sweet-tempered face that usually triumphed over admixtures. One of Aunt Bonnie's sisters, George's Aunt Louise, had married a man named Reed; the Reed boys—there were four—were so violently Fairlie, flax-blond, ham-handed, that the Reed parent (bony, brown) might have had no chromosomes at all and Aunt Louise's doubled in number to compensate. George would have considered this a natural law: their features were a concrete heritage, like the rings, brooches, and cups that passed without visible friction from one unit to the next. There was a family personality—decent, generous, conceited—and they carried their upbringing like a grain of sand on the heart.

They walked slowly now, all three in step, in and out of lamplight and the shadows of leaves. "I think you're a brave boy, Georgie, coming to Europe alone," his aunt said. "All alone in England! Flor never went anywhere without me. Do you feel brave?"

"Actually, it was pretty lonesome," George said. He hoped that nothing in his tone admitted how lonesome it had been; there would have been something degrading in sharing the truth that his holiday had failed. "I wouldn't do it like this again. I liked some things in England. I liked Scotland more. But when I got here this afternoon I was so lonesome I didn't know what to do. I went around to your place but nobody came to the door. I kept on phoning..." Did this sound like self-pity? He had been around to see them; nobody home. That was casual enough. Back in his hotel, he had telephoned. He heard the ringing for the tenth time and then Bob's voice, civil, surprised, "*George*? Your aunt isn't here just now, George, but I'm expecting her. Florence isn't too well. We've had to take her to a place...a sort of rest place. Your aunt'll tell you. Didn't you get the telegram? I guess you didn't. We thought maybe you shouldn't come." His voice was soft, for a man, full of the sounds and rhythms that meant New York. This came over to George with wild familiarity. Across Paris, the voice conveyed the existence of seasons, mornings, afternoons. The voice was not in the least like his own; the good disadvantages had been provided in a sense so that he would never sound like Bob. "Where are you, George?" said the voice. "Have you got a pencil or something?" He gave the name of a restaurant in a hotel not far from George's own and said he would be along shortly with George's aunt. Everything pertaining to danger and grief flowed and settled around that talk, leaving George free to stroll by the Seine with his aunt, holding her fan and her gloves.

"Of course Georgie's lonely," said his aunt. "No good being in Paris unless you're in love, eh?" and she tweaked her son-in-law's dark sleeve.

She didn't know what she was saying any more. That was the only explanation. She had gone crazy with shock. George heard Bob say, "Don't worry," as though he hadn't listened to her in years but had an answer for her comments and complaints.

"You need to be in love," his aunt said, so wickedly, her hand jumping now on George's arm, that he knew it was intended for him. That meant his mother had written about Barbara Sim. It had gone on for years: for four summers. When he was eighteen it was over. It was over for him, that is; not for her. Gracelessly, she persisted in loving. One day the thought of Barbara was shadowed by the memory of Flor. Flor had nothing to do with Barbara, didn't know she existed. But George remembered what it had been like to be with Flor just as, through a hole in time, one goes back to a lake, a room in a city, or the south. It was probably because of the bead. He had grasped it out of habit and it lay in his hand. It was the cheap glass bead from the necklace his cousin had broken when she was fourteen. He saw her hands flying outward and the burst of glass like water flying. When he thought about his cousin that was what he saw: a thin sunburned girl pulling on a string of beads and making the string break. She was frightening to him then; he was only seven. She had what Aunt Bonnie called "cold bad tempers." No matter what had happened since (the scene of the "little pieces of bread" was a swampy horror on which his mind refused to alight) she was fixed then and now and for all his life: a wild girl breaking a necklace, the circle of life closing in at fourteen, the family, the mother, the husband to come.

George kept the bead as if he had already known, when he was seven, that he was a sort of coward, and needed tokens in his hand. Soon after he had written the final, classic letter to Barbara he lost the bead. He put his hand in his pocket and the bead was gone. What remained was his habit of clutching air. He was still a coward, and too polite.

George's parents had followed the romance with Barbara first with indulgence and then with alarm. Now they could smile: George was not going to ruin his life with that girl. He thought they should have known better; he would never ruin his life over anybody. He had been accustomed for so many years to Barbara, to writing or telling her nearly everything, that it was to Barbara, now, he confided that his parents had got it wrong, and his mother had betrayed him to Aunt Bonnie. Then his eyes met the eyes of a girl coming toward them. The girl emerged in the most poetic way imaginable, out of the Paris night. That was the way he wanted something to happen; that was the thing he was ready for now. The girl held his gaze until she was level with the three of them and then she glanced away. She was fair, with high cheekbones, and wore a tight gray skirt and a suede coat.

"Nursemaid," said Aunt Bonnie into the night. "Millions of them come from Scandinavia every year. Warm little loves. They are supposed to be learning French."

She must always have been like that, a small bony cat waiting to jump. He decided to remember, in case it should ever be of any importance, that he had seen this girl on the Quai Anatole France. Aunt Bonnie moved with quick hopping steps, like a bird. She seemed to be enjoying the walk. She had always been the ailing one, but she had survived, and here she was, bobbing along, wound like a vine on the arms of two men, enjoying the night. The quai was quiet with the silence of a country road. Then they reached the Pont de la Concorde and the silence came to an end. A river of cars faster than the Seine ran past them and he saw at the other end of the bridge the lights of the Place de la Concorde strung unevenly, haunting and moving as the memory of lights across a lake, and the obelisk like a great lighted mast. "It's wonderful," he said dutifully. "But it sort of isn't a city." The answer, which should have come from Harris, was Aunt Bonnie's. She said as if it were wrenched from the heart: "New York is the only city." Her voice then resumed an artificial quaver; she had forgotten she was supposed to be an old lady. Now she remembered again. "If there was one thing my Florence hated, it was the way they light up all the monuments and things for the tourists. She said it made Paris seem like an old prostitute. She never would look. As a matter of fact, she hardly ever went out at night."

Half an hour earlier she had said that Florence loved the Paris night; but contradiction seemed to be typical of his aunt. She had told George that Harris was generous and kind, whereas in letters home she complained he was tight and thoughtless and had never given them—the women—a car. George couldn't very well ask, Are you stingy? even though Harris was there and able to defend himself—unlike Flor, who was past choosing. Now he became physically aware of the absence of Flor. He wondered where she was: in a sort of convalescent place, he supposed, hospital disguised as hotel where there was a significance, unknown to him, in the sound of a tap turned on or the color blue. Wondering where she was *really* he suspected she was in no special place. She was not anywhere. It would be nice to believe she was happier, calmer, more loving than ever, but he thought she was not anywhere.

The minute George went too far in his speculations he lost hold of the real situation. He could see three people walking, stopping for traffic, moving on; he could hear their voices, but he could not understand any of the things they said. That was normal; this had been a terrible day: there had been the journey from London, the transition, the idea of coming to Paris ("all unsuspecting…" as he kept telling himself), and then the telephone ringing in an unseen room, and Bob's voice saying, "Your aunt isn't here." His aunt's hand lay light now on George's arm, but her left hand clutched her son-in-law's sleeve, and he stroked her arm, muttering in his absent-minded way, "Don't worry"—the steady answer for keeping his female family quiet. They seemed to be joined for life, and, before thinking and deciding not to say it, George said, "God, I feel sorry for you, Bob," which would go down as another of the famous George remarks.

"You don't have to be," said Bob after a moment. "I knew when I met Flor there weren't two like her. She was never too much of anything. She had just enough. Just enough looks, just enough brains, just enough of what Bonnie here would call breeding." Aunt Bonnie began to flash in all directions and even George thought his cousin and the whole family with her were being undervalued. He wanted to say, Flor isn't queer from *our* side; as though Bob had anything to do with that! Well, Bob was being cool and objective now, but he hadn't behaved that way two years ago, on his honeymoon, because George had met him and he had seen and he remembered. This was probably a way of not hurting himself more than he could help, this distant "just enough," but George knew. Presently he realized that what Bob had said bore no relation to George's remark. It was simply a statement given into the night.

"What Flor had more of I think was a kind of purity," said Aunt Bonnie sadly. "You know, Georgie, when she was little, she never asked me one embarrassing question, you know what I mean, and as she wasn't the kind of girl other little girls would tell anything nasty to, well, she was spared all the shocks. She was fortunate," said Aunt Bonnie, "she grew up without any shocks. I don't suppose you did," she said, plucking at George's sleeve. Bob was abandoned. Georgie was her boy now. He saw that he was being made to change roles with Flor, and that George, who had grown up safely at home, overloved and overspoiled, was to be fitted out as his cousin—parents divorced, brought up just anywhere, breaking years of silence to send her father letters of abuse, quarreling in public with her mother and having public remorse. They were creating an unmarred Florence, and through her a spotless Bonnie; no one was to be blamed for anything. "I wouldn't have wanted a son," Aunt Bonnie said. "Your daughter's your daughter all your life. You know what *your* mother wrote me last spring, Georgie? She wrote, 'It's hard to understand it but he'll soon be finished with us.' And you were what, eighteen? Why, Flor at eighteen was like a little baby. She was never finished with me."

George thought, She is now.

Of course, he had said it. This time his reaction over the blunder was against the others. He was sick of his mistakes. He was sick of Aunt Bonnie and sick of Flor. If he had still owned the bead he would have got rid of it now. He would have reached out his hand and left it on the low wall beside the quai. He was sick of his aunt and he didn't like her. She was silly and mischievous and he didn't like her at all. It was all wrong, because she was in trouble now and he was part of the family; but there was no justice in liking and not liking people. He loved his parents, but here he was in Paris, without them. What his mother had said in the letter was true: he would soon be finished. He had loved Barbara but when he went to college he shook her off—couldn't shake her off fast enough. Hate might be easier than love, but he had never hated anybody and as far as he knew only one person had ever hated him, and that was Flor. He had seen it when he was seven and she was fourteen, and it was all the way she had turned her head and let him see her eyes. Perhaps she hated him because he was smug and fat and his parents adored him; or perhaps he was reading too much into that memory and she had behaved the way an impatient girl of fourteen might be with any small cousin who was a pest and a brat. His vanity was crucially engaged, for it was hard to swallow, even now, that, twelve years ago, Flor had hated Georgie Fairlie, whom everyone was supposed to love.

Aunt Bonnie brought him down to earth. It was one of her switches from nonsense to truth. Her voice would alter at such times and would become hard, practical, quite funny, a little bit hoarse, as if she were the sort of woman who might call a waitress "dear." She had levels of voice for her levels of truth. Now she dropped into reality and her voice hardened and fell. She seemed closer to George, and he had the feeling of walking with someone he knew, not watching three unknown people pacing into the foreign night. "You know, Georgie," said his aunt, turning to him, laughing like a girl, "one time Flor got herself mixed up with a fellow from Egypt. He said he had been something or other once, or his father had been. I never knew a girl like her for getting in with people who had been something but weren't now. He said that when all the troubles in the Middle East were over he would take Flor to Egypt and he would show her the nightclub where King Farouk used to go and where he used to go himself when he was a young bachelor. I may say he wasn't a bachelor any more but that was another of Flor's specialities, she always met them too late in more ways than one. Flor said what happens in this nightclub, and he said, oh you see such lovely girls. In this club you see toutes les Miss de l'Europe. Now, to Flor une Miss was a governess, but it turned out he didn't mean that. He meant Miss Oslo, Miss Vichy Water, Miss Baden-Baden. That was what he wanted to show my Flor, Georgie, toutes les Miss de l'Europe."

George laughed and then thought of Harris and stopped. They seemed to have been walking all night, halting, waiting for green lights, walking again. Harris was their guide. George was ashamed to look at him after Aunt Bonnie's story, but when they were on the Pont de l'Alma, obeying Aunt Bonnie's order to stop and see how beautiful the lighted bridges were, Bob leaned forward a little so that George could see his profile without seeming to stare. He was not the sleek, eager young man he remembered from the wedding trip, two years before, but someone soft and patient with the empty profile of the blind. He heard Harris say, "I used to wish we could be simple, but she couldn't be simple with the life she's had." The Seine was moving faster; the reflection of bridges cracked and shook. Bonnie took no notice of this plain provocation on the part of Bob and George guessed she hadn't heard: she had, though, for, choosing her moment, she said in an invalid's voice, "I can't ever tell you how sweet Florence was, George. Sweet and simple. And she was a high-spirited attractive girl. She could have had any one of a dozen tremendous men. A man tried to drown himself over Flor when she was only sixteen. Up there..." and she raised George's arm with her own to point back the way they had come.

"Don't worry," said Flor's husband soothingly. "Don't worry about a thing." He got his little group moving again and they went on. They were crossing into a different part of the city and Bob seemed rekindled with every step. This was his country: shops, nightclubs, well-dressed girls. He was emerging from the role that had been forced on him; he left off being soft and patient, neutral and blind. It had been their fault. They had excluded him. After all, he was the husband. George wanted to tell him, You know about Aunt Bonnie; it's only because I'm family, I use family words, I'm home. How could he explain that when she had said, "You're a real Fairlie," it left out Bob but took in Flor? Or what a comfort it was now, on the Pont de l'Alma, when everything said was wrong or hurting, to know that his features were armor and his behavior a shield? He tried to remember Flor, so as to place her in the family ranks; but her face kept avoiding him, like the girl seen that night and already lost. He supposed Flor was pretty; people said so. He forgot that he had once said so too. Now he thought, She had too much McCarthy in her, her eyes were too green. Then the face turned abruptly toward him and he could see her eyes, her mouth, and the part of her hair. He remembered Flor being very pretty, and proud, and he remembered her lifting her thick hair with her hands and looking around—as George's mother said, "knowing it." She couldn't help knowing; she probably looked in mirrors. "Flor was all Fairlie," Aunt Bonnie had said during dinner, as though Florence were dead. If she went on like that, in no time she would believe, and make George agree, that her daughter's hair was blond, her eyes blue. Flor was not anywhere now, so perhaps it didn't matter. Perhaps it was courtesy to accept the mother's mistakes. But he was stubborn and he knew that his isolated memories of Flor were right and Aunt Bonnie's fantasies wrong. He knew that Flor had red hair and a cold bad temper and perhaps didn't, or couldn't, care much for anything outside the span of the necklace. Bob, encased in silence and false calm, knew even more; but it was better not to explore that country. "I thought about Flor," said George, meaning that he had thought about her all the time, and it was almost true, but nobody heard him. They were skirting the Place de l'Alma and starting up the Avenue Montaigne and Bob was coming to life and Aunt Bonnie diminishing, going down. George sounded like his aunt, inconsequential. When the three separated that night, Flor would be lost. Their conversation and their thoughts were the last of the old Flor. If she was cured, she would be different. He was sure of that.

"You two boys have got to go back for the car," Aunt Bonnie said. "George, you've been a real comfort."

Bob said softly, "I'm glad you came."

They meant it. They would have been glad of anything. They were standing still on a quiet, dark street. This was where Bob and Aunt Bonnie lived. He recognized the double doors leading into the courtyard. He had come there that afternoon, looking for them. "Don't come up," Aunt Bonnie said. "I can get up and into the apartment by myself. I can get out of my clothes and into my bed without any help, and that's all I'm going to do. I'm going to do less and less now. Less and less."

Bob said, "Don't worry, you'll last longer than any of us." He sounded kind.

"Did the walk help you, George?" said Aunt Bonnie, before turning away.

"Help me?"

"I thought you'd had too much to drink, dear. I thought the night air would do you good. That's why I made us all walk." Suddenly she roared with laughter and said, "I must say, I used to adore drunks, I mean witty drunks. I must have, because I married one. Good gracious, when I think of Stanley holding forth, sometimes on the chair and sometimes under it..." She kissed George and she went in behind the double doors. George and Harris were alone. George wasn't certain how to behave. He might have said, I'm not drunk, you know, but he was afraid that Bob might answer, Don't worry. George was visiting Paris and Bob was forced to entertain him; it amounted to that. The whole family rose up saying, This man is in hell, be considerate, be decent. There was a lesser but distinct theme: He had no business marrying her. Keep him in his place. George ignored the whisper but he had heard it all the same. It seemed to him that the only atonement he could make was to give Florence back to her husband; to hand her back. Harris gave him an opportunity. They walked back to the Avenue Montaigne and stood on the curb. Harris was watching out for taxis. Suddenly he said, "They might let you see Flor. I could ask. She might recognize you. It would be a good thing. You were pretty close, weren't you?"

This was George's chance and he said the most considerate thing he could think of, which was: "To tell the truth, I hardly knew her. I think in my whole life I only saw my cousin six times."

Handing her back, he renounced all claim to her. She was outside the family. Harris seemed unaware of the magnitude of the stroke. He put up his hand for a cab, which drew up, and they got in. George was silent. Something had gone wrong. They rolled back the way they had walked and on the bridge George had an authentic hallucination.

He saw Aunt Bonnie and Flor and the girl on the Quai Anatole France as one person. She was a changeable figure, now menacing, now dear; a minute later behaving like a queen in exile, plaintive and haughty, eccentric by birth, unaware, or not caring, that the others were laughing behind their hands.

TITLES IN SERIES

For a complete list of titles, visit www.nyrb.com or write to:
Catalog Requests, NYRB, 435 Hudson Street, New York, NY 10014

J.R. ACKERLEY Hindoo Holiday*
J.R. ACKERLEY My Dog Tulip*
J.R. ACKERLEY My Father and Myself*
J.R. ACKERLEY We Think the World of You*
HENRY ADAMS The Jeffersonian Transformation
RENATA ADLER Pitch Dark*
RENATA ADLER Speedboat*
AESCHYLUS Prometheus Bound; translated by Joel Agee*
CÉLESTE ALBARET Monsieur Proust
DANTE ALIGHIERI The Inferno
DANTE ALIGHIERI The New Life
KINGSLEY AMIS The Alteration*
KINGSLEY AMIS Dear Illusion: Collected Stories*
KINGSLEY AMIS Ending Up*
KINGSLEY AMIS Girl, 20*
KINGSLEY AMIS The Green Man*
KINGSLEY AMIS Lucky Jim*
KINGSLEY AMIS The Old Devils*
KINGSLEY AMIS One Fat Englishman*
KINGSLEY AMIS Take a Girl Like You*
ROBERTO ARLT The Seven Madmen*
WILLIAM ATTAWAY Blood on the Forge
W.H. AUDEN (EDITOR) The Living Thoughts of Kierkegaard
W.H. AUDEN W.H. Auden's Book of Light Verse
ERICH AUERBACH Dante: Poet of the Secular World
DOROTHY BAKER Cassandra at the Wedding*
DOROTHY BAKER Young Man with a Horn*
J.A. BAKER The Peregrine
S. JOSEPHINE BAKER Fighting for Life*
HONORÉ DE BALZAC The Human Comedy: Selected Stories*
HONORÉ DE BALZAC The Unknown Masterpiece *and* Gambara*
SYBILLE BEDFORD A Legacy*
MAX BEERBOHM The Prince of Minor Writers: The Selected Essays of Max Beerbohm*
MAX BEERBOHM Seven Men
STEPHEN BENATAR Wish Her Safe at Home*
FRANS G. BENGTSSON The Long Ships*
ALEXANDER BERKMAN Prison Memoirs of an Anarchist
GEORGES BERNANOS Mouchette
MIRON BIAŁOSZEWSKI A Memoir of the Warsaw Uprising*
ADOLFO BIOY CASARES Asleep in the Sun
ADOLFO BIOY CASARES The Invention of Morel
EVE BABITZ Eve's Hollywood*
CAROLINE BLACKWOOD Corrigan*
CAROLINE BLACKWOOD Great Granny Webster*
RONALD BLYTHE Akenfield: Portrait of an English Village*
NICOLAS BOUVIER The Way of the World
EMMANUEL BOVE Henri Duchemin and His Shadows*

* *Also available as an electronic book.*

MALCOLM BRALY On the Yard*
MILLEN BRAND The Outward Room*
SIR THOMAS BROWNE Religio Medici and Urne-Buriall*
JOHN HORNE BURNS The Gallery
ROBERT BURTON The Anatomy of Melancholy
CAMARA LAYE The Radiance of the King
GIROLAMO CARDANO The Book of My Life
DON CARPENTER Hard Rain Falling*
J.L. CARR A Month in the Country*
BLAISE CENDRARS Moravagine
EILEEN CHANG Love in a Fallen City
EILEEN CHANG Naked Earth*
JOAN CHASE During the Reign of the Queen of Persia*
ELLIOTT CHAZE Black Wings Has My Angel*
UPAMANYU CHATTERJEE English, August: An Indian Story
NIRAD C. CHAUDHURI The Autobiography of an Unknown Indian
ANTON CHEKHOV Peasants and Other Stories
ANTON CHEKHOV The Prank: The Best of Young Chekhov*
GABRIEL CHEVALLIER Fear: A Novel of World War I*
JEAN-PAUL CLÉBERT Paris Vagabond*
RICHARD COBB Paris and Elsewhere
COLETTE The Pure and the Impure
JOHN COLLIER Fancies and Goodnights
CARLO COLLODI The Adventures of Pinocchio*
IVY COMPTON-BURNETT A House and Its Head
IVY COMPTON-BURNETT Manservant and Maidservant
BARBARA COMYNS The Vet's Daughter
BARBARA COMYNS Our Spoons Came from Woolworths*
ALBERT COSSERY The Jokers*
ALBERT COSSERY Proud Beggars*
HAROLD CRUSE The Crisis of the Negro Intellectual
ASTOLPHE DE CUSTINE Letters from Russia*
LORENZO DA PONTE Memoirs
ELIZABETH DAVID A Book of Mediterranean Food
ELIZABETH DAVID Summer Cooking
L.J. DAVIS A Meaningful Life*
AGNES DE MILLE Dance to the Piper*
VIVANT DENON No Tomorrow/Point de lendemain
MARIA DERMOÛT The Ten Thousand Things
DER NISTER The Family Mashber
TIBOR DÉRY Niki: The Story of a Dog
ARTHUR CONAN DOYLE The Exploits and Adventures of Brigadier Gerard
CHARLES DUFF A Handbook on Hanging
BRUCE DUFFY The World As I Found It*
DAPHNE DU MAURIER Don't Look Now: Stories
ELAINE DUNDY The Dud Avocado*
ELAINE DUNDY The Old Man and Me*
G.B. EDWARDS The Book of Ebenezer Le Page*
JOHN EHLE The Land Breakers*
MARCELLUS EMANTS A Posthumous Confession
EURIPIDES Grief Lessons: Four Plays; translated by Anne Carson
J.G. FARRELL Troubles*

J.G. FARRELL The Siege of Krishnapur*
J.G. FARRELL The Singapore Grip*
ELIZA FAY Original Letters from India
KENNETH FEARING The Big Clock
KENNETH FEARING Clark Gifford's Body
FÉLIX FÉNÉON Novels in Three Lines*
M.I. FINLEY The World of Odysseus
THOMAS FLANAGAN The Year of the French*
SANFORD FRIEDMAN Conversations with Beethoven*
SANFORD FRIEDMAN Totempole*
MASANOBU FUKUOKA The One-Straw Revolution*
MARC FUMAROLI When the World Spoke French
CARLO EMILIO GADDA That Awful Mess on the Via Merulana
BENITO PÉREZ GÁLDOS Tristana*
MAVIS GALLANT The Cost of Living: Early and Uncollected Stories*
MAVIS GALLANT Paris Stories*
MAVIS GALLANT A Fairly Good Time *with* Green Water, Green Sky*
MAVIS GALLANT Varieties of Exile*
GABRIEL GARCÍA MÁRQUEZ Clandestine in Chile: The Adventures of Miguel Littín
LEONARD GARDNER Fat City*
ALAN GARNER Red Shift*
WILLIAM H. GASS In the Heart of the Heart of the Country: And Other Stories*
WILLIAM H. GASS On Being Blue: A Philosophical Inquiry*
THÉOPHILE GAUTIER My Fantoms
JEAN GENET Prisoner of Love
ÉLISABETH GILLE The Mirador: Dreamed Memories of Irène Némirovsky by Her Daughter*
JEAN GIONO Hill*
JOHN GLASSCO Memoirs of Montparnasse*
P.V. GLOB The Bog People: Iron-Age Man Preserved
NIKOLAI GOGOL Dead Souls*
EDMOND AND JULES DE GONCOURT Pages from the Goncourt Journals
PAUL GOODMAN Growing Up Absurd: Problems of Youth in the Organized Society*
EDWARD GOREY (EDITOR) The Haunted Looking Glass
JEREMIAS GOTTHELF The Black Spider*
A.C. GRAHAM Poems of the Late T'ang
WILLIAM LINDSAY GRESHAM Nightmare Alley*
EMMETT GROGAN Ringolevio: A Life Played for Keeps
VASILY GROSSMAN An Armenian Sketchbook*
VASILY GROSSMAN Everything Flows*
VASILY GROSSMAN Life and Fate*
VASILY GROSSMAN The Road*
OAKLEY HALL Warlock
PATRICK HAMILTON The Slaves of Solitude*
PATRICK HAMILTON Twenty Thousand Streets Under the Sky*
PETER HANDKE Short Letter, Long Farewell
PETER HANDKE Slow Homecoming
ELIZABETH HARDWICK The New York Stories of Elizabeth Hardwick*
ELIZABETH HARDWICK Seduction and Betrayal*
ELIZABETH HARDWICK Sleepless Nights*
L.P. HARTLEY Eustace and Hilda: A Trilogy*
L.P. HARTLEY The Go-Between*
NATHANIEL HAWTHORNE Twenty Days with Julian & Little Bunny by Papa

ALFRED HAYES In Love*
ALFRED HAYES My Face for the World to See*
PAUL HAZARD The Crisis of the European Mind: 1680–1715*
GILBERT HIGHET Poets in a Landscape
RUSSELL HOBAN Turtle Diary*
JANET HOBHOUSE The Furies
HUGO VON HOFMANNSTHAL The Lord Chandos Letter*
JAMES HOGG The Private Memoirs and Confessions of a Justified Sinner
RICHARD HOLMES Shelley: The Pursuit*
ALISTAIR HORNE A Savage War of Peace: Algeria 1954–1962*
GEOFFREY HOUSEHOLD Rogue Male*
WILLIAM DEAN HOWELLS Indian Summer
BOHUMIL HRABAL Dancing Lessons for the Advanced in Age*
BOHUMIL HRABAL The Little Town Where Time Stood Still*
DOROTHY B. HUGHES The Expendable Man*
RICHARD HUGHES A High Wind in Jamaica*
RICHARD HUGHES In Hazard*
RICHARD HUGHES The Fox in the Attic (The Human Predicament, Vol. 1)*
RICHARD HUGHES The Wooden Shepherdess (The Human Predicament, Vol. 2)*
INTIZAR HUSAIN Basti*
MAUDE HUTCHINS Victorine
YASUSHI INOUE Tun-huang*
HENRY JAMES The Ivory Tower
HENRY JAMES The New York Stories of Henry James*
HENRY JAMES The Other House
HENRY JAMES The Outcry
TOVE JANSSON Fair Play *
TOVE JANSSON The Summer Book*
TOVE JANSSON The True Deceiver*
TOVE JANSSON The Woman Who Borrowed Memories: Selected Stories*
RANDALL JARRELL (EDITOR) Randall Jarrell's Book of Stories
DAVID JONES In Parenthesis
JOSEPH JOUBERT The Notebooks of Joseph Joubert; translated by Paul Auster
KABIR Songs of Kabir; translated by Arvind Krishna Mehrotra*
FRIGYES KARINTHY A Journey Round My Skull
ERICH KÄSTNER Going to the Dogs: The Story of a Moralist*
HELEN KELLER The World I Live In
YASHAR KEMAL Memed, My Hawk
YASHAR KEMAL They Burn the Thistles
MURRAY KEMPTON Part of Our Time: Some Ruins and Monuments of the Thirties*
RAYMOND KENNEDY Ride a Cockhorse*
DAVID KIDD Peking Story*
ROBERT KIRK The Secret Commonwealth of Elves, Fauns, and Fairies
ARUN KOLATKAR Jejuri
DEZSŐ KOSZTOLÁNYI Skylark*
TÉTÉ-MICHEL KPOMASSIE An African in Greenland
GYULA KRÚDY The Adventures of Sindbad*
GYULA KRÚDY Sunflower*
SIGIZMUND KRZHIZHANOVSKY Autobiography of a Corpse*
SIGIZMUND KRZHIZHANOVSKY The Letter Killers Club*
SIGIZMUND KRZHIZHANOVSKY Memories of the Future
K'UNG SHANG-JEN The Peach Blossom Fan*

GIUSEPPE TOMASI DI LAMPEDUSA The Professor and the Siren
GERT LEDIG The Stalin Front*
MARGARET LEECH Reveille in Washington: 1860–1865*
PATRICK LEIGH FERMOR Between the Woods and the Water*
PATRICK LEIGH FERMOR The Broken Road*
PATRICK LEIGH FERMOR Mani: Travels in the Southern Peloponnese*
PATRICK LEIGH FERMOR Roumeli: Travels in Northern Greece*
PATRICK LEIGH FERMOR A Time of Gifts*
PATRICK LEIGH FERMOR A Time to Keep Silence*
PATRICK LEIGH FERMOR The Traveller's Tree*
D.B. WYNDHAM LEWIS AND CHARLES LEE (EDITORS) The Stuffed Owl
SIMON LEYS The Death of Napoleon*
SIMON LEYS The Hall of Uselessness: Collected Essays*
GEORG CHRISTOPH LICHTENBERG The Waste Books
JAKOV LIND Soul of Wood and Other Stories
H.P. LOVECRAFT AND OTHERS Shadows of Carcosa: Tales of Cosmic Horror*
DWIGHT MACDONALD Masscult and Midcult: Essays Against the American Grain*
CURZIO MALAPARTE Kaputt
CURZIO MALAPARTE The Skin
JANET MALCOLM In the Freud Archives
JEAN-PATRICK MANCHETTE Fatale*
JEAN-PATRICK MANCHETTE The Mad and the Bad*
OSIP MANDELSTAM The Selected Poems of Osip Mandelstam
OLIVIA MANNING Fortunes of War: The Balkan Trilogy*
OLIVIA MANNING Fortunes of War: The Levant Trilogy*
OLIVIA MANNING School for Love*
JAMES VANCE MARSHALL Walkabout*
GUY DE MAUPASSANT Afloat
GUY DE MAUPASSANT Alien Hearts*
JAMES McCOURT Mawrdew Czgowchwz*
WILLIAM McPHERSON Testing the Current*
MEZZ MEZZROW AND BERNARD WOLFE Really the Blues*
HENRI MICHAUX Miserable Miracle
JESSICA MITFORD Hons and Rebels
JESSICA MITFORD Poison Penmanship*
NANCY MITFORD Frederick the Great*
NANCY MITFORD Madame de Pompadour*
NANCY MITFORD The Sun King*
NANCY MITFORD Voltaire in Love*
PATRICK MODIANO In the Café of Lost Youth*
PATRICK MODIANO Young Once*
MICHEL DE MONTAIGNE Shakespeare's Montaigne; translated by John Florio*
HENRY DE MONTHERLANT Chaos and Night
BRIAN MOORE The Lonely Passion of Judith Hearne*
BRIAN MOORE The Mangan Inheritance*
ALBERTO MORAVIA Agostino*
ALBERTO MORAVIA Boredom*
ALBERTO MORAVIA Contempt*
JAN MORRIS Conundrum*
JAN MORRIS Hav*
PENELOPE MORTIMER The Pumpkin Eater*
ÁLVARO MUTIS The Adventures and Misadventures of Maqroll

L.H. MYERS The Root and the Flower*
NESCIO Amsterdam Stories*
DARCY O'BRIEN A Way of Life, Like Any Other
SILVINA OCAMPO Thus Were Their Faces*
YURI OLESHA Envy*
IONA AND PETER OPIE The Lore and Language of Schoolchildren
IRIS OWENS After Claude*
RUSSELL PAGE The Education of a Gardener
ALEXANDROS PAPADIAMANTIS The Murderess
BORIS PASTERNAK, MARINA TSVETAYEVA, AND RAINER MARIA RILKE Letters, Summer 1926
CESARE PAVESE The Moon and the Bonfires
CESARE PAVESE The Selected Works of Cesare Pavese
BORISLAV PEKIĆ Houses*
ELEANOR PERÉNYI More Was Lost: A Memoir*
LUIGI PIRANDELLO The Late Mattia Pascal
JOSEP PLA The Gray Notebook
ANDREY PLATONOV The Foundation Pit
ANDREY PLATONOV Happy Moscow
ANDREY PLATONOV Soul and Other Stories
J.F. POWERS Morte d'Urban*
J.F. POWERS The Stories of J.F. Powers*
J.F. POWERS Wheat That Springeth Green*
CHRISTOPHER PRIEST Inverted World*
BOLESŁAW PRUS The Doll*
GEORGE PSYCHOUNDAKIS The Cretan Runner: His Story of the German Occupation*
ALEXANDER PUSHKIN The Captain's Daughter*
QIU MIAOJIN Last Words from Montmartre*
RAYMOND QUENEAU We Always Treat Women Too Well
RAYMOND QUENEAU Witch Grass
RAYMOND RADIGUET Count d'Orgel's Ball
FRIEDRICH RECK Diary of a Man in Despair*
JULES RENARD Nature Stories*
JEAN RENOIR Renoir, My Father
GREGOR VON REZZORI An Ermine in Czernopol*
GREGOR VON REZZORI Memoirs of an Anti-Semite*
GREGOR VON REZZORI The Snows of Yesteryear: Portraits for an Autobiography*
TIM ROBINSON Stones of Aran: Labyrinth
TIM ROBINSON Stones of Aran: Pilgrimage
MILTON ROKEACH The Three Christs of Ypsilanti*
FR. ROLFE Hadrian the Seventh
GILLIAN ROSE Love's Work
LINDA ROSENKRANTZ Talk*
WILLIAM ROUGHEAD Classic Crimes
CONSTANCE ROURKE American Humor: A Study of the National Character
SAKI The Unrest-Cure and Other Stories; illustrated by Edward Gorey
TAYEB SALIH Season of Migration to the North
TAYEB SALIH The Wedding of Zein*
JEAN-PAUL SARTRE We Have Only This Life to Live: Selected Essays. 1939–1975
GERSHOM SCHOLEM Walter Benjamin: The Story of a Friendship*
DANIEL PAUL SCHREBER Memoirs of My Nervous Illness
JAMES SCHUYLER Alfred and Guinevere
JAMES SCHUYLER What's for Dinner?*

SIMONE SCHWARZ-BART The Bridge of Beyond*
LEONARDO SCIASCIA The Day of the Owl
LEONARDO SCIASCIA Equal Danger
LEONARDO SCIASCIA The Moro Affair
LEONARDO SCIASCIA To Each His Own
LEONARDO SCIASCIA The Wine-Dark Sea
VICTOR SEGALEN René Leys*
ANNA SEGHERS Transit*
PHILIPE-PAUL DE SÉGUR Defeat: Napoleon's Russian Campaign
GILBERT SELDES The Stammering Century*
VICTOR SERGE The Case of Comrade Tulayev*
VICTOR SERGE Conquered City*
VICTOR SERGE Memoirs of a Revolutionary
VICTOR SERGE Midnight in the Century*
VICTOR SERGE Unforgiving Years
SHCHEDRIN The Golovlyov Family
ROBERT SHECKLEY The Store of the Worlds: The Stories of Robert Sheckley*
GEORGES SIMENON Act of Passion*
GEORGES SIMENON Dirty Snow*
GEORGES SIMENON Monsieur Monde Vanishes*
GEORGES SIMENON Pedigree*
GEORGES SIMENON Three Bedrooms in Manhattan*
GEORGES SIMENON Tropic Moon*
GEORGES SIMENON The Widow*
CHARLES SIMIC Dime-Store Alchemy: The Art of Joseph Cornell
MAY SINCLAIR Mary Olivier: A Life*
WILLIAM SLOANE The Rim of Morning: Two Tales of Cosmic Horror*
SASHA SOKOLOV A School for Fools*
VLADIMIR SOROKIN Ice Trilogy*
VLADIMIR SOROKIN The Queue
NATSUME SŌSEKI The Gate*
DAVID STACTON The Judges of the Secret Court*
JEAN STAFFORD The Mountain Lion
CHRISTINA STEAD Letty Fox: Her Luck
GEORGE R. STEWART Names on the Land
STENDHAL The Life of Henry Brulard
ADALBERT STIFTER Rock Crystal*
THEODOR STORM The Rider on the White Horse
JEAN STROUSE Alice James: A Biography*
HOWARD STURGIS Belchamber
ITALO SVEVO As a Man Grows Older
HARVEY SWADOS Nights in the Gardens of Brooklyn
A.J.A. SYMONS The Quest for Corvo
MAGDA SZABÓ The Door*
ANTAL SZERB Journey by Moonlight*
ELIZABETH TAYLOR Angel*
ELIZABETH TAYLOR A Game of Hide and Seek*
ELIZABETH TAYLOR A View of the Harbour*
ELIZABETH TAYLOR You'll Enjoy It When You Get There: The Stories of Elizabeth Taylor*
TEFFI Memories: From Moscow to the Black Sea*
TEFFI Tolstoy, Rasputin, Others, and Me: The Best of Teffi*
HENRY DAVID THOREAU The Journal: 1837–1861*

ALEKSANDAR TIŠMA The Book of Blam*
ALEKSANDAR TIŠMA The Use of Man*
TATYANA TOLSTAYA The Slynx
TATYANA TOLSTAYA White Walls: Collected Stories
EDWARD JOHN TRELAWNY Records of Shelley, Byron, and the Author
LIONEL TRILLING The Liberal Imagination*
LIONEL TRILLING The Middle of the Journey*
THOMAS TRYON The Other*
IVAN TURGENEV Virgin Soil
JULES VALLÈS The Child
RAMÓN DEL VALLE-INCLÁN Tyrant Banderas*
MARK VAN DOREN Shakespeare
CARL VAN VECHTEN The Tiger in the House
ELIZABETH VON ARNIM The Enchanted April*
EDWARD LEWIS WALLANT The Tenants of Moonbloom
ROBERT WALSER Berlin Stories*
ROBERT WALSER Jakob von Gunten
ROBERT WALSER A Schoolboy's Diary and Other Stories*
REX WARNER Men and Gods
SYLVIA TOWNSEND WARNER Lolly Willowes*
SYLVIA TOWNSEND WARNER Mr. Fortune*
SYLVIA TOWNSEND WARNER Summer Will Show*
JAKOB WASSERMANN My Marriage*
ALEKSANDER WAT My Century*
C.V. WEDGWOOD The Thirty Years War
SIMONE WEIL On the Abolition of All Political Parties*
SIMONE WEIL AND RACHEL BESPALOFF War and the Iliad
GLENWAY WESCOTT Apartment in Athens*
GLENWAY WESCOTT The Pilgrim Hawk*
REBECCA WEST The Fountain Overflows
EDITH WHARTON The New York Stories of Edith Wharton*
KATHARINE S. WHITE Onward and Upward in the Garden*
PATRICK WHITE Riders in the Chariot
T. H. WHITE The Goshawk*
JOHN WILLIAMS Augustus*
JOHN WILLIAMS Butcher's Crossing*
JOHN WILLIAMS (EDITOR) English Renaissance Poetry: A Collection of Shorter Poems*
JOHN WILLIAMS Stoner*
ANGUS WILSON Anglo-Saxon Attitudes
EDMUND WILSON Memoirs of Hecate County
RUDOLF AND MARGARET WITTKOWER Born Under Saturn
GEOFFREY WOLFF Black Sun*
FRANCIS WYNDHAM The Complete Fiction
JOHN WYNDHAM Chocky
JOHN WYNDHAM The Chrysalids
BÉLA ZOMBORY-MOLDOVÁN The Burning of the World: A Memoir of 1914*
STEFAN ZWEIG Beware of Pity*
STEFAN ZWEIG Chess Story*
STEFAN ZWEIG Confusion*
STEFAN ZWEIG Journey Into the Past*
STEFAN ZWEIG The Post-Office Girl*